Ornamen

1

1928 - 2018

Chris Fogg is a creative producer, writer, director and dramaturg, who has written and directed for the theatre for many years, as well as collaborating artistically with choreographers and contemporary dance companies.

Ornaments of Grace is a chronicle of twelve novels. *Pomona* is the first in the sequence.

He has previously written more than thirty works for the stage as well as four collections of poems, stories and essays. These are: *Special Relationships, Northern Songs, Painting by Numbers* and *Dawn Chorus* (with woodcut illustrations by Chris Waters), all published by Mudlark Press.

Several of Chris's poems have appeared in International Psychoanalysis (IP), a US online journal, as well as in *Climate of Opinion*, a selection of verse in response to the work of Sigmund Freud edited by Irene Willis, and *What They Bring: The Poetry of Migration & Immigration*, co-edited by Irene Willis and Jim Haba, each published by IP in 2017 and 2020.

Praise for Chris Fogg's previous work

"Chris Fogg takes us on a magical, whirlwind tale of his world... with eyes and ears and heart at full throttle... If it is possible to be exuberant, compassionate, politically and socially aware, wise, reflective and funny all at once, then Chris Fogg has achieved it here..."

Irene Willis – National Book Award & three times Pushcart Prize nominee; winner of Philip Levine & Violet Haas Awards

"Chris Fogg is a natural story-maker. These poems cut an arc across our times – they are travels of the heart and invite us to travel with them..."

Chris Waters – Winner of Bridport and Plough poetry prizes and author of *Arisaig, Through a Glass Lately* and *On London Clay*

"Evokes fundamental questions of now, who we are and where we are inside ourselves..."

Mark Bruce – Sky Arts / South Bank Award Winner, 2014

"Chris Fogg is a master at seeing the extraordinary in the everyday bits and pieces of modern life. I have an inextinguishable admiration for his gentle politic, for his ability to weave an apparently simple idea into a thoughtful reflection on what we should value most. Quietly urgent."

Gavin Stride – Director, Farnham Maltings

"Shifting between poetic and prose form, moments that shape a life are beautifully and unexpectedly etched..."

Lucy Cash – Artist in Residence, Whitechapel Gallery 2013

"In this arcane and ever complicated world that increasingly makes attempts to crush the soul, Chris Fogg reminds us that we have one. Astounding writing."

Ben Wright – Former Joint Artistic Director, Candoco; Associate Artistic Director, Skånes Dansteater Malmö and Jerwood Prize Winner

Theatre works written by Chris Fogg

The Tall Tree*
To See the Six Points* (*with music by Chris Dumigan*)
The Silent Princess
Changeling
Peterloo: The Greatest Show on Earth
Snapshot (*co-written with Andrew Pastor & Chris Phillips*)
Safe Haven
Firestarter
Trying to Get Back Home
Bogus
Heroes
It's Not Just The Jewels...
You Are Harry Kipper & I Claim My Five Pounds!
One of Us**
How To Build A Rocket** (*writing assistant to Gavin Stride*)
All The Ghosts Walk With Us (*with Laila Diallo & Phil King*)
Posting to Iraq
Tree House
The Time of Our Lives (*co-written with 6 others for Wassail Theatre*)

Adaptations:
1984
The Stone Book Quartet
Return of the Native
The Birdman

For young people and community companies:
The Ballad of Billy the Kid
Market Forces
Small Blue Thing
Inside
The Sleeping Clock
Titanic
The Posy Tree
Scheherazade
Persons Reported

Musicals: (*co-written with Chris Dumigan*)
Stag
Marilyn

Ornaments of Grace

(or *Unhistoric Acts*)

1

Pomona

by

Chris Fogg

flaxbooks

First published 2019
© Chris Fogg 2019

Chris Fogg has asserted his rights under Copyright Designs & Patents Act 1988 to be identified as the author of this book

ISBN Number: 9781076080783

Cover and design by: Kama Glover

Cover Image: The Opening of the Bridgewater Canal, one of the Manchester Murals by Ford Madox Brown, reprinted by kind permission of Manchester Libraries, Information & Archives

Printed in Great Britain by Amazon

Although some of the people featured in this book are real, and several of the events depicted actually happened, *Ornaments of Grace* remains a work of fiction.

For Amanda and Tim

dedicated to the memory

of my parents and grandparents

Ornaments of Grace (*or Unhistoric Acts*) is a sequence of twelve novels set in Manchester between 1761 and 2021. Collectively they tell the story of a city in four elements.

Pomona is the first book in the sequence.

The full list of titles is:

1. Pomona (Water)

2. Tulip (Earth)
    Vol 1: Enclave
    Vol 2: Nymphs & Shepherds
    Vol 3: The Spindle Tree
    Vol 4: Return

3. Laurel (Air)
    Vol 1: Victor
     part 1: Kettle
     part 2: Litmus
    Vol 2: Victrix
     part 1: A Grain of Mustard Seed
     part 2: The Waxing of a Great Tree
     part 3: All the Fowls of the Air

4. Moth (Fire)
    Vol 1: The Principal Thing
    Vol 2: A Crown of Glory

Each element can be read independently or as part of the sequence.

"It's always too soon to go home. And it's always too soon to calculate effect... Cause-and-effect assumes that history marches forward, but history is not an army. It is a crab scuttling sideways, a drip of soft water wearing away stone, an earthquake breaking centuries of tension."

Rebecca Solnit: Hope in the Dark
(*Untold Histories, Wild Possibilities*)

Manchester's Canal Network: circa 1928

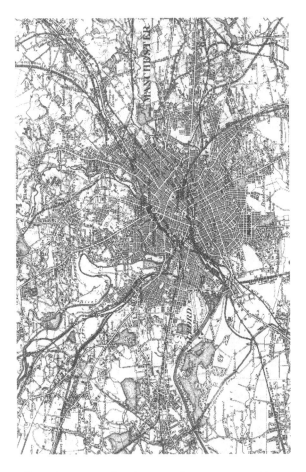

Follow the route taken by Hejaz from Barton Bridge to
Bradford Colliery, later recreated by Sol

Contents

Ornaments of Grace

"Wisdom is the principal thing. Therefore get wisdom and within all thy getting get understanding. Exalt her and she shall promote thee. She shall bring thee to honour when thou dost embrace her. She shall give to thine head an ornament of grace. A crown of glory shall she deliver to thee."

Proverbs: 4, verses 7 – 9

written around the domed ceiling of the Great Hall Reading Room
Central Reference Library, St Peter's Square, Manchester

"Fecisti patriam diversis de gentibus unam…"
"From differing peoples you have made one homeland…"

Rutilius Claudius Namatianus:
De Redito Suo, verse 63

"To be hopeful in bad times is not just foolishly romantic. It is based on the fact that human history is a history not only of cruelty, but also of compassion, sacrifice, courage, kindness. What we choose to emphasise in this complex history will determine our lives. If we see only the worst, it destroys our capacity to do something. If we remember those times and places—and there are so many—where people have behaved magnificently, this gives us the energy to act, and at least the possibility of sending this spinning top of a world in a different direction. And if we do act, in however small a way, we don't have to wait for some grand utopian future. The future is an infinite succession of presents, and to live now as we think human beings should live, in defiance of all that is bad around us, is itself a marvellous victory."

Howard Zinn: A Power Governments Cannot Suppress

Pomona

"No other dryad, or wood nymph, tended the gardens more skilfully, or was more devoted to the orchards' care – hence her name. She loved the fields and the branches loaded with ripe apples, and the woods and the rivers. She would not allow them to suffer from being parched, watering, in trickling streams, the twining tendrils and thirsting root. This was her love. This was her passion."

Ovid: Metamorphoses, Book XIV, verses 623-697

"As once I was so am I now
For evermore a hope unseen…"

William Morris: Pomona

Water

"And a river went out of Eden to water the garden; and from thence it was parted."

Genesis: 2, verse 10

"I to the world am like a drop of water
That in the ocean seeks another drop,
Who, falling there to find his fellow forth,
Unseen, inquisitive, confounds himself."

Shakespeare: A Comedy of Errors

1

2016

Molly stands on the footbridge leading across the Manchester Ship Canal away from the Imperial War Museum, Libeskind's sheet-metal shards glinting in a pale March morning. Her eyes blink from the watery sun as she adjusts to the daylight after several hours inside, staring at computer screens. She needs to collect her thoughts. She has found what she came looking for – an old silent Pathé Newsreel film showing different scenes from the visit by King Amanullah of Afghanistan to Britain some eighty years before, in the spring of 1928 – but infuriatingly there were significant gaps, long passages where the screen was just blank except for a few horizontal scratches.

Earlier she had wandered through the wasteland of Pomona, a slice of wilderness between the River Irwell and the Bridgewater Canal, where once huge cargo ships would dock and unload, when Manchester was the third largest port in England. Now it is overgrown and forgotten, a brackish, dune-like quality to the hulks of earth upturned by diggers, then abandoned. New saplings push through the concrete, gradually being covered by mosses and lichens, which clog generations of dumped rubbish. Swathes of meadowsweet grow through and around a burnt out motor cycle. Beetles writhe in the innards of an old mattress. Convolvulus binds round a rusting capstan.

Molly squatted low by the water's edge to watch hundreds of tiny fish, their gleaming backs giving way to the deep expanse of the dark canal beneath them. Birds scudded through the grasses. Larks, finches, she even saw lapwings, and a heron, perched like a ballet dancer *en pointe*, a grey statue poised above the surface of the black water. She sat in this well-thumbed fold in the map, this cracked crease in the page, a good hour, watching and sketching, trying to get her bearings, to uncover its special geometry of man-made canals and railway bridges, forging a spine through the city, and her own place within it. She watched a lone rat pick its way delicately and sure-footedly along the remnant of an old sewage pipe before dropping out of sight.

She packed away her sketch book, stood up and was just about to make her way back to the footbridge that connected the island to the twenty-first century above her, with its ceaseless traffic, electronic signs and billboards, when her foot caught on something sharp. She bent down and retrieved from beneath a dusty scrub of buddleia a broken piece of wood about a metre and a half long, the thickness of a skirting board, which perhaps was what it once had been. She examined it carefully. She could just make out flecks of coloured paint, reds and blues and yellows, and a thin black line that looked like a child's drawing of an umbrella. It, or something very much like it, was exactly what she had been hoping she would find...

Now she sits on a bench outside one of the cafés looking

out across the Canal towards Old Trafford, the home of Manchester United, smiling at the huge lettering emblazoned on the side of the stadium: *Theatre of Dreams.* Is that what she's doing too, she thinks, dreaming? She takes out her notebook and reads through what she has written, together with various photocopied sheets of information she has picked up during the time she has spent inside the Museum.

```
Ledger Title: Visit of the King of
Afghanistan to Britain

Catalogue Number: IWM 809
Number of Items: Reels (seven)
Type: 35mm
Creator: Foreign Office
Production Sponsor: India Office

Object Description:
Unfinished Film of King Amanullah
and Queen Surayya of Afghanistan
during their brief stay in
England, 13th March to 3rd April
1928

Content:
The film is partially completed.
It shows a few signs of proper
editing, but scenes may break off
abruptly in one reel and resume in
another.
```

That's putting it mildly, thinks Molly. At times she has found its narrative almost impossible to follow.

> Throughout the film numerous
> reporters, press photographers and
> newsreel cameramen can be seen
> recording the visit. (Reel 1)

She was particularly struck by the ease with which the press and the public could get so close to them, security seemingly nowhere in evidence.

> The King tours the BSA works,
> Small Heath, Birmingham, on 16th
> March, escorted by the deputy
> chairman, Sir Edward Manville. The
> factory makes both motor cycles
> and weapons. The King tries out a
> BSA-Thompson semi-automatic rifle
> and rides on a motor cycle.

But not at the same time, notes Molly with a smile.

> The film jumps to the King and
> Queen's visit to the Guildhall on
> 14th March, escorted by
> Lieutenant-General Sir Francis
> Humphries. They are met by the
> Lord Mayor, Sir J E Kynaston
> Studd, and various aldermen. The
> film jumps again to a royal
> reception in London on 13th March.
> The King and Queen leave in a
> carriage from outside Victoria
> Station, with lines of Grenadier
> Guards stretching down Wilton
> Street. It is almost snowing. The
> streets are decorated with British
> and Afghan flags.

What also strikes Molly is the sheer size of the crowds, several rows deep on both sides of the road, all waving white handkerchiefs and appearing to be cheering enthusiastically. Why was he such a draw, she thinks? But she knows. It was really Queen Surayya the crowds had come to see, with her glamorous mink coat and bobbed hair, more like a Hollywood film star than an exotic Middle Eastern Princess.

> The King inspects the guardsmen, who march off after his carriage leaves. The film jumps again to the arrival of the King and Queen at Dover harbour on board the SS Maid of Orleans, being met by Edward, Prince of Wales.

Molly frowns. She has been hoping there might have been scenes from the ship's departure from Aden, where it had stopped for provisions having set off the previous week from India. There was so little footage anywhere of her own family's homeland from that period.

> A jump to the King's escort of Royal Horse Guards and the state coaches arriving at Buckingham Palace, to the salute of the Irish Guards.

More cheering, handkerchief-waving crowds, notes Molly.

> Jump again to King George V, Queen Mary, the Duke of York, Stanley

> Baldwin and Lord Birkenhead (among
> others) waiting to greet the King
> and Queen as their train arrives
> at Victoria Station, also on the
> same day.(Reel 2)

Molly pauses, writes a question in the margin. With all of this jumping back and forth, how can they be certain this wasn't the King and Queen getting on the train to *leave* London?

> A continuation of the visit to
> Birmingham. Surayya is shown
> accepting a large bouquet of
> flowers, which she hands to some
> kind of servant as soon as can.

Almost as if she expects nothing less, thinks Molly.

> Another jump to Hatfield House and
> its grounds, where the King and
> Queen stay with the Marquess of
> Salisbury.

Surayya is looking bored.

> Yet another jump to the King and
> Queen visiting Portsmouth on 19th
> March. They are shown over HMS
> Victory and HMS Tiger, and the
> King is taken out on board
> submarine L22, which dives.

And Molly realises the true nature of the visit – it's a giant sales pitch. The King is eager to purchase the latest in weaponry and industry. He may, technically speaking, no longer be the King, having been overthrown in a surprise coup a few months previously, but clearly he expects to make a return and the British are keen to support him. The latest episode of The Great Game is being played out in front of the British public, Molly now sees.

> Jump to 17th March, the royal
> couple visit the RAF Technical
> Training Centre at Halton, where
> they are shown around several
> large workshops. (Reel 3)

The King loves planes. Molly knows this from other research she has carried out already. Less than ten years before he had formed the first ever Afghan Air Force, with old Soviet fighter planes, which had not gone down well with the British, but which had enabled Amanullah to finally bring about independence. Surayya, surprisingly, hates planes, has a morbid fear of flying, and only very rarely during her entire life can she be enticed to travel in one, preferring instead the glamour of luxury cruise ships, where she can be photographed wearing the latest western fashions.

> The King visits a Steel Works,
> probably Sheffield on 27th March,
> and a Railway Engine Works, where
> the steam train *King Charles II* is
> on display.

Now we're getting closer, thinks Molly, and she impatiently leans in closer to the screen – could the Steel

Works be at Irlam, rather than Sheffield, close to where she lived as a child? – only for frustration to set in once again.

> Jump to the L22 surfacing again at
> Portsmouth, and then returning
> alongside the Tiger.
>
> Jump to the Royal Tank Corps
> centre at Lulworth (Dorset) on
> 20th March, where an old Mark V
> Star tank demonstrates its hill
> climbing ability. As the King
> watches with the CIGS, Field
> Marshal Sir George Milne, a line
> of Vickers Medium Mark I tanks
> pulls up. The King climbs inside
> one.
>
> Jump again to the King and Queen
> at Hendon on 16th March watching a
> flying display by the latest RAF
> De Havilland DH9As, Gloucester
> Grebes, and Handley Page 0/1500s.
> Reel 4)
>
> On 22nd March the King, on board
> the river steamer Marchioness…

At last, thinks Molly, this is it. She hits pause on the museum's computer, but is again disappointed. This is not the Manchester Ship Canal, by which she now sits with her coffee. Instead The Marchioness…

> …sails down the Thames to
> Greenwich Observatory, where the

> Astronomer Royal, Sir Frank Dyson,
> shows the King around.

Shit.

> Jump to the boat setting out from
> Victoria Embankment and a repeat
> of the journey.

Boring.

> On the same day the King visits
> Woolwich Arsenal, where he is
> shown Vickers Mediums and 12-inch
> naval guns being made.

Boring, boring.

> Back to the trip down the river,
> the steamer comes in to the main
> dock at Woolwich, more of the
> works is shown.

But he visited, Molly knows from her reading, the Metro-Vickers plant in Trafford Park, just beyond United's ground, opposite to where she is now sitting. Why is there no footage of that?

> More of the river, showing the
> docks area and the various cargo
> ships. (Reel 5)
>
> The King and Queen visit the
> Rolls-Royce works at Derby on 27th
> March, followed by its Mappin and
> Webb factory, the Sheffield (or
> Irlam) Steel works again, Port

> Sunlight in Birkenhead, then a
> textile firm.

This is all over the place! Might the textile firm be Tootal's? The tie manufacturers on Manchester's Oxford Street? Molly knows the King visited there. Impossible to be sure.

> The royal party is taken across
> the Mersey and on to a formal
> reception at Liverpool Town Hall.

What? No! Don't say they've missed out Manchester altogether! Molly fast forwards, rewinds, but can find nothing of what she is searching for.

> The film jumps to the Grand
> National at Aintree on 30th March.
> In the enclosure before the race
> the horses "Grakle", "Koko" and
> "Billy Barton" are shown. The King
> and Queen watch the race.
> "Tipperary Tim" is shown winning.

Who cares?

> Jump to the King inspecting the
> cadets at RMA Sandhurst, probably
> on 26th March.
>
> Jump back to the Hendon display,
> with the King and Queen leaving.
>
> Jump again to the exterior of the
> Royal Geographical Society in
> Kensington Gore, visited by the

> royal couple on the evening of
> 22nd March. (Reel 6)
>
> The King's visit to a naval
> demonstration on 3rd April. Four R
> Class destroyers, led by HMS
> Thruster (nearest the camera),
> then HMS Salmon, HMS Torrid and
> HMS Rowena in line abreast drop
> depth charges in an anti-submarine
> exercise. The King, with the
> camera, is onboard HMS Nelson,
> whose sister ship HMS Rodney is
> also visible. The destroyer HMS
> Witch passes through the mist,
> followed by a Shakespeare Class
> destroyer and a C Class cruiser.

This is heavy duty propaganda, Molly realises. The sales pitch is now beginning to resemble more a serious show of strength. The message couldn't be clearer, she thinks. We're prepared to support you, Your Majesty, but if you renege on our agreements and continue your dalliance with the Soviets, then this is the kind of fire power you might expect to face as a consequence. Surayya, she notes, is nowhere to be seen in these passages. Where was she? What was she doing while her husband was playing soldiers?

> The film jumps to the King, in
> protective clothing, on 29th March
> descending into a coal mine in
> Derbyshire.

Whoa! Wait a minute. Derbyshire? No way. This has to be the part I've been searching for, she feels. She presses pause on the mouse and studies the freeze-frame meticulously, comparing it with the photocopied picture from an old newspaper she's brought with her from home. There's just no way of being certain either way. There's nothing on the film clip to indicate the name of the colliery, nor anything that can connect it with the photograph of what she knows absolutely is Bradford Pit, on the edge of Ancoats, sometimes referred to as Beswick Colliery, which has, ever since she can remember, been a part of her family's history, and this visit in particular, by King Amanullah and Queen Surayya, lies at the heart of it…

Now she sits outside, closes her notebook and looks back across the Ship Canal, where this story all started, ignoring the rest of the archive film which only shows the King trying his hand at the steering wheel of a brand new Rolls Royce, more visits to battleships, cruisers and aircraft carriers, more guns, more tanks, more marching bands, before it ends abruptly, shortly after he can be seen disappearing behind the doors of an English stately home beneath a long shot of an RAF fly-past…

She closes her i-pad and leans back. A straggle of starlings lands upon a bare patch of scrubby earth a few feet away from where she sits and begins scratching around. She checks her phone – one missed call from her boss at *The King's Arms* on Bloom Street, where she works part-time, where she's due in half an hour, plus a text from someone signing himself "Michael". She doesn't think she knows any Mikes – wait a minute, could it be the guy she bumped into in the College canteen? Though she doesn't remember giving him her number...

Frowning she gets up, wraps her scarf, the *qurqash*, tighter around her head, then walks away briskly back over the Lowry Bridge to catch the Metro. The starlings rise reluctantly as she passes them before returning to resume their steady foraging. Molly briefly pauses to make a lightning pencil drawing of their ragged flight to add to the growing collection of wings she is assembling in her sketch book.

2

Eccles & Patricroft Reporter

29th March 1928

RIGHT ROYAL WELCOME
FOR KING & QUEEN

Hundreds of well-wishers lined the streets near Barton Bridge to welcome the arrival of King Amanullah of Afghanistan, with his consort Queen Surayya, to inspect the world's first and only aqueduct swing bridge. Despite the inclement weather their spirits could not be dampened, as they waved their white handkerchiefs enthusiastically above their heads, a greeting which is fast becoming a feature of this Royal Visit. Everywhere this glamorous couple goes the crowds will follow, eager to show their support for these plucky and courageous survivors of the recent coup back in their home country, now welcome guests of their Majesties King George and Queen Mary.

Arriving first by the cargo vessel *Pioneer*, the flagship of the CWS, then transferring to the smaller pilot *Flying Breeze*, King Amanullah was played ashore by members of the 16th Service Battalion Band of the Manchester Regiment, affectionately known as the PALS. Waiting to greet him were Ernest

Terah Hooley, owner of Trafford Park Estates, Marshall Stevens, General Manager of The Manchester Ship Canal Company, Lt-Col George Westcott OBE, Lord Mayor of Manchester, Abraham Williamson, Civic Mayor of Salford, and Captain Linton of Manchester Liners, carrying the Silver Salver for Gallantry, recently awarded to him by the Board of Trade, in which Queen Surayya graciously took a keen interest, at one point balancing it on her head to the great delight of onlookers. What *will* they think of *next*?

The King took an especially keen interest in the workings of the Swing Bridge, which carries the waters of the Bridgewater Canal over those of the Ship Canal. He stood on the turning mechanism, built into a central island consisting of a twenty-seven foot race-plate embedded in granite blocks. Until this year sixty-four cast iron rollers sat atop this plate, held in position by a great spider ring, but these have recently been replaced by steel rollers which will be much more durable. Sir Edward Leader Williams, Chief Engineer to the Manchester Ship Canal Company, who designed the aqueduct, claimed it would last for a hundred years. With these new steel rollers, it could even last a millennium. Another reason why Manchester leads the way in the latest industrial innovations, making us the envy of the empire, if not the world.

Accompanying King Amanullah onto the aqueduct were Charles Heathcote, Chief Architect of British Westinghouse Electric Company, and Sir Philip Nash, Chair of

Metropolitan-Vickers, both of whom will be hosting His Majesty later during his visit, from where, it is hoped, new overseas orders may be placed, thus ensuring further long-term work for the skilled engineers of Trafford Park.

In addition to these two local worthies, the King was presented to several key workers from the Manchester Ship Canal Company, who had been part of the team responsible for these latest improvements to Barton Bridge, enabling even more water-borne traffic to ply their trade along both canals. Among these was one Yasser Halabi Wahid, aged 66, from the Sultanate of Aden on the coast of Yemen, where the King of Afghanistan's own ship had docked *en route* for British shores. Mr Wahid first came to England as a lascar in 1886, becoming part of the team that built the canal a year later. In 1889 Mr Wahid was badly disfigured during the dreadful chemical explosion at Pomona Docks, where he risked further injury in a valiant and successful attempt to rescue his comrades, for which he received a Special Mention in the subsequent report to Parliament. The King had a private word for Mr Wahid, no doubt speaking for us all in echoing our grateful appreciation.

So give three cheers for the stout-hearted men of the Manchester Ship Canal Company, for the engineers who make these great labours possible, and for the King of Afghanistan and his Queen, welcome friends, allies and visitors to our island realm.

*

SIR PHILIP NASH:

>Your Majesty, may I please present to you Mr Yasser Halabi Wahid from the Sultanate of Aden?

KING AMANULLAH: (*in Arabic*)

>Pashto is my native tongue, so I ask you please to forgive my faltering Arabic. I have heard great things about your courage and bravery, but why, I wonder, have you stayed here in this foreign land for so many years afterwards?

YASSER:

>The ways of Allah are mysterious, Your Majesty, but the ways of the heart even more so.

KING AMANULLAH:

>Ah, I believe we understand one another. You have an English wife?

YASSER:

>Yes, Excellency. Someone who took pity on a poor lascar and mended his broken body.

KING AMANULLAH:

>Such devotion is indeed to be treasured. And you have a family, a son, perhaps?

YASSER:

>Allah has been kind enough to bestow his

riches upon me. I do indeed have a son, Sir. He works for this good gentleman who stands beside us now.

KING AMANULLAH: (*in English*)

Sir Philip, I understand that this brave man's son works in your company?

A young aide leans in and whispers into Sir Philip's ear.

SIR PHILIP:

Ah yes, Your Majesty. Mr Wahid's son – er…

YASSER:

Hejaz, Sir.

SIR PHILIP:

Hejaz, yes, who is one of our young draughtsmen at Metropolitan Vickers, where we have high hopes for him, high hopes indeed. Now, if you will excuse us, Your Majesty, we have several other appointments today we must keep. May I please ask you, therefore, to press the switch that will swing the aqueduct back into position to allow the Bridgewater Canal to flow freely once more across the mighty waters of the Manchester Ship Canal? Time and tide, what?

King Amanullah presses the switch and the crowds

applaud as the aqueduct gracefully revolves. During the
cheering, the King whispers in Yasser's ear.

KING AMANULLAH: (*reverting to Arabic*)

> I know the ways of these men, believe me. I
> am to be at Bradford Colliery in the east of
> the city tomorrow at noon. Have your son
> introduce himself to me there. We may have
> something for him that might be more
> suitable to his talents.

YASSER:

> May Allah be praised. I thank you, Sir.

KING AMANULLAH:

> Hejaz, you say?

YASSER:

> The mountains of southern Arabia, Sir. Our
> homeland.

KING AMANULLAH:

> Yes indeed. I know what it is to lose a home.

YASSER:

> And also to find one, I hope? As I have, Sir.

KING AMANULLAH:

> Tell your son 'tomorrow'. Tomorrow at
> noon.

*

Hejaz comes home from work, exhausted and dissatisfied. Five years he has been in the draughtsmen's office at Metro-Vicks with not one sniff of promotion, while younger, less able, less dark-skinned employees come and go and rise above him. He sees a future filled only with more disappointment, so that when his father arrives back, wet and limping, proclaiming before he can even take off his hat and coat that he is the harbinger of wonderful news, and that at last his chance for betterment may have arrived, he is caught completely off guard.

Less than half an hour later, with time only for a bowl of his mother's neck-of-lamb soup, he is about to set off once more, back out into the cold and dark of this wet March evening. Jaz has tried to protest.

"But how will I get there?" he asks. "Tomorrow is Sunday. There are no buses or trains that will be running early enough."

Yasser is not listening. He waves his huge hands dismissively as he continues to thank Allah for this sudden blessing.

"I suppose," says Jaz uncomfortably, "I could walk. How far is it from Patricroft to Bradford Pit? Eight miles? Nine? If I set off early, I might make it in time."

"No, no, no," replies Yasser impatiently. "You cannot walk to meet a King. You must be conveyed by water, by canal. Like a prince in days of old. That way you can rest and be refreshed for your audience."

Jaz says nothing. He imagines the dust and grime of the hold in a canal barge, which will be the conveyance to which his father refers. This idea has not been thought through. But there is no gainsaying his father once he has fixed his mind upon an idea.

"Trust me," he says. "It is best. I know the canals. I helped build them."

Not even Rose, his wife, to whom he defers in most things, can dissuade him from his plan, and she silently shakes her head towards Jaz, a gesture unseen by Yasser, a gesture which Jaz understands all too easily to mean that this is an end to further discussion.

"It is all arranged," his father tells him. "They will be waiting for you at the back of *The Bridgewater Packet*."

And so he stands now beneath the gas lamp by the tow path as instructed. In a few minutes he sees the barge looming out of the mist rising from the canal, thickened by the steam and smoke from its chimney. It is, as he feared, a coal barge, making its slow nightly round of final deliveries and pick-ups along its return to Bradford Colliery where it will fill up once more. The bargemen nod and step aside to let Hejaz climb aboard. He doesn't recognise them, but they know who he is, or rather, they know his father, who is something of a legend around the canals, and has no doubt called in several favours to make this journey happen for him. As soon as he is settled, he offers the men some tobacco, which they each accept, folding the twist of paper deep within their pockets, then pull away once more. The bell on the Holy Cross Roman Catholic Church nearby begins to toll the hour. It is only 9 o'clock, but Hejaz knows it will be a close run thing if he is to make it to the Pit by noon the following day, when he is to meet with the King – at least according to his father, who was insistent Hejaz should go, but rather vague when it came to the details of how he should present himself. Don't worry, his father had told him. He is expecting you. After the bell has finished tolling, he settles down on some sacking on the upper deck, burrows deeper into his coat, glad that he has thought to bring along gloves. It is always cold by the water, and although Hejaz has known nothing else, having been born here thirty-three years ago, something of his genetic ancestry must still stir within him, longing for hot, dry desert air to take away the damp chill from his bones.

"Here," says one of the men, tossing him a small flask, as if reading his thoughts, "drink this. It's going to be a long night," and they push off once more into the centre of the channel. Hejaz unscrews the cap. At once the welcome smell and heat of rum escapes, and he is glad that, since arriving in England, his father no longer observes the stricter tenets of their religion concerning alcohol. He inhales the vapours as they rise, then screws back the cap. He must ration this in order to stay warm.

The journey will take them along the Bridgewater as far as the Pomona Dock, where they will take the short spur of the Ship Canal to the Castlefield Junction at the base of the city, from which they will pick up the busy Rochdale Canal as far as Ducie Street, where they will turn east along the Ashton for the final five and a quarter miles to Beswick, at which point Hejaz will disembark at the colliery steps and make his way to the pit yard, arriving in time, he hopes, to meet the King. Thinking about how he will manage this and what he will say when he does occupy his thoughts so completely that he takes little notice of his surroundings as they slowly make their dark passage, the thrumming of the engines below him gradually lulling him into a fitful sleep.

He is woken a little more than two hours later by the sound of a fog horn and the clanking of a buoy. It is now raining, cold and hard, and one of the men shakes his shoulder. "We're just entering the spur in to the Ship Canal," he tells him, "by Pomona Dock. It's more exposed here. Less shelter from the wind. Best you go below," and Hejaz wearily makes his way down a short ladder from the hatch the bargeman has opened for him and drops down. There is little comfort there either, for much of the cramped quarters are taken up with small bags of coal stacked in every available space, overflows from the main hold which is filled with loose slack fed directly from the chutes at each pit. These extra sacks are just drop-offs, sold to individual customers as separate deals, the money going straight into the skipper's pocket. Hejaz hunkers down between them, trying to find some comfort. As his eyes grow accustomed to the near Stygian gloom of the hold, he notices the faint glow of a stove at the far end, its embers dying, smoke seeping out from where the door doesn't quite fit. He sees a rat exploring the ash-filled grate. Despite the last sparks of the fire, there is a chill down here too, a mustiness, which Hejaz knows will make further sleep difficult, and he starts to cough from the smoke and dust.

Pomona Dock. This place, although he has only been there twice before, is etched in his memory. The scene of the chemical explosion in 1889, two years after his father began work on building the Ship Canal. He had been badly burned by the blast, including part of his face, and it was feared he would not recover, but the daughter of the landlady of the rooming house where many of the workers lodged had taken pity on him, had nursed him night and day back to health, through the worst of his fever, had bathed his raw skin with an infusion of oats, honey, tea leaves and wild herbs in lukewarm water, had encouraged him to believe he was strong enough to resume his work. And so it had proved. Yasser acquired a near mythical status over the next five years as the canal continued to be built, rising to gang master, and later to join the growing army of engineers brought in to oversee some of the trickier parts of the enterprise. He was a problem solver and by the time the Canal was nearing completion, he seemed to be everywhere at once. He and the landlady's daughter, Rose, remained close, and when the day came that he was offered a permanent position with the newly formed Manchester Liners, he asked her to marry him.

They moved to a house close to the Barton Aqueduct in 1894 where, a year later, Hejaz was born, and where they lived still, his father playing host to the ever-growing Yemeni community in and around Salford by the banks of the Canal, in Eccles, Patricroft, Peel Green and Weaste, on high days and holy days, when they would fling open their doors to anyone and everyone. Yasser was a powerful, formidable figure, with the livid scars from the burns on his neck now mostly concealed by the large beard he wore, with which he would rub Hejaz's cheeks when he was a small boy. In 1897 Rose gave birth to a girl, whom they named Pomona, the Roman goddess of fruit, in remembrance of the place that had brought Yasser and Rose together. On New Year's Day in 1900, to mark the new century, Yasser had taken the whole family to the banks of the canal by Pomona Dock, where he teased his now three-year-old daughter by telling her that the dock had been named after her. That was the first time Hejaz visited the scene. The second came fourteen years later, when Pomona had died after contracting tuberculosis, when his father and mother and he had stood at the water's edge to scatter rose petals in remembrance of her on the surface, which they watched float away towards the city till they were lost from sight. It was later that same day that Hejaz told his father he was joining the Manchester Regiment to fight against the Kaiser. Yasser shook him firmly by the hand and told him how proud he was. "Today you are a man," he said.

And now, ten years after that war's end, which saw Hejaz fight uncomfortably against the Ottoman in Aden, Greece and Turkey, before a final slog through Flanders, he is passing the Royal Pomona Dock a third time, on his way to meet the King of Afghanistan. He regards this third sighting accordingly with some foreboding. Down below deck the sound of the engine is louder but even that cannot quite drown out the sounds of scratching he hears in and among the sacks of coals he leans against, distant cousins of those rats he shared those mud-filled trenches with.

How has it come to this, he wonders? When he left for war, crowds lined the streets to cheer, throw flowers, wave flags, but when he returned, he crept back home down silent streets, hearing his feet echoing on the deserted cobbled streets on the late night walk from the railway station, from where, had it not been a Sunday when no trains ran, he would have been making this journey today. Finding work had not been easy and his father insisted that the way forward was through further education. Hejaz remembers a morning shortly after his return when his father banged his fist among the breakfast dishes, thrusting a leaflet advertising engineering courses at the Royal Salford Institute in nearby Pendleton. "You will start tomorrow," he roared. "With qualifications you will get good job, white collar job, management, no getting your hands dirty, like I have had to."

But it hadn't worked out quite so straightforwardly. He completed his diploma, applied for a position at Metro-Vicks (again through contacts and favours called in by his father) and joined the growing team of draughtsmen in a smart, new clean office. His father was delighted, but as the years slipped by, the hoped-for promotions failed to materialise, and now Hejaz found himself one of the older members of the team, where once he had been the new boy. There were dark mutterings at home. His father never, ever blamed him, lambasting instead what he saw as nepotism, as the nephews and cousins of managers climbed the ranks of the company instead of him, which only made Hejaz feel even worse. He was stuck, he knew it, but the rut he now found himself in would not have been so uncomfortable, had it not been for this all-pervading sense of disappointment that hung like a cloud over his father.

The hours crawl by. The final embers in the stove flicker and go out, and Hejaz hears himself coughing more and more as an icy chill envelops him.

*

"Lady Mayoress, my lords, ladies and gentlemen, I thank you with all due humility for your most generous invitation to speak before you today here in this most splendid Town Hall, and for those most kind words said during your welcome address. As some of you may know, my husband, the King, cannot be with us here today, as he is, at this very moment, visiting that Eighth Wonder of the World, the Barton Aqueduct, the world's first such swing bridge, which enables the waters of the Bridgewater Canal to be temporarily interrupted in order to allow ocean-going liners to navigate their way up the Manchester Ship Canal, making this great city of yours the third busiest port in the land, despite being forty miles distant from the sea, before making his way towards the Bradford Colliery – you see, I have been well briefed and have been paying close attention..."

A burst of laughter accompanied by warm applause greets this aside.

"... just a few miles to the east of us here at Beswick, where tomorrow he will inspect the latest technical innovations there, including a ceremonial opening of the recently installed state-of-the-art lift that will take workers down to the deepest shaft in the mine where a new seam has just been opened up. It is these

achievements of such ground-breaking ingenuity that we hope to take back to our own country, should circumstances change to enable us to do so, an event that we are hourly anticipating news of, so that we may continue the programme of modernisation we had lately embarked upon. My husband wishes me to convey to you his disappointment that he cannot be here with you today, therefore, at this most splendid luncheon provided for us by the Chef and staff of The Midland Hotel, which I shall describe to him in great detail when I rejoin him tomorrow.

"As you will note from this remark, we have no secrets from one another."

Polite laughter.

"Not even state ones."

More laughter.

"We share our thoughts on every single matter, which is why I can, with confidence, my lords, ladies and gentlemen, inform you that what I shall be discussing with you today carries with it my husband the King's full support and endorsement. We speak in one voice on this, as with all things."

Prolonged applause.

"We visit your country not just as guests of Their Royal Majesties King George and Queen Mary, with

whom we spent a most pleasant and gracious few days at Buckingham Palace, but as humble supplicants, for we are now exiles from our own homeland, the result of a cruel insurrection carried out by a small but troublesome minority of rural tribesmen, who took issue with some of the reforms my husband had introduced, many of which he had done so at my urging, reforms in particular to provide greater access to education for girls and young women, along with other basic freedoms hitherto denied them. It is about these reforms which I should like to say a few words this afternoon, if you will so permit me."

Further applause amid shouts of "Hear, hear!"

Sitting in the public gallery at the back of the Town Hall, in one of a very few limited places, for which she, along with the dozen or so others like her, had queued from earlier that morning, since before Queen Surayya had made her way in the Corporation's open-top Daimler the short distance from *The Midland Hotel* to Albert Square, Miss Esther Blundell, spinster of Gorton Parish, leant forward, entranced. She had seen photographs of the Queen in the newspapers that she read whenever she had time in the local library, and, along with everyone she knew, was fascinated by her fairy-tale glamour. To think that a real life Queen, an Arabian Princess, like someone from the Thousand and One Nights, was coming here, to Manchester, and was actually going to be visiting the place where she, Esther Blundell, worked, was like a scene from a romantic novel, the kind that generally she looked down her nose at, preferring instead something grittier and more contemporary, by the likes of Isabella Banks, Annie Besant, Sarah Grand or Ellen Wood. The librarians, she knew, all thought of her as something of a bluestocking, except for one, a Miss Nancy Cotton, who became for Esther a close and trusted friend. The other librarians' pursed lips and knitted brows would make Esther smile, for nothing could be further from the truth. She had not the time to be a bluestocking, she worked far too hard for that, but books and reading, especially writing by female authors grappling with the day-to-day realities of being a woman in a predominantly man's world, were her solace.

Esther was the second oldest of six children and the only girl. Consequently, when Alice, her mother died, exhausted, not long after giving birth to her sixth child, Freddie, it naturally fell upon Esther, barely thirteen herself, to assume the role of housekeeper and cook to the rest of the family. She watched all her brothers grow up, reluctantly go to school, then off to work at Bradford Pit as soon as they were old enough, two of them off to war, neither to return. She made their meals, washed their clothes, prepared their weekly baths, spruced them up when they began to go courting, and finally organised their wedding teas after each of them got married and left home. She was on friendly, if formal, terms with every one of her sisters-in-law, who would come to her from time to time with tearful concerns about their new husbands' occasional drunken Saturday nights, and she looked forward to the regular visits from the growing number of nephews and nieces who would pop round for

Sunday tea sometimes, though less so once their ailing grandfather, Walter, her father, grew too ill to receive them – Walter, who'd been forced to give up mining when barely into his forties because of a serious case of black lung, emphysema, and Esther had had to add nurse to her growing list of duties, as first his health, and then his mind, had gradually failed.

When, mercifully, he died, nearly two years ago now, she was still only thirty in a flat that was far too big for her, at a charge she could no longer afford, with little or no prospect of marriage. The Housing Association kindly offered her a much smaller 'widow's' flat, which she gratefully accepted, but there was still the rent to be found, and so she had gone, with some misgivings, to the Colliery Manager, the only person she could think of, to ask if there might be an opening for her somewhere. The Under Manager, a Mr Lomas, had looked up kindly at her from behind his desk, removing his spectacles to ponder the problem. Miss Blundell was known to him naturally, her father and five brothers had all been fixtures at the mine, and he liked to think that loyalty still counted for something, despite the ever-growing nature of the business. "Well," he had ventured after a few moments silence, "I believe there might be a vacancy in the Canteen…"

And so it had been settled. Esther now worked five and a half days a week in the Colliery Canteen, cooking and cleaning, and it was enough. The other girls who worked with her – and girls they all were, all but one of them younger than she was, and only working there till they found themselves a husband – looked upon her as some kind of older sister, a role she was quite accustomed to, and once again she found herself in the familiar position of listener, confidante, counsellor and, when the situation demanded it, rather stern teacher. The one older woman, a Miss Frangleton, was in her fifties, with a sweet tooth and a fondness for liquorice. She approved of Esther at once, could see that she was sensible and trustworthy, and that she could act as a much-needed buffer between herself and the ever-changing array of younger girls. The men were jocular but respectful when they came in for meals – they all knew that her brothers, all of whom had been fortunate enough to retain their jobs after the General Strike, would make them pay if they ever over-stepped the boundaries of propriety – and within a few months Mr Lomas approached Esther to see if she might be interested in "looking after" the Managers' Dining Rooms, which were much more salubrious and accorded her an extra two shillings a week on her wages.

But at nights, and during her brief periods of time away from work, Esther devoured her books, ordering her radical titles, which Nancy Cotton would save especially for her, hiding them away from the disapproving glances of the other librarians, and poring over articles in *The Manchester Guardian*. It was in one of these articles she had first read of the reforms being carried out by Queen Surayya for women and girls in Afghanistan, had seen advance notice of her arrival in England, accompanying her husband King Amanullah on a diplomatic trade visit to countries in Europe, and then learned, before it had even been announced at the pit, of their intended itinerary, which was to include an inspection of Bradford Colliery.

When Mr Lomas informed the entire work force, assembled in the pit yard one February Friday morning, there was both puzzlement and pride, puzzlement that a King from so far away should be coming to Manchester, and pride that of all the coal mines he might have visited, he was choosing theirs. Special arrangements were to be made, involving local dignitaries, and the colliery brass band put in extra hours of practice to master the Afghan national anthem, while Esther made the bold suggestion that perhaps they might decorate the Managers' Dining Rooms in red, green and black, the colours of the Afghan flag. Mr Lomas was delighted and handed over all the details to her, a responsibility she took great pleasure in, inspiring the other girls to be as excited as she was.

That Saturday, therefore, she had contrived to finish as early as possible so that she could catch a bus down to the Town Hall in Albert Square and queue for the Public Gallery, in the hope that she might get the chance to hear and to see Queen Surayya, who she knew was Guest of Honour of the Lady Mayoress for a special lunch that day. When the Queen finished speaking, Esther felt quietly elated. Here was a woman of genuine influence, trying to do something practical to improve the lives of women back in her home country who had been downtrodden for generations. The timing of the visit, coinciding as it did with Esther finally being accorded the right to vote, after having been such an active campaigner for women's suffrage, even though she had yet had the chance to exercise that right, Mr Baldwin giving no indication of calling an election just yet, only served to heighten her anticipation. Having been the only female in her home in Gorton, Esther knew all about being taken for granted, being occasionally invisible, but she also knew how much they all depended on her, and with this knowledge came a certain power. Her brothers knew not to cross her, or there would be no clean shirt for their Sunday afternoon courting. As she made her way back home to her widow's flat that afternoon, she was looking forward to seeing Queen Surayya at close quarters the following day, when she would serve her Sunday lunch, while her husband made his ceremonial descent down into the mine, and would watch eagerly for her appreciation of the decorations she had personally arranged to welcome her.

Gorton Reporter

31st March 1928

HISTORIC VISIT BY KING TO COLLIERY

Neither Inclement Weather nor Strange Incident Mars the Mood

Not even the Manchester rain could dampen the enthusiastic welcome given to King Amanullah of Afghanistan as he visited Bradford Colliery last week for the Grand Opening of the new lift that can convey miners to the recently-opened deep seams hundreds of feet below the surface.

Crowds lined the approaching streets as the King made his way by automobile, saluting and waving to his many well-wishers. Upon arrival he was greeted by Mr T.H. Fisher, the mine's owner, together with a delegation of staff, before being presented with a brand new miner's lamp as a token of his visit. Following the playing of both national anthems of Great Britain and Afghanistan by the Colliery Brass Band, Mr Fisher urged the crowd to give three hearty cheers for the King, which he acknowledged with a right royal salute.

Children from the nearby Christ Church School carried bouquets for Queen Surayya, who, to everyone's disappointment, was prevented from attending due to her feeling unwell, and the King accepted the flowers graciously on her behalf.

After declaring the new lift open with a short speech and the unveiling of a special plaque to commemorate the occasion, the King then duly stepped inside the cage, eagerly wishing to be among the very first to descend in it to the lower depths. Half an hour later, triumphantly waving his lamp, he showed off to the delighted crowds a lump of coal he himself had personally hewn while down below.

It was at this point that a potentially unpleasant incident was averted, when a rather dishevelled man in overcoat and hat rushed towards the King in a bid to attract his attention. Fearing he might be some sort of political agitator he was quickly removed by a couple of Constables, but not before he was within touching distance of the King, who, showing not the slightest alarm, turned and seemed to ask the young man a question, dropping a glove in the process. The man stooped to pick up the glove, which he offered back to the King from a semi-recumbent position, at which the King appeared, in the confusion, to hand the lump of coal he had just displayed to the now concerned crowds, to the man in question as he retrieved his glove. The confusion allowed the Constables time to intervene, marching the man off the premises, at which point the crowd burst into a round of spontaneous applause, both for the hasty actions of the police officers and the bravery of the King who did not flinch a muscle.

The people of Manchester wish *"God Speed"* to this plucky adventurer from across the seas. May he quickly recover his kingdom, for he will always be the People's Friend here at Bradford Colliery.

*

An hour after King Amanullah had left the colliery, two disappointed people stood by the gates to the pit yard, thinking back over the events that had just occurred.

Closing the canteen door and stepping out into the darkening afternoon, the rain having finally eased off, Esther paused. When she had heard Queen Surayya speaking at the Town Hall the previous day, there had appeared no sign that she was in any way unwell, but it was not in Esther's nature to be uncharitable. The Queen's schedule, she supposed, was a gruelling one, travelling the length and breadth of the country, a different destination each day, with all of their accompanying engagements and obligations, coming as it did after similarly packed programmes in other European countries previously. It was just unfortunate that, after all of Esther's hard work, the results were not appreciated by the person for whom they were intended, although she was gratified to learn from Mr Lomas that not only the mine owner, Mr Fisher, but the King himself had noticed all of her efforts and commented favourably upon them.

She was about to begin her journey back to Gorton when she became aware of another figure, standing motionless just a few yards away from her, who was suddenly seized by a violent bout of coughing.

Hejaz was feeling utterly desolate. He had made a fool of himself and now felt both embarrassed and humiliated, as well as fearful about how he was going to explain such abject failure to his father, who, Hejaz knew, would be even more disappointed about the turn of events than he was himself.

The moment he stepped off the barge as it moored into the canal basin by the pit, his fears that this whole enterprise had not been fully thought through were immediately realised. To begin with, as he approached the entrance to the yard, he could tell that he looked in no fit or proper condition to be meeting anyone, least of all a renowned former Head of State. He was quite filthy: his coat was covered in coal dust and pieces of sacking; his hands and fingernails were thick with dirt and grime; he was badly in need of a shave; his hair looked like it had been dragged through a hedge backwards; he felt certain that his clothes and body retained an unpleasant, unwashed aroma, and, to top it all, he was coming down with a severe cold. As he reached the top of the steps, he was at once overcome by a fit of coughing, causing the crowds who had gathered to greet the King to become aware of his presence and wrinkle their noses in disapproval. Just then the Colliery Brass Band struck up a fanfare and the King's Bentley drove into the yard. There was now no time for Hejaz to seek a washroom and at least make himself partly presentable. He could not approach the King like this, but nor could he disappoint his father, who had arranged this appointment for him.

But now that he was actually there, in the presence of the King, he realised that he had no idea how he was to make himself known. If he were to simply rush towards him, he would certainly cause consternation, if not downright alarm, especially looking the way that he did, but, having travelled all this way, he had to do something. But what?

He waited through the seemingly endless round of speeches, trying but failing to suppress further bouts of coughing, much to the irritation of the people standing nearby, who were clearly keen to catch every word the King spoke in his curiously accented English. Then, just when the ribbon had been cut and the lift declared officially open, Hejaz was on the point of approaching him when he disappeared into the lift and descended into the mine. Hejaz had to wait a further agonising three quarters of an hour, while the band played and the rain fell harder, and the crowds waited patiently.

When the King finally returned to the surface, Hejaz had grown quite desperate. Bursting through the crowds he ran towards the King, heedless of the shouts of warning all around him. The King turned, completely bemused but strangely calm and untroubled by this sudden intrusion into his inner circle. He looked Hejaz directly in the eye, but as Hejaz stammered his introduction, it was clear that the King had no idea to what he was alluding and was already turning away when Hejaz unpardonably grabbed his sleeve. In the ensuing confusion the King dropped his glove, and suddenly there were Constables and mine officials, together with members of the King's entourage, all jostling around this strange, wild-eyed young fellow kneeling before him. In a moment's sudden stillness, the King accepted the proffered glove, exchanging it for the lump of coal he had ceremonially hewn just a few moments earlier, before Hejaz was pulled away and the King was escorted indoors for the luncheon that was awaiting him.

Hejaz was dimly aware that he may have cried out to the King as he was being bustled away, and then a Constable was loosening his grip and advising him to go home before more serious charges might have to be brought against him. He heard words such as "affray" and "disturbing the peace" and "possible risk to His Majesty's person" and then, just as suddenly, he was alone. The band had started playing "*For He's A Jolly Good Fellow*", and gradually the crowds had dispersed until Hejaz found himself still in the yard, rooted to the spot, not moving, with a lump of coal in his right hand, and no clear understanding of how it had got there.

He looked at this piece of coal now, not in essence that different from the many scores of pieces he had unsuccessfully tried to lean against the previous night in a vain attempt at sleep, but at least this had the symbolic uniqueness of having been held by the King of Afghanistan. Perhaps there may be something to salvage from this debacle after all, he thought. He imagined a scenario where he might explain to his father a conversation that had taken place between himself and the King, which had not promised anything definite, but had resulted in the bestowing of this unusual gift, a gesture of understanding between two exiles from their homeland. But even as he played out this scenario in his head, he knew at once that he would never say such things. Hejaz was English; he had been born here; he had fought for King and Country in the war to end all wars; his grasp of Arabic was, at best, thin. His *father* was Yemeni, not him, and both had achieved established, if in his own case disappointed, lives here in Manchester. Still, this piece of coal would be useful to remind him of his hubris, of the foolishness and failure of the last twelve hours, and he would keep it, as a reminder of a lesson painfully learned.

Just at that moment, one of the Colliery's managers – at least that is who Hejaz took him to be by his dress and demeanour – approached him. "I say? Are you still here? Did you not hear what the Constable just said? We are not going to press charges, we simply want you to leave the premises at once – an act of extraordinary leniency, I would say, insisted upon by the generosity of the King, who said he was quite used to hot-headed young fellows and he was certain you meant no harm. Otherwise we may be forced to change our minds. Now – be off with you. Er – just a minute: what is that you are holding in your hand? Is that the piece of coal hewn from the new deep seam by His Majesty King Amanullah? I'd hand that over to me, if I were you. His Majesty has most graciously donated that to the Colliery, and we shall be sure to display it in our main entrance hall, along with other items of importance and significance regarding the mine's history. So – give that to me, there's a good chap, and then be on your way."

Now, standing outside the yard gates his humiliation feels complete. Without the piece of coal that little speech he had rehearsed delivering to his father would be impossible. There was nothing for it. He must begin his long journey back home and face the consequences. His father, he knew, would not be angry, just saddened on his behalf, and that would only make him feel worse. He was suitably wracked by a further bout of coughing, and, when it had finally abated, he gradually became aware of somebody standing quite close to him, followed by the touch of a gentle hand upon his arm.

*

"Are you quite recovered, sir?"

"Yes. Forgive me for troubling you."

"No trouble, sir."

"You are most kind." He raises his hat, then pauses. "I wonder if I might prevail upon you further?"

"Yes?"

"I need to take a bus into Manchester. Is there a stop nearby?"

"Yes indeed. I shall walk with you, for I too am to catch a bus, although in a different direction. If you will permit me…?"

"Yes. Of course. You are most kind. Here." He offers her his arm which, after a moment's hesitation, she takes.

They walk together in silence for a while.

"If you will pardon me for intruding on your thoughts, sir, but you seem… troubled. Is there something you would like to speak of?"

They stop walking. He turns and looks at her. She returns his gaze with a concerned smile, at which he is forced to break off, lapsing once more into violent coughing.

"I do apologise. This must be most unpleasant for you. I am… quite aware of the shortcomings of my appearance just now. I assure you that normally I would not be quite so…" He searches for the word. "… disarrayed."

"I am sure that is the case, sir, but I am anxious about that cough. You must take some medicine when you reach your home."

"Indeed, yes. I shall be sure to do so. Thank you." And he once again touches the brim of his hat.

"Is it far, sir, where you now travel?"

"Eccles. Or rather Patricroft. From Manchester I shall take another bus to Eccles and from there walk to Patricroft."

"That will take you a long time, I fear."

"Yes. I believe it may."

"You must cover your mouth with your scarf in order to avoid breathing in the smog and fumes. You do not want that cough to spread to your chest."

"I fear it is already too late for that." He turns away and once more coughs briefly. "And you?"

"Sir?"

"Do you travel far?"

"No indeed. To Gorton only. It is but a thirty minute single ride and the stop is opposite my front door."

They walk a little further in temporary silence. Hejaz surreptitiously tries to study the face and form of his companion. He notices that she walks with a barely perceptible limp, and he wonders how she may have come by that infirmity. He would like to turn their conversation away from the trivial to matters of more weight but cannot think how to do so without seeming forward or impertinent. But before he can think of anything, she is speaking once again herself.

"And here we are, sir, at your stop. Oh, you are in luck. Your bus has just turned the corner."

He raises his hat to bid her goodbye, but just as he is about to step aboard, he finds he cannot do so, and stands aside to let it pass. She looks at him with some surprise.

"And yet," he says, "I find that after all I do not wish to take it."

"So I observe, sir, and I cannot help thinking that perhaps you really are unwell, or at least a little worse than your outward demeanour would suggest. Your face remains quite pale."

"Yes…" He pauses, seemingly unable to continue.

"Sir?"

"Please," he says, "will you stop calling me 'sir'?"

"How else should I address you, for I do not know your name. And besides, I am so used to calling the managers at the Colliery 'sir' each day, it becomes habitual, I find."

"Hejaz."

"I beg your pardon?"

"Hejaz. My name. It is from the Yemen."

"I see." She tentatively tries out the name for herself. "He...jaz...?"

"Yes. But most people tend to call me Jaz. It's much simpler."

"Does it have a meaning?"

"I am named after the homeland of our ancestors. The mountains of Southern Arabia."

"How wonderful."

He smiles and inclines his head. "And your name? If I may...?"

"Miss Blundell. Esther. After my grandmother. It is a Jewish name, I believe, although as far as I know there are no Jewish branches of my family tree. I think my parents simply liked the name. My mother was an avid Bible reader, though not, in the conventional sense, particularly religious." She blushes, for she has never voiced these thoughts to anyone before. "A name is important, I think, don't you?"

"Less so perhaps if you have been given the name by somebody else."

"Why do you say that?"

"It can be a burden. Too much to live up to. Other people's expectations. Too much hope to carry."

"You speak as if from direct experience."

"Yes."

There is a long look passes between them as Hejaz looks up at Esther, who holds his gaze.

"Today," he continues, "today I have been…" He pauses.

"Yes?"

He turns away. "Humiliated. I have been made a fool of. Or rather, I have made a fool of myself." He looks back towards her. "As I fear I am in danger of doing so again." He coughs once more. She waits until he has composed himself before she replies.

"You must get yourself somewhere warm. You are shaking, Jaz. Your teeth… they are chattering."

He pulls himself away. "You are right of course. Is there another bus soon?"

"Not for twenty minutes more, I do not think. But mine…." She pauses before continuing. "Mine is due imminently. Might I be so bold as to suggest that you return with me? I have some medicines at home. I can light a fire, make you some hot tea."

He looks at her astonished.

"Please, sir – Jaz, I'm sorry – do not think me forward. I am certainly not in the habit of inviting young gentlemen I have barely met back to my lodgings, but you are unwell and I fear for your longer term health if you undertake such a long journey as you have in store without some sustenance and warmth beforehand, so that you may… recover yourself a little."

"That is extraordinarily kind of you, Miss Blundell."

"Esther – please."

"Esther. Yes. But I would not in any way wish to risk any damage to your reputation. Perhaps, instead, there is an inn somewhere near, a hotel?"

She smiles. "Yes there are, but not any that I would wish to enter, accompanied or unaccompanied. I fear my reputation, as you put it, would suffer even more if we entered such an establishment as those to be found nearby."

"I apologise," he says, inclining his head.

"Look," she says. "Here's my bus. Do come. Please. It will be better, I think."

He nods and together they board the bus to Gorton. There are not two seats together and so instead they sit one behind the other, Esther to the front, from where Hejaz can study this remarkable woman who is showing him such kindness, while Esther can keep her eyes fixed firmly ahead, relieved that he cannot see her blushes. She cannot quite comprehend her own boldness but has no regrets. It is as though, after inhabiting a twilit world that has been somewhat akin to surviving in a trench, she has at last lifted her eyes above the parapet and walked into the upper air.

This meeting, they both feel, each in their own separate thoughts as the bus makes its way to Darras Road where Esther lives in her "widow's flat", has rendered them rather like Joseph Smith's pioneers looking for sanctuary, thrown together as stones from a sling.

*

From that day on they were rarely away from one another's side.

After she had lit the fire, she drew some water for a bath, which she insisted he took, while she found him some fresh clothes and a dressing gown that had once been her father's. No sooner had he finished the soup she had warmed for him than he began to fall asleep on the sofa in front of the fire, and that is where Esther left him. She brushed down his coat and hung it over the door frame to dry, ironed and aired her father's clothes, then retired to her own bedroom where she did not sleep, but went over the day's events again and again, examining every word each of them had spoken, every look each of them had exchanged.

The next morning she crept into the living room where Hejaz still lay, deeply asleep. She leant over him and gently put her hand on his forehead, which was no longer clammy, though nor was it cool. In his sleep Hejaz briefly stirred. He lightly grasped Esther's hand in his own and then his breathing once more resumed its regular rhythm. Esther gently removed her hand from his and quietly got ready for work. Before leaving, she wrote a short note, which she left on the arm of the sofa.

Dear Jaz,

I hope that you have slept well and feel warmer and more rested. You looked so peaceful this morning I did not like to wake you. I have gone to work and shall not be back until this evening, when I expect you will have long left. There are some clothes that I have put out for you that should fit you – they were my father's – while your own clothes are hanging on the rack in front of the fire. I took the liberty of washing them last night – I hope you will excuse my presumptuousness – but I fear they will not be fully dried until later, and of course they will then need to be ironed. There is bread in the kitchen, butter and cheese. Please do help yourself.

May I be so bold as to ask you to leave me your address before you leave? I should very much like to write to you, if I may.

Yours
Esther Blundell, Miss

When Hejaz woke he felt extraordinarily calm. For a moment he could not recall where he was, and then the memories of the previous day returned to him, the humiliating and distressing events at the colliery, yes, but more, much more, the chance meeting with Esther and the conversation between them that had subsequently ensued. He did not remember saying good night or falling asleep, only the sense that a hand had rested on his forehead, a hand that he had briefly held, but that had since gone. He touched his forehead now and realised with a sense of wonder that, for the first time in many years, his mind was untroubled. He sat up and immediately found the note Esther had left behind. He read it and smiled. He would not be heading home just yet. He would wait for her to return from work. He had a question he needed to ask her.

*

They were married less than six weeks later.

The ceremony took place at Swinton Town Hall on a Friday lunch time. Hejaz declared to his father on his return from Bradford Pit, "I went to meet a King, I come home with a Princess." They took on the more easily pronounced Anglicised version of Hejaz's name. Wahid was shortened to Ward. Esther rolled the unfamiliar name around her tongue. Ward. Ward. From now on she would be Mrs Esther Ward.

Not many of Esther's family were able to take time off work to be able to attend. Two of her brothers' wives made it, along with their respective children, but sat stiff and uncomfortable throughout, and they did not follow on to the reception, which was held in Abdul's in Trafford Park, where they ate *mihshi* (stuffed vegetables with meat) followed by nuts and fruit, washed down with copious amounts of sweet tea, flavoured with mint, ginger and lemon. As Esther looked around at the dozens of faces smiling around her, faces that were unknown to her just a few weeks before, but which were now gradually becoming more and more familiar, and as she listened to the traditional songs accompanied by Hejaz's father playing the *oud*, Yasser, who insisted she call him *Babbi*, while Rose would simply be Rose as she was to everyone, she knew that she was crossing some sort of Rubicon. The sling shot that had flung her like Joseph Smith's stone was still in motion and who knew where it would alight? But one thing was certain: there would be no going back to Gorton, to her widow's flat, to the colliery canteen, to her old life. She looked across at Rose, who had welcomed her without hesitation the moment Hejaz brought her to his parents' home, who had recognised in Esther a kindred spirit, for she too had taken on a man who was broken, but who had now risen once more, and together they smiled as Hejaz was being passed between the older Yemeni women, from one to another, sitting together preparing a special drink with wreaths of knowing laughter. Yasser finished singing and a great roar went up as the drink was brought forward and Esther and Hejaz were carried into the centre of the room.

Esther had time to ask just one question before she was swept away. "What is it?" she mouthed towards Rose.

"This," said Yasser, before Rose had chance to answer, "is *qat*. Brewed from the leaves of the Flower of Paradise in North Yemen, which is where my son will be taking you after you have both drunk this."

"Yemen?" asked Esther naïvely.

"Paradise!" roared Yasser.

"And that," said Rose firmly, "is quite enough from you," as everyone laughed. She propelled Yasser back towards their table, whispering to Esther as she passed, "It's an aphrodisiac."

Although Esther and Hejaz had spent almost all of their time together since the day they first met, their love was not yet consummated. Later that night, back in Rose and Yasser's home, which was now to become *her* home too, Esther held Hejaz close. Their passion was fierce, intimate and intensely private.

3

1939 – 1950

Eleven years pass by.

*

Jaz returns to work at Metropolitan Vickers and stays in the same draughtsmen's office but is no longer fuelled by the feeling he is being passed over. He and Esther can now even talk jokingly about his failed attempt to gain an audience with King Amanullah, the snatching away of the piece of coal inadvertently given to him by the King, so that his sense of failure felt quite total. They recall his announcement to his father at the time, which Yasser is now pleased to pass off as his own: "You left to meet a King, but came home with a Princess." They smile as they remember this, sitting by the fire burning brightly with coal from Bradford Colliery, delivered to all the merchants along the Bridgewater and Ship Canals.

At Metro-Vicks Jaz continues to do meticulous work, which he knows is valued by his employers, and by 1939 a modest, informal ceremony takes place to mark his twenty five years of loyal service. Mr Puncknowle, (pronounced 'Punnel'), the managing director in charge of all manufacturing, presents him with a brass and mahogany barometer, made with parts supplied by their own factory, using drawings Jaz himself has produced, which he hangs by the front door in the hallway of his father's house, where he and Esther still live, where it is always fair weather, apart from those occasions he finds his father stepping into the kitchen, still expecting to find Rose there, Rose, who died suddenly and unexpectedly five years before from cancer, which she endured uncomplainingly, which only Esther knew about, for the two of them had become such close friends, and which they both agreed to keep from Yasser for as long as could be possible.

For the fourth time in his life Jaz found himself on the muddy tow path along the edge of the Bridgewater Canal by Pomona Docks, watching petals he had helped to scatter floating slowly away towards the sea some forty miles distant, as Esther began, softly, to sing something she had composed specially, after the fashion of Rumi, whose poems Rose had introduced her to.

> *My words hang in the air*
> *As a bird about to take flight*
>
> *But like the bird who does not wish*
> *To leave the safety of the nest*
>
> *My words stay caught in my throat*
> *Reluctant to take shape or be heard*
>
> *Lest they fall to the earth and break*
> *Before they have developed wings*
>
> *Strong enough to carry them*
> *From my heart into yours*

And so we stand here silent
Watching you float with the current

Petals of ash on the water
Making your way to the sea

To mingle with the waves at last
To carry you back to our homeland

Far beyond the horizon
Until they beach again

But for the most part life is good to them in Patricroft.

Esther looks after Jaz's father – Yasser will turn seventy-seven later this year – and carries on the voluntary work she previously shared with Rose. Now such a familiar figure in the growing local Yemeni community, it is as if she is one of them, *Ishtar*, as much as she remains Esther. She wears the *qurqash* on holy days and has been known even to paint the henna on her hands at wedding or engagement parties, or sometimes privately just for Jaz.

Much of her time she spends assisting in the Pendleton Ragged School at the New Windsor Chapel on Croft Street. She has never forgotten the inspiring words of Queen Surayya at Manchester Town Hall and dedicates several hours each week to helping young girls learn to read and believe in a future for themselves beyond the confines of the dark cellars and yards so many of them must return to each night.

Esther and Jaz have not had children themselves. In the first few years of their marriage Yasser would occasionally make unwelcome remarks, or drop unsubtle hints, but these would be instantly quashed by Rose, and since she died nothing further has been spoken of it. But when Jaz hangs up the barometer in the hall and taps the glass to test it is working, he is surprised, looking at the dark storm clouds hanging above the town, to see that it reads, "Expect change". The following week this surprise turns to astonishment as Esther informs him that she is three months pregnant. There are quiet celebrations in the household that evening, for Esther is now forty-two years old.

"If there's one thing I have learned in this life," says Yasser on hearing the news, "nothing is certain, but let us rejoice in the gift of this new imminent arrival into our home. *Insha'allah*. I shall make you some special tea, Ishtar," which he proceeds to do religiously each day from then on.

Esther/Ishtar continues with all of her activities for as long as she can. In her second trimester she experiences a huge surge in energy and finds herself walking from parish to parish, recruiting more and more young girls to attend the Ragged School, but in her final weeks she develops preeclampsia and is reluctantly forced to rest. Then, at a quarter past eleven one Sunday morning, 3rd September, just as Mr Chamberlain is speaking on the radio informing the nation that since "no such undertaking has been received", consequently "Britain is now at war with Germany", Jaz is called upstairs by the midwife to tell him that he is now the proud father of a baby boy, and that mother and son are both doing fine.

Some time later Yasser too climbs the stairs and knocks on their bedroom door. The scene that awaits him will stay etched in his mind for ever afterwards: Jaz and Ishtar, heads close together, bent over his new-born grandson. He says nothing until they smile up at him. "Come," he says. "Let me look at you. I am your *Jaddi*." Esther passes the baby for him to hold and he is immediately smitten and transfixed. He turns to Hejaz. "Have you decided on a name for him?"

"*Babbi*," he says, "I know it is our tradition for fathers to choose the names for our children, but I would like Esther to choose. When we first met and exchanged our own names, she told me then that the naming of children is very important, and I know that she will choose wisely."

Jaz and Yasser look towards Esther, who nods solemnly. "I should like him to be called Sulh."

They all look down on this tiny wriggling scrap as he seeks out his mother's breast. After a few moments Yasser speaks, trying to keep his tears in check. "Sulh," he says. "Peace. An excellent name for a boy born on a day that war is declared. May he bring his peace to all our lives. Come, Hejaz. Let us go downstairs and let Sulh get to know his mother without the two of us foolishly crowding around him."

*

They endured a safe war, as fraught and hazardous as thousands of others, but they survived.

Metro-Vicks gave over much of its operation to the construction of Avro bombers – Manchesters, Lincolns and ultimately Lancasters. Jaz suddenly found his highly developed draughtsman's skills in much demand, producing finely detailed drawing after drawing of undercarriages, fuselages, propeller fastenings. The factory switched to continuous twenty-four hour production and Jaz on occasion would work two eight hour shifts back to back, arriving home in the early hours, exhausted and coughing.

Esther meanwhile devoted what time she could to the WRVS, running soup kitchens, organising clothing banks for families who had lost their homes in the bombing raids that were becoming nightly occurrences, providing tea for the wardens, who would sometimes arrive at the makeshift canteens covered in plaster and brick dust, looking like ghosts. It was after talking to one of these, a purposeful, no-nonsense woman around the same age as her, that Esther volunteered to become an air raid warden herself. Sulh was three by this stage and Yasser agreed to look after him if her duties coincided with when Jaz too was on an all-nighter. She cycled the streets and alleys of her patch, expertly avoiding the pot holes and craters even on the darkest of nights, checking the blackouts, making her rounds of the various shelters, or in a morning checking for damage and casualties after another raid, liaising with her former colleagues in the WRVS to direct help where it was needed most. On especially cold nights she took to wearing her *qurqash* beneath her tin helmet, and people began to call her 'the lady of the veil', regarding it as a kind of good-luck charm, so that more and more she found herself answering to 'Ishtar'. She looked back to the First War, in which she had so angrily and reluctantly undertaken work manufacturing gas masks, or later as a Pit Brow girl at the colliery. Now she had found both her calling and her name.

Sulh, or 'Solly', as he increasingly came to be called, especially by other children, was unconcerned by the bombs, for he knew nothing different, and then later, towards the end of the War, when the raids on Trafford Park had long diminished, and he had started school at Lewis Street, the bomb sites were his playground, along with all his new-made friends, as they clambered in and out of the skeletal hulks of broken buildings, scavenging for shrapnel among the dust and debris, like armies of rats scuttling back indoors when their stomach clocks called for whatever their mothers might conjure up from their meagre rations.

Yasser still had many friends at Abdul's and from among the old bargemen on the canal, and occasionally he would return with treasure wrapped in newspaper, perch or chub or bream, which he would gut then grill on a toasting fork over the fire in the front room grate.

When the War ended, Ishtar hung her ARP uniform in the back of the wardrobe and used the helmet as a bowl for scrubbing potatoes. She helped organise the street party after VJ Night and then looked around and thought: what now? She walked Solly to school each morning, then met him each afternoon to fetch him home; in between she still helped out at the WRVS, for food rationing was, if anything, worse in the Peace than it had been in the War. She took to visiting those who were now alone, the elderly, the widowed, the soldiers returning to find their homes and families gone.

Then, in 1947, when Britain was gripped in a vice of iron frost, the swollen skies turned black with snow, and the water froze in the pipes, and the chill in the air was so deep, and the coal in the bunkers so damp, that the fires in the hearth would barely catch, Solly became ill. Despite the vicious cold, his head was burning. His throat swelled and he developed a barking, painful cough. While Ishtar stayed by his side and did what she could to try and bring his fever down, Jaz threw on an overcoat, took Ishtar's bicycle from the yard at the back and rushed to get help. The first doctor he tried was already out on a call, as was the second. Eventually he managed to rouse the district nurse, who agreed to come as soon as she could, as well as promising to telephone another doctor. By the time Jaz arrived back home, the doctor and nurse were already there, confirming a case of whooping cough, assuring them that, with the medicine they would leave with them, Solly would soon recover.

And so it proved. Within a few days Solly was back to normal. He regained his appetite, his cough subsided, and the following month he returned to school, joining in with all his usual games and activities in the streets with his friends. But for Jaz it was a different story. His coughing fits grew more painful and debilitating than they had ever been. He fell weaker and weaker, while outside the winter showed no signs of loosening its grip. Once more the doctor was summoned. After he had examined Jaz, listening carefully to his rattling chest and laboured breathing, he took Ishtar to one side. His expression was grave.

"Mrs Ward, I have to tell you that I'm seriously concerned. I recommend an X-Ray most urgently, although I feel bound to say that this will almost certainly merely confirm what my initial examination tells me. Your husband is suffering from acute pulmonary pneumonia, which, I fear, is already in such an advanced state, that I do not believe there will be much we shall be able to do for him, except to make him more comfortable."

In his final week Jaz calls his father, wife and son separately to his bedside to make his farewells:

"Father, I have tried always to follow your example, to live by your values, to be a good son to you. I hope I have not let you down."

"Ishtar, my Esther, I went to meet a King. Instead I found a Princess."

"Solly, soon you will become a man. I shall be sorry not to witness that. Look after your mother. Listen to what she says, for she is wise and strong. Stay true."

After he closed his eyes for the final time, and his rasping breaths at last quieted and ceased, Ishtar stayed by his side a long time. In her hand she clutched a letter that Jaz had written for Solly. On the envelope were written the words: *'To be opened on his 21st birthday.'*

He was fifty-two years old. He had been her husband for nineteen of them. The stone flung from the sling all those years ago had finally landed. For his funeral she wore white traditional Yemeni robes, which she vowed to wear from that point onwards.

As she and Yasser and Solly rode the bus back together from Pomona Docks where, as had become a custom for them now, they had scattered petals on the surface of the canal, Yasser turned to his daughter-in-law, gripping her hand tightly. "A father should not live to see the death of his son," he said. He did not speak again for several weeks.

*

Solly grew up. He played with the other kids among piles of bricks and broken windows, burnt out cars and cobbled courtyards, littered around the shells of roofless, boarded-up houses jostling cheek by jowl with those that were still being lived in, the ruins of bombed out homes built to celebrate victory after the First World War, laid to waste in the Second, still not demolished, still not rebuilt, but the perfect adventure playground for Sol and his friends, known universally as the Bama, short for Alabama, though no one could tell him why. The heart of the Victory estate.

The Victory. The Bomb Site. A home for heroes. With roads named after generals. Haig Avenue, Kitchener Close, Allenby Drive. The Victory. Older than time or wars, buried beneath the crush of hope and houses built since on the Bama. The bomb site. The Victory. Lollipoppa.

eeny-meeny macka-dacka der-die dum-a-racka
chick-a-lacka lollipoppa lom-pom-push

Between the barracks and the chapel, the slag-heap and the pithead, the Soap and Margarine Works, Steel Mill and Tar Pit, the railway and canal. The Victory.

The bonfires burned on the bomb site, Sol's stamping ground, hunting ground, for cowboys and dreams. The Wild West, Outer Space, anywhere but where it was. Pentecost and Tabernacle, Back Street Bethesda, Dante's Inferno, the Steel Works. The Victory.

They played there, fought there, recited prayers and tables there, accepting it, never questioning, where it came from, where it led to – *The Creature From The Black Lagoon It Came From Outer Space* – and landed here, the Victory, a maze, a rat-run of back-streets, brick alleys, cobbled squares, railway arches, then out into a clearing.

The Bama. The bomb site. The bonfires. The playground. The heart of the Victory Estate.

4

1957-58

Sol storms into the kitchen where his mother is preparing their supper, clutching an envelope tightly in his fist. He is seventeen and a half years old exactly.

"Look at this," he yells.

1st March 1957

Dear Mr Ward,

In accordance with the 1948 National Service Act passed by HM Government in order to extend compulsory conscription for all able-bodied British-born men between the ages of 18 years and 30 years, you are formally summoned to report for duty at Catterick Garrison four weeks from today for an initial period of preliminary training, after which you will be assigned to a posting for the duration of your service.

A separate sheet is enclosed with this letter listing everything you are required to bring with you.

Yours etc
Major K.G. Birkett, DSM

Ishtar reads it carefully, twice, then quietly sits at the table.

Sol continues to rail. "I thought I was exempt. If you're black or Asian, they don't call you up. Everyone knows that."

Ishtar says nothing. She goes into the front room, to the bureau where all the important papers are kept, and after a few moments pulls out the document she has been looking for, which she hands to Sol. It is his birth certificate. It lists his name as Solomon Ward, his mother's name as Esther, his father's as Henry James.

He looks at her uncomprehendingly.

"When your grandfather first came to this country to work on the Canal, they couldn't spell or pronounce his surname properly – Wahid – and so they shortened it to Ward – you know that. Then your grandmother, Rose, took over all the official business for the family. "We must assimilate," your grandfather would say. "We are British now. But we never forget our home." So that when your father was born, although he was named Hejaz, Rose wrote on the birth certificate "Henry James", explaining that her husband's accent rendered this as "Hejaz", and this became shortened to "Jaz". And so I simply carried on with that tradition. You were born the day war was declared on Germany, and so we called you 'Sulh', the Yemeni word for 'peace', short for Sulheyman, but on the birth certificate we wrote 'Solomon', which also happens to mean 'peace', but which is much more readily understood by people here in England, knowing that we would probably end up calling you 'Sol' – as we do. I imagine that the civil servants processing the registers of births for National Service simply read your name, 'Solomon Ward', where you were born, 'Salford', and didn't think to check further. Why would they?"

"Well they should have." He throws the letter onto the floor.

"You can explain to someone at the Town Hall if you really don't want to go. But you're only a quarter Yemeni in terms of blood, you know, and it's not as if you look that different from millions of other English boys with dark hair. Do you really not want to go? It'll be much simpler for you if you do. It's only for eighteen months, after all. You'll be back before you know it."

"You sound like you want to be rid of me."

"That remark is too foolish to warrant an answer, Sol."

*

Sol slams out of the kitchen door, through the yard into the alley that runs between the backs of two streets of houses, pauses just long enough to light up a cigarette, and then, scowling, turns his collar up as he hunches into the wind and heads towards *The Black Boy*, the pub on the nearest corner. It's name feels fitting. But it's Friday night after all and there may be some action, something to distract him from the scramble in his head.

On the corner, shielding their cigarettes with their hands from the stiff breeze blowing up from the Canal, Eric and Ray call him across.

ERIC:

What's with you? You've a face like thunder.

SOL:

This. (*He thrusts the call up letter in front of them*).

ERIC:

Oh. Right. Best get plastered then.

RAY:

I reckon ours'll be arriving too any day now, eh Eric?

ERIC:

Could be worse.

RAY:

How's that?

ERIC:

At least it's not a twelve month ago.

RAY:

What difference does that make? We've all got to go at some point.

ERIC:

Don't you ever read the papers?

RAY:

Not if I can help it. Except for the gee gees. (*He shoves Eric playfully*).

SOL:

What he means is, if it had been this time last year, I might have been sent to Suez.

RAY:

Oh, right. I see. Where *do* you fancy then?

SOL:

Nowhere.

RAY:

Join the Army, see the world.

ERIC:

Germany, Cyprus, Singapore.

RAY:

Or maybe you'll just get stuck in Catterick. Like our Stephen did when it was his turn.

SOL:

Where *is* Catterick?

ERIC:

Yorkshire.

RAY:

Ay, a right dump, our Stephen said. Like Eccles on a wet weekend.

ERIC:

> Like tonight, you mean. Eh up, it's pissing down. If
> we're to get to *The Majestic*,we'd best get a shift on.

SOL:

> You two go, lads. I'm not in the mood tonight.

ERIC:

> That's exactly why you should go. You might get
> lucky.

RAY:

> Ay, ay – Skirt Alert at ten o'clock. Don't fancy yours,
> mate.

*Ray straightens his tie, stubs out his cigarette and heads
across the road to the bus stop where three girls are
waiting with umbrellas.*

RAY:

> Good evening, ladies. Ray's the name, dancing's the
> game. (*He shows off some moves*). Might you three
> beauties be going to *The Majestic* tonight?

SUSAN:

> Not with you.

RAY: (*singing*):

> 'Uh-huh-huh, I'm all shook up…'

ERIC:

Just ignore him, girls.

SUSAN:

That's what I *am* doing.

ERIC:

He can't help himself. He was stood under a tree that got struck by lightning. It fell on his head and he's not been the same since.

BRENDA:

What was he like before?

ERIC:

Twice as daft and just as ugly. (*Brenda giggles*).

SUSAN:

Shut it, Brenda.

RAY:

Brenda? Like Brenda Lee? (*He launches into 'Jambalaya'*).
'Son of a gun, we'll have big fun on the bayou...'

SUSAN: (*spoken*):

'Goodbye, Joe – we gotta go.'

RAY: (*still singing*):

'Me, oh my, oh...'

BRENDA:

He's funny.

SUSAN:

Yeah, funny peculiar. Come on, girls. Let's walk to the next stop.

ERIC:

Wait. Why don't we start over and introduce ourselves? I'm Eric. This one who thinks he can sing is Ray. He says we're mates, though honestly, girls, I never clapped eyes on him till just this minute. And the good-looking feller over there, who looks like Tyrone Power, that's Sol.

SUSAN:

He doesn't say much, does he?

ERIC:

The strong silent type.

BRENDA:

I like Tyrone Power.

ERIC:

And won't you tell us *your* names?

SUSAN:

Susan. This is Brenda – but you know that already.

BRENDA:

Mutual, I'm sure.

Susan rolls her eyes and removes the chewing gum from her mouth, wrapping it in a tissue, which she drops into her handbag.

SUSAN:

And this is Nadia. (*Nadia nods her head*). She's quiet too. (*She looks across to Sol*). Maybe the two of you should get together and say nothing to each other.

RAY *(sings):*

'My baby whispers in my ear –
Mm, sweet nothings
He knows the things I like to hear –
Mm, sweet nothings…'

Ray continues to sing Brenda Lee's 'Sweet Nothings'. Brenda laughs until Eric kicks him and he stops.

ERIC:

Saved by the bell. The conductor's bell. Here comes the bus.

NADIA:

I don't think I'll bother tonight.

SUSAN:

Oh Nadia, come on. It'll be fun.

NADIA:

No. You two go. I'll see you Monday.

CONDUCTOR:

Make your mind up, girls.

SUSAN:

Are you're sure?

NADIA:

Yeah, I'll be fine.

The bus pulls away as Brenda shrieks, contriving to fall into Ray, who slips his arm smoothly round her waist and guides her upstairs towards a double seat, followed closely by Eric and Susan.

BRENDA:

Where's Tyrone Power?

RAY (*looking round*):

Sol?

ERIC:

I expect he stayed behind to escort your friend safely home.

SUSAN:

He's a dark horse and no mistake.

ERIC:

Still waters, Susan. Cigarette?

SUSAN:

Don't mind if I do. Ta.

Back at the stop, as the bus disappears round the corner, Nadia becomes aware that Sol is still there. They stand silent and awkward for a moment, then both begin to speak at once.

SOL:

I'm sorry about Ray, he...]

NADIA:

Well, I'd better be going...]

SOL:

Sorry. Go on.

NADIA:

No. After you.

SOL:

I'm afraid I've forgotten your name. I wasn't really...

NADIA:

Nadia.

SOL:

Nadia. Yes. My name's...

NADIA:

Sol. I know who you are.

SOL:

You do?

NADIA:

I've seen you at Abdul's. You were at my cousin's wedding a couple of years ago.

SOL:

Sorry. I don't remember.

NADIA:

I've changed since then. (*Sol nods*). Other times too.

SOL:

How come you know my name?

NADIA:

You're Yasser's grandson. Everyone knows Yasser.

SOL: (*smiling*):

I suppose so.

NADIA:

He was the first of us to come and live here. And your mother's a legend. 'The Woman in White'. 'The Lady of the Veil'.

SOL:

She's embarrassing.

NADIA:

She's amazing.

SOL:

Not if you live in the same house.

NADIA:

She does anything for anyone.

Sol looks away, lights a cigarette. He offers one to Nadia, who shakes her head.

NADIA:

I haven't seen you at Abdul's in a while.

SOL:

No.

NADIA:

Why's that?

SOL:

You ask a lot of questions.

NADIA:

That's what my dad says.

SOL:

Your dad's right.

NADIA:

He'd agree with you.

They smile.

SOL:

Since I started work, I don't really have time for much else.

Nadia:

I see. What do you do?

Pause. Sol does not answer right away.

SOL:

Metro-Vicks. Machine Shop. You?

Nadia:

Typist. Turner's.

SOL:

You want to be careful.

NADIA:

How do you mean?

SOL:

Turner's. Asbestos.

NADIA:

I'm in the office all day. I don't go near the factory.

SOL:

All the same…

She nods.

SOL:

Your friends? Do they work there too?

NADIA:

They're not really my friends. But yeah, they do.

SOL:

So why were you going out dancing with them?

NADIA:

I could ask you the same question.

SOL:

Ray and Eric? Oh, they're not so bad. We went to the same school, that's all.

NADIA:

I didn't really want to go out with Susan and Brenda tonight, but they're always asking, and my sister says I ought to say yes once in a while, or they'll think I'm stuck up.

SOL:

Sister?

NADIA:

Farida.

SOL:

And *are* you?

NADIA:

What?

SOL:

Stuck up.

She looks at him sharply.

NADIA:

I think I'd better be getting back. (*She begins to walk away*).

SOL:

Wait. I'm sorry. I shouldn't have said that.

NADIA:

No. You shouldn't.

She hurries away from him, putting up her umbrella as she leaves the bus shelter. It is now raining hard. Sol watches her go, then angrily stubs out his cigarette and chases after her.

SOL:

Wait. Look – I've said I'm sorry. I just…

NADIA:

What?

Sol has caught up with, and then run in front of, Nadia, momentarily preventing her from walking further. She tries to sidestep him only to step off the kerb into a puddle.

NADIA:

Now look what you've made me do.

SOL:

Let me walk you home. It's the least I can do.

NADIA:

No. I'll be fine. I only live a couple of streets away.

She hurries on her way. Sol stares after her for a while till she reaches a corner, then decides to follow her. He rounds the corner himself just in time to see which house she enters and stands under a street lamp, diagonally across the road from where she lives. He watches as she draws the curtains shut in the front room. He is sure that she has seen him and so he decides to wait. The rain continues to fall. He waits ten minutes, then another ten, then another. He is completely drenched. He is just about to give up and go back home, when the door opens. It is Nadia's sister, Farida.

FARIDA:

What are you doing? What do you want?

Sol doesn't answer.

FARIDA:

Just go away. You'll catch your death.

Farida looks back inside. Nadia is evidently speaking to her.

FARIDA: (*to Nadia*):

Really? Are you sure? (*She turns back towards Sol*). She says: would you like to come in?

Sol nods.

FARIDA:

Hurry up then. I'm letting all the cold air in here.

Sol crosses the street, hesitates a moment at the doorway, then steps inside.

FARIDA:

You're soaked! Take your shoes and jacket off, then go through there and stand by the fire. Understand this – if our parents weren't away, in Nafaj, on a pilgrimage, there's no way you'd be allowed in here. And Nadia – half an hour, that's all. Then he's got to go. Alright? Before Salim gets home.

Nadia nods.

FARIDA:

I'll make some hot chocolate.

Farida shows Sol into the front room, where a coal fire is burning, before she goes out to the kitchen. He stands close to the fire but still cannot stop shivering. Nadia comes in with a towel and looks at him.

NADIA:

What do you want?

Sol looks back towards her. She meets his gaze.

SOL:

I don't know.

There is a long pause.

Nadia wraps the towel round Sol's shoulders. He begins silently to weep. Slowly and carefully Nadia holds his shoulders through the towel, then gently leaves the room, closing the door behind her.

*

Later, after he has drunk a mug of hot chocolate and begun to get dry, Sol finally begins to speak, quietly and bitterly. He does not look once at Nadia, staring instead deep into the fire as he talks, while she, sitting across the room from him on the hearth rug, her face in shadow, scrutinises him intently.

SOL:

I was just seven when my dad died. He called me to his bedside and made me make a promise. To look after my mother and grandfather. To become a man. I think in his way he was trying to make me feel better, convincing me that I was strong and that I would be able to cope after he'd gone. But I took him at his word. When I passed the eleven plus and went to the grammar school, I was proud to put on the uniform on that first day. This was the first step, I thought. But when I turned fifteen, I could see things were difficult at home. My grandfather was too old and ill to work any more, so my mother had to be on hand to look after him. This still didn't stop her from keeping up with all of her community activities though, and often I'd arrive home from school to find her not there, just my grandfather asleep in the kitchen. It was clear I had to get a job. My teachers tried to persuade me to stay on, take my exams. One of them even came round to the house. My mother prepared *harissa*. He was enchanted by her, as everyone is….

The scene dissolves into the one Sol now describes, an incident that took place back in his own home, two years previously.

SOL:

You do realise, he said, just how clever your son is.

MR MEAKIN:

He's top of his class in many subjects, and he has a

real gift in art.

SOL:

My mother raised an eyebrow when he said that, but said nothing. My teacher even mentioned the possibility of university.

YASSER:

Of course he is intelligent…

SOL:

…my grandfather replied, in one of his now rare lucid moments…

YASSER

He's my grandson, we only want what is best for him. Haven't I always said, Sulh, you work hard, anything is possible?

SOL:

My teacher now warmed to his theme.

MR MEAKIN:

There are grants too, so you needn't worry about the cost.

SOL:

It was at this point my mother chose to speak. She coughed slightly, in that annoying way she has, as if she doesn't want to interrupt, but in fact she always does.

ISHTAR:

Yes –

SOL:

– she said…

ISHTAR:

…we understand what you are saying to us. Solly is a bright boy, he always has been, and as for his art, well – you know that his father was a skilful draughtsman, perhaps he inherited this gift from him, but…

MR MEAKIN:

Forgive me, Mrs Ward –

SOL:

Mr Meakin couldn't help himself from saying…

MR MEAKIN:

– but I am not just talking technical ability here, with which Sol is most fortunately blessed, but something else, something harder to define, something like…

ISHTAR:

Yes –

SOL:

– my mother asked?

MR MEAKIN:

He has real talent, Mrs Ward, the potential to be a

genuinely fine artist.

SOL:

There was a long silence after that. I didn't know where to look. My teacher just didn't understand, this is not the way we talk in our house, it sounded so... boastful somehow, and that is something we must never do.

Nadia nods.

ISHTAR:

I see –

SOL:

– said my mother.

ISHTAR:

Thank you. Would you like some more tea?

SOL:

Mr Meakin shook his head. He didn't realise that, as far as my mother was concerned, the conversation was now at an end.

ISHTAR:

We thank you so much for coming to see us, Mr Meakin, and we really appreciate the very kind things you have had to say about Solly, don't we, *Babbi*?

SOL:

> But by now my grandfather had sunk back into himself, staring at the fire, and didn't answer.

ISHTAR:

> The thing is, Mr Meakin, we had been rather counting on Solly getting a job as soon as he is able to leave school. Since my husband died, things have been... well, I'm sure I don't need to say any more. Metro-Vicks have already offered Solly a position, on the shop floor for now, but with prospects, and there's always night school for him to be able to continue with his art, isn't there?

SOL:

> It was at this point, when an awkward silence had descended, that my grandfather stood up suddenly and shouted to Mr Meakin:

YASSER:

> I spoke with the King of Afghanistan. He has promised he will find him something.

There is a sharp intake of breath from Nadia.

SOL:

> I turned to him and led him gently back to his chair. "That was my father, *Jaddi*, not me." There were tears in his eyes.

ISHTAR:

Well, Mr Meakin, we thank you again for coming out to see us in your own time like this, but as you can see, we are a family, and we look after one another.

The scene dissolves back to the front room in Nadia's house. The fire in the heart is now red with the fading embers.

SOL:

I left school the next day and went to work at Metro-Vicks the day after that, loading crates of ball-bearings onto lorries. At the end of my first week, I went home and emptied my pay packet on to the kitchen table. My mother separated a small amount from it, which she put into a jar on the dresser.

Her voice can be heard in the darkness, rising out of the crackling sparks of the fire.

ISHTAR:

For night school, Solly, so that you can carry on with your art.

Her voice dies away.

SOL:

That was two years ago. I haven't touched a penny of it. I haven't picked up a pencil since, and today this arrived. (*He holds up his call-up letter*). Bloody National Service. Two more wasted fucking years...

For a long time neither of them says a word. Nadia remains where she is, watching Sol, his back towards her. His shoulders begin to shake a little, and at first she thinks he must still be shivering from having got so wet. It takes her a while to realise that he is crying once again. She goes to approach him, but finds that she cannot. Instead, after a further pause, she finally speaks.

NADIA:

Your mother loves you, Sol.

She slowly creeps from the room.

When she checks on him half an hour later, he is lying fast asleep on the front room floor. She fetches a blanket from the airing cupboard, which she gently lays across him before Farida leads her away. She slowly climbs the stairs to her own room.

When she comes downstairs early the next morning, he is nowhere to be found. The blanket lies neatly folded on the sofa, and Salim, Farida's husband, is sitting in the kitchen with a mug of coffee.

NADIA:

Have you seen Sol? The boy? (*She gestures towards the front room*). Did he say anything?

Salim looks hard at Nadia.

SALIM:

He was never here, do you understand?

NADIA:

Perhaps he left a note…?

Salim catches her elbow as she turns to go.

SALIM:

He wasn't here.

Nadia bows her head. A few moments after she has left the kitchen and gone back upstairs, Salim takes a note from his jacket pocket, a note Sol had written before leaving, which he tosses onto the last few embers of the fire in the grate.

*

Ten years earlier. 1947.

Three months after the death of Hejaz, Yasser took the seven year old Solly for a walk. It was a damp, grey Sunday morning. The worst winter of the century was finally beginning to thaw, but there were still slabs of ice gathered at the edge of the Ship Canal, knocking against the bank. Rooks, feathers plumped against the cold, shouldered into the wind, cawing from the rooftops of terraced houses as Yasser and Solly walked hand in hand through the narrow, dark labyrinth of cobbled streets and alleyways towards the lock gates. Solly was wrapped up in a big coat over an extra jumper, scarf tightly wound around his chest and pinned at the back, a navy blue woollen balaclava on his head and matching knitted gloves on his frozen fingers, which Yasser had to keep reminding him not to chew.

After a brisk ten minute walk they drew near to the Canal. As always an iron mist hung like a pall over the still, murky water, its surface stiff with a slick sheen of oil and sewage. A small coil of rats shivered in the weeds at the Canal bank, their keen eyes foraging among the scraps of bones and rubbish. Solly aimed a stick at them, which they easily dodged before continuing their scrape and scratch.

Yasser stooped so that his eyes were on a level with Solly's as his huge hands gripped his grandson's thin shoulders. "Let them be," he said. "They're doing no harm here, are they? If they were underneath your bed, that would be different, but out here in the open, they're just going about their business. Like you and me."

"Sorry, *Jaddi*. I'll remember." As ever, Solly hung on his grandfather's every word. "What are we doing here? It's so cold."

Yasser stood up and looked around. "You'll see," he said. "Shouldn't be long now." He scanned the Canal to his left and right, while Solly tried to draw a picture of the Swing Bridge, which loomed above them. A distant ship's horn sounded and, dimly through the mist, which a pale sun had still not broken through, he began to discern a large liner making its slow way up the Canal from Liverpool towards Manchester. At the same moment,

Yasser tugged Solly's sleeve and pointed in the opposite direction. "Look," he said, and Solly saw a light being held up against the smeared glass of a window in the small brick building standing next to the bridge. "That's our signal," said Yasser. "Best be sharp. Put your pencil and paper back in your pocket."

He took hold of Solly's hand once more and quickly walked towards the light. Gates on either side of the bridge had come down so that vehicles could not drive across it, and a small queue of cars, bicycles and vans was already beginning to form as Yasser and Solly reached the small brick building with the light. A voice called out from inside.

"Perfect timing, Yasser. You and the boy there, step onto the bridge. That's it."

"Thanks, Ron," Yasser called back, and with his arm around Solly's shoulder, he guided him onto the bridge. "Now, Sulh, hold tight."

There was a metallic whirring sound of wheels turning and wires tightening, and Solly felt a deep vibration beneath his feet as slowly, incredibly, the bridge began to move. He looked up at his grandfather in wonder. Yasser smiled back, nodding. It took several minutes for the bridge to swing round completely, so that by the time its motion had ceased, instead of spanning the Canal, it now hovered alongside it, in parallel with its flow. Each end of it was completely open and Yasser, keeping a tight grip on Solly's hand, walked him the entire length of it, from one open end to the other, so that they had an unbroken view of the huge ship, which needed clear passage to be able to continue through.

Solly gazed wide-eyed as the giant leviathan sailed slowly past him. It was so immense that, as he strained his neck to look all the way up to its very top, it appeared to block out the entire sky. He could make out writing on the side of the hull as it passed him – '*SS Pioneer*' – followed by something in an Arabic script. Although Solly could understand and speak some Arabic, for Yasser frequently spoke it at home and his mother had taught herself the language too, becoming quite fluent, he could not yet read it, and he turned back towards his grandfather, who was staring up at it, his eyes cloudy with tears.

Solly could dimly make out the shapes of men busily working on the ship's different levels, coiling ropes, carrying crates, or leaning over a rail as they lowered buckets from one deck down to another. Solly waved, hoping that one of them might see him. He waved until he thought his arm might drop off with the effort, but he would not stop. Eventually he was rewarded by one man, standing precariously in a kind of cradle from where he was repainting one of the signs in Arabic. He saw Solly just as he was being hoisted back up towards the upper deck and waved back. Solly turned towards his grandfather and beamed.

Finally the ship sailed past and the bridge slowly began to swing back towards the road. While they were still suspended over the centre of the Canal, they both continued to look towards the mighty liner as it slipped back into the mist, making its steady way towards the Royal Pomona Docks and then to the Port of Manchester, before the bridge completed its graceful passage. Yasser and Solly stepped off, and cars once more flowed freely across.

Yasser led Solly silently by the hand further along the bank towards the Bridgewater Canal, which crawled alongside. They climbed the steps towards the aqueduct. Yasser lifted Solly up to sit astride a girder, from where he could see out along both canals to where they joined. It was high but Solly felt quite safe with his grandfather's arms wrapped tightly around his waist. They were quiet for some time, and then Yasser began to speak, slowly and deliberately in Arabic, pausing to look at Solly, to make sure he was understanding him.

"It is more than sixty years since I first came here. I was not yet seventeen years old. I remember as a small boy in Aden running down to the harbour to greet the fishing boats coming in from their overnight trips. The quaysides were wet and slippery, and there would be birds everywhere, flying above us, diving between us. Then, as I grew older, and the port became larger, the trading vessels would land there. From all over the world they came – wood and ivory from Zanzibar, coloured cloth from India, nutmeg and spices from the Moluccas – and I would help the men unload them, sometimes managing to carry something back, something that might have spilled and otherwise gone to waste, home for my mother – and then, later, the British were there, in greater and greater numbers, with bigger and bigger ships, men o' war with guns and rigging, merchant ships with oil and coal. It was around then that the fighting broke out, wars between the tribes and the Turks, the Hashid and the Bakil, with the British as peacemakers, or so it seemed to me as a young boy. Aden was by then a true city of the world, with Zaydi and Ottomans, Saudis from the north, Ethiopes from the south, Persians and Jews, Indians and Afghans, all of them jostling and fighting to get their share. Then, when the Suez Canal was opened, more and more ships and people crowded the quayside, and the fighting grew worse. Nobody knew whose side anyone was on any more. One night a fire broke out in the city – some said it was the Pasha, others said it was the Imam, it was impossible to know – and by the time I made it back to where we lived, the whole district was in flames. I found my father carrying the burnt body of my mother. He was wild with grief. 'Run,' he shouted. 'Flee. Get as far away from here as you can.' That was the last time I saw him. A beam, ablaze from a nearby building, came crashing to the ground between us, and I was swept along by the human tide of screaming, frightened people back towards the sea. I leapt on board the first ship I came to, a British merchant ferrying coal between Liverpool and Bombay, and her captain granted me safe passage in return for free labour, which I gladly gave. Half a year later we reached Liverpool. While we were unloading goods onto wagons, amid the crush of crowds and horses, I overheard someone talking of a scheme to build a great canal linking Liverpool with Manchester, where so many of these goods were bound, and that soon they would be hiring labourers. In less than a year I was part of a gang blasting out the land, digging huge cuttings, excavating mountains of earth for embankments. I was a quick learner, a keen solver of problems, and it was not long before I was put in charge of my own gang, eventually working my way to becoming part of the main construction team led by Thomas Walker himself. He was a great man, Sulh. He had a dream, a dream that would not only link these two cities, but that would link Manchester to the rest of the world. He died shortly before we reached the Weaver Navigation, but his dream lived on, and soon the canal was ready to be filled with water and welcome ocean-going ships from the four corners of the empire. I am sounding like a true Englishman, am I not? For that is what I felt I had become. The British had rescued me from almost certain death when the riots swept across Aden and brought me to this cold, wet city, and I was grateful. I had work, I had respect, I had friends, but for all that I was lonely, so that when the call went out for people to work on the aqueduct to take the Bridgewater across the Ship Canal, I volunteered without hesitation. Where we are standing now, Sulh, this island, is a pivot, which houses the turning mechanism. Sixty-four iron rollers sit on top of a revolving plate, held in position by a great spider ring. I helped build that ring, Sulh, and it has kept turning ever since. Twenty years ago, we replaced the iron rollers with ones made from reinforced steel, forged over at Irlam, a couple of miles up the Canal, and they will last another hundred years at least. We made these new rollers just before King Amanullah made his visit from Afghanistan, and I stood on this very spot with him that day, Sulh, and spoke to him about your father. It is about that conversation that I wish to speak with you this morning."

Solly looked up at his grandfather, who was watching him carefully.

"What do you know about that meeting?"

"Not very much, *Jaddi*. Only what my father used to say every year on my birthday, how he went to see the King but came back with a Princess."

"Meaning your mother, boy."

"Yes."

"And there isn't a day goes by that we do not count that as a blessing."

"*Jaddi?*"

"She reminds me so much of your Grandmother Rose. She came to my rescue just as your mother came to your father's. You see this, don't you, boy?" he asked, pulling back the collar on his shirt to reveal where his skin had never quite fully grown back. "Do you know what it is?"

"Yes. I think so. You were burnt."

"Burnt and left for dead after the explosion at Pomona, and I would have been for sure had it not been for the man who found me, who carried me to your grandmother, who took me in and nursed me back to health again."

Solly was staring at the scar. "Does it still hurt?"

"Sometimes, yes. Especially on days like today. But do you want to know something? I'm glad that it does. It reminds me."

Solly shook his head, puzzled.

"It reminds me of how I met your grandmother, and I can never be sad about that, but more than that, it makes me remember that life can be hard sometimes, but that if you stay true, you can come through those times the

111

stronger for it."

"I'm sorry, *Jaddi*. I don't know what you mean."

"I'm talking about your father. After I had spoken with King Amanullah, your father travelled all through the night along four different canals to get to Bradford Pit in time to meet him and present himself to him. Only things didn't quite work out like they were meant to. Did he ever tell you about the piece of coal?"

"No, *Jaddi*, he didn't."

"No. I don't suppose he did. The thing is, the King, just before your father tried to speak with him, had been down the mine. He actually dug a piece of coal from the newly-opened seam, and when he came back to the surface, he accidentally dropped one of his gloves. Your father rushed across the yard to pick it up for him, and when he presented it back to him, like a knight offering his services…"

"A knight?" said Solly in wonder.

"… a knight, yes – the King presented him with the piece of coal he had just brought to the surface. As tribute."

"What happened to it?"

"That's what I'm telling you, Sulh. They took it from him."

"Who?"

"The big bosses at the mine. They thought, you see, that the coal belonged to them, but…"

"… the King had given it to my father?"

"Yes." Yasser was breathing hard. He gripped his grandson's shoulders and looked him in the eye. "And I want you to promise me that one day, when you're older, you will bring it back."

They looked at each other a long time until eventually Solly spoke.

"Yes, *Jaddi*. I promise. For you."

"Not for me, my boy."

"For my father?"

"For yourself."

He slowly relaxed his grip on Solly's shoulders, then placed the boy's small gloved hand back inside his own giant one. Together they walked back home as the pale sun at last began to break through the ragged wisps of grey cloud, and the ice on the branches of the few bare spindly trees on the piece of waste ground near the lock gates slowly started to melt. Neither of them spoke as they quickened their pace, their breath rising above them to form strange statues. Solly would never forget this day, but for years it lay buried far back in his brain. Occasionally it would resurface, and then he would take it out from its dusty corner, brush the cobwebs from it and hold it to the light, but it would always cloud over again before he had chance to examine it properly and grasp what it meant.

*

Less than a fortnight after he had fallen asleep in front of the fire in Nadia's front room, Sol was on the train up to Catterick in Yorkshire to begin his National Service. Their paths did not cross before he had to leave. Six weeks after that, training duly completed, he received news of his posting – of all places, to Aden – and a month later he was sitting in the large tent that served as his unit's sleeping quarters by the Seedaseer Lines, not far from *The Sharnaz Club* and the *Qat Market*, writing the first of several letters to England in the course of the next twelve months.

*

74825871 Pte S. Ward
British Army Arabian Peninsula Forces
Aden
BFPO 667

3rd June 1957

Dear Nadia,

It has taken me almost three months to write this letter to you. Several times I tried to begin but on each occasion I tore it up without finishing it. This time I finally hope to manage it. I wonder if after all this time you will have forgotten me?

I am sitting in the tent that I share with some of the other boys. There are twelve of us in all who try to sleep here each night, though we are plagued by mosquitoes. It seems we have arrived at exactly the wrong time of year, the end of the rainy season, and the air is hot and sticky. Right now it is late afternoon. We have an hour during which we have no drill, no manoeuvres, in which we are left pretty much to ourselves, unless it is our turn to be on jankers (that's kitchen duty), which today I'm not, so here goes.

First of all, I want to apologise, for the way I behaved that night we met – I don't know what you must have thought – and then for just disappearing early the following morning without so much as a word. I hope you got the note I left you? But in case you didn't, sorry, and please say thanks to your sister too.

As you can see from my BFPO address, I've been stationed in Aden. Of all the places it might have been! I mean it's not like anyone knew. My army papers simply say, 'Solomon Ward' and 'born in Salford', so nobody here knows my connection with this place, and for some reason – I'm not sure why – I haven't let on that I speak a bit of the language, or that my grandfather sailed for England from here more than seventy years ago. Not that he'd recognise it now. It's all changed, with roads, and airfields, and enormous ships everywhere you look. There's still an old town, though, with a fish market, and all kinds of fruit and spices – our mothers would think they were in heaven – but more and more new buildings are going up, so that it's hard to get a sense of the place as it once must have been.

When we're out on patrol, I look and listen and try to take it all in, but I don't really feel a connection, not yet anyway. Is this really my homeland, I ask myself?

Anyway, that is not what I wanted to say, but somehow, being with you, or imagining I am with you, as I'm doing now, makes me want to talk about all kinds of things I didn't even know were in my head. What I want to ask you is this – will you write to me? Will you be my pen friend? Will it be OK for me to keep writing to you?

Yours hopefully,
Sol

64 Mellor Street
Patricroft
Eccles
Salford

23 June 1957

Dear Sol,

I received your letter yesterday. Thank you for not sending it directly to my home address. That would not have been a good idea, and I am so relieved you sensed that. Eric was standing outside the gates at Turner's as I left from work. At first I thought he must be waiting for Susan – did you know that they were going out together now? – but as I headed for the bus stop he called me over. Honestly, Sol, he looked like he thought he was in some kind of spy film, with his collar turned up high and his hat pulled firmly down upon his brow. I wondered what he could possibly want, and then he reached inside his jacket pocket, looked furtively over his shoulder to check nobody was watching him, before he handed over your letter.

"This came for you," he muttered. "Sol sent it inside one he'd written to me."

"Sol?" I asked, not understanding.

"Sorry it's got a bit creased," he said, shoving it into my hands. "Don't worry, I haven't read it." And then he was off, like a greyhound out of a trap. He looked quite comical, I must say.

Anyway, I got it. I have to admit I was really surprised. But pleased. And the answer is yes – as you can see. I will be your pen pal.

This is all for now, as I need to catch the last post before anyone notices I'm not helping with dinner, and I wanted you to know that yours had arrived safely, and that I've read it a dozen times.

Your pen friend
Nadia

5 July 1957

Dear Nadia,

We have just returned from our first expedition into the desert, where there had been reports of minor tribal uprisings. We saw no evidence of this, everyone was incredibly friendly, though we've been told you can never be too careful. As we drove in our convoy of jeeps past tiny roadside villages, where men and women would stare and children wave, I wondered if these were the sorts of places our families had come from originally, for little appears to have changed here for centuries, unlike Aden itself.

I don't know about you, but in our house it is rarely spoken of. My father visited here briefly, during World War 1, but he never spoke of it, and my mother is English, in spite of all her efforts to pretend otherwise. She's never been further than Derbyshire, where she went once as part of the Mass Trespass. Before I was born. My grandfather still remembers the old country of course, though his memory's not too reliable these days...

But if you could only see the desert for yourself, Nadia! I can't do it justice – the light, the colour, the way the heat shimmers on the horizon, the clothes worn by the people, the women especially. When we returned to base, I rooted out some paper and pencils, and for the first time since I left school, I started to draw again.

Yours gratefully,
Sol

17 July 1957

Dear Sol,

It's different for us. We came over to England much later than your family did. Farida and I are the first in our family to be born here. My father still expects us to go back some day. But I don't want to. I'm more English than Yemeni, and I like it here. I like the cold and the rain, and I like how friendly the people are towards us. People like your mother. Why are you so hard on her? She's been such a friend to our community. Still, I expect you have your reasons. It's difficult growing up, isn't it? Mothers and sons, fathers and daughters...

Farida is the apple of my parents' eyes. First she marries a good-looking boy from a well connected Yemeni family. Not only that, he works in a bank, with "good prospects". My father still works on the Steel Works in Irlam, like so many of our people do, and for him and my mother the whole purpose of our coming here, apart from leaving behind the civil strife that was always threatening to boil over back at home, was to make a better life for their children.

Us.

My brother, Hilal, died when he was just a boy, before I was born. I think that was what finally convinced my parents to come over to England, and they have always wanted my sister and me to do well, at school and now at work. When I got the job at Turner's, they were thrilled and proud. Even now, they pay for me to go to night school to get Advanced Shorthand, so that my chances of becoming a secretary to someone higher up, one of the managers maybe, will be that much better. But of course, what they hope for most of all is that I should marry well, like Farida has done. But I have my own ideas. I look at Farida and I wonder, is she really so happy? Her husband, Salim, is not a kind man, I think. I sometimes hear my sister crying in the night, and in the mornings her eyes look tired, as if she has worries.

I hope that the enclosed parcel will arrive safely. Think of it as an early birthday present. I was overjoyed to read that you have started to draw again.

Yours happily,
Nadia

10 August 1957

Dear Nadia,

This will have to be just a short note, I'm afraid, as we are headed back to the Interior again later today to try to calm things down there. Our C/O says there's a bit of a flap on, some trouble between Houthi tribesmen from Lahej and Saudi Arabs from the north. I expect you know more about the history than I do, something to do with rival claims over oil fields, but stretching much further back, Sunnis and Shi'a. I've never really understood all that. My grandfather always says we are all equal before Allah, and my mother, who reads the Qur'an every day, appears to be drawn towards the Sufis.

Anyway, I don't know when I'll next get a chance to write, all leave has been cancelled, and the C/O says we might not get back to base for several weeks, so I wanted to let you know that the drawing paper and pastels arrived safely yesterday. I can't tell you just how much your kindness means to me, Nadia. Thank you. I shall try not to disappoint you with the results of my efforts, and I have already packed them to take with me into the desert.

I hope all goes well with you.

Yours, in haste
Sol

*

Ishtar parks her bicycle in the backyard, next to the privy, and covers it with the black tarpaulin, before letting herself in by the back door. She calls to Yasser, who she can hear tending to the fire in the back room, that she's home, then goes into the hallway to hang up her coat. Lying on the mat by the front door is a large envelope. It bears a British Army postmark. Curious, she takes it into the kitchen where she sits to open it. It is too large to signify bad news and the handwriting is clearly Sol's. This is unusual. Since his posting Sol has written regularly, at the beginning of each month, but more out of obligation, she feels, than a genuine desire to communicate.

His letters follow a predictable pattern:

"The days are hot, the nights hotter..."

"The lads aren't too bad, we have a laugh together..."

"The Sgt Major's alright if you keep your head down..."

"The food's improved since we reached Aden..."

"How is Jaddi?"

Never a sense of how he is feeling, what his impressions of the country are, the nature of his duties, what his plans might be when his National Service comes to an end. But he has always been a drifter, she thinks. School came easy to him, he never needed to apply himself, his was a natural facility for storing and retrieving facts, for writing stories, for drawing...

She pauses. She knows the heart went out of him after that evening Mr Meakin, his form teacher, came round, and she made it clear that staying on at school a further one, two, or even three years, was just not possible. Sol's sense of drift deepened after that, became his general condition, even, in the end, diminishing his anger, which had burnt so fiercely at first. She was proud of that anger, thought it would spur him on to continue his studies at night school, but he simply gave up, and this continues to be a source of disappointment for her.

And so, as she considers this envelope bearing his handwriting, she wonders what has happened? He has already sent his cursory letter this month. What has prompted this additional communication from him? She turns the letter over and notices that it is in fact not addressed to her, but to Yasser, and the knot in her stomach that is always there tightens further.

"*Babbi*," she calls, "there's a letter for you, from Solly."

Yasser comes in, rubbing his forehead. "From Solly? Here, let me look. Have you seen my glasses?"

She points to the top of his head and he pops them down onto the bridge of his nose. "He's a good boy."

Yasser begins to tear impatiently at the envelope.

"Careful, *Babbi*. You don't know what's inside."

He nods and slows down. His big hands fumble over the sealed flap until eventually he manages to open it. From inside he pulls out a large piece of paper folded precisely into four, which Yasser smoothes out on the kitchen table. As what is on the paper reveals itself to him, an involuntary gasp escapes from his lips and he leans back, removing his glasses to cover his eyes.

Ishtar reaches inside the envelope from which a smaller piece of paper falls. "There's a note," she says. "Shall I read it?"

Yasser nods.

" *'Dear Jaddi',*" she reads, then pauses.

Dear Jaddi,

Last week we drove out across the desert to the

mountains, to Hejaz, the place you named my father after. They are so beautiful, these mountains, rising out of the plains towards the sky. I can't find the words to do them justice, Jaddi, and so instead I have tried to draw them for you. I hope you can recognise them and that they bring back happy memories for you.

With love
Your grandson
Sulh

In barely a dozen sure pencil strokes, with less than half of these edged in pastel, an entire landscape floats out of the paper before them. Yasser and Ishtar sit in silence a long time staring into it, conjuring the vast empty desert of Southern Arabia, the sharp mountain peaks piercing the heat haze.

So this is where my Jaz is named after, thinks Ishtar, and not for the first time marvels at the sheer randomness that they met at all, that Yasser walked out of this terrain, down to the sea more than a hundred miles to the south, boarded a British ship, sailed to Liverpool, survived a chemical explosion, married his landlady's daughter and had a son, this same son who travelled by barge and canal to Bradford Colliery to meet the King of Afghanistan, and instead alighted upon her, and brought her back, here, to this overcrowded maze of back streets and brick alleys that have become as familiar to her as her own hand. That Solly could have created all of this with just a few bold marks on a creased and folded page.

Yasser looks up at her, his face wreathed in tears.

"Rose," he says, "our boy is back."

Ishtar looks away hastily so that she might compose herself, before turning back to her father-in-law and patting the back of his hand.

"Yes," she says. "He's back."

*

On the first Sunday in December, 1957, at exactly twelve noon, ten million households across Britain were tuning in to *Two Way Family Favourites* with Jean Metcalfe and Cliff Michelmore. Among these was the Raqeeb household in Mellor Street, Patricroft. No sooner had the familiar theme tune of *With A Song In My Heart* begun to fade than Nadia was helping to set the table for Sunday lunch, a special lunch which the whole extended family were attending, for today was her birthday. She was seventeen. Her mother had made her favourite dish – *shakshouka* – eggs, meat, tomatoes and peppers, spiced with cumin, turmeric and chilli, served on a bed of *laxoox*, a Yemeni flat bread – and now she was preparing *zabib*, a cold raisin drink that Nadia would offer the guests when they arrived. As well as her parents, together with her sister Farida and her husband Salim, aunts, uncles and cousins were expected, and many of the women were already helping Nadia's mother in the kitchen, unwrapping the various dishes each had brought, while the men were smoking, teasing Nadia as she handed round the glasses of *zabib*.

The talk and laughter continued unceasingly throughout the first course of the meal, on through to the dessert, *bint-al-sahn*, the 'daughter of the plate', a layered cake of doughs and clarified butter drizzled with honey, adorned with a single candle, around which Nadia's name in Arabic script had been iced by her mother, which was carried in ceremonially by Farida.

"Make a wish," she said, and all fell silent as Nadia closed her eyes, before blowing out the candle.

In the lull that followed the applause, Jean Metcalfe's mellifluous tones oozed from the radio, which had not been switched off.

"And here's a request from Private Solomon Ward stationed with the British Army Arabian Peninsula Forces, Aden. 'Please could you play for my pen friend, Nadia, of Patricroft, Manchester, who is seventeen today,' he writes, '*Look Homeward Angel* by Johnnie Ray?' Of course we can, Private Ward, and so for you, Nadia Raqeeb of Patricroft, Happy Birthday."

As Johnnie Ray crooned across the airwaves, a silence fell on 64 Mellor Street, all eyes trained and darkening, narrowing on Nadia.

"To your room," her father said quietly, and without protest, in mortified embarrassment, Nadia consented.

Look homeward, Angel
Tell me what you see
Do the folks I used to know
Remember me...?

Two hours later, when all the guests had departed and the tables cleared, the furniture put back and the dishes washed and dried, Nadia heard her mother's gentle knock on her bedroom door.

"Go away," she moaned, turning over onto her side as her mother walked quickly in and sat down on the edge of the bed beside her.

"Who is this Private Ward person? And what does he mean with this pen friend nonsense? I've asked your sister and she tells me nothing."

"Because there's nothing to tell."

"A soldier boy gets a silly pop song played for you on your birthday, on the radio, BBC Light Programme, listened to by millions, and you say it's nothing? How will I ever walk outside this house again? Oh, the shame you have brought on this family."

"It's nothing, *Ommi*. We write letters, that's all."

"Letters? What kind of letters? Let me see them."

"No, *Ommi*, they're private."

"There – you see, what did I tell you? You're ashamed to show me. If you've nothing to hide, you'd let me read them."

"No, *Ommi*. That wouldn't be fair."

"Fair? What do you know about fair? Only Allah knows this."

"To *him*, *Ommi*. It wouldn't be fair to *him*."

"At least tell me who he is."

Nadia turned away and sighed. "He's called Sol. Solomon Ward."

"An English boy?"

"But his real name is Sulh Wahid. He's Yasser's grandson. His mother is…"

"I know who his mother is. The Woman in White. The Lady with the Veil. She's a saint, that woman, there's nobody she hasn't helped at one time or another, and Yasser, well… everyone knows Yasser. He was the first among us. But this boy – Sulh, Sol – what does he do? What are his prospects?"

"He's a soldier, *Ommi*. He's doing his National Service. He's stationed in Aden, our old country, and I write to him, because he misses his home."

Her mother looked her sharply up and down, like a magpie searching for something shiny that she might pounce upon, then turned away disappointed that she had not been able to find it. "You're a good girl, Nadia. Now wash your face and come downstairs so you can tell all of this to your father." At the doorway she paused a moment. "And when you next write to that soldier boy of yours, make sure he understands – no more silly pop songs on the radio."

*

The months pass. The end of Sol's National Service draws closer. Back home Yasser retreats further and further back in time. Ishtar looks after him as best she can. More and more he calls her Rose, his wife's name. She has long stopped correcting him. What does it matter now, she thinks? She is reminded of when she nursed her own father, how, in his last days, he began calling her by her mother's name, his wife's, as his fever rose and his breaths came in short, painful rasps. But Yasser is not physically ill. He may not be quite as strong as he once was, but he can still carry in sacks of coal from the yard like they were bags of apples, or lift the ladder onto his shoulders to lean against the house wall when gutters are to be cleaned out. But often she will find him just sitting, staring at Solly's drawing of the mountains of Hejaz, which he has insisted they pin to the front room wall above the fireplace, singing songs in Arabic, tracing the lines on the page with his huge trembling hands.

And so it comes as a great shock when one afternoon, after she has felt it safe to leave him for an hour, while she visits Mrs Ahmed, who has just come out of hospital following an operation, and has then gone to collect another neighbour's children from school, taken them back to their house, given them their tea, she comes home, calls Yasser's name as she always does, not worried that he has not answered her, goes into the kitchen to make him a glass of mint tea, his favourite, even in this hot weather, takes it into the front room, where she is not surprised to see him sitting in front of Solly's drawing, sleeping, she thinks, until gradually she realises that she cannot hear his breathing.

"*Babbi?*" she calls softly. "*Babbi?*"

She kneels beside him, gently strokes his hand, then walks to the kiosk at the end of the street to telephone the doctor.

The funeral is the biggest the town has ever known.

In keeping with Muslim tradition, he is to be buried within twenty-four hours of his death. Ishtar, a convert and more zealous than Yasser ever was himself, wishes everything to be done correctly – except in certain key instances. After telephoning the doctor she returns home.

She asks a neighbour's child to hurry to Mr Hassan al-Haideri, the spiritual leader of the Yemeni community in Eccles, who has set up a small *zawiyah* on Peel Road, a converted house, where prayers and meetings are held, to come as soon as he can. While she waits for him to arrive, she reads softly verses from the *Qur'an*. Mr al-Haideri offers his condolences, speaks a *salat*, a special mourning prayer, then, in a rare concession, permits Ishtar to assist him with the ritual washing of the body. Together they wash Yasser three times, before wrapping him in a simple, plain *kafan*, a burial cloth of modest cotton.

Afterwards, while Ishtar sits with the body to begin her period of mourning, the *iddah*, which will last for four months and ten days, Mr al-Haideri contacts key members of the local community to tell them the news and to ask them to let as many people know as they can. It is not long before a steady stream of friends and neighbours arrives to pay their respects and offer their prayers. Ishtar stays up all night. Sometimes she sits by Yasser's side, sometimes she lets others keep the vigil while she goes into the kitchen to prepare dishes for after the ceremony.

The next morning it is another warm spring day. Mr al-Haideri returns early with four men who bring the coffin with them and who will act as bearers. Ishtar thanks them and by ten o'clock everything is ready. Several people have gathered at the house and, at a signal from Mr al-Haideri, the procession begins. The streets are lined with people, not just from the Yemeni community, not just other Muslims, but, it seems to Ishtar, the whole of Patricroft is there. Non-Muslims bow their heads, remove their hats, draw their curtains out of respect for this man who was loved and venerated by all, and who has finally died aged ninety-five. The local Police Constable halts the traffic as the procession turns into Liverpool Road, before winding its way down towards the Ship Canal and onto Barton Bridge, where the coffin is temporarily placed while the bridge swings out over the water as a mark of respect and recognition to Yasser and the role he played in the aqueduct's construction. He was the first to arrive there from Yemen. There then followed a growing trickle, which in the last decade, since the end of the War, has turned into a steady stream. Hundreds of families now live nearby, in Eccles, Weaste, Swinton and Salford, in Irlam, Cadishead, Rixton and Patricroft, working on the Canal, at Trafford Park, at Metro-Vickers, Regent Tyres, Pilkington's Tiles, at the Soap, Tar and Margarine Factories, and of course at the Steel Works just a couple of miles further along, and everyone, it seems, has turned out to say their farewells. A slight breeze ripples the surface of the canal. A lone rat scurries along the water's edge. A large ship passes, its flag lowering, before sounding its horn three times. The seamen all line the port bow, presenting a salute to the coffin on the bridge.

Ishtar, dressed from top to toe in her familiar white, her head covered in a white *qurqash* which had formerly been Rose's, worn on her wedding day to Yasser, walks against tradition directly behind the coffin, is the only person to accompany it on to the swing bridge, then back onto Peel Green Road for the final stretch towards the cemetery, where Mr al-Haideri conducts the last remaining acts of the ceremony, leading the mourners in the *janazah* prayer, before inviting everyone present to pour three handfuls of soil into the open grave, while intoning the *Qur'anic* verse: "We created you from it, we return you to it, and from it we will raise you a second time."

After everyone has finally left, only Ishtar remains. The gravediggers complete their task of burial before patting down by hand the final pieces of earth into a raised mound. Ishtar scatters petals upon it, petals of the kind she will later drop upon the waters of the canal at Pomona Dock, as was done for Rose and Jaz, then pours scented water over the ground.

As she turns at last to leave, she sees a young girl whose face she recognises but whose name she does not know. She carries a small wreath. She bows and covers her face with a veil as Ishtar approaches her.

"On behalf of Sol," the girl says, then lays the wreath by the side of the grave before walking quickly away.

Ishtar watches her go. She has not, she realises, during the course of these last twenty-four tumultuous hours, when time has not run normally, thought about how she might let her Solly know.

5

1958 – 1963

Seedaseer Lines, 7 July 1958

Internal Briefing chaired jointly by Major-General Douglas Harrington, Commanding Officer, Yorkshire & Lancashire Regiment, British Army Arabian Peninsula Forces, and Sir Vivien Carstairs, representative of Her Majesty's Government, Legislative Council, Aden Colony.

What follows is a brief transcript of the summary of information presented by Captain Jackson, acting C/O of the Aden Protectorate Levies, to members of the 4th Brigade as important background ahead of their continuing operations in the Interior.

MAJOR-GENERAL HARRINGTON:

At ease, gentlemen. Please remain seated. Sir Vivien and I have just hot-footed it from Government House with fresh orders to root out insurgents from the hinterland. But before we get into detailed operational matters, I'd like you to listen to Captain Jackson of the Aden Protectorate Levies. I'm sure he won't mind me telling you that he came to his current position by an unusual route. After World War II he chose a civilian role as Head of Municipal Police in Muscat, from where he has gained the first hand experience of liaising with local native officers that we ourselves might need right now here in Aden. What he has to say to you this morning, gentlemen, may surprise, even shock, some of you, but I want you to be certain of one thing: he speaks today with my full authority behind him. Captain Jackson, gentlemen.

The Officers applaud, briefly but politely, as Captain Jackson joins the Major on the podium, then lean forward attentively to hear what he has to say.

CAPT. JACKSON:

Thank you, Major. What I am about to tell you may be familiar already to some, but possibly quite new to most of you. It goes without saying that much of what I shall be relating is confidential and not to be shared with your various units unless deemed absolutely necessary. There is no desire here to spread panic or alarm, but forewarned is as ever forearmed.

Since the Legislative Council, at the urging of our Arab and Indian partners, concerned for the general health and well-being of the native population, passed the law on 1st April last year outlawing the importation, sale, possession, distribution and consumption of *qat* throughout the territory, there have been unforeseen consequences not predicted at the time, which have created particular repercussions for the British Army Arabian Peninsula Forces. As we all know only too well, that law has been enforced here in Aden itself, but throughout the rest of the

Protectorate the trade continues more or less unimpeded, though arguably in even greater quantities than before.

Qat is a Yemeni cultural institution, much like tobacco is for our chaps, and since the ban there has been, as I am sure you have witnessed for yourselves, an outbreak of loud and angry protests in the streets, a massive increase necessary in the recruitment of the Municipal Police, many of whom are sympathisers with the agitators, and a state of emergency has been declared. Many of you will, I am certain, have been deployed in quelling such disturbances in recent months. As a result the law prohibiting *qat* was repealed in the hinterland, while still being retained here in Aden itself. This has subsequently led to a large exodus of people from across the Protectorate to the adjoining Sultanate of Lahej, which has become a gathering point for a growing number of nationalist sympathisers, as many as five thousand if our Intelligence Services are to be believed, and I have no reason to doubt the veracity of their claims, not only clogging up the roads, but leaving the city bereft of much of its necessary daily work force, at the same time as fuelling the rising discontent among the indigenous population.

We have to wonder, gentlemen, whether the motives of our Arab and Indian partners in urging the ban in the first place were as truly altruistic as they claim. Be that as it may, there is no doubting the enormous economic impact the ban and its consequences have been having on the coffers of Her Majesty's Government. Whilst British forces were initially able to halt the flow of illegal *qat* from Yemen's external borders, via Al-Dhali, Yafi and the Northern Imamate, Harari *qat* from Ethiopia has flooded the market. Prior to the ban only £550 of Harari *qat* was sold *per annum* in the Protectorate. Since last April that figure has sky-rocketed to an unimaginable £101,650 in a single month. An estimated further £50,000 loss in revenues has accrued from our no longer collecting tax and duties on the leaf, together with uncountable losses to Aden Airways, which can no longer service our Commonwealth cousins in Africa, since Ethiopia has revoked the license of Aden Airways to fly across her territory to reach our other destinations on that continent. I hope Sir Vivien will forgive my bluntness in revealing these figures, but the bald truth is that the Treasury cannot continue to endure such heavy losses and still maintain a fully equipped fighting force here in the Protectorate.

Moreover, gentlemen, it will not surprise you to learn that criminal elements have infiltrated the caravans of *qat* making their way across the hinterland and, we have discovered, (and this is where we arrive at how this rapid escalation of unlawful activity becomes a concern for our military role here in the Protectorate), guns, as well as drugs, are being smuggled into the Colony.

We took a pounding at Suez a couple of years ago – there's no point pretending otherwise – and the last thing we want to do now is find ourselves in another situation where Britain is perceived as the aggressor, the wrong-doer, thereby alienating our international allies. But I believe in this case our consciences can be clear. Laws are currently being broken and it is our job to enforce them, even if, in the fullness of time, those laws are subsequently repealed. The whole thing's a dog's breakfast and no mistake, and it now falls on us to clean up the mess.

I mention all of this because we have recently received most disturbing reports of defections within both the Arabian National Police, who accompany us on so many of our operations, and the Aden Protectorate Levies, currently under my supervision, and it may well be that you will come across such defectors when you yourselves are out in the field.

Thank you, gentlemen. Any questions?

*

11 January 1959

To Whom It May Concern

Reference for Lance Corporal Solomon Ward

I am writing this reference for Lance Corporal Solomon Ward, formerly of the Combined Yorkshire & Lancashire Regiment, as part of the wider British Army Arabian Peninsula Forces, Aden, in order to shed further light upon his character and achievements during his time in the Armed Forces.

Ward was called up for National Service in Catterick in 1957 and after an initial period of training was posted overseas to Aden.

He at once showed tremendous ability and talent, with a marked aptitude for acquiring new skills, and very quickly he was looked up to by his fellow soldiers as a natural leader. He first came to my notice as a Private, where I was his Commanding Officer in operations around Crater. I was immediately impressed by his facility in adapting so quickly to the alien conditions, allied with his calmness and attention to detail while carrying out the highly dangerous operation of identifying roadside bombs.

138

Such was his proficiency in his allotted tasks that it was my great pleasure to recommend him for promotion to Lance Corporal, at which time I also discussed with him the possibility of his staying on after the duration of his National Service, in order to become a regular soldier, a career which, in my opinion, would have most assuredly suited his skills and provided him with a potentially distinguished and honourable career. He declined this invitation, however, citing family commitments back at home – an ageing, ailing grandfather – to which he felt he owed an obligation. I must say that I was deeply impressed by this quiet awareness of his sense of duty and responsibility.

Ward is also an excellent artist, a talent he kept hidden from his fellow soldiers for several months, but which, when it emerged, was much in demand to record important impressions of his unit's surroundings, tasks and terrain.

It was during what would have been his last month of service that the unfortunate incident occurred, which saw the tragic death of one of his closest comrades, due to the actions of a young Yemeni insurgent, little more than a boy, who had been acting as a local interpreter for the unit while out on patrol, following yet another outbreak of tribal conflict between the different warring factions beyond the Protectorate. Ward felt he had personally let his comrades down by befriending this boy in the first place, and he suffered an acute sense of guilt, followed by a nervous breakdown as a consequence of these events. This was further compounded by the injury he himself sustained in attempting to intervene between the boy and his target, resulting in the loss of fingers from his left hand, as well as severe scarring injuries to his arm and upper body which, it is hoped, will improve with time. These injuries led to his medical discharge from the Army in August 1958. They were treated in field hospitals, initially in Aden, subsequently in Djibouti, where his necessary rehabilitation caused an inevitable delay in his being well enough to return to England until December of that year.

Since his discharge, I have had no contact with Lance Corporal Ward, for which I am truly sorry. I make no apology for declaring that I liked the man: he was a good soldier, who served his unit, his regiment and his country with distinction and courage, despite its unfortunate outcome. I believe he deserves all due consideration for a second chance on his re-entry into civilian life.

Yours faithfully,

Capt. Michael James Bradley
Commanding Officer, 4th Brigade
Yorkshire & Lancashire Regiment
British Army Arabian Peninsula Forces
Aden

*

I am riding in the second of the two vehicle patrols heading towards Crater on what is supposed to be a routine operation. We head up country like this quite often these days and so at first everything seems normal. A member of the Arab National Police is accompanying us. Hakkim. Like all Yemenis he is chewing qat, which is usual, but for some reason, today the smell is overpowering, and I wish he would just spit it out. The lead vehicle pulls off the track and we follow for several hundred yards before stopping as we reach a steep rocky hillside leading up to a volcano. These cones and craters are everywhere here though none of them are active any longer. They're murder to climb because the ground is so hard and uneven, pitted with sharp outcrops of dried lava from eruptions that must have taken place thousands of years ago.

Corporal Carter – Roy – signals for us to wait. The Levies are joining us – the Aden Protectorate Levies – local conscripts who are often sent on ahead as scouting parties if we're having to sort out local difficulties. Because everyone knows now that I can speak a bit of Arabic, I often go with them. What started out as little more than minor skirmishes between rival villages has started to escalate. I used to have this romantic notion that these tribal warriors were freedom fighters, wanting to reclaim their homeland, first from the Turks, then from the British, but I've come to realise that it's much older than that – Sunnis and Shi'a, who'd rather fight amongst themselves than unite in a common cause. That's why when we go, and we all know that one day we'll have to, the fighting here will continue. I can't see it ever becoming one country. Which breaks my heart, because it's so beautiful, so stark and rugged here in the desert, where the light is so pure, the land so unforgiving, you have to make your peace with it.

But things have got much worse lately, ever since we tried to outlaw the qat trade. We can enforce the ban in Aden, but not out here in the hinterland, where smugglers of the drug have also been caught gun-running. Roy comes back from talking on the field radio and tells us the Levies have been held up and won't be with us for hours yet. Best make camp, he says. In the shelter of the jeeps. Just in case, you never know. He's talking about the possibility of snipers up on the peaks, but he doesn't say so. He doesn't need to, we know what he means.

When everything's set up, Hakkim makes a fire to boil water from the canteen for some tea, and I take out my sketch pad. Up above the mountains I see an eagle hanging on the high thermals, hear its mewing cry, and I try to draw it. This occupies me for a good half hour, so I don't notice the woman and the boy arrive.

It seems like a law of nature out here. Even in the emptiest of quarters, where it doesn't seem possible that any form of life can survive, as soon as we get anywhere, it's only a matter of seconds before we start to notice the flies. If we sleep out in the open, which we've done many times, when we wake up in the morning, we'll see animal tracks in the sand, though we'll never have seen the actual animals, or heard them in the night. So it is with advance parties like today. Within an hour of making camp, someone will turn up, usually women with their children, selling things, and so it's no surprise that these *two are here now. Hakkim half-heartedly tries to shoo them away, but the woman just squats a few yards further down, waiting patiently with her few pitiful bits and pieces, her face and head covered by a red scarf, the only scrap of colour in this bleached out landscape.*

The boy, however, is bolder. He wants to see what I'm doing and he peeps over my shoulder. When he sees the eagle I have drawn he beams, then points back up to the sky, where the bird is still to be seen circling, looking for prey as the sun slowly sets.

I ask him his name.

Taii, he says. Willing, obedient.

Soon Roy and the others from the lead jeep have brought out a ball and Taii plays soccer with them.

Eventually, in a flurry of dust and screech of tyres, the main body of the Levies arrives. Their C/O, Capt. Jackson, is brisk and cross.

What a bloody shambles, he says. HQ's got us checking every hilltop in Crater. We're meant to be somewhere else by nightfall, so best get a move on. My lads will shimmy up here while you provide cover, then we'll have to leave you to it, I'm afraid.

At once some of the Levies run up to the summit like mountain goats, while others quickly set up mobile gun placements, and we position ourselves with rifles behind our jeeps. I haven't time to be scared but I can feel my heart racing. They don't like National Service call-ups to do any actual fighting unless we really have to, and though I've fired a gun plenty of times in training on the ranges, I haven't fired one in anger as yet. The truth is, I don't feel anger, just confusion.

But suddenly all hell lets loose. It seems there are *snipers just beyond the ridge, who must have been waiting till there were more of us they could inflict damage on. They start firing and throwing grenades at the Levies still running up the mountainside. We suffer several losses, but we greatly outnumber the small band of Nationalists at the summit, and pretty soon the firing stops. It is just as the smoke is clearing and Capt Jackson is cautiously standing to assess the situation, that Hakkim pulls out his revolver and appears to aim it towards the C/O. I shout out a warning and Roy leaps on Hakkim from behind, so that his shot goes wide, before knocking the gun from his hand. He handcuffs him to the side of the jeep, and it is then that I notice the boy, creeping along the ground towards Roy. His right hand is closed tightly around something. I yell at Roy to get down, then charge towards the boy. But I'm too late. He releases the pin on the grenade just as he reaches Roy, killing both of them instantly. I feel a pain shoot through my arm and chest as I hit the ground just where the boy had been crawling. I hear the eagle's mewing call high above me as I drift further and further away...*

*

Sol is having another of his nightmares. Nadia tries to calm him as he thrashes his arms and shouts. His body is wet with sweat and his face is hot. Eventually he quietens and drifts back to a still-troubled sleep.

The year is 1963. February. The big freeze. The worst winter since 1947.

Nadia and Sol have been married for just under a year, and he has the dreams nightly. When he wakes, he says, he can't remember them, just the fear, which remains with him always, even, often, when he is awake. He doesn't tell Nadia just how much this fear stays with him, but she knows. She sees him flinch at every loud noise, hears his speech falter for no clear reason, watches him as he stops in the middle of walking, looking past the streets and houses, to somewhere else, far away. She senses this has grown worse since their wedding, and especially since the birth of their daughter a few weeks ago. She wonders why she didn't notice it while they were courting. Perhaps it was because then she did not see him every hour of every day, as she does now, as she has done since Christmas, when the Tyre Factory began laying people off and he was one of the less fortunate ones.

"Last in, first out," they had said, as if, somehow, the decision to let him go was not theirs to make, but because of some external universal law, and now, she knows, that as well as the nightmares he is worrying about how they will make ends meet, here in this two-roomed flat above the fish and chip shop, with its permanent smell of grease and fat, which makes Nadia feel queasy still, much worse before when she was pregnant, but still bad nevertheless, bad enough to pierce the iron frost that holds the town in its grip as it has for almost three months now, that it will not release yet for nearly three more, so that the condensation, which ran like a cataract down the windows in summer, is now a permanent crust of ice that each morning she must scrape away as she tries to keep her daughter warm – they have already had one scare with croup – so that between her daughter's waking still every two or three hours to be fed and her husband's tortured dreams, it seems as though she has not slept herself in months. Her eyes have ever-darkening circles around them, her body feels as though it were weighted with stones, her breasts sore, her stomach cramping, and yet, perverse as it is, she is not without contentment. This life they all inhabit, this cheerless flat they must call home, this permanent winter they must endure, they have made together, freely, with determination and hope, a hope that is still a long way from being kindled, and as Sol's breathing begins to calm at last, and as she nurses their brown-eyed daughter, who gradually grows less fretful, Nadia can raise a weak smile in these last dregs of night, as a pale sun makes vain efforts to peel back the blanket of cloud, and look down on how she, Sol and their daughter Jenna, meaning a bird in flight, born at a hospital called Hope, have come to find themselves alighting here in this particular place, in this particular year, as this particular dawn breaks.

*

Four years earlier.

A slow, insidious shower was just beginning to fall at a quarter before five on a cold Wednesday evening towards the end of a blustery March in 1959. Standing outside the main gates of the entrance to Turner's Asbestos Company on the edge of Trafford Park, Sol was anxiously waiting.

The dozens of buses that would be taking the three thousand office and factory workers home in just a few minutes time were lined up ready, their engines idling, with clouds of fumes rising as if from a swamp, and Sol was concerned that, in the press of people, he would miss her. He moved further towards the side, away from the fumes, from where he hoped he might stand a better chance of seeing her as she left with all of the other girls as soon as the factory hooter sounded at five o'clock.

She had amused him in one of her letters with her observations of the ways of the typing pool. The girls would clack away at their typewriters all day long, more than fifty of them in the main hall beneath the mezzanine walkway that girdled the floor above, where the offices of the various managers were sited. The noise was so loud that you could barely hear yourself think, she told him, but the factory hooter was louder, so that as soon as it sounded the girls would stop their typing immediately, mid-sentence, with no thought of finishing whichever letter or memo they happened to be working on, and their chairs would all scrape back simultaneously. There would then be the briefest of lulls between the cessation of their typing and the end of the hooter's call before, as starlings obeying some unseen signal, they would all flock as one towards the main door, the clacking of typewriter keys now replaced by that of their stiletto heels on the hard tiled floor, together with the girls' chatter, like birdsong, as they exchanged their plans for the evening ahead, interspersed with shrieks and squeals and cries of "See ya."

Recently Nadia had been promoted. Her night school

classes in shorthand had paid off and she had been invited to become the personal secretary to one of the Export Managers in an office located off the mezzanine walkway above the typing pool. This meant more money, but a less rigorous adherence to the sound of the factory hooter, and sometimes Mr Tunstall, her boss, would want her to finish off an urgent letter before he would let her leave, or he would need her to go over the following day's appointments with him, and this could delay her leaving for several minutes, so that she might have to catch a later bus. She missed the easy camaraderie of the typing pool, but not so much that she wished to return there. She was ambitious to do well for herself, while the extra money she was now earning was extremely welcome at home, and all in all Mr Tunstall wasn't a bad boss. As often as he kept her late in an evening (and rarely for more than a few minutes), he was just as likely to let her go early if she had finished all she had to do on a particular day, and he was not like some of the bosses she heard the other secretaries describing in the canteen over lunch. He didn't ask her to sit on his knee or try to look up her skirt. He was married, with a photograph of his wife and their two children on his desk, and Nadia had already conformed to that other secretarial cliché by having been asked to find a card for their wedding anniversary the previous week.

Outside the rain was falling harder and there was nowhere for Sol to shelter in the new position he had chosen to wait in. His hand, arm and chest began to throb from his injuries. After the roadside incident at Crater, when he had failed to save his mate Roy, he'd been taken to a nearby field hospital where his wounds had been cleaned and patched up as best they could, before being transferred to the military hospital in Aden. The situation there, in the aftermath of the attack and other copycat incidents, meant that, for a while, things threatened to escalate into a full-scale rebellion, and so Sol had been flown out to Djibouti, where he was allowed to convalesce in calmer surroundings. In a few weeks the flap in Aden had calmed down, the insurgents had been crushed, the ban on the *qat* trade repealed, and life in the Protectorate for a time reverted to how it had used to be. Sol was flown back to rejoin his unit. But by then his period of National Service had expired, and new arrangements were made for him to return to England when the next troop ship set sail, which was six weeks later. It was a slow voyage, which had to deliver and pick up freight and passengers at several ports along the way, and it took Sol a further twenty-seven days before he disembarked at Liverpool. From there a transfer was arranged for him on an oil tanker, which took him down the Ship Canal, a further twenty-four hours, dropping him off at Pomona Docks, from where he had caught a bus to Trafford Park, to Metro-Vickers, where all the buses went, and had walked the final half mile to Turner's from there.

He'd arrived at the gates in good time, at about half past three, and he had been sitting on a wall opposite the gates since then. He'd told no one he was coming back, not Nadia, not his mother. The last letters he had received had been forwarded to him in Djibouti, to which he'd replied, briefly, saying he was hoping to be on his way home as soon as the hospital, and then the army, released him. Now, as the factory hooter sounded, and the thousands of workers began to pour through the gates towards the waiting, fume-filled buses, with the rain now falling in stair rods, he began to have doubts. Perhaps this hadn't been such a good idea after all. What if he didn't see her? What if he did, but she didn't recognise him? What if she did recognise him, but wasn't pleased to see him? What if she had a boyfriend…?

Back inside Turner's Nadia was just putting on her coat, when Mr Tunstall coughed apologetically and asked her if she wouldn't mind staying on a few extra minutes this evening. There were some figures he needed checking for a report that needed typing for the following day's board meeting. "Of course, Mr Tunstall," replied Nadia, taking off her coat and walking back into the office.

It was almost an hour later that Nadia finally left the building. The cleaners were busy mopping the tiled floor, and Terry, the night time caretaker, was already doing his rounds. "Goodnight, Miss," he called, as he always did. "You've just missed the last works bus, I'm afraid," he added, "but there'll be a regular service in ten minutes. Have you got your umbrella? It's a regular downpour out there now."

Nadia thanked him, put up her umbrella and ran through the rain bouncing off the pavement towards the bus stop. As she approached it, she noticed a forlorn figure step into the light cast by an overhead street lamp. It was a young man, in army uniform, completely drenched and shivering. She paused.

"This is becoming a habit," she said, "and not a very

good one."

The young man looked at her nervously.

"I seem to recall you were soaked through the last time I saw you."

He smiled and nodded.

"Well don't just stand there. Come and stand under the brolly, you'll catch your death."

He hesitated, then did so, and at once they became aware of the proximity of each to the other.

"Sol," she said, handing him the umbrella to hold and linking her arm through his. "Why didn't you tell me you were coming home?"

Sol felt the weight and tension of the last months leave his body all at once. "I wanted to surprise you," he said.

"Shock me, more like."

They smiled. She saw Sol's smile turn into a wince slightly, as he rubbed his shoulder. It was then that she noticed the missing fingers on his left hand. She stretched out her own hand towards his and held it. "Here's the bus," she said. "Let's sit upstairs and you can tell me all about it."

They talked without stopping all the way back to Patricroft, happy, inconsequential things, continuing as they walked the few streets from the bus stop to Nadia's house. It was only the second time they had seen one another, yet there was an intimacy between them that felt easy and natural, a simple extension of all they had shared in their letters over the past two years. Only when they reached her front door did a silence finally fall. The rain had eased and they looked at each other a long time.

"I'm glad you're back," said Nadia. "And safe. One day you must tell me what it was like, what you saw, what you felt, what happened. When you're ready."

"I'm not sure I ever will be," he said. "But I brought you these," he added, and he delved deep into his kit bag, from where he pulled out a large cardboard tube. "Here," he said, handing it over. "In there. Drawings. They'll tell you."

She held the tube reverently in her hands and nodded. Her eyes were shining.

After a long pause, she took her key from her coat pocket. "I'll have to go in now," she said. "They'll be wondering why I'm so late. Does your mother know you're back?"

Sol shook his head.

"Then go home. Surprise her too. Put some dry clothes on. Get warm. Go on."

"But…"

"I'll see you tomorrow," she said. "Come for tea. Six o'clock."

Sol stood on the step smiling for several seconds after Nadia had gone inside and shut the door. His reverie was abruptly broken by the flap of the letter box suddenly being lifted and Nadia hissing out to him. "Go home, Sol. Before my dad sees you."

Laughing, Sol was on his way. His feet took him automatically back to Stanley Road and his own house before he'd even registered the fact. He hadn't got his key with him, he realised, and so he knocked sharply twice. After a moment he heard his mother walking down the hallway. "Who is it?" she called. "Is everything alright?"

When she opened the door, her eyes widened, her hand raised to her mouth and she took a step backwards. "Sol?" she whispered. "Is it you? Why didn't you tell me you were coming?"

"I wrote," he lied. "My letter must have gone astray."

"Never mind, you're here now. Come in," she urged. "Your room's all ready for you. It has been ever since we heard the news about your accident."

"We...?"

"The whole neighbourhood, Sol. Everyone's been asking after you. When's he coming home, they all say? Well, here you are, at last. You'll be able to tell them yourself now, won't you?"

She ushered him into the sitting room, where a fire had been lit. Sol was standing in front of it, not really feeling the heat from it. Instead his eye was caught by the drawing he had sent that was hanging on the wall.

"Your grandfather looked at that picture every day, Solly."

Sol nodded grimly, turning back towards his mother. "I think I should get out of these wet clothes," he said and climbed upstairs. He was, whether he liked it or not, home.

*

Tea the following night could be considered a success, thought Nadia afterwards, as she replayed the minutiae of all that had happened. Not that very much had. It was more in the covert looks she saw her parents exchange when they thought she wasn't looking, rather than what was actually spoken, where the real drama had played out.

Sol had been polite, respectful, had dressed smartly, answered all the questions that were put to him, complimented her mother on her *fattoush*, a salad of vegetables, tomatoes and mixed greens served on flat bread, and *tabouleh*, containing chopped parsley, mint and onions mixed with bulgar wheat, followed by the *saltah*, a meat broth with fenugreek and spiced herbs, and did not raise the subject of Aden, except once when Nadia's father asked whether he had visited Al Mahrah in the east of the Protectorate, which fortunately he had, and so he was able to describe with genuine enthusiasm his impressions of the lush valleys and forests of Hauf that he had come across so suddenly and surprisingly after crossing the vast and forbidding empty quarter, which had once been home to Nadia's father's ancestors.

All proceeded smoothly until after the meal, when, over a bowl of strong mocha, Sol was asked about his future plans now that he was back.

"Well," he said, "first I have to make an appointment with the hospital to check that my wounds are healing as they should." (Appropriate nods of sympathy and concern). "Then I shall, to begin with at any rate, see about getting my old job back at Metro-Vickers. I need to be contributing towards the housekeeping for my mother." (Further murmurs of approval).

"To begin with?" asked Nadia's father. "Do you have

longer term plans or ambitions?"

At this point, Nadia's mother paused in mid-pour, and Salim, Farida's husband, leaned across to offer Sol some *qat*, which he politely declined. Nadia and Farida looked at one another anxiously, as Sol, seemingly unperturbed, continued to expand.

"Yes I do. I've enrolled at the Royal Technical College, at Pendleton – you know? – what used to be the Mechanics Institute, to study Art at evening class."

"Ah yes," said Nadia's father, "this is excellent. Every man should have a hobby. But I was asking more about your career prospects…"

Sensing everyone's eyes upon him, Sol looked down, sipped the hot mocha, and then replied, "I don't intend to stay in the warehouse for longer than I have to, but it's early days yet. I've only just got back."

"Yes, of course," purred Nadia's mother. "Nadia tells me that your father was a draughtsman, in an office, white collar? Your Art classes may be useful, no?"

"*Ommi*," interrupted Farida quickly, taking the chance to clear away some of Sol's dishes, "I think that's enough questions for one night, don't you? Sol only returned back to England yesterday," and she moved across to the gramophone, which took pride of place in the front room where they were all sitting. "Let's have some music, shall we?" And she proceeded to put on a record by Fatimah al-Zaelaeyah.

"I know this," said Sol suddenly. "We'd hear it in the streets and markets of Tawahi, just off the Esplanade Road."

"Esplanade Road? I remember Esplanade Road,"

roared Nadia's father, who at once began to dance around the room, urging Sol and Salim to join him, beaming as Sol did, then laughing as Salim did not.

The ice was broken, the tension noticeably dissipated, and Nadia's mother nodded, smiling towards her daughters.

But although the evening had gone reasonably well, it was clear to Nadia that unless Sol was able to secure that all important 'white collar' job, which her parents viewed as the passport to success, acceptance and approval, he would not be invited back. Nor would he be deemed a suitable potential husband for her, which in turn meant that there was no easy way for the two of them to meet without subterfuge. Fortunately, Farida had warmed to Sol, right from that first occasion more than two years ago, when he had waited patiently outside in the rain, while their parents were away on their pilgrimage, for just one word with her sister, and she had agreed to let him come in. It was Farida who came up with the plan.

There were two cinemas in Eccles: *The Broadway*, which showed all the latest British and American films, and *The Regent*, which, on Friday evenings, had just begun to show Arabian language films for the growing Yemeni community. Salim wasn't interested in going, but Farida longed to, though could not respectably go alone. Similarly, there was no possibility of her parents consenting to let Nadia see Sol. Evenings out to local dances with girls from the office were only possible on those occasions when Mr and Mrs Raqeeb might be away visiting family in Sheffield, where another large Yemeni community had first settled more than fifty years before, and so Farida suggested that Nadia might accompany *her* to *The Regent* to see Arabian films on Friday nights, to which her parents happily agreed, as did Salim, who felt less guilty about spending the evening with other male friends at Abdul's, where they could talk politics without having to worry about boring their wives.

In reality, Nadia would instead go with Sol to *The Broadway* to watch an English film, and then hurry across to *The Regent* to meet Farida as she came out, together with a couple of other local young wives, who were sworn to secrecy. Farida and Nadia would then catch the bus home together, so that Farida could fill Nadia in on what she had just seen, in case anyone asked them what the film had been about, not that they ever did. Salim would meet them off the bus and escort them the five-minute walk back from the bus stop to their home in Mellor Street, usually still full of what he had been discussing at Abdul's to take much interest in their silly romantic films.

But the films that Nadia saw with Sol were far from silly and hardly what you might call romantic. They were gritty and modern and shone a light into the worlds of other young couples like themselves, struggling to find their place in a rapidly changing world, and for more than two years Farida's plan worked perfectly.

*

1960: Saturday Night & Sunday Morning

"Nine hundred and fifty-four… Nine hundred and fifty-bloody-five…. Another few more and that's your lot for a Friday… I could do 'em in half the time if I worked like a bull, but they'd only slash my wages… Don't let the bastards grind you down, that's one thing I've learned… What I'm out for is a good time, all the rest is propaganda…"

Sitting in the dark of the cinema, Sol and Nadia, holding hands, watch different stories unfold. Sol sees in the Raleigh factory where Albert Finney's character Arthur works a mirror image of his own experiences at Metro-Vicks. He's no longer in the warehouse packing the lorries that will carry the precision tools to all corners of the Empire. Now he's on the shop floor, making the tools himself, along with a couple of hundred other lads, with whom he's formed a kind of kinship, all of them in it together, workers against bosses, us against them, yes-men against rebels. Which of those is *he*, he thinks now, watching the film, sharing Arthur's contempt for those who settle for less? If he really does side with Arthur, which deep down he feels certain he does, why does he do nothing about the discrimination he witnesses daily? Or speak out against the ritual humiliations, simply accepting whatever is thrown at him? Perhaps, he thinks, he has always played it safe, kept his head down, his mouth shut, taking out all of his frustration on his mother instead, who never retaliates, never argues, simply averts her gaze and turns away. Unlike Nadia now who, he can sense, is watching him intently.

Nadia can feel Sol shift uncomfortably, his hip pressed up close to hers in this back-row double-seat, where, unlike all the other courting couples on either side of them, who, inspired perhaps by the film's certificate, seem intent on creating X-rated scenes of their own, breaking the world record for the longest uninterrupted kiss without once coming up for air, they focus their attention on the picture, while remaining acutely aware of the closeness of each other's body. She knows he is identifying strongly with Arthur, just as she is with Shirley Anne Field's clear-eyed Doreen. Nadia wonders if she might be the one to save Sol from himself, to help him pursue his dreams. At the same time she is not so naïve as to think life has such neatly contrived outcomes, not so much a happy as pragmatic ending. She is sure she isn't the first girl Sol has taken to the cinema, and in the Army he is bound to have acquired what her sister describes as "experience", (though not of the kind Arthur is currently enjoying up there on the screen with an older married woman, she hopes), but she is certain that she's the first girl who he's really talked to, as he did so freely in his letters to her, and as increasingly he is beginning to on these Friday nights, which she knows he is sure to again as soon as they step outside *The Broadway's* warmth and fug into the cold night air when the film has finished. What will he make, she wonders, of Arthur's decision, finally, to ask Doreen to marry him? Will he think he's selling out, becoming like all those yes-men he (and Sol) dismiss so witheringly, or will he see him as simply growing up, accepting that he needs a soul mate to

159

share the quest he has embarked on? Are she and Sol soul mates, Nadia asks herself? All well and good, but she wouldn't mind as well the occasional attempt at one of those all-time kissing records their cinema neighbours have just set.

Siraa fal Wadi (Struggle in the Valley: The Blazing Sun)

"Or *Lust in the Dust*," laughs Farida. "*Sex in the Sand*. The two leads practically devoured one another with such passionate staring into each other's eyes. I don't know how they managed it. I wouldn't have been able to stop laughing. Even so, when the actor playing Ahmed seemed to look directly at you in enormous close-up, I'm telling you, Sis, I felt myself blushing, even in the dark. I had to cross my legs or I swear I would have wet myself. That Omar Sharif, he's proper gorgeous. Don't tell Salim I said that, nor *Ommi* neither! What she'll want to know is…" She begins to list each item on the thumb and fingers of her right hand. "… did we enjoy it? Yes, but a bit slow. What was it about? The struggle between poor farmers and their cruel master – all very dramatic with meaningful long shots of water wheels and camels. Nice music but no songs, and no – it didn't have a happy ending." She links her arm through Nadia's. "I don't know why you want to see such rubbish, she'll say." She smiles ruefully. "Come on, Sis, Salim will be waiting. Let's hope the next one's more cheerful."

1961: A Taste of Honey

Geoffrey: You're just a bit depressed, that's all. You'll be your usual self once you get used to the idea.

Jo: And what is my usual self? My usual self is a very unusual self, and don't you forget that, Geoffrey Ingram. I'm an extraordinary person. There's only one of me, like there's only one of you.

Geoffrey: We're unique.

Jo: Young.

Geoffrey: Unrivalled.

Jo: Free.

Geoffrey: We're bloody marvellous.

Watching this, another film without a happy ending, Nadia is struck by how many of the locations she recognises. Buildings, statues, streets, bus rides. I've been there, she thinks. I know that corner. I've walked along that stretch of canal, stood on that swing bridge. It's as if suddenly she and Sol are at the centre of the universe.

"Just imagine," she says, as the picture finishes, "people all over the world are looking at where we live."

Sol nods.

"Blimey," she continues, "look at the time. We'll have to leg it if we're to meet Farida in time for the bus."

They run down the middle of the road singing.

"The big ship sails down the alley, alley-oh
The alley, alley-oh
The alley, alley-oh
The big ship sails down the alley, alley-oh
On the last day of September."

Breathless, they reach the stop just as the bus is pulling out and Nadia has to leap to make it on board. They don't talk about Jo becoming pregnant even though she's still a school girl, or Geoffrey being homosexual, though Nadia would have liked to. They don't talk about anything very much, and Nadia wishes they didn't have to be so secretive all the time. It's like walking on eggshells, speaking in code.

Instead she merely yells to Sol's receding figure, waving as the bus pulls away, "We're bloody marvellous!" to which Sol roars back, his voice growing gradually quieter, until she can barely make out what he's saying.

"There's only one of you...." he calls.

"And there's only one of me," she answers, almost inaudibly to herself, and smiles, running her tongue slowly over the roof of her mouth, as if seeking out that last drop of honey.

Ana Horra (I Am Free)

Farida is quieter than usual on the bus journey home.

When Nadia asks her what film she had seen and what it was about, so that she can be fully prepared to answer any of her mother's questions when they get home, Farida turns away.

"*Ommi* wouldn't like this film either," she says. "It's about this girl – Amina – who goes to college to study. She has big plans, dreams, but her family force her to leave, to marry a boy of their choosing, who she's never met, and who treats her badly. He won't let her try for a job, he doesn't even allow her out of the house. But no matter how cruel they all are to her, they cannot crush her spirit."

She turns towards Nadia and takes hold of both her hands firmly in her own.

"You did well at school, Nadia, and now you have a good job. Don't let anyone take it away from you. This is 1961. They're sending rockets into space now. We mustn't live in the past." She kisses her sister's cheek. "Don't listen to me, Nadia. I'm talking nonsense. Look – there's Salim, tapping his foot impatiently. Well, he'll have to wait a little longer yet. My period started today."

1962: A Kind of Loving

Ingrid: Was that a wedding I saw you at the other Saturday?

Vic: Yes. My sister's.

Ingrid: How's married life suiting her?

163

Vic: She likes it. They've got a nice flat. They're dead lucky.

Ingrid: I love weddings.

Vic: I like your perfume.

Ingrid: It's called 'Desire'.

Vic: Living dangerously, aren't you?

Ingrid: I only wear it for special occasions.

(They kiss).

When the picture finishes, it's still light as they step outside, the clocks having sprung forward the previous weekend. They have more than an hour before they're due to meet up with Farida, and Sol suggests a walk. In a few minutes they find themselves in Peel Park, with its blackened granite statues where jackdaws strut like Teddy boys. Leaves are beginning to open on the scraggy sycamores. They reach a quiet spot beneath the one of Queen Victoria and sit down on the grass, hidden from what Nadia is sure would be a stern, unamused stare by a scrub of laurel which has spread nearby, providing a kind of canopy, beneath which they might sit unseen. A black-bodied peppered moth, a Manchester moth, lands softly on Nadia's shoulder, with no more weight than a breath.

"Hold still," whispers Sol, as he coaxes it to flutter gently onto his finger, where they watch it slowly opening then closing its paper-thin wings. For several seconds neither of them speaks, before eventually it takes off and flies back to the shelter of the laurel tree, where it basks camouflaged against the soot-stained bark. Sol leans in towards Nadia.

"I like your perfume," he says, nuzzling into her neck.

"Give over," she says, laughing, but almost at once they are kissing, fierce and hungry. Sol pulls Nadia greedily towards him, before rolling her onto her back. She pauses, puts her hands gently on his shoulders. "Let's not," she says. "Please. Not like this. Not here." But the next moment she is kissing him harder than ever.

Afterwards, walking back towards the bus stop, they are both quiet. Nadia is thinking once again about the film, remembering the conversation between Ingrid and Vic after *their* first time...

Ingrid: I don't want you to feel there's anyone here holding you back.

Vic: I don't know what I feel half the time. Sometimes I feel rotten, sometimes I feel it's not fair on either of us, and sometimes I feel like I do now.

Ingrid: I've always wanted you, you know that, don't you?

Vic: Well – now you've got me.

... while Sol recalls the scene where Vic walks out in the

middle of the night, after they've married and are living with Ingrid's monster of a mother, and he feels trapped. Vic walks all night, having failed to snatch some sleep on a deserted railway platform, before heading back to his childhood home just as it's getting light, crossing the iron bridge, becoming enveloped in clouds of steam from an early morning train, to find his mother, already up and doing, even at this hour, outside washing the front room windows and giving him short shrift, so that he goes to seek out his father, who he knows will be up on his allotment...

Sol thinks about Vic being a draughtsman, like his father, Jaz, and how he misses him, and Yasser too, how, since coming back from National Service, he has had no man he can confide in, ask advice from. He turns back towards Nadia. It's up to him now, he thinks, no one else. He knows, if he has to, he will do the right thing, and smiles. Nadia takes his hand.

"Come on," she says, "Farida will be wondering where we've got to."

Inta Habibi (My One And Only Love)

Farida begins talking as soon as they arrive, not noticing the quietness that has fallen on Sol and Nadia.

"This is an easy one to tell you about. *Ommi* would have loved it, so no awkward questions this time. It stars Shadia, and we know how much she likes *her*, though you have to wait till right before the end until she sings a song – that's when... Wait – let me start from the beginning… Oh, goodnight, Sol. Same time next week?"

Sol walks away without a word to either of them.

"He's a bit moody, isn't he?" asks Farida. "Have you two had a row or summat? Anyway, what happens in the film is this. Two poor families learn that a distant relation they both share is leaving them a fortune, provided that the son from one of them – Farid – and the daughter of the other – Yasmina – marry each other. The only trouble is Farid and Yasmina can't stand each other, and each of them is secretly having an affair with someone else. By conniving together to dupe their families, they end up falling in love of course and live richly and happily ever after, which they celebrate with a song and a belly dance…"

She breaks off, realising that Nadia is not listening.

"What's the matter with you? Cat got your tongue?"

Nadia runs on ahead.

"It's lucky Salim can't meet us tonight," continues Farida, hurrying to catch up with her, "or you'd have some explaining to do, my girl."

They reach the front door. Just before Nadia can fetch her key from her handbag, Farida puts her hand on her shoulder. "You'd better wipe your face first," she says, handing her a tissue, and while Nadia dries her eyes, Farida surreptitiously brushes the grass stains from the back of her sister's coat. "Things will sort out," she says, "you'll see. Sol's a good boy."

*

The wedding is set for the end of May.

As crowds line the streets for the annual Whit Walks, Nadia's family are putting the finishing touches to the decorations in the front room before the guests will start to arrive, although there will be far fewer than when Farida was married. Nadia's mother, Salwa, dabs her eyes as she thinks back to that time, only five years ago. Such a grand occasion that had been, everything done properly according to tradition, just as if they were back home in Sana'a, with events taking place over five glorious days, as she had described to a gathering at the Eccles Women's Institute, where she had been invited to speak about Yemeni customs, and her husband had said that "that would be acceptable since there would only be ladies present".

"First there is *Thebal*, or 'Green Day', begins Salwa. "Brass vases are filled with *rihan*, a mixture of basil and rose petals, and placed all over the house. We turned the front room into a *mafraj*, an open spacious place full of light and air. We hung small jewels from the windows, *qamariyas*, which sparkled in the sunlight. We burned *bochor*, incense, in *madah*, hookah pipes, you know, bubbling away, and drank *gishar*, a kind of coffee made with cardamom. I have brought some for you all to try later. Farida wore a *qamis* of traditional green, not her favourite colour, but she looked very nice, I think – see, I have some photographs you may wish to pass around – with a veil, which she removed when it was just the women together, which for most of the day it was, but not before Salim, her husband-to-be, who arrived early to

168

present her with an *aswaqa*, a wedding gift. It is a small camel, made of clay or wood, painted in bright colours, with tiny packets of rice and salt and oil upon its back, symbolising that he will never allow her to go hungry once they are married. Salim looked so handsome, with his white suit and red turban and sash, with his jewelled dagger, so different from the clothes he wears every day for the bank! Then after he had gone, we all laughed and sang traditional songs and planned what we would do over the next three days before the actual wedding day itself, enjoying sweets and mint tea." She pauses while she hands round a box of home made confections. "Please," she says, "try some. I make them myself. Pretty colours, hah?" She looks around, beaming.

"Second day is *Hamam*, which is our word for the Turkish Bath. All the ladies who had been present the day before arrived bright and early this day and together we took the 49 bus to Piccadilly, then changed to the number 50, which took us all the way to Victoria Baths on Hathersage Road, such a beautiful building, marble pillars, tiled floors, stained glass windows, where Farida was scrubbed from head to toe in a special room – we could hear her squealing all the while we waited – and then an even louder shriek as all of her body hair was removed with a paste of lemon and sugar. Ai! Don't ask. Then we made our way back home. My sister, Farida's Auntie, went on ahead to let people know we were coming, so that as we turned the corner into our road, all the neighbours could be there to welcome us with fireworks and the banging of pots and pans. Such a lot of noise! Fortunately our neighbours did not complain – no, they join in! Farida went upstairs and changed into a beautiful dress picked out by her and bought specially for this day – not a traditional one of antique silver, but very modern – I don't need to tell you, ladies, how the young ones are today with their fashions – see, I have more photos – and we served everyone more food and tea and coffee, and there was singing and dancing until very late. Still no men, you understand? But we ladies know how to enjoy ourselves, don't we?

"Next day, not so early, is *Al-Naqsh*, Henna Day. The young girls today don't always do this like we used to, but I was so happy that Farida chose to. We all stay home for the day, wearing pyjamas, very lazy, and a lady comes round to paint the bride, and anyone else who wishes to be, with henna in patterns on the hands and feet, sometimes on the face, and sometimes, in olden times, here…" and she giggles, pointing to her breasts. "But Farida is a good girl and only wanted her hands to be painted. Here – more photos coming round… I also bring some henna with me – we can all try if you like – afterwards, with the coffee, I show you how it is done. You can all go home, surprise your husbands," and she wiggles her fingers mischievously towards them.

"Then comes Gold Day, when the bride goes to the Hairdresser's to have her hair done in that special way – as well as the Bride's mother, I wanted to look my best too – and afterwards we returned home. Farida put on another new dress, traditional in style but this time in her favourite colour, which is a shocking pink, so bright, ladies, you need sun glasses just to look at her, together with some of the family jewellery that my grandmother had passed down to me and which I had worn on my own wedding day, necklaces, ear rings, bracelets – here, let me show you, I am wearing one of these bracelets today – and then afterwards she was marched upstairs to relax, so she can be fully ready for the big day ahead, while the rest of us prepared the food for all the guests who would be coming. Brides are supposed to read verses from the *Qur'an* to settle their minds and calm their nerves, but I hear her listening to that Johnnie Ray on the radio and I have to go up and tell her to turn it down, unless she wants her father coming up to speak to her.

"Finally comes the Wedding Day itself. I was up before it was light, making sure that the house is ready and all of the food just right. Guests began arriving early in the morning and I was rushed off my feet, as you can imagine. Then, just after six o'clock, Salim and his family arrived in a great procession, with more fireworks, more music and car horns blaring, such a racket. It was only then that Farida emerged from her bedroom, wearing a snow white dress, sparkling with sequins – which I had spent many weeks sewing on by hand, ladies – a crystal crown on her head, carrying a bouquet of bright red flowers, which she handed to her younger sister Nadia to hold as she came down the stairs. What a picture she looked. Like a princess from the Arabian Nights. The whole house fell silent and then burst into applause. Tears are running down my face – and my husband's too. Salim lay his *jambiyah*, his curved ceremonial dagger, down before her feet, placing an egg upon the ground, which Farida daintily stepped over, a symbol that she was now entering her husband's home – although actually they are living with us until they can afford a house of their own, but no matter, this way I still get to see her every day. My little girl was married. All that remains to make my happiness complete is to become a grandmother."

Salwa sat down to warm applause as the W.I. secretary thanked her for her "most interesting and enlightening talk, I am sure we have learned a great deal this afternoon, and now we can all look forward to sampling the delights of the cardamom coffee you have so kindly brought with you and, for those of us daring enough to try, painting our hands in those colourful patterns."

Now, on the eve of her younger daughter's wedding, Salwa sits down forlornly as the last of the Whit Friday Walks process past her front room window, accompanied by the incessant (to her ears) mournful English hymns played by a brass band, their melancholy tunes matching perfectly her own mood of disappointment.

Nadia wants nothing to do with a traditional Yemeni wedding. She has at least consented to a small reception here at home afterwards for other family and friends, but Salwa finds she doesn't have the heart, or the energy, and the decorations, unpacked from their box where they have been stored since Farida's wedding day, lie strewn about her feet. In spite of herself, she finds herself going over and over the time, just two weeks before, when Nadia had announced her plans.

"*Ommi*, I need to talk to you."

"Yes, *Arnouba*, but I'm very busy. Can't it wait?"

"No, *Ommi*, it can't."

"Well, talk to me while I am putting away the washing."

"No, *Ommi*, I need you to sit down."

"Very well. What is it?"

"I want to get married."

"Of course you do, Nadia. Every girl wants to get married."

"I mean that I want to get married *now*."

"Oh…"

"Yes. Sol and I have discussed it and we…"

"Sol? That young man you brought round for tea? I didn't know you were serious. We'll need to speak to your father. Can't this wait until he comes home later?"

"No, *Ommi*. We'll talk to *Babbi*, yes, but I want to talk to you first."

"But he will need to seek your father's permission…"

"No, *Ommi*. We are both twenty-one now. We can decide for ourselves. But I… I would like you to be happy for us."

"I see. Yes. But there will be so much to do. These things cost a lot of money, and your father will not want you to leave this house not properly provided for."

"I don't want a traditional wedding, *Ommi*. Just something simple. We've already booked the Town Hall."

"When for?"

Nadia lowered her head. "Two weeks."

"Ai!" Salwa raised her hands to her head and began to

173

rock back and forth where she sat.

"Please, *Ommi*, don't be upset."

"But why so fast? Young people today, you are always in such a rush about everything…" She stopped suddenly as the realisation struck. "Nadia. No."

Salwa began to whirl around, her voice growing louder and shriller, as Farida came running down from upstairs. "Did you know?" she demanded, wheeling round at her.

"Yes," said Farida, moving across to Nadia and putting her arms around her.

"When?"

"Just yesterday."

"This can't be happening."

"*Ommi*," said Nadia, breaking free of Farida and walking towards Salwa, "you are jumping to conclusions. Sol has managed to get us a flat, but if we don't take it at once we run the risk of losing it, that's why we have to be quick."

"Really? I may not be as clever as you, Madam. I may not have gone to school and passed my exams, or gone out to work and got a good job, but I can still do arithmetic. Let's see what the end of the year brings, shall we?"

Nadia reddened.

Farida sat down beside her mother. "It's 1962, *Ommi*. This is Manchester, not Aden. Let them get married their own way, and wish them joy."

Nadia mouthed a silent 'thank you' across the room, and Farida motioned for her to go upstairs. She let her mother calm herself down, then kissed her on her forehead. "Be happy for them, *Ommi*, and when *Babbi* comes home, let's all tell him together and persuade him how modern we all are now, how British."

Salwa dried her eyes and nodded. After Farida had left her to join her sister upstairs, she stood up to check her appearance in the front room mirror before her husband came home and noticed anything amiss. "This is God's way of punishing me," she thought, "for wanting too badly to have a grandchild."

*

"Yes?"

"Mrs Ward?"

"Yes."

"I'm…

"I know who you are."

"Yes."

"I was wondering when you would. Whether you might."

"Can I come in?"

"Of course you can."

Nadia steps into the hallway and is led through into the front room.

"Oh…" She stops in front of the drawing of the Hejaz Mountains. "Is that…?"

"Sol's, yes."

"It's…"

"Yes."

"… remarkable."

"Yes."

"I had no idea."

"No."

"I have a few that he gave me when he first came home, but they're nothing like this one."

"No?"

"This is so…"

"Yes."

"I bought him a sketch book."

Ishtar nods her head silently.

"I sent it to him."

"Yes. I know."

"Did he tell you?"

"No. I guessed."

Nadia bows her head.

"He sent this with a letter for his grandfather. He would stand in front of it for hours every day."

"Did he ever go back?"

"No. He didn't. And after he looked at this, he never needed to, he said. But I'd have liked to. Just once. I don't suppose I shall now. How about you?"

Nadia shakes her head. "I was born here. So was my sister. Not long after my mum joined our father. I listen to all their stories, but I don't feel the same connection as they do. I'm English, Mancunian. This is where I live and this is where I belong. I don't feel I could call anywhere else home."

"But you're so young. The world's a big place, Nadia."

"You know my name?"

"You brought those flowers, didn't you, when Sol's grandfather died?"

Nadia nods.

"I thought it was you."

"I'm pregnant."

"Ah. Yes. I thought you might be."

"Didn't he…?

"No. He didn't."

"Oh."

"Don't take it personally. He doesn't talk to me about very much at all. He's not done for years. Not since he left school. Which he blames me for. But like I said at the time, he could always go to Night School."

"He does."

Ishtar turns sharply towards Nadia.

"Every Tuesday. Hasn't he said?"

Ishtar shakes her head.

"The Institute. He takes Art classes."

"I'd no idea. I thought he'd stopped again after he came home." She sits down wearily on the sofa and pats the space next to her, indicating that Nadia might join her. "You should ask him to do a drawing of you."

"I might, at that," says Nadia smiling, sitting next to her.

"So – what are you going to do?"

"Sol's offered to marry me."

"You don't have to, you know? But it'll be harder if you don't."

"I want to."

"Well then, that's alright, isn't it?"

"Is it?"

"What does your mother say? No, don't tell me. I can imagine. She'll come round."

"I haven't told her I'm…"

"Do you not think she'll have guessed?"

"She still thinks of *me* as a baby. But I'm twenty-one now, so…"

"Where are you going to live? Is that why you've come round? To ask if you can stay here? You can, you know, there's plenty of room…"

"No, Mrs Ward, thank you. But Sol's found us a flat. It's not much, but it's a start. We want to try and make a go of it on our own. But we'll come round for a visit, if that's alright, after the baby's born."

"I'll hope you'll come before then."

"*I* will, but I can't speak for Sol."

"No. I don't expect you can."

They move back into the hallway towards the front door where Ishtar pauses. "Nadia?"

"Yes?"

"Thanks for coming round. And for telling me. I appreciate that."

"Yes, Mrs Ward."

"And let's dispense with the 'Mrs Ward', shall we? Call me 'Ishtar', everyone else does, and it seems to have stuck."

"Don't you mind?"

"Why should I mind?"

"Well – you're not…"

"Not one of you?"

"I didn't say that. I've already said. I was born here, in Patricroft."

"And I was born in Gorton. I was christened Esther, but when I married Sol's father, after a few years I decided to convert. Jaz wasn't particularly religious, nor was Yasser, but they each had a deep quiet strength about them that drew me more and more to want to find out where that all came from. And so I became '*Ishtar*'. Mr al-Haideri at the mosque told me it means '*She who Waters*'. I rather liked that notion, and so I've tried to live up to it."

Nadia nods. "Can I ask you a question?"

"Anything."

"Has Sol ever talked about what happened? You know? When he got wounded?"

"No, love, he hasn't. I wish he would. He dreams about it sometimes, I think. I hear him shouting in the night. But when I go in…"

"He's fast asleep again?"

"Or pretending."

"He goes very quiet sometimes when he's with me, too, and I think I've lost him."

"You'll find him. Deep down, he's a good boy."

"That's what my sister says."

After the front door has been closed, each of them pauses on either side of it for a moment, before Nadia strides back down Stanley Road towards Mellor Street and her home for only a few weeks more, while Ishtar pads back along the hallway and into the front room, where she stands in front of the drawing Sol had sent to his grandfather.

Nadia, just as she reaches the turning she needs for home, on an impulse goes right, instead of left, and heads for the Canal. The swing bridge, which she travels across twice each day to and from work on the bus, is opening. Work. One of the most awkward of the many difficult conversations she has had to have these past few days was with her boss, Mr Tunstall…

"I'm getting married," she said without any preliminaries one morning last week.

"Oh," he replied, clearly taken aback, before nervously coughing, as he always did when conversation veered away from work duties. "Congratulations."

"Thank you."

"And who is the lucky fellow, might I ask?"

"Oh, you don't know him, Mr Tunstall. He doesn't work here. He's a neighbour."

"I see." He coughed again. "What does he do?"

Nadia was expecting this question and had her answer prepared. "He's not long returned from National Service and he's still finding his feet. He's at Metro-Vicks at the moment, but he has plans. He's going to Night School at The Institute." She did not elaborate and Mr Tunstall was too polite to press further.

"Well, I shall be sorry to lose you, Nadia."

"Sir?"

"I don't mean now of course, but well…" As he began to cough once more, his face and the back of his neck coloured brightly. "I don't expect it will be very long before… well, you know…?"

Nadia looked down, saying nothing.

"But let's not get ahead of ourselves, shall we? I am

being terribly selfish, for you are the best secretary I have ever had. I shall miss you greatly when the time does indeed come for you to step away to attend to more domestic duties, and in the meantime, I shall have to desist from keeping you late in an evening. Your husband-to-be would not thank me for that, would he? Now, do you have those letters ready for me that we began yesterday?"

"Yes, Mr Tunstall. They're on your desk already."

"Thank you, my dear, and very many congratulations to you. Mrs Tunstall will be so pleased when I tell her..."

Now, standing by the Canal in a light spring rain that has just begun to fall, Nadia brushes away some wisps of hair that have blown across her face and looks out over the dark expanse of water, its slick sheen of oil caught in the pale evening sun flitting between the clouds. She is shaken from her reverie by the sudden sound of a ship's siren, loud and close, as a large tanker, its deck stacked high with brightly coloured, rusting containers, sails by. It flies a flag she doesn't recognise and on the side of its hull she can make out a mixture of Cyrillic and Arabic script. As her eyes focus and adjust, she begins to pick out different men going about their various tasks, African, Asian, Middle Eastern, as well as white, all these different nationalities converging on this one spot, being funnelled down the Canal towards the Port of Manchester just a few miles away. One young black man, being lowered over the side in a flimsy cradle suspended by chains jerking from side to side, appears to be scraping barnacles away from the ship's name, which is partially obscured by the man's body, but which she eventually makes out –

هِجْرَة

– *hejira*, the flight to freedom, notably that taken by Mohammad from Mecca to Medina, and she thinks of how, five years ago, it was because her parents were away on a pilgrimage themselves, that she was allowed by her sister to invite a rain-drenched Sol into their house, to hear him open up as he dried in front of their coal fire, talking himself into an exhausted sleep while she herself awoke.

The young black man on the side of the ship nearly loses his balance, catches hold of the supporting chain at the last moment, regains his footing, turns and sees her looking up at him. He whistles and waves and she finds herself smiling and waving back, before a sharp word from one of the officers above makes him turn back to continue with his scraping and cleaning. Nadia is reminded of Jo in *A Taste of Honey*, her brief fling with the black sailor on leave, here by the Barton Docks, and how he had returned to sea, not even aware that she was pregnant, a future Jo had no choice but to face alone.

The ship continues to sail past, and Nadia watches it till it is almost out of sight as it rounds the bend in the Canal, glides beneath the rising concrete skeleton of the M63 motorway viaduct still under construction, and the bridge swings back and traffic continues to cross it once more. She turns up the collar on her jacket and heads smartly back towards Mellor Street with renewed hope and vigour.

*

On the morning of the wedding Sol stands before the cracked mirror in the tiny bathroom at the end of the landing about to shave. He has not slept well. His movements are sluggish and slow. It's as if he is sleep-walking into this marriage, feeling neither enthusiasm nor reluctance for it.

When Nadia told him the news, he was, he realises now, almost relieved, as if at last he was being prompted into action. Although he knew that arrangements could be made for them to live with either Nadia's parents or with his mother, he saw this as a chance to strike out and break free from the yoke he had felt himself under since he left school. The very next day he had found them a flat above the fish and chip shop on Barton Road, and Nadia, when he had shown it to her, looked grim but nodded silently. He was reminded of the ending of *A Kind of Loving*, the film they had watched just before their snatched and fumbled sex in Peel Park, which had led to this hasty marriage, and he quoted the words Vic had used back to Nadia. "I know it's not much, and we might end up throwing pots and pans at one another within six months, but at least we'll have no one else to blame."

Nadia had smiled and put her arms around him. "I couldn't stand it if we had to stay at home. *Ommi* would be for ever fussing around us, while *Babbi* would always be watching me disapproving."

He was grateful she hadn't pressed him about moving

into *his* house with Ishtar.

Now, standing before the cracked bathroom mirror, he takes a deep breath, content that this will be the last time he ever has to. It feels like the start of a new chapter, and he contemplates with incredulity that unknown microscopic life wriggling away in Nadia's belly that has propelled him at last to take decisive action. He wonders if, without it, he might just have continued to drift.

The Army had brought such a rupture to his life. He had been so angry when he had received the call-up papers, so certain had he been that he would have been exempt, so outraged that his mother had entered completely English names on to his birth certificate, just when he had reconciled himself to climbing the social and property ladders that promotion at the factory might bring him, had begun to envision a possible future, from which National Service would set him back more than the two years he would be away. But when he learned of his posting to Aden, he was intrigued, and once he was there he found himself falling under the spell of its deserts and mountains, feeling, in spite of himself, a connection with the country, with the people, and most especially with his grandfather. He began to grow into himself, become more at ease in both his body and his mind. But then came the incident – the explosion, the death of Roy, his foolish trust in the boy Taii, the betrayal, the wound – and the sense of guilt that still to this day has not left him. It was Nadia who saved him, quite literally, her letters, her faith in him, her knowing not to ask him direct questions, her unshakeable optimism. It was Nadia who'd sent him the sketch book, the pencils, the pastels. And it was Nadia who had suggested he might at last go to Night School for Art classes, who had found out all about the Institute. He is determined he will not let her down.

The Institute. The Salford Royal Technical College. Formed when the Salford Working Men's College was merged with the Pendleton Mechanics Institute, as his Art tutor is so fond of reminding them. "We're like Shakespeare's 'rude mechanicals'," he declared, and Sol had smiled. He had read and enjoyed *A Midsummer Night's Dream* at school, one of the few of them who had, or at least who would admit to it.

"Like Bottom the Weaver," his Art tutor, Mr Wright – "but please call me George" – continued, "or Flute the Bellows Mender, Snout the Tinker, Snug the Joiner, and Peter Quince the Carpenter, we're all of us getting our hands dirty, rolling up our sleeves, creating something out of nothing, things that endure. Believe me, I know what I'm talking about. My father was a printer. He taught me to read by letting me trace the letters of his wooden printing blocks. 'We've got a good name,' he used to say, 'Wright. We come from a long line of people who make things'."

Sol had liked that comparison. It made him feel like what he was doing was less of a hobby, more about something that mattered. Each week when he turned up he found himself walking the same corridors as engineers and builders, plumbers and electricians, in a long line that stretched back to spinners and weavers, cutters and dyers. Lowry had studied there, like Sol, at night school, when he wasn't working as a rent collector. He'd go to Peel Park in his lunch hour to practise drawing, Peel Park of all places…

The classes covered everything – still-life, landscape, portraits, life drawing. For the still-life classes George would bring in engine-parts, bits of machinery, which reminded Sol of when he would draw tanks and jeeps out in the desert, how he had liked to rub his fingers along the metal to scrape off flakes of rust, which he'd then mix in with the marks of his pencil. When they drew from life, Sol approached the sketches in the same visceral manner, grinding his pencil hard into the paper to convey work-strong arms, wire-taut muscles.

George would come up to him afterwards, wreathed in pipe smoke, nodding in approval. "You draw as though your life depended on it," he'd say.

"It does," Sol had replied…

He runs hot water into the sink, lathers the shaving brush with soap, but then, just before he is about to start shaving, he pauses. The old doubts surface and return. Since coming back from Aden he has lost touch with all his old Army pals, deliberately resisted all invitations to drinks or reunions, cutting himself off. He returned to Metro-Vickers, but the injury to his hand made working in the warehouse, and then the machine shop, problematic, and so he was moved to "less demanding" duties, such as sweeping the floor or hosing down the yard. He felt useless and demeaned, something that has stayed with him ever since, even though he now drives the fork-lift trucks to manoeuvre the crates around the factory yard. Cocooned inside his cabin as he drives the truck each day, literally screened off from his work mates and the world, he finds himself increasingly isolated, experiencing flash backs, sometimes not hearing what people are saying to him, so that they have to repeat the simplest of instructions several times just to get through to him. Once or twice he has found himself lashing out and has been reprimanded for getting into fights. He is reminded of Arthur in *Saturday Night & Sunday Morning* and he smiles grimly: "Don't let the bastards grind you down."

He steps back from the sink and contemplates his reflection, his face fragmented by the cracks in the mirror. He rubs the shaving lather onto the face he sees there rather than his own and looks at the shape he has made. He does not recognise it, a blur. He wipes it clean with a flannel, smearing the suds across the glass so that now he can see nothing at all.

He is shaken from his reverie by a sudden, sharp knocking on the front door. It takes him several seconds to realise what it is, and then he hears his mother's voice answering it, inviting someone in, then directing them upstairs. It's Eric, his friend from before the Army, who delivered his first letter to Nadia when he had first arrived in Aden, and who today is his best man.

"Eh up, Sol? Not ready yet? Best get a move on, eh?"

*

Nadia and Sol will marry at the Registry Office in Eccles Town Hall with only a few people present – Nadia's mother, her father, Farida, Salim, Ishtar, Sol's friend Eric as best man, Ray, and two of Nadia's girl friends from the office, Brenda and Susan, who will throw confetti over them as they leave, which will blow away in a gust of wind, swirling among the lunch time shoppers, before gathering in pink and white grimy drifts by the side of the kerb. Nadia will wear a short, navy-blue shapeless shift-dress, with a drop-waist and contrasting collar and cuffs in white, flat Mary-Jane shoes with a T-strap, her hair loose and long, beneath a white crocheted beret, while Sol will wear a suit he has borrowed from Eric and a tie of his father's he will grab at the last minute.

In the photographs that Mr Tunstall will pay for as a wedding gift, Nadia and Sol will look at how everyone will appear to be standing awkwardly, as if uncertain of how to behave, everyone, that is, except for Nadia and Sol themselves, who will have eyes only for each other, and who will smile like a pair of skaters venturing onto the ice for the very first time, not caring if one of them will slip or fall, because they know that the other will catch them.

Afterwards they will go back to Mellor Street for the small reception Farida will have helped Salwa to prepare, and Salwa will afterwards remember, with some small degree of satisfaction, just how much Sol will praise the wedding cake she has baked specially. Nadia's father, Mr Raqeeb, will shake Sol by the hand and insist that now he is a married man he must call him Jamil. He will look him in the eye and say, "So – you are the young army private who requested a song to be played for Nadia's 17th birthday?"

"Yes, sir. Jamil, sir."

"You caused quite a stir that day, let me tell you. Just as you are doing today."

Sol will shift uncomfortably from one foot to the other.

"Pen pal, hah?"

Sol will smile and nod, and then Jamil will clap him hard across the back and roar with laughter, and Nadia will see this from across the room, where she will be doing the rounds of all the guests, and will feel all the remaining tension drain from her shoulders.

And a few hours later she and Sol, with Brenda and Susan, Eric and Ray, will be dancing at *The Majestic*, as they had all of them almost done five years before, and the DJ will be playing *Walking Back to Happiness* by Helen Shapiro, and the six of them will sing along at the tops of their voices –

Walking back to happiness – woopah oh yeah yeah
Said goodbye to loneliness – woopah oh yeah yeah

– before a local group from Eccles will take to the stage, one of whose members lives in the same street as Susan, who will wink at her as they sing:

Just one look
That's all it took yeah...

Just one look
And I knew that you were the only one...

And back in Mellor Street, when all the guests have gone, Farida will help Salwa to clear up, while Jamil will go on to Abdul's with the other men to talk and drink and celebrate. Farida will climb upstairs to her bedroom, where she will wait for Salim to join her.

But he will surprise her by already being there, sitting on the edge of the bed. He will watch her as she removes her ear rings, takes off her dress. He will stub out the last of his cigarette and walk towards the dressing table, where she will be brushing her hair, and he will take the brush from her and run his fingers gently through her long, silky black hair, before suddenly pulling it hard, jerking her head back, bringing his face close up to hers, waiting until he sees the faintest trace of tears begin to prick her eyes. And then he will throw her onto the bed, turn her roughly on to her stomach, cover her mouth with his hand, and fuck her hard from behind, until he will come with a moan and a shudder, and roll over onto his side.

Farida will lie motionless, waiting until she will know he is asleep, and then quietly she will creep into the bathroom, where she will sit on the edge of the bath, shaking soundlessly. After a few moments, she will collect herself, wash herself with warm, soothing water, careful to be certain that she will leave no trace of blood anywhere, and then she will return to her room and crawl into bed beside her snoring husband, who will not now wake until morning, until after she will have already got up.

Downstairs Salwa will be dozing peacefully. She will not hear her husband quietly let himself in, nor will she notice him, standing over her with a deep smile of contentment. He will gently wake her and say to her in a whisper, "Well now, Mrs Raqeeb, both our daughters are married, and earlier Salim is telling me that he has at last found a house for Farida and him. They will be moving next week. Our little birds will have flown the nest."

*

Almost a year later, in their tiny flat above the fish and chip shop, where ice is encrusted on the inside of the windows, Nadia stands looking out towards the frozen Canal, the sky lightening, her own tiny bird in flight, baby Jenna, nuzzling her shoulder, as Sol's breathing finally calms and the nightmare leaves him. She sees two children, a boy and a girl, wrapped up in scarves and gloves and woolly hats, venture carefully onto the ice. When they are sure it will take their weight, they begin to skate, holding hands, in ever-widening circles, making scratched and doodled bird-tracks across its surface. She is just about to turn away when a sudden flurry of movement alerts her. The ice has begun to crack, and the boy has fallen into the freezing water. He flaps his arms frantically until the girl manages to catch hold of him and pull him to safety. He stands rooted to the spot as she hugs him close, then takes hold of his hand and marches him quickly back in the direction of where they live. Nadia breathes a sigh of relief, kisses the top of Jenna's head, and looks back towards Sol, who is just beginning to wake up.

"You're up early," he says. "What are you looking at?"

"I think," she says, "it's starting to thaw."

6

1963-68

"Cheering crowds braved Manchester's inclement weather to greet His Royal Highness Prince Phillip, Duke of Edinburgh, accompanied by Home Secretary Mr RAB Butler, as he made a special tour of the University's research laboratories to witness for himself the exciting new strides being taken by the country's leading scientists and captains of industry.

"First stop was a chance to see the latest in robot technology. Here's Professor Meredith Thring demonstrating his Robot Fire Cart, nicknamed 'Robbie'. There it is – yes, that funny-looking metal crate on four wheels. It may not seem like much, but that Robot Fire Cart's got a mind of its own. It slowly circles a building, rather like a Night Watchman – so watch out, all you caretakers out there, this metal crate might just be after your job! That dish on its top revolving slowly is a Gyro

Compass Oscillator. Or 'GCO' for short. If it detects a fire, which it does with the aid of a heat-sensor, its automatic steering mechanism guides it towards the source of the flames. Whoa there! Not too close! That should do it! Now a robotic finger swings back round to open a valve and direct the extinguisher nozzles to spray the fire with water and prevent it from spreading further. Who needs a Fire Engine when you've got Robbie?

"Early tests have not been without their setbacks, however. The first prototype was liable to keep chasing the sun! But now, with new inventions like these by Professor Thring and his colleagues, Britain can once again lead the world in science and technology. That's what Prince Phillip thinks anyway. Here he is, leading this gathering of white-coated boffins in three hearty cheers for Robbie the Robot Fire Cart!

"What *will* they think of next?"

*

Sol's art tutor, George Wright, was re-lighting his pipe as he stepped out of *The Broadway* cinema, having just enjoyed Joseph Losey's *The Servant*.

"Perhaps it needs a foreigner," he thought ruefully to himself, striding towards *The Old Bull* for a quick half before closing time, "and an American at that, to really get under the skin of the British class system."

He had loved everything about the film – Harold Pinter's script, the actors' performances (especially Dirk

Bogarde's), Johnny Dankworth's music. He found he was humming the song *All Gone*, which had snaked its way repeatedly through it, as he walked along Church Street away from the cinema. He looked around at the demolition sites everywhere. Not just houses, whole streets were being cleared. Flattened and wiped, erased from maps and memory. Soon it would indeed be 'all gone', except, he presumed, somehow the old class-divides would survive, mutated possibly, but still there.

His thoughts now turned to that ridiculous newsreel from Movietone, which had preceded the film. He'd chuckled along, as he usually did, deriding the customary patronising tone and pukka accent, but deep down he'd been disturbed. George was an old-fashioned socialist, a Fabian idealist, whose heart beat a little faster to the martial tunes of Soviet marching bands, the propaganda posters of huge collective farms, the grandiose ten-year plans, the permanent state of revolution, though he rejected outright the Stalinist purges and had been appalled by the embarrassing spectacle of Kruschev banging his shoe on the podium at the United Nations. And now this stupid newsreel. Despite its gentle mockery, its message could not be clearer. The white heat of technology made for fine rhetoric but the reality could only mean huge job losses. What kind of future lay in store for the young men who attended his Evening Classes, young men like Sol, reduced to collateral damage in the unstoppable march of progress? And you really couldn't stop it, thought George. Macmillan had been right with his "never-had-it-so-good" talk at the last election, much as George hated to admit it. He thought of how hard his mother had worked while she was still a child, all those years of domestic drudgery in the tripe colony at Miles Platting. What wouldn't she have given for all the latest household appliances, the fridges, the cookers, the washing machines, soon, it seemed, all to be mass-produced by robots? Would the working man also become a thing of the past, a forgotten folk memory, like these bulldozed streets around him?

He stepped inside the warm smoke-filled fug of *The Old Bull*, ordered his half of mild, brooding over it at the end of the bar. He resolved that he'd focus on industrial scenes for his next term of classes. He'd show his students slides of brick fields, cement plants, steel works and coal mines, factories, forges, cotton mills and shop floors, photographs he'd been taking for the past couple of decades recording and capturing change, as well as paintings by Cornish, Braaq, Ormsby and Burton, Downie, Millar, Owen and Harris. Lowry, too, of course. Maybe he might tell them about when he met the great man, painting St Michael's Church at Angel Meadow. Or perhaps they should start with Holman Hunt's *Work*, followed by a critique of Soviet posters, peopled with heroic figures driving trains and tractors, wielding spanners and wrenches aloft like weapons, bathed in the blood-red glow of the forge? Yes, he smiled. That would do it. He looked round the pub, hoping his friend Francis might be there, but he wasn't. Pubs were not his habitat. Perhaps he might ride over to him on his DOT Villiers motor cycle before going home, he thought.

Feeling better, George downed the rest of his beer and headed back out into the once-familiar landscape as it continued to shift before his eyes.

*

Despite his initial bravado, it did not take long before Sol was regretting his stubbornness in refusing to live either at home with his mother or with Nadia's parents after he and Nadia were married, even though offers were made from both quarters, for as soon as Nadia had to give up work as her pregnancy progressed, it was clear that Sol's wage as a fork-lift truck-driver alone would not be sufficient, even for their basic flat above the chippy. To make matters worse, however hard Nadia tried to brighten the place up, the lingering smell of grease and fat was all-pervasive, while the windows and walls dripped with condensation. But Sol's pride would not permit him to give in, and Nadia never once suggested they should leave. She remained determinedly cheerful, enjoying the distant view of the Canal, watching the progress of the motorway bridge arching over it as it neared completion, pointing out the changing seasons on the spindly sycamores just visible if you leaned out of the window and craned your neck to the left.

Sol enquired about a better-paid office-job but was given short shrift. There were younger men, it seemed, with 'O' levels, queuing up for it, and in a fit of pique he left Metro-Vickers. Once again Nadia said nothing by way of rebuke, merely agreeing with him that he was worth better than that, and besides, there were plenty of jobs to be found.

And so it proved. He found one at Kellogg's, as a

ludicrously titled "Quality Assurance Operative", which in reality required him to wear a white coat and hat, stand beside conveyor belts along which poured thousands of corn flakes hour after hour, from which his task was to try and pick out the black ones every time he saw them. After a few weeks of this, he thought he would go mad. He even dreamed of corn flakes and in the end the sight of them proved so mesmeric he found he could no longer distinguish the black ones from the rest and was dismissed for taking too long one afternoon over a cigarette break.

From Kellogg's he went to Kilvert's, where his job was to clean out the vast ovens that cooked the lard, but even Nadia blanched at this, complaining that she could never get the smell of it out of his clothes. From Kilvert's he went to Palmolive, and from Palmolive to Regent's Tyres, but as the big freeze descended on Manchester, as 1962 turned stiffly into 1963, he was laid off, and as the ice thickened on the Canal, and their flat grew colder and colder, and as their baby Jenna developed a nasty bout of croup, Sol found himself out of work. He would leave early each morning with the purpose of scrolling down the lists at the Labour Exchange, but it was mainly to get out of the flat and away from the seemingly ceaseless crying of Jenna, noting the anxious look in Nadia's eyes, but not knowing what to say or do about any of it.

He avoided going to the Arab Workers' Union, where he knew they would find him something, for fear of running into Nadia's father, who, now that he had reduced his hours at the Steel Works, spent more and more of his time there as a volunteer to support new arrivals, and whom Sol felt too ashamed and defeated to face.

He eventually found work at the Cussons Soap Factory in Kersal, on the edge of the Ship Canal, which he would set off for early each morning, both to save money on the bus fare and to spend as little time in the flat as he had to. No longer a 'quality assurance operative', Sol now found himself working at what was uncompromisingly but accurately referred to as 'breaking out'. This involved him back on another conveyor belt carrying sheets of cardboard in stacks of fifty. Printed around the edges of these sheets was a perforated pattern, which Sol, along with other young men, had to 'break out'. This required them to remove the excess cardboard from beyond the outline of the pattern, throwing that onto the floor at their feet, which, when this pile threatened to bury them completely, a young boy would come to sweep away, before placing the newly-shaped stacks back on to the conveyor belt, which would transport them across the floor to where girls and young women, correctly deemed more skilled, would fold each sheet, using the perforated pattern as a guide, into cardboard boxes. These boxes would then be returned to the conveyor belt where, further down the line, packs of soap, which had been cellophane-wrapped by more experienced women operating a machine set up for the purpose, would be dropped into and fill each one, which another team would remove, seal their tops, then load into piles to be fork-lifted to the warehouse for storage and delivery. On several occasions these boxes were found to have 'accidentally' split, spilling their contents of freshly-packed bars of soap, and Sol would smuggle these back home, making him an instant hit with Nadia and Farida, for Cussons Imperial Leather was a rare treat, and they'd smooth the lather on their cheeks in imitation of the television adverts.

" *'One of life's luxuries one should never be without'*," they'd purr and giggle, mimicking the Home Counties accent.

"You wouldn't be so fond of them if you saw the colour of the Canal that flows past the factory," Sol would tease them, "a kind of dirty brown sludge full of what you wouldn't believe."

When he started, Sol had to divide his stacks of fifty sheets into three or four smaller piles to be able to break out the excess card cleanly enough, but after he had been there a week he was able to manage the whole stack in a single thump, bend, break and tear. It was physically exerting, he worked up a real sweat in no time, and it encouraged, Sol discovered, the kind of push-and-shove among the other lads he remembered from his time in National Service. Every afternoon, he noticed, the pace of the work seemed to get quicker and quicker, with piles of fifties stacking up, waiting to be broken out, while the Supervisor looked on disapprovingly, tapping his watch and urging them to work faster. It was only after a few days that Sol realised, as every new person did who came later, that as the piles of finished boxes grew steadily higher while the day wore on, waiting for the fork-lift truck driver to whisk them away towards the end of the shift, so the more experienced workers would take this as their cue to slope off behind these piles, where they could remain hidden from the Supervisor's office window, for a smoke and a game of cards, and every single day, without fail, a fight would break out, the punching of the packs of cardboard leeching into the punching of another body, as tempers sparked and flared, before fizzling out as quickly as they had started.

It was behind one of these mountains of boxes, late one afternoon while Sol was taking a breather, that he had his first real conversation with Cadge. He had seen him around, of course, had nodded, grunted the occasional hello, but never properly spoken to him. Sol almost stumbled over him, sitting on one of the boxes, leaning his back up against another of the taller piles, reading the racing page of *The Daily Sketch*, a cigarette in one hand, a pencil in the other, with which he would underline the name of a particular horse, before tucking it behind a cauliflower ear.

"*Bob's Your Uncle* for the 4.30 at Haydock. Eleven to two. Five pound seventeen and six for a pound bet. It's a dead cert. I'd bet my house on it – if I had one. What d'you reckon?"

Sol shook his head.

"What? You don't do the gee-gees? It's the only thing that keeps me sane around here. Listen – what are you doing after work tonight?"

It was a Tuesday – when Sol had his Art class at night school – but lately he'd found it harder and harder to motivate himself, and George had noticed. "What's the matter with you, Sol? You've lost your spark these days." Sol had made some excuse about the baby and broken nights and feeling tired, and George had smiled and urged him to channel his exhaustion into his mark-making on the page, but nothing seemed to come out right, and he was growing discouraged.

"Well," he said to Cadge therefore, "I usually do something on a Tuesday, but what did you have in mind?"

"A drink first, obviously. All this cardboard and dust works up one hell of a thirst. Then a crowd of us goes down The Albion."

"The Albion?"

"The dog track. There's greyhounds every night of the week if you want them. Except Sundays of course. Mondays and Thursdays it's White City, Wednesdays and Saturdays Belle Vue, and Tuesdays and Fridays The Albion."

Sol realised what Cadge was talking about. He'd passed it on Seaford Road on his way to Pendleton, where the Institute stood, and noticed the crowds walking away from it as he travelled home on the bus, but had never really taken it in properly, his head normally full of whatever he'd been wrestling with in the art studio just a few minutes before. Why not, he thought? He could do with a night out, and Nadia would be none the wiser. He might try his hand at drawing some of the people there. Yes. He could show them to George the following week. George would peer up close at the charcoal on the paper, smudge a line here and a mark there, nod his head, say something cryptic about authenticity, before relighting his pipe...

And so it began.

He did indeed take his sketch pad along, and he revelled in the whole basket of delights that was laid out before him – not only the gallery of different faces he encountered with their gamut of mixed emotions (joy, despair, elation, disappointment; loneliness, loss, hope and communion), the range of characters he observed (the fast-talking bookies chalking up the dogs' names race after race, then rubbing them out with the backs of their hands; the rapid exchange of single, five and even ten pound notes; the tic-tac men in their black bowler hats and white gloves signalling the odds from one side of the track to the other, one hundred to thirty the favourite, fifteen to two bar, the yankees, the ponies, the each-way-treble-accumulators; the ferret-faced men in caps and mufflers, pencil stub behind their ears, woodbine wedged permanently between their lips, tearing up betting slips with nicotine-stained fingers; the old girls with their glasses of milk stout in the Tote bar; the West Indian cricketers he recognised from the papers; the office parties on their works' night out, the girls tottering on their heels with Babychams and Cherry B's, hungrily being eyed up by the young wide-boys in their crumpled suits and creased gabardines downing another pint of mild to summon up the courage to try and entice one round the back of the stands in between races) – but the whole machinery of the meeting (the parading of the dogs on leashes before each race by stewards in white coats; the numbers and colours of each dog grubbily displayed on their tattered jackets, red for trap one, blue for two, white for three, orange for four, black-and-white stripes for five; the rickety wooden traps wheeled on and off the track for the start of each race, a rough mixture of bare earth, parched grass, cinders and sand; the rusty iron grilles at the front of the traps through which the dogs pawed and peered as they waited for them to rise, to release them in pursuit of the moth-eaten, mechanical hare that whirled around the outside of each bend, which they chased to the accompaniment of the deep-throated roar from the seven to eight thousand people crammed into the stands). Sol ingested all of this greedily, sucked in by the noise and grit and life of it, the rawness like a slap in the face, the sharp tang of sweetness in his mouth, from the strong mugs of tea at Mick's Transport Café across the street, scanning the photos on the walls of past champions, *Pigalle Wonder*, *Brilliant Bob* and of course *Mick the Miller*, after whom the café was named.

He found himself going again on the Friday, and then again the following Tuesday. On this third visit one of the stewards noticed him sketching the dogs during the pre-race parade and came over to him.

"You're becoming quite a regular, old son," he said. "What's that you're drawing?"

"Anything," said Sol, "and everything."

"That's what I thought," said the steward, who introduced himself as Pat. "The thing is, my old son, you've got people asking questions. They're wondering whether you might be one of those undercover cops posing as an artist, when really you're just compiling a file of identikits that you might then use to frame people with. Know what I mean?"

"Nothing could be further from the truth. But if it's annoying you, I'll stop right away."

"It's not me, son," said Pat, "but some of the others round here are not as trusting as I am. Might you be interested in a job by any chance? Evenings, twice a week? That way I can keep an eye on you, make sure you don't get yourself into any trouble…?"

Sol accepted on the spot. It was, he realised, as soon as Pat had made the offer, exactly what he had been hoping for, and the extra money would certainly come in handy for Nadia and the baby. He'd have to give up his Art classes of course, but he was sure George would understand, and the money he saved from that would be a further bonus. Perhaps he might surprise Nadia with some flowers on his way home…

The arrangement suited Sol down to the ground. He enjoyed handling the dogs, grooming them, feeding them, watching the trainers working them, parading them before the races, loading them into the traps, tossing in a real rabbit after the race was over and the electric hare had sped back to its starting gate, then separating them from each other as they fought over the fresh meat. He was quickly on first name terms with several of the bookies, their assistants, the regular punters, who would frequently sound him out for tips – how was *this* dog doing in training, or *that* dog recovering from injury? He found he had an eye for spotting just when a particular dog was in peak condition, or when it was starting to look stale or jaded, and though he wasn't strictly permitted to place bets himself, he found that he could get others to place them for him, and pretty soon he had a slate with two or three of the bookies around the track.

But knowing what condition a dog looked in was no guarantee of how it might run on any given day. There were so many variables – the trap the dog was drawn in, the weather, the going, the other dogs in the race – and it wasn't long before Sol found himself losing heavily. The money he'd saved from his Art classes was not buying flowers for Nadia, nor were many of his extra wages finding their way home either. Soon he was digging into his salary from Cussons to try and meet his debts, until one week he found that he'd gambled away the lot.

By this time he was also going to the Castle Irwell Racecourse across the way from The Albion every time they had a meeting. If anything, he found the atmosphere of horse racing even more intoxicating than the dogs. The crowds were larger, noisier, with more of a press and jostle, while the speed of the horses created a visceral thrill deep within him, the pounding of their hooves across the turf vibrating right through his body. The sweat and steam rising from them as their saddles were removed after an especially hard race would transport him high into the air, from where he could look down on the whole scene, seemingly unchanged since races had first been run there, almost two hundred years before, captured in those paintings by Frith, reproductions of which George had shown him once on a trip to Manchester Art Gallery, the whole of humanity spread out before him, like so much flotsam washed up on the tide, the sport of kings, men in top hats cheek by jowl with trilbies, cloth caps, bowlers, women in fine dresses, clutching wide extravagant hats in the wind, the jockeys in their bright silks, and there in the centre of it all, parting the waves of people like Moses on the Red Sea, Prince Monolulu, the celebrated tipster, resplendent in his head dress and feathers, brandishing a ceremonial spear and shield, dancing like a Watusi warrior, shouting out to all who cared to listen: "I got a horse! I got a horse!"

Sol let himself be swept along by it all, tossed by the tide till finally he was spat out like a flounder, flapping and gasping for air on the shore, his clothes awry, his shoes scuffed and trampled on, his pockets empty. He felt a hand on his shoulder, shaking him awake. It was Pat from The Albion.

"You seem to be in a bit of trouble, my old son."

Sol found that he had nothing he could say.

"Maybe I can lend you a hand? Come on. Up you get. Let me buy you a mug of tea over at Mick's."

They sat down in the warm fug of the Transport Café. Pat waited while Sol drank his tea and his shivering gradually ceased.

"So tell me, son, how much do you owe them now?"

Sol shook his head. "I don't know. A lot. More than I can pay back."

"How would you like to have all of that wiped out?"

Sol looked up. "How...?

And Pat leaned across the table and whispered in Sol's ear for several minutes, at the end of which he sat back and waited. "Well?"

"Do I have a choice?"

"Frankly, my son, you've run out of options."

The Albion was what was known as a "flapper" track. That meant that it did not fall under the auspices of the GRA, the Greyhound Racing Authority. It was still legal – just – but was largely unregulated, especially when it came to doping. Doping could give dog owners or trainers an underhand advantage when it came to gambling. By illegally drugging their dogs, they could control their performance on the track and in the betting ring. Sometimes, dogs were sedated in races to lengthen their odds for a future target race. Dogs were then raced without sedatives, or given stimulant drugs or steroids in order to improve their performance, earning those in the know big cash rewards. Sol's task was a simple one. He was given access to a wide range of prescription tablets. Each week he would be given a list of names of those dogs to which these were to be given, mixed in with their meat, along with dates as to when to begin, increase, or stop the dosage. In return, a set amount was reduced from what he owed the bookmakers on a week-by-week basis, provided the dogs produced the required results. If everything went to plan, if Sol did as he was bid, and if the dogs won or lost as they were meant to, he would, he was told, be debt-free by the end of the year.

On a cold Tuesday night in December, when there was a sharp frost in the air, and Sol had paid back his final installment, Pat sought him out just as he was about to set off back for home. "You've done good, my son. Time for a little holiday. You've earned it, I think, don't you? So don't come back to the track till after Christmas, when we can sit down and have a nice little chat and see what else you might be able to do for us."

Pat was smiling and Sol understood that he would never be free of it. "What if I don't want to come back?"

"Well that's up to you, my son. It's a free country. But just you make sure you'll not be telling anyone about this special arrangement we've had between us, alright? We wouldn't want that pretty young wife of yours to know what's been going on, now would we? Or for her to have a little accident. Do we understand one another?" He patted Sol's cheek in a way that appeared to be friendly, but was an unmistakable warning, which Sol grasped immediately. "Merry Christmas, old son," said a smiling Pat before he left Sol nursing the dregs of a mug of tea in Mick's. He felt trapped. He was under no illusions about what might lie in store.

Later that night, while Sol and Nadia and Jenna were all sleeping in their refrigerator of a flat, they were suddenly awakened by a loud banging on the outside door, followed by the sound of splintering wood as it was forced off its hinges, then heavy footsteps pounding up the stairs, forcing their way into their bedroom.

A terrified Nadia clutched a screaming Jenna to her, while Sol meekly raised his hands in the air in surrender, which one of the police officers thrust behind his back where he roughly cuffed them, before bundling Sol down the stairs and into the waiting van, which drove him speedily away. The whole incident took barely sixty seconds. After they'd gone, Nadia, still trying to quieten Jenna, surveyed the wreckage.

*

"Solomon Ward, you have been found guilty by the Magistrates Court of one count of illegal possession of a prescribed valoid drug, namely Cyclizine, obtained by you fraudulently under the pretence of treating dizziness, with actual intent to administer surreptitiously to greyhounds kennelled at The Albion Race Track, Seaford Road, Pendleton, Salford, plus one count of perverting the course of justice by misdirecting a police investigation, and have been passed here, to the Crown Court, for sentencing. You have deliberately deceived, misguided and cheated the public into placing lawful bets on dogs that were prevented from performing to their true capabilities because of the adverse influence of the drugs you administered, which acted in the form of a sedative. You committed these actions on more than one occasion for your own unlawful financial gain. Despite your claim that you were at all times acting under instructions imposed on you by a party or parties unknown, you can produce no evidence to substantiate this, nor that you were in any way forced, coerced or threatened, and so this court can come to only one conclusion, which is that you did act knowingly and alone. We have heard from Prosecuting Counsel how doping is the scourge of greyhound racing today, a pastime innocently enjoyed by thousands of hard working people right across the country. You have been instrumental in hoodwinking these people for your own avaricious ends."

The judge waits, looking Sol directly in the eye. "Before I pass sentence, is there anything by way of circumstance extenuating you wish to say to me?"

Sol lowers his head, remaining mute, as he has done throughout the trial.

The judge sighs and shakes his head. "Very well. You give me no alternative but to commit you for a term of six years at Her Majesty's pleasure, where you may repent at leisure upon this judgement by a jury of your peers."

"I needed money to pay our rent, keep our heads above water," Sol suddenly blurts out. "I made sure none of the dogs suffered any real harm…"

The judge raps his gavel sharply. "You will have plenty of time to indulge in such self-pity during the period of your sentence. You have squandered every opportunity afforded you, by your family, your school, your employers, by the Armed Forces, for whom you carried out two years creditable National Service overseas. You have betrayed the faith entrusted in you by your Commanding Officer, wilfully I might add, who nevertheless took time to provide this glowing detailed reference by way of mitigation…" He brandishes an official document. "…with its full account and explanation of those most distressing incidents which led to your medical discharge, an act of extraordinary lenience in my view, requesting a second chance, and it is within this context I urge you not to forfeit any further right to clemency this court might choose to exercise, if it so thought it might improve your coarse demeanour." He brings his gavel down one last time hard. "Take him down."

The Attending Officer gently guides him down the corridor towards the holding cell. "Keep your head down, lad, that's my advice. With good behaviour you could be out in less than four, no matter what the Beak says. Stay focused, sharp, and always on your guard."

Sol manages to catch a final glimpse of Nadia gazing down upon him from the Public Gallery. She puts her fingers to her lips, kisses them, proffers them in his direction, then places the same hand upon her heart. It is more than he can bear.

*

Sol had been held on remand at Strangeways Prison in Manchester, and the following day he was transferred to Walton Gaol, a few miles outside Liverpool looking out across the Mersey towards the Wirral, to begin serving his sentence. It was 11th January 1964, his daughter Jenna's first birthday.

He was allowed two visits per month, but the paperwork required for permission and authorisation to be granted took a few weeks, and so it was not until the second Friday in March that Nadia was able to attend. When Sol emerged from the cells into the Visiting Room it took him a while before he spotted her among the thirty or so people, mostly women, who were anxiously waiting. She was sitting in an allocated chair, still wearing a raincoat, a bag by her side. Her hair was tied back and she was nervously twisting the cheap wedding ring on her finger that they had bought from a jeweller's stall on Eccles Market one giddy Saturday afternoon shortly after he had proposed to her. That was less than two years ago but seemed a lifetime away. She was scanning the other prisoners as they entered, frowning, until eventually she saw him, stood up and waved, a thin, tight smile briefly crossing her face.

Before Sol had had a chance to say anything, she began to speak.

"Sol. You're looking tired. To be expected, I suppose. How are they treating you? No, don't tell me, not yet, I don't want to know, not really, so long as you're OK, and you seem to be. I'm rambling – sorry. It's nerves, I expect. I haven't got long. I left Jenna with Farida, but I have to be back before Salim gets in from work. He doesn't like me to go round, especially since… well, you know? And it took ages to get here. I had to get a bus from Patricroft to Eccles, then a train to Lime Street, where I had to change for West Kirkby, getting off at James Street, followed by a half mile walk to Moorfields, where I had to catch another train, this time towards Ormskirk and get off here at Walton, and a further half mile walk from the station. It's taken me two and a half hours, so I'll have to be setting off again in half an hour if I'm to be back in time so that Farida doesn't get into trouble. God, I wish I had a cigarette."

"You don't smoke."

"I do now."

"Sorry."

"Don't, Sol. Just don't. What's done is done and we've got to make the best of it, so I've been thinking."

"Yes. So have I…"

"Stop right there, Sol. I've got a speech prepared, which I've been practising all the way here, so please don't interrupt me till I've finished. Alright?"

"Alright."

She took a deep breath. "Right. This is what's going to happen. I'll stand by you, Sol. I think it's terrible, what you've done, and you've only yourself to blame, but I think you know that too deep down, so I'm going to give you another chance. You said in court that you did what you did for me and Jenna, and in a peculiar sort of way I think you did, but if only you'd talked to me first, about how worried you were, or how unhappy, then we might have sorted something out, together, and avoided all of this, but the judge was right, Sol. You've now got plenty of time to think about what you've done, and not only that, but to think about how things might change in the future, because believe me, Sol, they're going to have to. No more secrets, no more bottling things up, understand?"

Sol nodded but said nothing.

"So what I've decided is this. Jenna and I are moving out of that awful flat. The landlord wanted to put up the rent, charge us for the cost of repairing the damage after the police broke down the door, and when I said I couldn't pay any more, he just shrugged his shoulders and said that was up to me. But then a Chinese family came along and bought the shop and they need the whole place for their own family. They're going to do it all up and I'm sure it'll be very nice, but I have to be gone before they can start. They're being really good about it, Sol, saying I don't have to leave for another three months, not till I've found somewhere else, but the truth is, I can't really afford it, not even at the old rent, not now you're in here – family allowance doesn't stretch that far – and I hate the place if I'm honest. We were right to give it a go, just the two of us, then the three of us once Jenna came along, but it's so full of unhappy memories, Sol, I just need to get out."

She paused and took another deep breath. Sol looked back at her. He knew what was coming next.

"So I went over to your mother's, Sol – no, don't interrupt, she's been a good friend to me, I've been to see her a few times, just me, then with Jenna. I don't know what it was that went wrong between the two of you, Sol, not really, but whatever it was, it's all in the past. You have to move on. So your mother said that me and Jenna could stay with her as long as we need, for always if we have to, so that's what we're doing. Then I'm going to get a job, maybe a couple of jobs. Susan says I could go back to Turner's, but I don't think I could, not back to the typing pool, not after having been Mr Tunstall's secretary, it wouldn't seem right, so I've spoken to my father at the Arab Worker's Union, and he's got me a part-time job a couple of mornings a week teaching English to the wives of the men coming over from Lahej, helping them to settle, find their feet, how to use our money in the shops, that kind of thing, and your mother has got me an interview at Lewis Street Primary in Eccles as a teacher's help and assistant on three other half days. If I get it, Farida and your mother will share looking after Jenna till I get back each day, and if I have to, I'll get some evening work too, cleaning offices after they've closed, stuff like that."

She was gripping the sides of her chair tightly, so that her knuckles were white.

"Right," she said. "That's it."

"You seem to have got it all sorted."

"Someone had to, Sol."

They held each other's gaze. Eventually Sol spoke.

"It sounds good," he said. "Thank you."

"OK." She let out a long, deep breath. "There's a couple of other things. First of all, I shan't probably be coming again. Not often, anyway. They don't do weekend visiting and I won't be able to make it all the way here and back in time to fit in with these jobs, or with Jenna. And I'm not bringing her with me. This is no place for a kiddie, Sol. Maybe over Christmas, eh? But we've managed being apart before, haven't we? When you were on National Service? I seem to remember you were a pretty good letter writer back then," she said with a smile, her body relaxing a little. "Perhaps you can be again?"

He nodded.

"And I've brought you this." She passed a large envelope across the table towards him.

"What is it?"

"Open it and find out."

"I'm not allowed to here. I'll have to wait till I go back to the cell. They check everything that gets brought in."

"Well, you'll have to write and let me know what it is, won't you? I found it while your mother was showing me and Jenna where we could put our things once we move in. She's moving out of her room, so that we can have the

215

larger one, and it was in a drawer in the dressing table. 'I'd forgotten about this,' she said. 'This is what Sol's father left him just before he died. Look what it says on the front'."

Sol picked it up and read: " *'For Solly. To be opened on his 21st birthday.'* I remember him showing me this. He was sitting up in bed, with a blanket round his shoulders. He lay it on his lap and then started coughing really badly, and my grandfather whisked me out of the room, while my mother fetched a bowl and towel. She must have put it away to keep it safe…"

"It's best you open it then. You're nearly twenty-four now. You need to make up for lost time."

"Yes," he said, looking back at her. "I do."

She leant across to kiss him, just as a loud bell rang to signal the end of Visiting Hours. "I'll have to dash," she said. "I mustn't miss that train."

Sol reluctantly let go of her hand.

"Think on what I've said, Sol. Make sure you write." And with that she was gone.

Sol clutched the envelope tightly, imagining her rapid stride hurrying towards the station, away from him, back to the house he'd been a child in.

Nadia flew down the road towards the station, just leaping aboard as it pulled away. She flitted down the gangway till she found a compartment with no one else in it, slid back the door, sat down and silently started to cry, all the tension finally draining away from her. She looked out across the Mersey towards Birkenhead, the New Brighton ferry plying its way along the estuary and out towards the open sea. So many people on the move, she thought, all of them trying to find their way to somewhere else. She dried her eyes and thought of Jenna, how in a couple of hours she would be picking her up from Farida, how she would push her across the park towards their new home, and how she'd look up from her pram, mesmerised, as she always was, by the clouds passing above her in the sky.

*

Sol was cleared to take the envelope back to his cell. He decided not to open it just yet, but let it wait, till he'd had time to think about what Nadia had said and properly take it in. He had a cell to himself for the moment, for which he was grateful. He climbed onto the single chair and peered through the smeared glass of the broken window high up near the ceiling, trying to get his bearings. Looking up he could see a rectangle of sky, while below was an unused passage between different wings of the prison. It was almost knee deep in rubbish and litter. An open drain ran down the centre, carrying what looked like sewage and effluent, and in which he could make out a rat foraging among the detritus.

Over the coming weeks and months he would regularly look out onto this less than salubrious view. On most occasions he would see the same rat, or one of his cousins, and took to looking forward to seeing the way he made a home for himself, even down there among the scrap and discard of a part of the prison the outside world never got to see. The rat, it seemed, thrived on neglect, completely in his element. Except that he wasn't neglected. Not entirely. Sol was watching out for him. He'd worry if he didn't see him each time he looked out through the cracked skylight. Sometimes a whole week might go by without Sol catching a single glance of him. He wondered then whether he might never see him again. But always, eventually, he'd show up once more, raising his head above a piece of broken pipe, nosing the air, going about his business, always on the alert for signs of danger, blithely unaware that someone else was looking out for him.

*

Nadia secured the two jobs she had told Sol about. She especially enjoyed working with the recent arrivals from overseas as they made their first few tentative steps in this strange new world they found themselves in. She found she had a real aptitude when it came to teaching them to read and write in an unfamiliar tongue, and a small seed was planted in the back of her mind. "I wonder," she thought, "when this is all over…"

In addition she took on whatever extra work came her way, cleaning the offices in Orbit House, one of the many new tower blocks rising from the rubble of bomb sites and waste ground that still lay broken and smouldering everywhere around her, which she did for two hours each morning from 6am, to which she could take Jenna, who would happily toddle around after her; or serving chop suey and chips two nights a week in the Chinese Take Away that had replaced the fish and chip shop where they had all lived together previously; and now here she was, in the run-up to Christmas, working for five nights in Kendal Milne's Department Store on Deansgate in the centre of Manchester, assisting with the window displays.

She would arrive at six-thirty in the evening, having left Jenna with Ishtar, just as the regular employees were heading for home, and she would work straight through until five the next morning. She knew this wasn't sustainable, but it was only for one week, while the displays throughout the entire store were changed over for Christmas, and it was well paid because of the unsociable hours. Most of her co-workers were students, younger than she was, and beside them she felt very old indeed. Once she would have enjoyed mixing in with their banter, but now they inhabited completely different worlds, and they seemed to look on her as some wise older sister, to whom they could come for advice, or a shoulder to cry on if they'd just broken up with their latest boyfriend. She said nothing of her circumstances to any of them, nor did they ask her. It was as if they sensed some sadness in her, born of experience, while to her they represented a road that was no longer one she could travel down, a gate that had been closed, which she might lean on, look over and observe the scenery from, but not one she would ever again open. There was one other young woman, whom she might have confided in, Anita, who was about the same age, a single mother struggling, like Nadia, to keep things going. One morning, she said, her husband, Roy, had simply walked out of the front door of their Moss Side bed-sit and never come back, leaving her with no money and a three year-old boy – Lance – to bring up by herself.

For the most part, though, they simply worked, packing bolts of brightly coloured material into wicker hampers to be transported up and down the elevators to whichever floor they were needed, unrolling yards and yards of cotton wool snow to be spread across every available surface, or carrying various mannequins up and down the stairs waiting to be dressed as angels, Santas, elves or snowmen, or tableaux of happy, smiling families.

All through each night piped music would be playing the latest hits from the Top Twenty, and, to Nadia, in her current hyper-sensitive state, when every sound made her head spin and her body feel like broken glass, each song seemed to carry a message just for her, freighted with meaning.

"When you're alone and life is making you lonely
You can always go
Downtown..."

"I walk along the city streets you used to walk along with me
And every step I take reminds me of just how we used to be
How can I forget you
When there is always something there to remind me...?"

"The dogs begin to bark, hounds begin to howl
The dogs begin to bark, hounds begin to howl
Watch out, strange cat people
Little Red Rooster's on the prowl..."

"All day and all of the night
All day and all of the night
All day and all of the night..."

Over and over, on an endless loop, these tunes filled every floor of the store, and Nadia found herself singing along with them too, just like everyone else, even though they were driving her mad.

On the final night, with emotions running high and time running out, boxes were spilled, tinsel was torn and Christmas trees tumbled, as tempers and temperaments frayed. But it wasn't Little Red Rooster who was on the prowl, it was Miss Gresty. Miss Gresty, the Shop Window Designer, who they were all in awe of, who always dressed from head to toe entirely in black, with black bobbed hair, black lipstick, theatrically held cigarette holder with a black Sobranie permanently attached, black tights and black ballet pumps, who cultivated a Russian accent (even though she was from Bury) and called everyone "Darling", and who clapped her hands to bring them all together for one last motivational speech.

"Darlings, tomorrow we open. In few hours time, when customers queue to see Christmas Grotto, we must be ready. No second chances, no wait till next day, so please – no more this bish-bash pell-mell helter-skelter."

Even Nadia had to bite the inside of her cheeks to stop herself from giggling but Miss Gresty was unstoppable.

"Take deep breath. Relax. Ten minute break, then start again. But first..." She flung open one of the emergency exits behind her and waved an arm theatrically. "Follow me."

They trooped behind her, up a back staircase, which led all the way up to a narrow landing and another set of double doors.

"Up," she said, "up, up, and away. Watch out, strange cat people," and she gently pushed the two doors outwards, from where a final couple of steps led everyone out on to the roof of the department store.

It was approaching half past three in the morning. A sharp frost had formed on the rail that ran around the top of the flat roof. Overhead the stars in the Milky Way arched above them, hard and glittering. From the other side of Deansgate they could hear the bell of St Ann's Church toll the half hour. Everyone fell silent, their breath forming statues in the clear, crisp air. Someone saw a shooting star and pointed. Then nothing. They stood, singly or in small clusters, awestruck, not moving, holding their breath so as not to break the spell, the whole city stretched out before them, empty and sleeping in a sparkling moonlit monochrome. This was a true winter wonderland, not the pastiche they had been labouring to create in the store below them, and even Miss Gresty was, for once, lost for words.

Then, as if someone had lifted the tiniest corner of this blanket of silence that lay across the world, Nadia thought she detected the faintest of sounds, like when she would wake sometimes in the middle of the night just seconds before Jenna had made even the slightest murmur. Some of the others had heard it too, their heads turning in the direction of what now began to resemble an infinitesimal squeaking. Like a fingernail gently scraping down a rusty kettle. This grew. The squeaking became many-voiced, high-pitched, ultra-sonic, on the very edge of human hearing, like a hundred wine glasses singing when moistened fingers circle their rims, then a thousand, then a hundred thousand. The air began to tremble, the whole sky felt alive with the sound, which had now become so loud that it seemed to be right inside Nadia's head, like a shaken tin of six inch nails, as she, along with everyone else, stood transfixed, straining to see where the noise could be coming from. Even had anyone spoke, by now they could not have been heard. Instead Miss Gresty merely gestured, sweeping out an arm, her long black fingernail pointing down to the street. As one, everyone looked, craning their necks, leaning over the rail.

There, below them, spanning the entire breadth of Deansgate, writhing, rolling, in wave after wave, boiled an entire sea of rat. Thousands upon thousands of them, tumbling together, climbing, scrabbling, crawling, layer upon layer, several feet deep, so that had any of those watching been unfortunate enough to have been standing where now this seething mass of skin and fur, tail and snout bulged and surged, they would have been wading waist-deep.

Behind them, like giant locusts, two City Corporation lorries, with snow ploughs the width of the street, their huge headlamps raking the sky like search lights, herded the rats with mechanical efficiency the entire length of Deansgate. Nadia heard someone say that the city's sewers, built more than a century before, in Queen

Victoria's time, were starting to collapse, and that in order to begin the repairs, first they had to move the rats to a different sewer in another part of the city.

It took almost half an hour for the whole convulsive wildebeest of rat to pour beneath them, as they swarmed towards Shudehill and the slimy granite flagstones of Angel Meadow beyond. The silence that they left behind was like the one to be found on a battlefield, when the last few survivors crawl through the early morning mist, across the piles of stiff corpses, in the vain hope of finding a loved one still alive.

Nadia heard in that hungry silence Jenna's urgent cry, demanding to be fed. She felt Anita's hand upon her arm. They turned and headed back down to finish their shift.

*

Sol tried to keep himself as busy as he could at all times. He worked in the sewing room, stitching donkey jackets several hours each day. He played basketball in the gym, table tennis in the association room, volunteered at the library, did press-ups in his cell. But he did none of these things willingly, except possibly the press-ups, and even these he carried out in order to maintain the sense of heightened physical and mental alertness that had gripped him since he was first arrested. But mostly he just felt numb, in shock, dislocated from himself, like he did when he first came round after the roadside attack in Aden, something else he could only blame himself for.

He was lost.

When he was in Strangeways, waiting for his trial to

begin, he was visited one afternoon by Ray and Eric. Gone was the usual banter between them. None of them made any jokes, not even Ray. Instead an awkward, protracted silence hung in the air between them.

"It might not be so bad," said Ray eventually, passing a cigarette across the table towards Sol. "It might be like being back in the Army."

"You're presuming I'll be found guilty then?" Ray shifted uncomfortably in his chair.

"Well, you are," said Eric. These were the first words he had spoken. "Aren't you."

Sol glanced at him sharply, then looked away. A few seconds later he nodded.

Eric shook his head. "You're a tosser, do you know that?"

"Steady on, mate," said Ray. "All he's done is nobble a few dogs."

Eric kept his eyes firmly on Sol. "I'm not talking about that."

Ray frowned. "What then?"

"*He* knows. Don't you, Sol?"

Sol said nothing. He simply looked up, a moment of frightened panic in his briefly unclouded eyes.

"Has Nadia been to see you yet?"

Sol nodded.

"What did she say?"

"Not much. She just asked me if it was true."

"And did you tell her?"

Sol nodded again.

Eric leaned back. "That's something."

"Not everything." Sol reached across the table back

225

towards his two former pals. "They threatened me."

"Who?" said Ray.

"Who do you think?" said Eric, ignoring him, looking instead directly at Sol.

"They said that if I knew what was good for me, by which they meant if I knew what was good for Nadia and Jenna, I'd say nowt."

"Better late than never."

"I suppose."

"You should've thought about them in the first place, before you got mixed up with any of this."

"I know." Sol looked back at Eric. "You'll keep an eye out for them, won't you?"

"Course we will, mate," said Ray, "won't we, Eric?"

"Nadia'll be all right," said Eric. "She's a lot stronger than you give her credit for. If you'd spoken to her sooner, you might've…"

"What?"

"Avoided all this," he continued, and he spread out his hands, indicating the prison waiting room where the three of them now sat.

A buzzer sounded for the end of visiting time. Ray immediately got up. This place was giving him the creeps, the way everything echoed so loudly, the scraping back of their chairs, the heavy doors constantly slamming in the distance, the jangling of keys from the officers' belts, the smell.

"Thanks for coming," said Sol. He looked suddenly very young.

"Don't mention it, mate," said Ray, jiggling his foot up and down. He couldn't wait to get outside again. If it were him in here instead of Sol, he'd not last five minutes.

Eric stood up. "She'll be all right," he said. "Nadia. You're fucking lucky. You know that, don't you?"

Sol nodded. He found that he couldn't speak.

"You take care in here," Eric added, more softly. "Keep your eyes peeled, eh?"

Ray watched Sol being led away by a large bull of an officer back towards his holding cell, then turned on his heels and practically sprinted out into the watery spring sunshine. A magpie's machine gun rattle mocked him from the spiked railings on the top of the prison wall.

"He's made his bed," said Eric when he joined him.

"Ay," said Ray. "I suppose. He's still our mate, though."

Eric spat onto the pavement. "Course he is," he said. "He knows that. Come on." And he strode off angrily towards the bus stop, his hands jammed into his pockets.

Sol was determined not to let Nadia down a second time. Eric's words had struck him keenly. "She'll be all right," he'd said, and now, Sol could see, she would be. He felt acutely aware of the truth of that other thing Eric had said to him. "You're fucking lucky." Nadia would be much better off without him, yet somehow she was standing by him. It was something he told himself every night.

But even so, those first few weeks in Walton, Sol was terrified. Inside, doing time was seen as some kind of crazy game of survival, which everyone knew the rules of, it seemed, apart from him. A few of the inmates were friendly. They tried to show him the ropes, which of the screws were all right, which ones were best to avoid, how to do trade for a snout, which of the narks to steer clear of, but some of them saw him as the latest newbie to torment, just another pilchard, who was so green he would swim straight into whatever trap they set for him, or spit into his diesel, the prison tea, with its rainbow coloured scum on the surface, like the slick oily sheen of the Ship Canal. Diesel.

Mostly he simply tried to follow the advice of the Attending Officer who had led him away to the police van after his trial and keep his head down. Gradually he began to recognise the terrain, the lie of the land, and stake his own small place within it.

He read newspapers, trying to keep up with what was happening in the world outside, so that he would be ready for what he might face when the time came for him to leave. Every day he wrote letters to Nadia, about what he did, what he saw, what he read, what he thought, and if he didn't hear back from her some weeks, he reminded himself that she was much busier than he was, that he had time on his hands whereas she was raising a child, his child too, though he realised he didn't know Jenna, was missing these first precious years of her growing, that he could never have that time back, and that he would have to work extra hard to establish any sort of relationship with her when he came back out, when she would be seven, would have started school, and he might be an unwelcome stranger arriving in her well-ordered life. He would have to make her proud of him, but first, he knew, he had to win back Nadia's trust.

He had been completely taken aback by her strength of purpose, her single-mindedness, her certainty that the solution to the situation she found herself in, a situation caused solely by *him*, lay within *her* power to resolve, and her power alone. She would simply take charge, leave him no room for manoeuvre, take it or leave it, which she had done, and he knew, he absolutely knew, that he must acquiesce to all she was proposing, or risk losing her. She took his breath away. She'd be *more* than all right, even better without him hanging round her neck like an albatross. He had to make sure, he knew this now, to use his time inside to let those broken wings mend so that he might learn, if not to fly again exactly, at least to try some clumsy, stuttering take-off, and find his way back home again.

He looked now at the contents of the envelope she had brought him from his father, like a message from beyond the grave. He carefully opened it out and smoothed the creases on the paper as best as he could, creases that had first been folded more than seventeen years ago, and which had not seen the light of day since. It was thin but strong paper, a light grey in colour, the sort used for architect's drawings and, when he had finally unfolded it all, enormous, almost four feet by three feet, too large to lay out on the floor of his cell and still have space to look at it. He requested and was given the end of a roll of sellotape and stuck it on the one wall large enough to accommodate it, opposite his bunk.

It was a map of the waterways of Manchester and Salford, the rivers Irwell, Irk and Medlock, the routes of several canals – the Bridgewater, the Rochdale, the

Ashton, Manchester Ship, Pomona Dock, Castlefield Junction, Irwell Navigation – together with various landmarks along the water's edge – wharves, docks, basins, bridges, factories, mills and mines. It was exquisitely drawn, down to the minutest detail, but large enough to be clear and uncluttered. Sol had had no idea just how skilled a draughtsman his father had been, and he wondered if after all it was from him he had inherited his skill in drawing.

Poring over it now, as he did first thing every morning when he woke in his cell and last thing every evening just before lights out, he marvelled at its precision, its neatness, but also at his father's hand writing, an immaculate copper plate, tiny but flawless, added afterwards with a fountain pen and not a hint of a smudge or spill of ink.

Despite being overwhelmed by the sheer scale and wonder of its achievement, Sol was at first puzzled as to why his father had selected to leave behind this as a parting gift, for it must have been executed in his final months, when he was so very ill, frequently coughing blood, when he must surely have known that his days were limited. The courage and determination to complete it, against such almighty odds, and not to sacrifice one iota to the overall quality, moved Sol beyond words.

He had not, he realised now, thought much about his father in the years since he had died. Sol had only been seven when that had happened, and although he was sorrowful at first, he quickly got over it, accepting it as one of those facts about his life, like a grandfather who spoke a different language and a mother who had begun always dressing in white, and simply got on with the business of daily living, going to school, playing with other children on the bomb sites, kicking a football, learning to ride a bike, and so the years had passed, and memories of his father had simply faded.

What had also faded over the years, and what Sol at first did not notice, was a faint, narrow pathway, traced in a draughtsman's blue pencil across the map. A thin blue line. What had his father meant by this, Sol asked himself each time he bent over it? The line picked out a route, from a spot on the Bridgewater Canal, which Sol recognised as being close to the street he had lived in as a child, the same street Nadia had now taken herself and Jenna to, snaking its way along the different waterways towards a short arm of the Ashton Canal, marked by his father as "Beswick Lock", where the blue line ended next to a small sketch of a pithead, labelled "Bradford Colliery".

Sol recalled a cold winter's morning, shortly after his father died, when his grandfather had taken him down to the Canal and spoken to him, mostly in Arabic, much of which he had not understood, about how he had first come to England as a merchant seaman, something about a journey his father had taken overnight by narrow boat to meet a King, and finally a story about a lost piece of coal, which his grandfather wanted Sol to bring back...

As the weeks in Walton Gaol passed into months, and the months into years, Sol studied this map more and more, and pondered that story for what it might mean, what the message was his father had so painstakingly marked out for him to read when he turned twenty-one, and the beginnings of an idea slowly began to form in his brain. Each night he would watch what little he could see of the orange night sky from the tiny barred window with its smeared, broken pane at the top of his cell, before finally slipping into a fitful sleep. Outside, as the moon crossed and re-crossed the small rectangle above Sol's head, the world turned.

*

13 August 1964

Ever since the story first broke (a month before when the appeal had failed), the whole of Walton Gaol was agog with the news that there was to be a hanging there.

Peter Anthony Allen, together with Gwynne Owen Evans, had been found guilty of the joint murder of John 'Jack' West, a van driver from Workington. Following their failed appeal, they were to be the first people to be executed in England in 1964 and, as events unfolded, the last ever to receive an unreprieved death sentence anywhere in the United Kingdom. They were to be hanged simultaneously, Evans at Strangeways, where Sol had been held while awaiting his own trial, and Allen at Walton, where now he resided. It was all any of them could talk about.

The murder had happened as a result of what appeared to be a bungled robbery of West's home. During the trial Allen and Evans each attempted to pin the blame on the other.

Extract from Officer's Case Notes

Detective Sgt. Bagnall, Cumberland & Westmorland Police

Investigation into the Murder of John 'Jack' West 6th April 1964

West had returned home after a normal working day just after six o'clock on the evening of Monday 6th April. At around three the following morning a next door neighbour had been awoken by a noise in West's house and, on looking out of his window, had seen a car disappearing down the street. He telephoned the Cumberland Police, and Officers arrived to discover West dead with severe head injuries and a stab wound to his chest.

Evans and Allen had stolen a car, a black 1959 Ford Prefect, Registration Number NXC 771, to go to West's house, and later abandoned it the following day in a builders' yard in Ormskirk, where Evans had asked a nearby tenant whether he could leave it there. The tenant thought his behaviour suspicious. She reported it to the local police, who matched it to the description given by West's neighbour, and, with these and pictures of Evans, colleagues in Liverpool traced its route back to Lancashire. Officers in Workington Police Station also tracked Evans, through his parents, as well as through previous criminal and army records, to Allen's address in Preston.

At lunch time on the Wednesday, less

than thirty-six hours after West's murder, Detective Inspector Byrnes, assisted by Detective Sgt Bagnall, turned up at Allen's home in Preston, hoping to find Allen there. Which he was. Allen was driven up to Kendal, and from there on to Workington, where the rest of the murder squad were based. In questioning he claimed to have been at home with his wife, Mary, and Evans on the night of the murder. He said he had no idea where Evans might be, but that his wife was currently visiting her mother in Bolton. Officers from there kept a watch on the house until she showed up. She immediately informed them where they might find Evans, who was quickly discovered on a street corner at Philips Park Road in Miles Platting. A search carried out by Constables from Manchester City Police revealed West's watch inside Evans' jacket pocket, and he was arrested on suspicion of murder.

Initially Evans admitted that he, together with Allen, had gone to borrow money from West, but accused Allen of sole responsibility for the murder. He too was then driven up to Workington, where Allen was still being held. To begin with, Allen stood by his claim not to have done anything on the Monday night, but changed his mind when he was told that his wife and Evans were now also in custody. He explained that *Evans* had suggested robbing West, not he, and had initially gone into West's house on his own. Evans had then let Allen in, hoping that West would not notice, but West had come downstairs and discovered them. Allen then admitted he had fought West, but only in self-defence. He said that Evans had an iron bar which he had used to hit West.

Evans, on the other hand, claimed West had told him that he should see him if ever he was in Workington and needed money, so he had gone to ask for a loan. However, he said that _Allen_ had forced his way into West's house intent on robbery, and that _Allen_ had been the only one to attack West. During questioning, Evans spontaneously mentioned that he knew nothing about a knife and did not have one. Until this point, neither Detective Inspector Byrnes nor Detective Sgt Bagnall had revealed that West had been stabbed. Evans admitted only to stealing West's watch.

Mary Allen's statement supported her husband's account that Evans had come out to invite him in. She reported that she had asked the two men what had happened in the house, and that Evans had said _both_ had attacked West.

At a quarter past one in the morning of Thursday 9th April, less than forty-eight hours after the discovery of West's body, both Evans and Allen were charged with his murder.

*

It was a shabby affair. A key witness at the trial, held at the Manchester Assizes, was Mary Allen. She testified that Evans had thrown the knife used to murder West out of the stolen car into Lake Windermere. She also revealed that Evans was more than a lodger to her, and affectionate letters written by her to him while he was awaiting trial were produced. These feelings had changed, though, when she heard how Evans had tried to pin the blame onto her husband during the preliminary hearings at the Magistrates Court. Judge Mr Justice Ashworth urged the jury to treat her evidence with caution but deemed it admissible nevertheless, for there was consistency between it and her initial statement to the police. In summing up he directed them to consider whether the murder had been convicted by one or both or neither of the defendants. They took less than three hours and returned a guilty verdict on both men, who were duly sentenced to "suffer death in the manner authorised by law".

The Daily Herald

11th August 1964

WEST MURDERERS TO HANG IN TWO DAYS

Home Secretary Refuses Clemency Request

Following last month's unsuccessful appeals by Peter Anthony Allen and Gwynne Owen Evans to have their death sentences for the murder of John 'Jack' West overturned, an eleventh hour plea to the Home Secretary for clemency and a reprieve was last night turned down.

On 20th July Lord Chief Justice Lord Parker of Waddington and Justices Winn and Widgery upheld the original sentence, much to the general surprise of the public, for only two hangings had taken place in 1963, and none up to this point in 1964, with 19 reprieves granted since 1957.

Petitions on both sides were launched, with the much larger one calling for the hangings to proceed, spearheaded by this newspaper.

Under the law the Home Secretary has to decide whether to advise the Queen to exercise the royal prerogative of mercy and commute the death sentences to life imprisonment, but late last night, the Right Honourable Henry Brooke MP, *"failed to discover any sufficient ground to justify him in advising Her Majesty to interfere with the due course of law"* in either case, and simultaneous executions have now been announced for 8am on 13th August in just two days time, Evans in Manchester and Allen in Liverpool.

*

The night before, nobody slept in Walton Gaol.

For weeks the atmosphere inside had become increasingly feverish. No one could talk of anything else, all of them knowing that a sealed, windowless room on Landing 2 in I-Wing was the location for the gallows in a ten-feet-deep, ten-feet-wide and twelve-feet-long chamber, and that just the other side of this lay the cell where Allen awaited his fate.

Opinion was fiercely divided among the inmates over whether he was guilty or not, some favouring the theory that it was Evans who wielded the knife that had killed West, others equally certain it was Allen, who admitted using the iron bar, but even more of them vitriolic in their low regard for Mary, who, they argued, had effectively sold both men down the river in exchange for her own freedom.

Sol said little during this time, preferring to keep his own counsel. He saw in both men, from what he had read in the newspapers, uncomfortable echoes of his own situation, a stint in the army, difficulty in settling back into civilian life, being drawn towards a series of petty criminal acts. Maybe, he thought, in the darkest reaches of the night, alone in his cell, if he had not been caught when he was, he too might have drifted towards more serious crime. He hoped that something in the way he had been brought up, the proud examples of service and selflessness practised by Yasser, Jaz and Ishtar, might have stayed deep within him somewhere and would have prevented him from crossing the line that Allen and Evans had so irrevocably done when they attacked West, whichever of them it was who had dealt the fatal blow. Of one thing he was certain, though. It must have taken enormous courage by Mary to have admitted in open court to her marital betrayal of Allen, her affair with Evans, and then to confess to what she had heard Evans say about the murder weapon.

He knew from first hand experience the strength and resilience of women. Nadia had already been as good as her word in that long breathless speech she had uttered when she came to visit him when he was first transferred to Walton. She was now working in several jobs, while her sister and his mother supported her with minding Jenna, who in the meantime continued to grow and thrive. Nadia's letters, which arrived as regularly as clockwork every fortnight, were full of descriptions of their daughter's many achievements – her first steps, her first words, including a photograph, taken by Nadia's mother, of her first birthday, her smiling face lit by the single candle on her cake. Sol wondered if she sometimes might catch sight of him in one of their wedding photos, point towards him with a wondering expression to her mother in her eyes, or whether all photos of him had now been put away. Nadia had made a promise and she was keeping it, no matter what the cost to her must be, he thought, while he continued to watch the moon cross and re-cross the skylight in his cell, night after night, mouldering away until he was granted a release. Would he be worth her sacrifice, he would ask himself, when the time came?

But such thoughts would fade with the dawn, when once again the more pressing issue of Allen's impending execution would resurface and dominate the day. There would be no release for *him*, except that to be granted by the executioner, Robert Leslie Stewart.

Robert Leslie Stewart, universally known as 'Jock', together with another Allen, Harry, had between them replaced the legendary Albert Pierrepoint, as Chief Executioners to the Crown, when Pierrepoint suddenly, and without explanation, resigned. Rumours spread that, having dispatched more than four hundred condemned men and women to their deaths (some sources claimed the true figure to have been more than *six* hundred), including Lord Haw-Haw and John Christie, he was piqued by not receiving payment for one man whose sentence was commuted to life just minutes before his hanging was to take place, even though he had put in place all of his customary meticulous arrangements. He prided himself in being able to carry out the entire proceedings, from entry into the gallows chamber to pronouncement of death by the prison doctor, in ten seconds. Only paid for each execution he actually carried out, he was also a publican, where he lived with his wife in Newton Heath, East Manchester, before retiring to Southport. He was something of a dandy, a flamboyant figure, noted for the hats he wore at a jaunty angle and the cigars he liked to smoke after each hanging.

Harry Allen and Jock Stewart, who jointly succeeded him, could not have been more different from one another. Chalk and cheese. Allen, with slicked back hair parted in the middle and a pencil thin moustache, had a penchant for showmanship and a flair for the dramatic. He would don a bowler hat and sport one of a selection of many differently colourful bow ties he kept especially for the purpose, while Stewart was a quiet, driven man, sober and reserved, who set himself the target of reducing Pierrepoint's ten second completion time to just eight. Gwynne Owen Evans was to be hanged by Harry 'The Hat' Allen at Strangeways, while Peter Anthony Allen was to be executed by Robert Leslie 'Jock' Stewart at Walton.

Stewart reported to Walton Prison at 4pm on the day before the hanging and checked that all the necessary preparations were in place. He had one-to-one meetings with the representative of the County Sheriff, the Prison Governor, the Prison Doctor and Chaplain, before satisfying himself that the gallows and trap were in perfect working order. He may have heard Allen struggling violently when news came through that there was to be no last minute reprieve, but he would not have seen him. Bound by the Official Secrets Act he would say nothing, but rumours of Allen's last night spread around the Gaol like wild fire. Some said he threw himself at the glass partition that separated him from his wife, smashing the glass and breaking his hand, others that he struggled violently and cried for his mother as restraints were applied to his wrists and ankles. Later it emerged that in a last audience with the Chaplain he had prepared a short statement, which concluded: "I am glad I was caught as I could not have lived knowing I had helped in taking a human life." But many of the inmates doubted that this was true. Sol rather hoped that it was.

At half past seven in the morning, all the prisoners began a faint, rhythmic tapping, quiet and insistent, on their cell doors – bang, bang, bang – with fists and feet and enamel mugs. Bang, bang, bang – on and on and on. As it got nearer to eight o'clock they started banging quicker – quicker and louder – and at eight o'clock exactly they all banged as one, once, hard, and then stopped dead.

And Sol knew. That was the moment that Allen had been hanged.

The hairs on the back of his neck stood up, and all at once there was pandemonium, as everyone gave voice to their feelings, each of them relieved for once to be confined and locked up in the privacy of their cells.

Stewart had placed a white hood over the head of Peter Anthony Allen, followed by the noose. Then the hangman had pulled the lever which released the trap doors, and the condemned man had dropped. Stewart noted later in his diary that Allen had shouted "Jesus!" as he was led to the drop. There was an enormous boom, which over half the prison must have heard, when the massive trap doors crashed against the wall of the pit. It was over. Allen, at just twenty-four years old, was dead.

Sol was a fortnight shy of turning twenty-four himself.

*

30 January 1965

The flag in the exercise yard was flown at half mast and shortly after nine o'clock on a cold, grey winter's morning, all of the prisoners were made to stand to attention for a minute's silence in respect of the passing of the old warrior. The Governor made a short speech and then everyone was marched back to their respective wings to watch on television the funeral of Sir Winston Churchill.

Sol had been in Walton just over a year and although now it all seemed less strange and new to him, even so he was surprised by the passive compliance in everyone's reaction to having no choice in the matter. He thought that they would, by default, be resistant to doing anything under orders, that they would be to a man anti-

Establishment, and so would have little time, and even fewer tears, for a man who seemed to Sol to belong to a different era, but to his surprise most of them sat in respectful silence, watching the events of the day unfold before them on the wall-mounted set in the free association room where they were now all gathered.

They watched as his flag-draped coffin rested on the gun carriage beneath the tower of Big Ben, a biting wind carrying the roars of ninety cannons thundering, one for each year of his life, in nearby Hyde Park, before a single drum began to beat, merging into the rhythmic pounding of boots upon pavement, as more than a hundred Royal Navy seamen moved in lockstep to draw the funeral cortège through the streets of London towards St Paul's Cathedral, where representatives of more than a hundred countries from around the world had assembled to pay their homage.

Sol regarded all this with curiosity. He stayed watching more out of a regard for his grandfather than for Churchill himself, for Yasser had always admired him, would often quote him, especially the stuff about "blood, sweat and tears", whenever he felt the occasion demanded it, which was often. Sol looked at all these kings and princes, many of them no longer in power, but living in sequestered exile somewhere, dressed up in their tassels and braids, brocaded uniforms, cockade hats, with gleaming belts and buckles and swords, and thought they appeared faintly ridiculous, more like characters from a story book than real life leaders of the world today. It seemed to him that they were witnessing not just the funeral of one man, but the passing of an old order, and about time too. He was reminded of how his grandfather would tell him of the day he met King Amanullah of Afghanistan, another deposed despot dressed in a silly costume, and how his father had travelled through the night to try and meet him, only to have been publicly humiliated, his journey marked out in thin blue pencil on the drawing now on Sol's cell wall. He began to feel more and more uncomfortable as the pomp and ceremony passed before him on the flickering black-and-white TV screen, which eventually gave up the ghost, receding to a spiralling white dot, the image shrinking to the size of a pin head before disappearing completely.

It was shortly after this day that Sol received the first of several postcards from his mother. It seemed she had taken to reading the obituary columns in the newspapers in the local library, and she began to send him, at random intervals, a series of blank white postcards with no picture on the front, just his address, c/o Walton Gaol, each with a quotation from someone who had died that year. The first contained a quote from Churchill, not one Sol could remember Yasser ever speaking, and for some reason he could not explain, even to himself, he stuck it on the back of his door, where, over the years, a display of more than a hundred such postcards would accumulate.

"I am an optimist. It does not seem too much use being anything else..."

*

18 March 1965

When Sol was still working at Metro-Vicks, driving a fork-lift truck in the warehouse, in the July of 1961, just a few weeks before his twenty-first birthday, the whole factory was buzzing with the sudden news that they were about to receive a visit from Yuri Gagarin.

Just three months after becoming the first man to orbit the earth in space, Gagarin was launched on another mission, a propaganda world tour. While most of his visits were to heads of state, he also received an invitation from the Amalgamated Union of Foundry Workers, whose headquarters were in Manchester, and in a deliberate attempt to forge solidarity between the workers in England and the Soviet Union, Manchester became the second stop on Gagarin's world tour.

The cosmonaut arrived at Ringway Airport on a specially chartered Viscount 800, the appropriately named *Sir Isaac Newton*, which Gagarin briefly took the controls of as it made its final descent. He was then driven in a Bentley convertible, which he insisted kept its hood open despite the pouring rain, so that the thousands of cheering crowds lining the streets could see him and wave to him.

"If all of these people can stand in the rain," he said through his interpreter, "then so can I."

For the whole length of the drive, he was showered with flowers – roses, poppies, daffodils and tulips – until he finally reached Trafford Park, where thousands more had been waiting in the rain for hours to welcome him. When his car pulled into the forecourt at Metro-Vicks, the crowds broke through the police cordon and mobbed the cosmonaut, shaking him by the hand, clapping him on the back. One young woman was wildly ringing a hand bell, while Sol, together with three other work mates, climbed to the top of a red telephone kiosk, where they clung to each other to avoid slipping off and to get a better view of this hero of the people.

In a crowded ceremony Gagarin was presented with a uniquely commissioned gold medal, made the first ever honorary member of the Foundry Workers' Amalgamation, and the first Soviet citizen in *any* British Trade Union. The medal depicted the hands of two people cradling the globe with the words '*Together Moulding A Better World*', which Gagarin immediately pinned to his uniform, alongside all of his many other medals, and made a short speech in Russian, which was simultaneously relayed to the adoring crowds both inside and outside the factory.

"Although I was not able to see the British Isles while up in space," he said, adding, "they were always covered in cloud…" – a remark which provoked much laughter – "…I truly felt the eyes of the world were looking up at me, for which I will always be grateful."

To further cheers and applause, he was then driven away to his next destination.

It was a day Sol never forgot – to have been so close to the first man ever to look down on the Earth from outer space, who was now within touching distance of him and his pals.

Now, nearly four years later, in the association room of Walton Gaol, he found himself with another bunch of quite different pals, looking up at the recently-repaired television set, showing the first ever walk in space.

Along with millions of others around the world, he watched in wonder as Alexei Leonov squeezed out of the narrow airlock tube of *Voshkod 2*, 'Sunrise', his space suit inflating like a moth emerging from its pupa, tethered to the space craft by just a five-metre-long umbilical cord to prevent him from drifting off into nothingness.

Sol watched him floating free in weightless slow motion, despite, according to the television commentary, actually moving at twice the speed of the fastest jet, while below him the earth wheeled and turned on its axis. Sol could clearly see the outlines of continents and oceans, as Leonov, nicknamed *Little Eagle* by Sergei Korolev, the mastermind behind the Soviet space programme, hung suspended above them.

"A sailor must be able to swim in the sea," the commentator continued. "Likewise a cosmonaut must be able to swim in outer space."

Twelve heart-stopping minutes later, *Little Eagle* returned to his eyrie and the first ever space-walk had ended. When asked how he felt, he replied simply, "Like a grain of sand."

Sol remembered the William Blake poem from primary school he'd had to learn by heart and tried to imagine what it must have been like to hold infinity in the palm of his hand.

Later, back in his cell, he looked out through the smeared, barred window, pressed his face close to the cracked pane to gain the best view he could of the night sky. It was cloudless and clear. The stars arched above him. He wondered if *Voshkod 2* might be passing directly over his head, unseen, but looking down on him at that very moment. Sol waited, eternity in an hour, an insignificant grain of sand, for another slow sunrise.

*

30 July 1966

"Some people are on the pitch. They think it's all over. It is now!"

While many of the inmates crowded round the television set in the free association room as Geoff Hurst scored that unforgettable fourth goal to secure England the World Cup may not at the time have contemplated a deeper meaning as to what the "it" in Kenneth Wolstenholme's iconic commentary might have been referring to, it would have surely returned to them a few short hours later, back in their cells, once the euphoria had begun to subside. It certainly resonated with Sol.

Unless he got any sort of remission, he was now just over a third of the way through his sentence. Although he had got used to the routines of each day, had established a set of familiar patterns to help him navigate the boredom of prison life, and had reconciled himself for the most part to his current reality, by focusing his eyes on some kind of hazy future after his release, when he could return to Nadia and to normal life, he experienced, as they all did, regular bouts of depression, when that longed-for future seemed like a mirage, shimmering out of reach beyond the limited horizon of his dreaming.

What if Nadia no longer wanted him back? What if he found himself slipping back into his old bad habits of before? Not that he worried about the latter so much these days, not since, out of the blue a couple of months before, he had received an unexpected visitor. He had had nobody come to see him since that first, and so far only, visit from Nadia just after he had been transferred to Walton from Strangeways, but on a wet Wednesday afternoon in May, his second wedding anniversary, he had recalled ruefully, standing waiting for him in the Visiting Room was Pat, from The Albion Greyhound Track.

"Hello, old son. How's tricks? How're they treatin' you? You been in the gym, son? You look fitter, sharper."

"Why are you here?"

"Now that's no way to greet an old mate, is it? I was just passin', you know? Had to see a man about a dog, and so I thought, why don't I see how young Sol's getting along?"

"Well, now you've seen me…"

"Yeah, I have, and I've got a little message for you. So why don't we just sit down for a minute, like old pals, and then you can listen to what your Uncle Pat's got to say?"

Something in Pat's manner made Sol sit down at once, that way he had of suddenly switching from jokey banter to deadly seriousness.

Pat leaned across the table towards Sol and lowered his voice. "Listen, my friend. Some mutual acquaintances of ours, whose names we needn't mention just now, have asked me to pass on a message to you. They was very impressed by the way you took the rap without complaining, without even saying a word to anyone that might have attracted any unwanted attention to their legitimate business interests, you know what I mean? They wanted me to tell you, that as far as they was concerned, your debt's been repaid, in full, you don't owe them nothing, and that pretty little wife of yours won't be getting any sort of social call from them or any of their friends, so you needn't worry yourself on that score. Alright? And besides, The Albion's not what it was, so we're moving on to pastures new, down Haringey way, my old patch, mate. *Plus ça change*, eh?" He gave Sol a friendly pat on the side of his face. "So I reckon this is goodbye, my old son." And with that, he was gone.

When Sol made his way back to the association room, one of the warders called him over. "There's a letter for you, Ward. Special delivery." And he handed him a large envelope. Inside was a card, from Nadia, wishing him *"Happy Anniversary"*, and a pressed laurel leaf that reminded him achingly of that first time in Peel Park, which from that day on he placed between the pages of each book he took out of the prison library.

Now, as he joined in the celebrations that greeted Geoff Hurst's wonder goal, and delighted in the antics of the players on the pitch when they'd collected the Jules Rimet trophy and were holding aloft their nine carat gold medals, he led the rest of the prisoners who had crowded round the television set in the same jaunty dance as Nobby Stiles, up there on the screen, socks rolled down, with his gappy toothless grin, and they all spontaneously began to sing, so joyfully that even the screws joined in:

"We all live in a yellow submarine
A yellow submarine, a yellow submarine…"

*

More Postcards from Ishtar:

"I should like to bury something precious in every place where I've been happy and then, when I'm old, I could come back, dig it up and remember."

Evelyn Waugh

"If I see a thing that needs doing, I do it."

Margery Allingham

*

8 April 1967

TV was the great leveller, bringing the outside world into the prison on those occasions they all gathered together to watch it. On a wet and miserable Saturday afternoon the association room had been packed for the Grand National, being run just a few miles down the road at Aintree.

Everyone stared in disbelief at the carnage that took place at the fence after Beecher's Brook, where horse after horse fell, unseated its rider, or refused to jump at all, except for one, that is, the one hundred-to-one shot, Foinavon, who somehow manoeuvred his way around the melee, to be virtually the last horse standing. Several jockeys remounted and set off in desperate pursuit, vainly trying to close the gap between them, but they couldn't get near him. The inmates, to a man, suddenly began urging Foinavon on, even though not a single one of them had placed a bet on him, seeing in his mad dash for freedom and victory something of themselves, a rank outsider, destined for the knacker's yard, but on this one magical afternoon capturing the hearts of a nation. When his jockey, John Buckingham, crossed the line first, he threw his cap into the air in joy and disbelief. He was only riding him because several others had turned down the opportunity, thinking the horse had simply no chance, and the cheers rang loud and long around every wing of Walton Gaol.

Also cheering were the bookmakers, on the course and off, up and down the country, who were cleaning up and pocketing thousands. Sol's mind inevitably went back to those dark days at The Albion, where his actions had led to rank outsiders surprisingly winning, but on this particular rain-swept Saturday afternoon there wasn't the slightest shadow of foul play. The men all chanted Foinavon's name in sheer delight that miracles do occasionally happen and even the last can be first.

The following week, Sol had a second surprise visitor. He had to be fetched from his cell, where he'd been trying to write some kind of suitable message to put inside a card for Jenna's 4th birthday. But the task was defeating him. What could he say to this child he no longer knew? He pictured her trying to read it, puzzling over his unfamiliar handwriting, coming across the words, *"Happy Birthday, Jenna, with love from your Daddy,"* then turning back to her Mummy with her face scrunched up and frowning, saying, "Who's my Daddy?" He wondered how Nadia would answer her, and how she might then go on to answer the question that would inevitably follow. "Where is he?" He hoped she would tell her the truth. "He's in prison," she'd answer as matter-of-factly as possible. "Why?" Jenna would ask, and then Nadia would turn her to face her, so that there could be no doubting what she would say next. "He's not a bad man, Jenna, but he did a bad thing." Jenna nods, taking this in. "Is he sorry?" Yes, whispers Sol out loud in his cell. Tell her I am. But Jenna has already turned her thoughts to the cake that Farida has just carried in from the kitchen...

Sol was roused from his reverie by one of the screws hammering on his cell door.

"Get a move on, Ward. You've got a visitor. You don't want to keep the young lady waiting, do you?"

Sol put down the card and followed the officer into the Visiting Room. Young lady? He felt a sudden fluttering in his chest – maybe it was Nadia? Maybe she'd brought Jenna with her? No. She'd said she wouldn't do that. But maybe she'd changed her mind?

He hurried after the officer with pounding anticipation. He scanned the Visiting Room looking for Nadia. But of course, she wasn't there. Eventually, he noticed a young woman sitting by herself, anxiously looking about her, untying a scarf from her head. They saw each other at the same time and she nervously raised her hand in something approaching a wave, half stood up, then sat down again, as Sol walked over to her.

"Hello," she said. "You're probably wondering who I am and what I'm doing here, aren't you?"

Sol said nothing.

"Aren't you going to sit down?" she said, now opening the white plastic handbag perched on her knee.

Sol stood facing her. She looked familiar, but he couldn't place her.

"Sheila Carter," she said.

Christ, thought Sol. Carter. He sat down quickly before his legs gave way beneath him.

Sheila fished a photograph out of her handbag and slid it across towards him. "That's me and Roy on our wedding day."

Sol forced himself to look at it. There was no mistaking now. Roy. His Corporal. His pal. Standing to attention by his young bride, this nervous-looking woman fumbling with a match as she tried to light a cigarette, glancing across to him. In the photograph she was smiling. Sol remembered her now. Roy had had the same picture in his locker.

"He was always so handsome in his uniform," she said, blowing smoke from the corner of her mouth.

"I'm sorry," he said.

"I know you are," said Sheila. "That's why I'm here."

Eight years, thought Sol, eight years since that terrible day in Crater, but the memory of it was still as fierce as the sun which had beat down upon him so mercilessly then. It still had the power to clench him in its fist like it was yesterday. Like it did now.

"It was my fault," he said.

"No," she said. "I thought so at first. But it wasn't."

"The young boy. I encouraged him."

"You couldn't've known."

"I should've been more careful."

"You were just a boy yourself. Roy was the one in charge."

Sol could feel the day flooding back. The sun knifing down. The woman squatting by the roadside. The jeep. The boy with the football. The ambush.

He looked down at his hand, the missing fingers. Sheila saw and turned away.

"I couldn't go to the funeral," he said.

"I know," she said.

"I was in the hospital."

"I know."

"I wanted to."

"It's OK."

"Then afterwards… when I got back… I just wanted to forget it…"

"But you can't."

"No."

"That's what your wife said."

Sol looked up sharply. "Nadia? You've spoken to her?"

Sheila shook her head. "She wrote. She got my address from Captain Bradley. She told me where you were, what you'd done. She said you have nightmares.

Do you still?"

Sol nodded. "Sometimes."

Eight years.

"I used to," she said, "try to picture it, imagine it, but... I couldn't. The letter said it was quick, that he wouldn't have had time..." She stopped and looked directly at Sol. "... to be frightened."

"No."

"No?"

"I mean yes. It was quick. He wouldn't have had time."

Sheila breathed out deeply.

"But even if he had," said Sol, "he wouldn't have been frightened. Nothing phased him. He took everything in his stride. Like he'd seen it all before. He made us feel safe."

"Yes," she said. "He used to make me feel that way too."

In Sol's dreams, when the snipers started shooting, and they'd ducked down behind the jeep, Roy would turn towards him and smile, just before the boy was there, with the grenade. If only, thought Sol...

"If only what?" said Sheila, and Sol realised he must have spoken his thoughts aloud.

"Nothing," he said.

"Tell me," she said. "You were there. I'd rather know. However bad it is. Knowing's better than imagining."

"Can I have a cigarette?" he said.

She passed one across. He lit it, drew on it deeply, then looked away from her, somewhere over her left shoulder, seeing only an eagle making slow, wide circles in the desert sky above him...

When he'd finished telling her, coils of smoke wreathed both their faces. Slowly they cleared, like after a fire's been put out, mingling with the thick pall that hung above all the other tables in the Visiting Room.

She let a few more seconds pass, then wafted the few remaining wisps away with the back of her hand.

"Thank you," she said at last. She sat there, dry eyed. "I thought I'd cry," she said, "but I reckon I'm all cried out."

Sol did not trust himself to speak further.

"Your wife tells me you draw," she said after a moment.

"I used to," he said.

"Maybe you should take it up again."

"Maybe."

"If you do, perhaps you could send me one." She wrote down her address on a piece of paper and pushed it across the table towards him. "I'd like that."

Sol said nothing. He folded the piece of paper and put it in his shirt pocket. Then he tapped it with his right hand.

Sheila looked at the clock on the far wall. "I'd best be making a move," she said. "That's good advice for both of us, I reckon. You don't have to be in a place like this to feel like you're doing time."

"I know."

"What's happened's happened. No amount of guilt, or feeling sorry for ourselves can change any of it. Time we let it go. Both of us. Look forward, not back."

Sol nodded.

"Your wife tells me you've got a little girl?"

"Yes."

"How old?"

"Four. I was just writing her a card when they told me you were here."

"Four," she said and smiled. "That's a lovely age. I've got two. One of each. Both teenagers now. They think the whole world's against them. But it's not, is it?"

Sol thought of his mother, how he'd been carrying so much rage and anger towards her for so many years, and shook his head.

"What?" said Sheila.

"Nothing," said Sol. "I was just remembering how *I* used to feel like that when I was their age."

"It'll pass."

"Yes," said Sol, feeling the knot inside his stomach begin to loosen a little. "It will."

"Thank you," she said, extending her hand towards him, "for telling me."

Sol took her hand and shook it. "Thank you for coming."

Later that night, back in his cell, Sol took out the piece of paper with Sheila's address written on it. He turned it over and, with the pen he'd been using to write Jenna's card, he sketched a few lines on the page. When he'd finished, he looked it for a long time. It wasn't good enough yet. He'd keep trying till it was.

He thought back to Foinavon winning the Grand National. He did not, he now realised, identify with John

Buckingham, the jockey who had picked up the ride on this rank outsider only by chance. No. He was more like those other jockeys who'd fallen at the fence after Beecher's, chasing after their mounts, somehow getting back up into the saddle and giving chase. They knew that they'd never catch him, but it was the trying that mattered, the not giving up, the making the best of things, hoping that they might at least make the frame.

From that night on, his nightmares started to fade. They did not cease altogether, but they began to diminish, in both their frequency and their intensity, and, as his sentence progressed, they gradually loosened their grip on him. The knot in his stomach continued to untighten.

*

25 June 1967

Far fewer inmates gathered round the television just over a couple of months later, however, on a hot, sticky Saturday evening, preferring instead to stay outside in the exercise yard while the long, light nights permitted, but Sol was there, front and centre, having read about the event in the newspaper a few days before, intrigued.

Our World was to be the first ever instantaneous broadcast, transmitting via the Early Bird, Canary Bird and Lani Bird satellites, to every continent except Antarctica live across the globe. At the last minute the Soviet Union and Eastern Bloc countries pulled out, while the major US networks refused to screen whole sections of it because they thought the rest of the world would not be of interest to their regular audiences, and French TV was worried that it might clash with their usual Saturday night sports programmes, but in the end more than twenty different countries provided content for the programme, which was beamed right across the world to an estimated audience of more than three hundred million people, including Sol and a few other die-hards in Walton Gaol.

It began with the Vienna Boys Choir singing in Austria, to the accompaniment of a montage of images of the world's oceans, mountains and deserts, earthquakes, volcanoes and waterfalls. It then cut between hospitals in Japan, Denmark, Mexico and Canada to see four of the eighteen hundred babies born throughout the world in the first two minutes the programme had been on air, lives born worlds apart at a moment in history, when it became possible to see right around the globe in a heartbeat.

The sun circled the equator at a thousand miles an hour, but the camera outran it. At the flick of a switch it could move at the speed of light. It could be where it was sunrise or sunset, summer or winter, today or tomorrow, all at the push of a button.

From the grimy association room Sol was transported – from a summer's evening in Paris, to a winter's morning in Melbourne, from just before lunch in Vancouver, to mid-afternoon in New York. Suddenly the world had become smaller but the opportunities larger. Less than a hundred years before, when his grandfather first travelled to England from Arabia, no one could travel faster than the speed of a horse. In 1518 it took Magellan three years to sail around the world. In 1929 a zeppelin circled the globe in just three weeks, and in 1961 Yuri Gagarin orbited the earth in less than three hours. Now, with the aid of cables, microwave links and satellite dishes, it took a mere three seconds. Sol could see what different people were doing, at that very moment, right across the world, and the thought intoxicated him – steel workers in West Germany, fishermen in Spain, cowboys in Canada, Presidents in New Jersey. He heard Marshall MacLuhan describe the younger generation, which he took to include himself still, as the "children of tomorrow", living in a "global village", viewing the world as a "huge mosaic", an "X-ray of world cultures" in which "everyone would participate". Most of us, he argued, were terrified of the present, preferring to live our lives by looking through the rear-view mirror. Only artists, he insisted, could look life in the eye. He reminded Sol of the way his night-school tutor, George, used to talk, when he had spoken of how art was a job, you had to roll up your sleeves and be prepared to get your hands dirty, ten percent inspiration, but ninety percent perspiration, and that it was in the sweat you might bring things to life. He began, for the first time since that evening when Mr Meakin, his form teacher from school, called round to visit them just before he left school, to imagine a future.

The programme ended back in London. The Beatles, four northern lads roughly the same age as Sol, who'd grown up just a few miles further down the Ship Canal from where *he* had, barely a stone's throw from where he now sat in Walton Gaol, sang *All You Need Is Love*, while across the Atlantic the Ku Klux Klan burned their records on Alabama bonfires.

The Bama. Alabama. Choctaw for scorched earth.

When Sol returned to his cell that night, he looked closely at the drawing his father had made of the waterways of Manchester, the canals and rivers, linking the city to the rest of the world, and bringing the rest of the world right back to its heart. He closed his eyes and ran his finger blindfold over the thin blue line he now knew by heart that traced the journey his father had made almost forty years before.

*

Further Postcards from Ishtar:

"To most of us the future seems unsure. But then it always has been; and we who have witnessed great changes must have great hopes. I have seen flowers come in stony places..."

John Masefield

"I've found you've got to look back at the old things and see them in a new light."

John Coltrane

*

Case of Solomon Ward

Ex-Lance Corporal Solomon Ward, formerly of the Yorkshire & Lancashire Regiment, was found guilty of the crimes of one count of possession of an illegally obtained prescription drug, several counts of fraud, plus one count of attempting to pervert the course of justice, and was formally sentenced to a term of imprisonment of six years.

He was duly committed to HM Prison Liverpool (Walton), where, having served two thirds of his sentence, his case has come up for review in respect of whether the said Solomon Ward is eligible for consideration for early release.

During his incarceration, Ward has committed no offences or misdemeanours and there has been no cause for reprimand regarding his conduct by any of the Prison Officers.

He is a quiet inmate, who, although he did not initially mix freely with his fellow prisoners, has since integrated well; neither has he shown any signs of aggression or hostility towards them, nor has he been on the receiving end of any untoward bullying or other form of misconduct.

He has had few external visitors during

his time here.

He works hard in the machine room, regularly partakes of exercise in the prison gym, and, according to his most recent report from the Prison Psychiatrist, he displays little outward sign of any mental disorder that might mitigate his chances of re-integration into society upon his eventual release.

Consequently, it is my view to propose to the Parole Board that, given all of the information available, Ward no longer represents any threat to the general public and is ready to be referred to the Resettlement Wing, where preparations for his imminent release from custody can be more effectively transitioned and managed.

It is therefore the recommendation of HM Prisons that the said Solomon Ward be approved for early release after serving four years of his sentence.

Signed:

Sir James Peter Coatman, Prison Governor

Date: 11 January 1968

*

Sol had to wait a further three months before hearing whether the Governor's recommendation had been accepted by the Parole Board. It finally came through with a release date set a further three months from then, on 11th July.

In these final weeks he began to grow increasingly nervous about what to expect when he got out. What at first, four years ago, seemed alien and strange, had now grown familiar and safe. He was used to the pattern of his days, as unchanging as the passage of the moon across the broken skylight at the top of his cell, in which the only decisions he had to make for himself were which books to take out of the prison library. As his release date grew nearer, he became increasingly uncertain about what would await him once he walked free. Free. Such a simple word, just four letters, one for each of the years he had spent inside, but one which contained an entire dictionary of complexity and ambiguity, which he found himself getting lost and ravelled in.

Once again, it was Nadia who provided clarity, her words like scissors, expertly shaping a much-needed army-issue crew-cut, shearing away the tangled, knotted locks he'd grown while in prison, which now threatened to fall across his eyes, so that he could not see what lay before him. Her letter was like the mirror held up after the cutting has finished and the hair from around the neck and shoulders swept away into a tidy heap on the floor, raised up behind and tilted all around, so that Sol might examine those parts of himself he normally did not get to see.

Dear Sol,

What wonderful news! I am so relieved that you will finally be coming home. It must have been agony for you these last few weeks, waiting on the decision by the Parole Board. Thank heaven that this long nightmare is at last coming to an end.

Your mother and I are already getting the house prepared for your return – and before you say anything, please understand that if we are to make this work, there have to be clear rules. I hate that word, but I can't think of a better one. The last thing either of us wants is for this to happen again. We can't pretend it will all be plain sailing the moment you step out of prison. It's bound to feel strange at first, you're going to need some time to get used to things once more, and so I have made certain arrangements in preparation for this moment. Please don't be angry with me, for it is only meant to help us.

So – what is going to happen is this.

You, me and Jenna will all live here with your mother in Stanley Road, at least to begin with. There is plenty of room – as you know – and we can all get along very well together, I am sure. She's been so kind to us while you've been inside, never asking for anything. All she wants is for you to find your way again. We both think that, for the time being, until things settle and become clearer, it would be best for all of us to stay here together. But first of all, Sol, you <u>must</u> make your peace with her. I don't *know what it was that drove such a wedge between you, but it's time now to build bridges. Will you do that please? For me?*

The next thing of course is that you will need a job. I have some good news. I went to see my old boss at Turner's – Mr Tunstall, you remember him? He was always very nice, and we have kept in touch over the years since I left – you know, Christmas cards and the like – and so I went to see him one day after I had finished work. I explained you were coming home soon and asked if he might be able to suggest anything. He said he'd think about it. Within a few days he wrote to me to say that he had been speaking to some contacts he had (probably at the Lodge or the Rotary, but that's what they're for, aren't they, to help each other?) and that he'd found you a position as a trainee draughtsman at British Westinghouse. I'd told him how good you are at drawing, and how your dad had been a draughtsman, and how much you liked that drawing he'd left you for your 21st, and so this is what he came up with. It's a six month trial period, to see how you get on, though I'm sure you'll do fine, and there's one evening a week of night school, which is compulsory, to get you qualified, but the firm pays for it, so that's very good, isn't it?

And the last thing is, I really want you to go back to your drawing again, Sol, properly this time. You were so good. I made enquiries at the Mechanics Institute, and George is still there. He said he'd gladly take you back, so long as – and these are his words, Sol, not mine – so long as you didn't piss about this time. He's funny, isn't he? I can see why you liked him. He gave me a lift home afterwards on the back of his motor bike. And you needn't worry about the cost of it either. When you left school, your mother put aside some money every week from your wages to pay for any evening classes you might want to take up, because she knew how disappointed you were to have to leave school early, but you never asked her for it, never said what you wanted to do. Perhaps that's when this rift really grew between the two of you? But anyway, she's kept that money all these years, and she's been adding to it ever since you got called up for National Service, so there's more than a hundred pounds, Sol, more than enough for you to start up at the Institute again, and keep attending for quite some considerable time.

Please don't be angry with me for organising everything like this. I know how impossible it is for you to do that while you're over there in Walton, and I knew you wouldn't want to be kicking your heels when you came home, that you'd want to make up for lost time, and so I went ahead. I want this second chance to work for us, Sol, but to begin with it has to be on these terms. I'm sure you can understand that. Oh, and I'll be carrying on with my own jobs too. I love them. And I might have some more news about that before you come home. I've an interview next week with the Local Education Authority for a promotion, coordinating

Adult Literacy programmes for all new arrivals across Salford. Wish me luck!

Not long to go now, before we can say goodbye to these last few years, hello to the future, and be together again. I cannot wait to hold you in my arms and to kiss you like we used to. And I cannot wait for you to begin to get to know Jenna, who is quite the young lady now that she has started school!

With all my love,
Nadia xx

She astonished him.

As Sol waited for the final weeks to tick down, the world outside seemed to be in a permanent state of upheaval and convulsion, and he increasingly wondered what he would find once he was free. That word again. Freedom seemed to be on everyone's lips, the freedom to speak out, say no, protest and sit in, burn flags and burn bras, to march and let your voice be heard.

The days of Sol having a cell all to himself had long since gone, and over the years he had had to share with a succession of other men, all of whom were either waiting on remand, or serving shorter sentences, several of them for causing disturbances at anti-war rallies. The latest of these, Lenny, a long-haired student from Manchester University, kept up a ceaseless running commentary on the seemingly unstoppable flow of events happening round the world. "Power to the People," he'd sing. "Right on," he'd say as he rolled another joint, and then, "Peace, man," to the screws who confiscated his weed.

When he first stepped inside the cell, his eyes were drawn at once to the series of postcards from Ishtar with quotes from people who'd died that Sol had arranged on the back of the cell door.

"Whoa, man!" he'd said. "Messages from beyond the Grave! It's like the Tibetan Book of the Dead," and he proceeded to sit cross-legged on the top bunk and chant, while the outside world turned on, tuned in, dropped out, shook, rattled and rolled, turned itself upside down.

5 January: Alexander Dubcek succeeds the Stalinist Antonin Novotny as First Secretary of Czechoslovakia, heralding the dawn of the Prague Spring.

Lennie makes paper flowers, which he hands out to everyone, inmates and screws alike, who each regard him with the same dismissive bafflement. Unconcerned, he sings to them.

"Call out the instigators
Because there's something in the air
We've got to get together sooner or later
Because the revolution's here…"

30 January: the Tet Offensive begins.

1 February: Nguyen van Lem, a Viet Cong officer, is executed by a South Vietnamese police officer.

The photograph of this execution, by Eddie Adams,

makes headlines right around the world and is pinned up by Lennie in Sol's cell. Sol remembers George talking to him in one of his Evening Classes about his work as a photographer and who his influences had been. One of these had been the American Lee Miller, with whom George had worked briefly during the Second World War, who had taken some of the first photographs of the liberated concentration camps in Belsen, Dachau and Buchenwald. I want to take pictures that matter, she'd said. That was when Sol began to stop drawing. Nothing he drew, he felt, really mattered, but George had tried to persuade him otherwise. They must matter to *you*, he'd said, nobody else. That's what counts in the end. Sol wonders now whether he'll discover what that might be, what it is that might matter to him.

16 March: the My Lai massacre takes place in which US troops kill scores of civilians.

4 April: Martin Luther King is assassinated in Memphis. Riots erupt across America.

Lennie tries to recite from memory the entire *'I Have A Dream'* peroration, which Sol falls asleep to every night for a fortnight, waking up each morning to hear Lennie still wrestling with it. He never makes it through to its end.

20 April: Enoch Powell delivers his Rivers of Blood speech.

Lennie cuts out a picture of Powell from one of the newspapers and pastes it to the centre of the dart board in the free association room, inviting the inmates to test their skill. Powell's eyes become the new double top, his open angry mouth the bull's eye, till the screws take it down to boos of disapproval and derision.

13 May: Protesters take to the streets in Paris. More than a million people march down the Champs Elysées. Barricades are set on fire as the police charge students with horses and water cannon.

Lennie stages a one man sit-in in the Gaol Canteen.

16 May: Ronan Point, a twenty-three storey tower block in East London, collapses after a gas explosion, killing five people.

Sol watches this in disbelief on the television screen. As the high rise tumbles, like a flimsy house of cards, he feels the whole assemblage of his own body crumbling inside him too, his skeleton imploding, his bones shattering like glass, his breath escaping as if from a punctured tyre. He's due to rejoin this new world of demolitions, slum clearances and steel towers in less than two months. He's not ready.

29 May: Manchester United become the first English team to win the European Cup.

Walton Gaol rings out to a mixture of prolonged

cheering and good-natured booing.

5 June: Robert Kennedy is shot dead by Sirhan Sirhan in The Ambassador Hotel, Los Angeles.

"Some people see things as they are and say why. I dream things that never were and say why not?"

11 July: Sol is released.

"The future is not a gift. It is an achievement."

*

Final Postcards from Ishtar:

"A joyous daybreak to end the long night of captivity....But let us not seek to satisfy our thirst for freedom by drinking from the cup of bitterness and hatred."

Martin Luther King

"Few will have the greatness to bend history itself, but each of us can work to change a small portion of events. It is from numberless diverse acts of courage and belief that human history is shaped."

Robert Kennedy

*

Lennie gives Sol a hug the morning he is to leave.
"I wish I was coming with you, man."

"Just a few more weeks and you'll be out yourself."

"Right. See you on the barricades."

"Not me. I'm keeping my head down."

"Play it as it comes."

"All the rest is propaganda."

They smile briefly at one another and then Lenny tries to slip some weed into Sol's pocket, which Sol refuses.

"Don't want to get busted on my last day."

Lenny nods. "Stay in touch?"

"Sure."

They both know that they won't.

Sol takes a last look round, stands on the single chair and peers down into the rank passageway between the adjoining prison wings for a final time. The rat is nowhere to be seen.

Sol collects his few possessions from a desk close to the outer gate, where he changes back into the clothes he first arrived in over four years previously. They no longer fit him, and once again he feels acutely ill equipped and unready for whatever the outside world will fling at him. One of the Prison Officers gives him a few shillings for the bus and train fare back to Patricroft. Sol thanks him and asks if he might do him a small favour.

"Depends what it is," says the Prison Officer, looking uncomfortably over his shoulder.

"Could you post this for me?"

Sol hands him an envelope. It's addressed to Mrs Sheila Carter. Inside is a drawing that Sol has managed to complete in his final weeks inside. It captures that day in Crater. Roy is leaning against a jeep. He is rolling a cigarette. Something has caught his attention. He is looking up. An eagle climbs overhead, trying to catch the high thermals. Yes, thinks Sol. This was how it was, how it remains.

The Prison Officer nods, relieved. "Sure thing."

"Thanks," says Sol.

As he steps through the gate to the street beyond, where people are going about their daily business, passing the prison as though it were just another building, he feels a near paralysing mixture of elation and fear. He hoists the rucksack containing his few precious possessions onto his back, the postcards from his mother, the letters from Nadia, the photos of Jenna, the drawing made by his father, breathes in deeply and takes his first few steps of freedom.

Just as he reaches the corner, he is stopped short by the sudden blaring of a car horn. He turns, and there, waving to him from across the street, of all people, standing by the open door of a white Mini Cooper, wearing a T-shirt and jeans, is Farida.

Farida?

"Come on, she says, "I'm parked on a double yellow. Get in quick and let's be on our way."

Reeling, Sol staggers across the road and climbs in beside her. "Farida?" he says. "How…?"

Laughing, she turns on the ignition and pumps the accelerator as if she's driving a getaway car, which, in many ways, she is.

*

Almost six years ago to the day, Farida and Salim were moving into their new home, a large three-bedroom semi on leafy Hawthorne Avenue in Monton, less than a mile from Farida's parents' house, but a world away in affluence and aspiration. When Salim proudly showed it off to Salwa and Jamal, they walked around it in hushed awe, all the while turning to Farida and beaming. Jamal could barely keep the tears of joy from his eyes as he shook Salim firmly by the hand and said, "This is what I always dreamed of. When I first arrived in this country, I saw hope, opportunity and I thought one day, maybe, if I work hard and Allah is merciful, my grandchildren might achieve something like this."

Salim inclined his head in silent respect and said that it was he who would be eternally grateful to Jamal, for his generous hospitality, welcoming him into the bosom of their family, allowing him to live there for so many years while he saved enough for the deposit on this house, the kind of house, he added, that a wife of such special quality as their daughter, who he was blessed to be sharing his life with, truly deserved.

Salwa looked across towards Farida, standing quietly in a corner of the main lounge by the inglenook fireplace, and shook her head, smiling in disbelief. "Oh my daughter, what a husband you have!"

Farida smiled in reply. "Come and see the kitchen, *Ommi*, while I make some coffee."

After Salwa and Jamal had left, with more grateful *salaams* and declarations of joy, Salim allowed himself a small moment of quiet satisfaction, standing before the ornate mirror above the fireplace, while Farida cleared away the supper. He took out a comb from the inside pocket of his jacket and attended to a strand of hair that had fallen out of place, before scrutinising his fingernails which, as always, were flawlessly polished. Yes, he thought to himself, the evening could be counted an unqualified success. Duty had been done, obligations met. He would not need to have them back for several weeks now. They would accept that he and Farida needed time to settle in. A pattern would quickly emerge of alternate months for Sunday lunch between Farida's and his own parents, with judicious invitations to the manager of the bank and his wife for supper on occasional Fridays, with the rest of the time devoted to just the two of them. Farida's sister Nadia, and that ne'er-do-well husband of hers, would not be welcome. He would make sure that Farida was under no illusion about that.

Yes, a most agreeable evening. He looked around the room with its new, modern furnishings and allowed himself another rare smile. He had hated living with Farida's parents, but he had been prepared to play a waiting game. They had in fact stayed there for far longer than he would have wished, more than five years. He had saved enough for a deposit on a smaller house in less than three, for he was frugal and scrupulously counted every penny, but he had, from the beginning, set his sights much higher than the back-to-back terraces of Eccles and Patricroft.

He first spotted the house on Hawthorne Avenue more than a year ago, when the bank was requested to look into

277

selling it after the previous owner, an elderly bachelor, had retired intestate, and it became part of Salim's portfolio. He managed to draw out the affairs just long enough for him not only to raise the sufficient capital for the deposit, but also for its complete refurbishment, which was carried out to his exact specifications and taste. Farida had not been consulted. About any of it. "I wanted it to be a surprise," he had said, when he finally showed it to her. It was then that his promotion to Assistant Branch Manager had come through, and so Salim acted. Once his mind was made up about a thing, he was swift and decisive. He glanced back towards the mirror, combed, quickly and expertly, the thin moustache above his top lip and marched towards the kitchen.

"Come, Farida," he said. "It's time for bed."

"Yes, Salim," she said and squeezed past him in the doorway towards the stairs in the hall. But before she had placed one foot on the first stair, Salim was at her side. He grabbed her hair with his right hand and pulled her sharply towards him, so that she was bending sideways. Involuntarily she winced and exhaled a small cry of pain. He placed the forefinger of his left hand to her lips.

"Not a sound," he said, and then proceeded to drag her by the hair up the stairs towards their bedroom.

Freed from the constraints of occupying a bedroom in close proximity to Farida's sister and parents, Salim, now they had at last moved into their own house, no longer felt the need to take the same precautions, the same preventative measures that might have led to some

278

awkward misunderstandings. Now he could give his needs and desires a freer rein.

Farida took to wearing the full *burqa* whenever she ventured out – to the shops, the market, or when she arranged to meet Nadia in some neutral territory, like a park. The two sisters had come to an unspoken agreement not to invite the other to where they each now lived. For Nadia there was simply no room in the flat above the chip shop and Farida did not wish to emphasise the contrast in their current circumstances. The *burqa* made her feel invisible, safe from prying eyes and questions, and also enabled her to hide the angry welts on her arms, the bruised face.

But she could not hide these things from her doctor, who she still went to see from time to time about the trouble she was having with keeping a baby. She had had several miscarriages already, and so, when she became pregnant once more, she knew she had to run the gauntlet of her doctor's concern.

She waited until the worst of the marks on her face had begun to fade and then covered these as best as she could with creams and make up, but even so, when her doctor asked her to partially undress, she could hear her intake of breath. She did not ask Farida directly what might have happened, probably knowing that she would hear the usual excuses of walking into a door, or tripping over a kerb. Instead she simply looked Farida in the eye and asked, "Is there anything you wish me to do? I can, you know, alert the authorities…"

Farida quickly shook her head and turned away while she dressed as hastily as she could. "Thank you, Doctor, but there's nothing to tell. I am such a clumsy person. My husband is always telling me. Goodbye."

But when she lost this baby as well, which she did one weekday morning, shortly after Salim had left for work at the bank, when she was suddenly wracked with cramps and she started to pass blood clots with large amounts of tissue, she was so overwhelmed with grief that, after she had cleaned herself up, she spent the rest of the day in bed. When Salim arrived back home, he began to shout at her coldly and continuously. Why was the house so dirty? Why had she not made dinner? Why was she still lying in bed like a slattern?

After that she stopped going out altogether. She asked Salim to arrange to have all of their groceries delivered, an arrangement which pleased him greatly, for he could now oversee every last detail of the household expenses, delighted when he saw opportunities for further economies. Instead Farida spent her days meticulously cleaning and polishing, washing and ironing, preparing the food that Salim now ordered, cooking it, then starting all over again the following day. The house was spotless and sterile.

When Nadia had not seen her sister for several weeks, she began to worry. She went round to her mother's one afternoon on her way back home after an appointment at the ante-natal clinic. By now she was seven months pregnant and already huge. She flopped down onto the front room couch, propped herself up with cushions as she drank a glass of Guinness that she had found she

couldn't do without as each week of her pregnancy passed, and asked her mother outright. "Have you seen Farida lately?"

"Not since we were last there for Sunday lunch."

"And how was she?"

"The same as always. Quiet. They have a new washing machine. Twin tub. It takes half the time my old thing does. That husband of hers, he is so good to her. Always spoiling her with the latest mod cons."

"I haven't seen her in ages."

"Well, I expect she's very busy. Now drink that disgusting stout. I want to show you something I saw in the catalogue for baby…"

A fortnight later, still not having seen or heard anything from her, Nadia decided to take matters into her own hands. She had never visited her sister in her new home, but she knew where she lived and set out to go there one Wednesday around lunch time in early December. It was only about a mile and a half away from the chip shop, but, in her advanced pregnant state, it felt too far to walk, so she caught the number 52 bus to Eccles Library, changed to the number 33, which dropped her off at Monton Green. Christmas lights were up in the town centre and in all the shops, and here on Hawthorne Avenue one or two houses had put decorations up already in their front room windows and around their front doors. Nadia felt the baby kicking against the wall of her stomach and paused. She was vacillating daily between being excited and scared, but on this particular day, as she rubbed her belly, while inside the baby shifted position and settled again, she was filled with anticipation. Sol had changed jobs yet again, but she was hopeful that this one might last and that when the baby was born he might shake off whatever it was that seemed to be holding him back. They rarely said much these days, apart from the necessary day-to-day stuff. She had finished at Turner's a few weeks ago and already she was missing it, while when Sol came in from work he was simply too exhausted to do anything but fall asleep. The flat was dispiriting, but if they both made an effort it could be brightened up a bit.

When she approached her sister's house, she felt suddenly nervous. This was a neighbourhood that felt like an altogether different world from the one she and Sol lived in, or from where she and Farida had grown up as kids. What if she wasn't in? What if she was, but she didn't want to see her?

Pushing aside her doubts she walked up the drive and knocked loudly three times on the windowless front door.

From inside she heard a voice call out, "It's open. Just come in and leave whatever it is on the floor in the hall."

Puzzled, Nadia walked in. The silence that greeted her felt immense. Her feet sank in the deep pile of the fitted carpets sucking out all noise. Instinctively she bent to take off her shoes. Still nothing. She crept slowly forward along the hall towards the back of the house, where she could see a door that was not quite shut. Pushing it slowly open she walked through and found herself in the kitchen. There on the floor, on her hands and knees, wearing only a pale slip, scrubbing so hard that her breath was expelled in every forward motion, was her sister. She was shockingly thin. Nadia involuntarily gasped. She put her hand to her mouth before lowering herself beside her as gently and as quietly as she could, so as not to startle her. She laid a hand upon her shoulder. Only eventually did Farida stop. When she finally did so, Nadia could hear she was crying. She turned her face towards her. It was heavily swollen, not just with tears, but with bruises. She had a black eye and a split lip, and her hair, usually so lustrous and shining, was dirty and lank. Nadia pulled her towards her and held her.

After a time, Farida composed herself, wiped her eyes and glanced towards the clock on the kitchen wall. "You must go," she said. These were the first words she had spoken since Nadia had arrived. "He will be home in two hours and I have so much I must do before then. I must finish the floor, prepare the supper and make sure I am washed and dressed. If I don't, Nadia, it will only make things worse. Please. Go. I shall arrange to see you again soon. I promise. Before your baby is born. And please – don't tell *Ommi* or *Babbi*." Her eyes were pleading and Nadia simply nodded, kissed the top of her sister's head, then left.

Three months later, after Jenna was born and Nadia had begun to establish a new pattern to her days, she managed to persuade Farida to come and meet them once a week in Buile Hill Park, which was roughly equidistant between both of them. Farida would still wear the *burqa*, which caused Nadia concern, but as the weeks passed, and the days grew warmer, so Farida gradually cast off various layers, until she began to resemble more closely how

Nadia remembered her before she went to live in Monton Green. Her face was clearer too and Farida explained that Salim was planning to embark on what he termed a "charm offensive" to impress his superiors at Head Office in Manchester, for he now had his eyes firmly set on becoming Branch Manager when Mr Callan, the current incumbent, retired in twelve months' time. Salim, she continued, liked to speak in military language. He talked of his long-term campaign, his strategy, tactics – hence the "charm offensive" – planning his targets for each phase of the mission. The current phase, Farida told Nadia with a shrug, was to make sure she looked at her best for when he launched his next attack, in the form of dinner parties for every member of the Bank's Board of Trustees and their wives over the coming year.

"Does that mean he's stopped hitting you?" Nadia asked bluntly.

Farida looked away awkwardly. "He finds other ways," she said. "Less visible."

Nadia tensed physically with revulsion at the thought.

"Don't worry. I have power too."

She didn't elaborate further and Nadia didn't like to delve. She guessed it was something to do with learning how to use these pauses between his attacks, these comparative periods of respite, to her own advantage.

"I know what he likes, Nadia. Until he changes, that is, and comes up with something new he wants to try."

They both fell quiet for a while, walking in step, taking turns to push a sleeping Jenna in her pram round and round the pond with the ducks eyeing them from the water's edge, hopeful that a few crusts of bread might be heading their way. A breeze picked up, flicking the surface, stirring the trees. A fresh green newly-minted laurel leaf, broad as a plate, floated to the ground in front of them. Nadia, remembering, picked it up and smiled to herself. "I'm going to press this in a book," she said, "and give it to Sol."

Farida linked her arm through her sister's. "Come on," she said, "I need to be getting back."

This arrangement carried on undisturbed for the next six months, but what shook the ground beneath them then was not Salim, but Sol.

"He's been arrested, Far. The police came last night. It was terrifying. They broke down the door and dragged him away."

"What's he done?"

"I've no idea. I've hardly seen him these last few months. He's said he's been working double shifts. He gets in late, reeking of drink. He seems like a different person."

Farida waited until her sister had calmed down, and then sat her down on a bench in the park. Jenna was nearly a year old now and was almost walking. Farida lifted her out of her push chair and tried to settle her on her lap, but she wriggled away and began crawling towards the ducks, who endlessly fascinated her. Farida trailed after her, picking her up and swinging her round in a high wide circle above her head, which she loved and which always made her squeal and shout, "More, more!"

"I don't know what to do," said Nadia miserably.

"We'll go to the police station. Together. We'll find out what he's been charged with. Whether he's got a solicitor. They have to, I think. And then we'll ask them what's going to happen next."

"What if they don't tell us?"

"Then we'll keep asking till they do." She set Jenna back down on the grass.

"Nadia, look," said Farida suddenly. She held her sister's arm and together they watched, as Jenna pulled herself up by the side of the bench until she was standing upright. She took her hands away and steadied herself, her arms outstretched. Then she tottered precariously back towards Farida, who looked back at Nadia with the widest of smiles. "That's what we have to do, love. Put one foot in front of the other till we get where we need to."

Nadia lowered herself down from the bench and stretched out her own arms towards her daughter's, urging her on, until she fell with a giggle into her waiting embrace.

Once Sol had been sentenced and transferred to Walton, what to do suddenly became clear to both Nadia and Farida. Farida adored Jenna and was secretly delighted when her sister asked if she might mind her for three afternoons each week, while Nadia was out at work, to share this task with Sol's mother. In no time at all a pattern established itself and Farida arranged her whole week around those days when she'd fetch Jenna from Ishtar's and take her back to her spotless house. She had a stash of toys that she hid at the back of the airing cupboard, where Salim never ventured, which she would bring out every time Jenna was round, and which she'd put away afterwards. On some afternoons Jenna would be tired and need a nap, which Farida would be disappointed about, for she loved to play with her, to let her help her in the kitchen, to hear her ceaseless song and chatter, but only briefly, for when she lay her down under the covers of her bed, where she'd fall asleep almost instantly, Farida would lie next to her, stroking her hair, whispering in her ear. She never minded making the bed up afterwards and ensuring that no trace of Jenna's fine black hair could be found afterwards by Salim.

The arrangement was that, on no account, must Nadia arrive to pick up Jenna later than four o'clock. That would then give Farida two hours to remove all evidence that Jenna had been there, to clean and tidy and make the supper, which Salim insisted must be ready by six-thirty, half an hour precisely after he returned from work himself each day, allowing him time to wash and change before eating.

This all worked perfectly for almost nine months until one afternoon when Salim arrived back at home in the middle of the afternoon. He had wanted to surprise Farida. He had the most wonderful news. He had learned that his year-long military campaign had been successful. Mr Callan had called him into his office that morning and informed him that the bank's Board had telephoned him just a few minutes before to confirm that he, Salim, would be the next Branch Manager as soon as Mr Callan retired, which was to be the following month.

"Congratulations," Mr Callan had said, shaking his hand and offering him a cigar. Salim did not smoke cigars, but he did not refuse, and as he puffed contentedly on this, his first one, he thought that this was a new habit he might indulge in again when the occasion merited it. "I say," continued Callan, "we're a bit quiet today. Why don't you push off early, buy a bunch of flowers, surprise that pretty little wife of yours, and have a celebratory dinner, what?" He winked at Salim as he drew deeper on his cigar, a tiny fleck of spittle dribbling from the corner of his mouth.

Salim was privately disgusted by him, but he smiled back and laughed. "Well, if you're sure, Mr Callan." He stubbed out the cigar as soon as he left the office, wrapped it in a tissue to save until later, and hopped on to a bus just as he reached the stop. To his surprised delight, he discovered he was whistling.

"Someone's cheerful," quipped the conductor as he punched his ticket.

"Yes," said Salim, "I've just received some rather good news. Thank you."

He continued whistling throughout the entire journey, noting with pleasure that, at this time of day, it took only thirteen, instead of seventeen, minutes, and then began to walk briskly in the direction of Hawthorne Avenue. He remembered Mr Callan's suggestion about flowers for Farida, and he thought yes, why not, turning left for the shop instead of right for home, only to be disappointed as he passed the florist's to realise that today was a Wednesday, a half-day, and that the shop had closed early. Never mind, he thought. What she did not expect, she would not miss.

He turned the lock in the door, and, as soon as he stepped inside, he knew at once that something was wrong, different. He was about to call out Farida's name when he saw it, parked on a plastic rolled-out mat that he did not recognise, a child's pushchair.

As soon as Salim placed his key into the lock, Farida's senses went into overdrive. She crept to the top of the stairs and waited, not daring to breathe. She couldn't understand why he should be home so early, unless it was simply to check up on her. When he was moving from one phase of behaviour to another, this would frequently be presaged by a sudden unexpected change in his routine. She listened to him enter the house, close the door behind him, then stop. He would be looking at the pushchair. He would be trying to work out whose it must be and would be rapidly coming to the conclusion that it could only be Nadia's. She heard a sharp intake of breath. He had worked it out. His immediate thought was to call upstairs, to demand that she come down at once, explain herself, but now, in that infinitesimal pause, his killer instinct had kicked in. He would creep up the stairs, stealthily, like a wolf, to come upon her unsuspecting, unawares. She waited, not moving a muscle. She waited, feeling the pressure of each step through the carpet as he climbed. She waited, knowing that the first words he might say, or rather, not the words themselves, but the tone in which he spoke them, would tell her at once how she would need to act next.

"Farida?" he said, barely above a whisper. "Are you asleep?" His voice oozed like dripping honey. "Is there

289

something you need to tell me?"

She sprang at once to her feet. Whenever he adopted that sweet, overly concerned tone, she knew to be on high alert. If he shouted, it was much simpler. That meant he would simply strike her. But when he wheedled like this, it was as if he were caressing her neck with a silk scarf, just before he tightened the noose. She needed to act quickly and decisively, to surprise him and take the initiative away from him. Somehow, with Jenna asleep in their bedroom just behind her, it all became so much clearer, so much easier. She would not let him near the child. Even for him to see her, to look down on her while she slept so innocently, would be like a violation.

"Salim," she said quietly, springing suddenly right in front of him at the top of the stairs.

"I thought I'd surprise you," he replied, "but it seems like you're the one with surprises today, and you know, don't you, that I don't like surprises?"

"Please don't raise your voice, Salim."

"Why shouldn't I?" he hissed.

"Because I have a headache."

He looked at her witheringly and began to chuckle mirthlessly. "A headache?"

"Yes." She looked at him steadfastly, never taking her eyes from his face, where she saw his left cheek begin to flicker and pulse.

Suddenly he made a dart to get past her in a lunge towards their bedroom, but she was ready for him. Before he had taken more than a step, Farida thrust herself in front of him. Expecting her to retreat from him, as she usually did, he stopped abruptly. He was poised on the very top of the stairs, his hands momentarily away from the banister. After a fraction's hesitation Farida placed a hand on each of his shoulders in front of her and pushed, once, firmly. Salim's eyes widened in disbelieving surprise. He reached out towards one of the stair rails, but his fingers slid agonisingly away from it before they could properly take hold. He toppled backwards and fell in a slow motion cartwheel, tumbling down the stairs until his head hit the floor at the bottom with a sickening thud. Farida stared for a moment, waiting to see if he stirred, but he didn't. With grim satisfaction she saw a trickle of blood seeping from his head, which was tilted at a pleasingly unnatural angle, leaching into their new cream-coloured fitted carpet. That would be a difficult stain to clean, she thought.

Instantly she dashed back to the bedroom, picked up the still-sleeping Jenna in her arms, rushed down the stairs, neatly stepped over Salim's lifeless body, placed her into the pushchair, opened the front door and rushed down the drive towards the bus stop, where, she knew, Nadia's bus would be shortly arriving, and sure enough, there it was, just pulling in as Farida turned the corner. She waved urgently to Nadia, handed Jenna, just beginning to stir in the pushchair, over to her, and immediately turned to head back to her house.

"Emergency," she said. "Salim is coming back early. See you next week." And with that, she was gone, leaving Nadia staring after her as she scurried round the corner. Jenna was now beginning to whimper and Nadia turned her attention back to her. "Come on, sleepy head. Are you hungry? What's the matter with Auntie Far today?" And they crossed the road to wait for the bus back to Eccles.

Making sure that no one had seen her, Farida returned to her house, opened the front door, hastily rolled up and put away the plastic mat, and then, with extreme self-consciousness, began to scream. The sound raised a neighbour, who came hurrying round, where she saw Farida kneeling on the carpet over the prostrate body.

"Please," she cried, "can you call an ambulance? It's my husband. He's just fallen down the stairs and hit his head. He's not breathing."

Salim had never had a telephone installed. He hated, as he said, to be surprised, and so the neighbour quickly returned next door, dialled 999, and within minutes the separate blue lights of an ambulance and police car were flashing in their driveway, while a small crowd of onlookers gathered on the pavement just beyond. The neighbour wrapped a blanket around Farida's shoulders, still kneeling by Salim's body, where she stayed, not moving, until someone pronounced him dead and he was taken away in the ambulance.

*

Court 1 in Manchester Town Hall, reached via the Mount Street entrance, is less than half full as Mr Alan Carmichael, LLB, Attorney at Law, the Coroner assigned to this case, sits down at his desk. The Clerk to the Court reads out the various preliminaries – case number, name of the appellants – before handing over to the Coroner himself.

Mr Carmichael flips open the case file in front of him, reviewing the contents of the various documents inside – statements from the attending Police Constable, the Chief Ambulanceman who was first on the scene, the Doctor who had formally pronounced death, the Pathologist, the neighbour who had telephoned the emergency services, the employer of the deceased, and finally the wife and the wife's sister. He sees nothing to change his mind from two weeks earlier when, at a Preliminary Inquest held on the morning after the death of Mr ul-Haq in order to release the body for burial to conform with the standard Muslim practice of funerals taking place within twenty-four hours of cessation of life if at all possible, he regarded the case as being a straightforward one. However, he is nothing if not diligent and so he has re-read all the statements the previous evening, and the Clerk has arranged for all of the necessary witnesses to be present and available for further questioning.

SALFORD CITY POLICE
Case No: *TK/1204849*

Date of Incident: 14th July 1965

Address: 48 Hawthorne Avenue, Monton

Crime/Incident (Primary)
Discovery of Dead Body

Narrative Report
On Wednesday 14th July 1965 at 3.57pm,
while patrolling my usual beat, I was
alerted by the blue light flashing on the
top of the Police Telephone Box on Green
Lane, Monton. I picked up the call
informing me of an incident that had taken
place at 48 Hawthorne Avenue, Monton,
reported to Eccles Police Station
following an Emergency 999 call placed by
a next-door neighbour, Mrs Margaret Pullen
of Number 50. I proceeded immediately on
foot to Number 48.

Upon arrival at the property, some five
minutes later, an ambulance was already
there, parked across the entrance to the
driveway, its engine still running and its
emergency light flashing. I walked up the
drive and noticed the front door to the
house was open. I was aware of a woman
crying. Another woman, identifying herself
as Mrs Pullen, the next-door neighbour,
confirmed that it was she who had called
for the police and ambulance.

One of the ambulancemen was kneeling at
the foot of the stairs, where he was
examining the prostrate body of a man of

Middle Eastern colouring, dark, well-trimmed hair, early thirties, dressed in a suit and tie. The ambulanceman confirmed that he was not able to detect a pulse in the man, who, Mrs Pullen informed me, was her neighbour and the owner of the property, Mr Salim ul-Haq, Assistant Manager of Martin's Bank, Liverpool Road, Eccles. The ambulanceman also reported that he had telephoned for a Doctor, who was now on his way and was expected imminently.

The second ambulanceman was attending to the woman whom I had heard crying when entering the property. She confirmed that she was Mrs ul-Haq and that it was her husband lying on the floor.

At this point Dr Julius Sandler, physician on call at Hope Hospital, arrived and confirmed that Mr ul-Haq was dead. It was now 4.11pm and Dr Sandler then proceeded to attend to Mrs ul-Haq, who was in a state of great shock.

I noted that the body of the deceased lay crumpled awkwardly at the foot of the stairs, with the neck twisted at an extreme angle, and there was blood on the carpet, which appeared to have issued from a cut on the back of the deceased's head. Both ambulancemen, Mrs Pullen and Mrs ul-Haq all separately stated that they had not attempted to move the body at any time.

I then climbed the stairs myself and noticed that one of the banister rails just below the top of the staircase had splintered and partially come loose.

I asked Mrs Pullen to recount what had happened and she explained that she had been in the kitchen, baking a cake for her and her husband's supper later that evening. She was listening to Mrs Dale's Diary on the radio, and when she heard someone screaming and shouting for help, at first she thought it must be part of the programme, until it persisted and grew louder. She switched off the radio and it was then she realised that it was her neighbour, Mrs ul-Haq, who she could hear. She rushed round at once and discovered Mrs ul-Haq standing by the open front door, her hands to her face, looking down at the body of Mr ul-Haq, who was lying "as you see him" at the foot of the stairs. "They don't have a telephone and so I rushed back next door and called 999." Mrs Pullen later repeated this version of events, which I took down in a formal statement, and which was submitted as a separate document to the Coroner's Office.

I then requested permission from Dr Sandler to ask Mrs ul-Haq a few questions. He looked at her and she nodded. She explained that she had been looking after her sister's eighteen-month-old daughter for the afternoon, while her sister, Mrs Nadia Ward of 64 Stanley Road, Patricroft, was at work. Because the weather was warm, Mrs ul-Haq had decided to take the baby for a short walk in her push chair to meet her sister at the bus stop. This is what she did. She handed the baby and all of her things to her sister. They parted at the bus stop agreeing that Mrs ul-Haq would again look after her sister's daughter the following week as usual. Mrs ul-Haq then returned at once to her home. Upon entering the house she found her husband lying at the foot of the stairs. She noticed the bleeding and immediately shouted for her neighbour to help. When asked if this was the time her husband normally came home from work, she said no, he was back much earlier than expected. Normally, she said, he came home at six o'clock, and no, she could not explain why he was so early on this particular afternoon. There was nothing further she could add and at this point she became once more extremely distressed and Dr Sandler advised that I should cease any further questioning.

Later, when she had recovered somewhat, Mrs ul-Haq repeated her story in a written statement, a copy of which was forwarded to the Coroner's Office.

I subsequently contacted Mr ul-Haq's employer, Mr Godfrey Callan, Branch Manager of Martin's Bank on Liverpool Road, Eccles, who confirmed that Mr ul-Haq had indeed left the bank early that afternoon at Mr Callan's insistence on account of having just been appointed as the next Manager once Mr Callan retires, which, prior to the events of this day, had been scheduled for one month's time. He had suggested Mr ul-Haq should go home early, buy some flowers and surprise his wife with the good news.

I contacted a local florist's, a Mrs Mabel Monks, whose shop is situated at Number 42 Canal Bank, Monton, who explained that, it being a Wednesday, a half-day, she was closed on the afternoon in question, but she was still present in the shop, where she was checking various invoices, and she did remember a man in a business suit peering in the window at around twenty past three, which, when shown a photograph of the deceased, she said could very possibly have been the same man. This would also explain why Mrs ul-Haq did not see her husband while walking to and from the local bus stop with her sister's baby, for the florist's is on a side street, which would have caused Mr ul-Haq to return home via a different route.

I also contacted Mrs ul-Haq's sister, Mrs Nadia Ward, who corroborated the timings of when she collected her daughter from her sister.

I related all of the above events to my Supervising Officer, Sgt Banks, who agreed with my own initial findings that there appeared to be no grounds for further investigation.

Officer ID: **KINSELLA, T. PC 0825**
Reviewed by: **BANKS, B. SGT**
Approved: **YES**

Date: **19/07/65**

*

CORONER:

PC Kinsella, I have reviewed your most detailed report, together with the attached statements. Do you have anything further to add to what is already written here?

PC KINSELLA:

No, sir.

CORONER:

Very well. That will be all. Thank you.

Mr Carmichael once more looks down at the accumulation of statements on his desk. The Pathologist has confirmed that death was due to a catastrophic fracture of two cervical vertebrae in the neck of the deceased and that death would have been instant. He has placed the time of death at approximately 4pm on the day in question. Everything seems to be in accordance with PC Kinsella's initial findings. Mr Carmichael has noticed who he has assumed to be the grieving widow waiting outside the Court as he arrived, dressed from head to toe in what he believes is called a burqa. He sees no reason to prolong her misery further. The case seems clear, better to bring matters to a swift conclusion, issue the Death Certificate and allow the family to begin the process of moving on.

CORONER:

Clerk, will you please ask Mrs ul-Haq to enter the Court?

CLERK:

    Certainly, sir.

Farida enters and sits down in the chair indicated for her by the Clerk near the front of the Court. Even through the burqa it is clear she is trembling.

CORONER:

    It is the decision of this Court, having reviewed all of the evidence, that this has been a tragic and most regrettable accident, a still-young man dying on the very day he learns of his promotion and has hurried home to share this good fortune with his wife. The verdict is Accidental Death. Mrs ul-Haq, please accept the Court's deepest condolences.

*

After Mr Carmichael had issued his decision and risen to leave, everyone collected their papers and brief cases and made their way out of the court back to their offices and homes and daily lives, until only Farida remained. She had not moved from her seat and eventually one of the officials had to quietly ask her to leave, as they needed to prepare for the next case. She roused herself from her thoughts, picked up her bag and hurried down a corridor.

It was over.

The long period of waiting and uncertainty had at last come to an end. She felt as though she could finally breathe, look around and begin to think about the rest of her life. As she walked down the marble staircase, past the stained glass windows, looking up at the huge vaulted stone ceiling, with its confident array of busts and statues, the weight of history and commerce pressing all around her, she realised she did not know where she was going. She wandered down one corridor after another, with rows of large, heavy, carved mahogany doors, most of them shut, but some open, offering glimpses into council chambers, committee rooms, with their polished tables and oak-panelled walls, with rolls of honour and large oil paintings of councillors and mayors in coloured robes with chains of office.

She found herself in a Great Hall, whose walls were lined with twelve enormous murals, six on either side of her, depicting, she supposed, scenes from the city's past. She saw ancient kings and warriors, knights in armour, soldiers on horseback. She saw scientists conducting experiments, with telescopes and test tubes. She saw Romans constructing a fort and a priest standing trial with a bonfire burning behind him. What had all these people, she wondered, to do with her? But then she saw Flemish Weavers greeting a Queen riding in triumph on a horse, the opening of the Bridgewater Canal and the aqueduct carrying it over the Irwell, which she recognised immediately, and finally she saw a merchant sitting in a window having a dream. In this dream he imagined his garden becoming a haven, a sanctuary for the poor children of hard working parents, and this gave Farida an idea.

A voice from behind her asked if she was lost.

"Not any more," she answered. "I'm just on my way. Thank you."

She walked quickly out of the Great Hall. Her eye was instantly caught by the mosaic of bees worked into the floor beneath her feet, bees and cotton flowers. She paused briefly to look at one closely, smiled and then made her way towards the exit.

Once outside it took her some time for her eyes to readjust to the brightness of the day. Dozens of people were criss-crossing Albert Square and she felt herself becoming dizzy. She sat on one of the benches to re-orientate herself and tried to steady her breathing. Flocks of grimy pigeons were taking off in small gusts and then landing again a few feet away as the people walked through them. One pigeon, she noticed, had come quite close to where she was sitting. It was foraging for scraps, paddling in staccato pools of sunlight that fell in flecked patterns on the dusty pavement, its stained back a sheen of blues and greens glistening beneath the black, its head tapping like a tiny hammer at imaginary nails. Scratching in the dirt between her feet, its hobbled strut concealed a certain unbowed strength.

She knew what she would do. She stood and watched it fountain into the air before coming back to earth again just beneath the bench where she'd been sitting to continue its determined scrabble.

She walked up Cross Street, past the recently rebuilt Unitarian Chapel, and cut through Spring Gardens towards Piccadilly to catch her bus back to Eccles. She sat on the upper deck and watched the streets and neighbourhoods roll by, Ancoats, Chethams, Wallness, Pendleton, Seedley, Winton, past the demolition, waste ground and building sites of slum clearances from which high-rise tower-blocks of concrete and steel were mushrooming the sky. She saw men digging roads, laying cables, mending pipes. She saw women weaving in and out of scaffolding and ladders, stepping over broken paving slabs, navigating between lines of cars, delivery vans and trucks tipping cement, coughing in the clouds of dust as they walked from shop to shop. And everywhere she saw children, coming from school on bicycles, or holding their mothers' hands and skipping, or lines of little ones in pairs walking in crocodile fashion in brightly-coloured bibs, waiting at the zebra crossings for lollipop ladies to see them safely to the other side.

Farida knew that she would never have children. She would not remarry. But she also knew how much she loved looking after Jenna while Nadia was at work, and as the bus slowly crawled its way through the traffic back to Eccles she formulated a plan.

The case was closed. Accidental death. That was what the Coroner had pronounced, reinforcing it with those kind words of sympathy saved directly for her. No further investigation required. Everyone was satisfied. She was free. Free of Salim and free of any guilt. At the funeral, which had taken place immediately after the initial Interim Inquest, when Salim's body had been released for burial, she had sat silent and stony-faced throughout. She had said nothing to anybody, not to Salim's family, not to her own parents, not even to Nadia. Nobody commented on this. She's in shock, they had all murmured. It's only to be expected. She'll come round. Just give her time. Time and space. And they had. She had been left alone. She had cleaned up the stain on the carpet where Salim had hit his head. She had taken his clothes round to Ishtar, knowing that she would know what to do with them, where they could be of most use. Ishtar had thanked her and said that it was good to get all this sorting done quickly, before it had chance to fester. The only question she had asked Farida was about money.

"Will you be able to manage?" she had said.

Farida had nodded, grateful for Ishtar's practicality, for she hadn't given such matters much thought.

She went the following day to the bank where Salim had worked. Mr Callan, who had been persuaded to stay on a few extra weeks while they sought a new manager, was there to greet her personally. He had been to the funeral, but she hadn't spoken to him then, hadn't spoken to anyone. Now he took both her hands in his, offered his condolences, on behalf not only of the bank, where Salim had been such a highly valued and respected member of the family ("That's what we consider ourselves here," he had said, "a family") but also on behalf of himself and his wife, for they had come to look upon Salim as not just a trusted colleague but a loyal friend, and he invited her into his office at the back of the bank, where his secretary brought her a cup of tea. She thanked them, but as she listened to their glowing eulogies about her husband, she did not recognise him as the same man she had intercepted at the top of the stairs, his face twisted in silent fury. As she looked around, she supposed that this would have been his office had he lived, and she imagined how he would have customised it, a photograph of the two of them, she assumed, from their wedding perhaps, smiling for the cameras, before everything that followed.

Mr Callan was now speaking to her seriously. "I expected that you'd be here to see us before too long," he was saying, "and so I have taken the liberty of looking through your late husband's various accounts, and I am satisfied that everything is in order. Your husband was a most scrupulous man, Mrs ul-Haq." She inclined her head and smiled thinly. "Well of course," he went on, "you don't need me to tell you that. His attention to detail was quite ferocious. Nothing would escape him, however seemingly inconsequential." Farida nodded once more and took another sip of the tea, which was weak and too sweet. "And so I can state with absolute certainty that there is nothing you need concern yourself with, as far as money matters are concerned. The house is now yours. Salim had in fact only recently paid off a significant portion of the mortgage with savings he had made, and he had also been extremely prudent and successful with certain investments he had taken out. The interest from these is not insubstantial, and, even allowing for the vagaries of the stock market, your husband's portfolio is extremely low risk, but currently high yield, a situation I anticipate continuing for the foreseeable future, Mrs ul-Haq, and so the remaining mortgage repayments will easily be covered by the return. In addition…" He paused and cleared his throat nervously, as if aware that what he was about to say might seem a little indelicate. "In addition, the bank has generously agreed to pay you a widow's pension based on what your husband *would* have earned had he taken up his duties as Branch Manager, which he was of course due to have done the week after

305

he… Yes."

"That is indeed most generous, Mr Callan," said Farida, putting down her cup and saucer, "and so characteristic of my husband to have been so forward-thinking. He never liked to leave anything to chance. That is why this accident…" She broke off and turned away.

"Yes. So distressing." He offered Farida a handkerchief, which she gratefully accepted. "I think we may safely say that at least you shall not have anything to worry about financially. May we assume, for the time being at least, that you will be staying with us?"

"Of course, Mr Callan. It is what my husband would have wanted, I am sure." Farida stood up. "Thank you."

"Thank *you*, Mrs ul-Haq, and if there is anything else we can do for you, anything at all, please don't hesitate to come in and see us. There will be no need to make an appointment. Our door will always be open."

"Thank you. I shall, but you have explained everything so clearly to me that I do not believe there will be any need. Goodbye."

Now, as she walked along Hawthorne Avenue, she stood at the end of her drive looking up towards the house. She pictured again those mosaics of bees and flowers waiting to be pollinated in the tiled floor of Manchester Town Hall. Yes. She was sure. The idea had come to her fully formed on the journey home. She may not be ever able to have children of her own, but she loved them, and she was good with them. There must be many other young women, like her sister, who needed to keep going out to work, with small children not yet old enough for school, who would welcome a child minding service, a nursery, a play group.

She could see at once what would need to be done. She would take out most of the furniture, furniture that Salim had chosen, not her, and replace it with cushions and bean bags and child-sized chairs. She would take up the fitted carpets and have in their stead the wooden floors that lay underneath, scrubbed and polished and hard wearing, and easy to clean if drinks were spilled, or paint was knocked over. She would paper the walls with wipeable surfaces, so that the children could draw on them and use crayons. She would put transfers of bees on to the walls and front windows, and she would hang a sign here at the entrance to the drive, where now she stood, imagining it all. *Busy Bees*, she would call it, and they would all of them be busy, she and the children, busy and happy, smiling at the flowers.

*

Three years later, when Farida picked up Sol from outside Walton Gaol in her white Mini Cooper, in answer to his astonished question, "How…?", she told him none of this. She knew he was aware Salim had died, Nadia had written to him about that, mentioning the accident, but nothing more, and so as he sat down next to her in the passenger seat and they drove off together into the Friday afternoon traffic, she simply said instead, "I have my own business, a nursery for children before they start school. At first it was very small, just Jenna and one or two others, but pretty soon word got round and I started receiving requests from complete strangers. I advertised in Yellow Pages..." She noticed Sol's puzzled look. "It's an extra part of the phone book. It began a couple of years ago. Before I knew what was happening, I had a waiting list. Then your mother suggested I hired the Community Hall at Holy Cross, which I now do for four hours every day, and that's full too. I pay someone to be in charge there. I use students from the college on placements, and I need to be able to get between the two spaces as quickly as I can. That's why I bought this," she said, tapping the steering wheel. Sol sat back, shaking his head. Farida was the first person in either his or Nadia's family to own a car. Now here she was, wearing jeans and driving a Mini.

It was all so overwhelming. Sol found that it was not just the amount of change that had been going on in the wider world while he'd been inside that was hard to get his head round, but things much closer to home. After the initial pleasantries were over, Farida could see that Sol was reeling with the shock of his release. The euphoria and the strangeness combined were proving exhausting, so she stopped speaking, and they drove together in silence for most of the rest of the way, broken only by her pointing something out to him that had gone or was new, or by Sol scratching his head over a street he no longer recognised.

The demolition sites of his childhood were gradually being swept away and replaced by brand new tower-blocks. The juxtaposition of old and new, jostling together side by side, was both exhilarating and unsettling. When he saw a landmark he remembered, he would exclaim and point, and Farida would smile, not really understanding exactly what it was he was seeing or remembering…

You can see me there now if you look hard, he thinks, (we all of us carry our past lives with us, like the locks and chains of Marley's Ghost), tethering my imaginary horse to the railings by the school yard. I tip my Wyatt Earp hat with my Colt 45, blow across its barrel, twirl it once, twice, before dropping it from my fingers blindfold into my hip-slung holster, scraping off the Wanted posters 'Dead or Alive', in case somebody might recognise this stranger who's just blown into town. I scan the scene before moseying down past the Sheriff's Office to the local saloon to drink sarsaparillas. A coyote cries. I look up. It's Ray, from across the way, or the Cisco Kid as he prefers, and this is his signal and everyone clears. This town ain't big enough for the both of us, Wyatt against Cisco, me against Ray…

Turn the page, spin the kaleidoscope
Past the hopscotch, whip-and-top, skipping rope
The big ship sails down the alley, alley-o
The Cowboys and Indians come and they go…

There I am again, with a ray gun, space helmet from a cardboard box, climbing slow-motion up the pile of coke stacked in the yard, planting home-made flags, conquering the dark side of the moon…

Or again, though much later, as James Dean – hours and hours perfecting that quiff, the curl of the lip, the shrug, the what-if, the cocky conviction I'd carry it off, this scrawny, pale-faced northern teen…

I un-tether my horse from the railings by the school gate, stroke his muzzle, give him some sugar. It's time to let you go, boy, I whisper, it's time to take our separate ways. He nods his head, nuzzles me, neighs, before galloping off into the unimagined night...

The Bama. The Bomb Site.

Bulldozers, giant crabs with iron jaws and steel teeth, gouge the guts and entrails, chew the coke and concrete, spit the steel and slag heaps into huge storm drains, staunching wounds and gashes, stitching scars and lacerations, leaving multi-coloured Legoland to seize the future, heal the nation, air-brushing history...

But look closely now and see – we're still there, shadows, ghosts, palimpsests shimmering, Wyatt and Cisco, Ray and me, Eric and all of us, the whole posse, the Bomb Site, the Victory.

Ground Zero.

In the ashes of the bonfires, beneath the ruins far below, a horse lies sleeping, flanks like bellows heaving, expanding, contracting, expanding, contracting...

Just before they finally reached home, Farida swung the car up onto the high motorway viaduct of the M63, little more than a concrete skeleton when Sol was last there, now complete, a vast arch spanning the Ship Canal. The mighty oil tankers, which loomed so large when viewed from ground level as they passed by Barton Bridge, now seemed insignificant and tiny from this new height, this altered perspective, little more than a speck in the eye.

"Well – here we are," said Farida, as they turned into

Stanley Road. "But you can see that."

"Yes. Thanks." He made no move to get out the car, just sat there, staring at the house he was born in, the house he thought he'd left for good when he and Nadia had married more than six years ago.

Farida placed a hand on his arm. "Come on," she said. "I'll pick up your stuff from the boot," and she got out of the car.

Still Sol did nothing. It was as though, after all the weeks, months and years of dreaming of this moment, the day he would be released from prison and would see his wife and daughter again, he couldn't bring himself to accept it, now that it was here.

Farida walked round to his side of the car and opened the door for him. "Gently does it," she whispered. "They're probably watching us from inside. They'll be thinking you don't want to see them at this rate."

Did he, he wondered, did he really want to see them, Nadia, Jenna, his mother? It all felt suddenly too much for him, when here was Farida again, putting his rucksack into his arms and speaking to him once more. "I'll be off then. It's best you do this by yourself."

He nodded, as she kissed him lightly on the cheek. "You'll be alright," she said, and then she was back in her car and roaring off down the street.

Sol watched her go, hoisted the rucksack onto one shoulder, and then walked up towards the front door of his mother's house. A dark-coloured moth, basking on the step, its body camouflaged to blend in with the blackened brick, opened its wings to receive the last of the sun. Sol observed it briefly, remembering, before the door swung open, and there was Nadia, her eyes shining. She took the rucksack from him, placed a hand beneath his elbow and slowly led him indoors. She shut the door behind them, put the rucksack on the floor and pulled him towards her. They did not kiss but held each other tightly for a long time.

Sol opened his eyes and became aware of a small child peeping round from behind a door frame. Sol lowered himself slowly down until he was at her level. "Hello?" he said. "You must be Jenna. I'm your…"

"I know who you are," she said and fled upstairs, banging her bedroom door behind her.

"Give her time," whispered Nadia. "It's a lot to get used to."

Sol nodded.

"Let's go into the kitchen," she said. "Your mother's waiting."

7

15th – 22nd September 1968

Manchester Evening News

15th September 1968

BRADFORD COLLIERY TO CLOSE

The winding gear at the headstocks of Bradford Colliery turned for the last time today as miners working the final shift were brought to the surface. Singing, cheering crowds accompanied them as they made their way through the pit-yard gates, which were then padlocked behind them.

But these songs of defiance masked the grim reality of almost two thousand men and women, who have now lost their jobs, with little prospect of alternative employment in the near future. One miner's wife, who wished to remain anonymous, told us, "This is a sad day for the town, for once the mine goes, what will happen to the rest of the community?"

News first broke of the possible closure when several houses in nearby Miles Platting collapsed because of subsidence beneath them, due to the unstable conditions of the extensive seams of the colliery, which stretch for several miles underground. With the National Coal Board not in a position to guarantee the long-term safety and security of houses in the vicinity, closure became the only option.

The Manchester Evening News requested an interview with a representative from the NCB but no-one was available to comment. However they did issue the following brief statement:

"It is with great regret that we announce today the formal closure of Bradford Colliery. As we made clear in the Government enquiry two years ago, it has become uneconomic for us to continue to extract coal from this site."

There was deep anger at the brevity of this statement, indicating an apparent lack of feeling from the Management. Union officials confirmed that while it is true the costs of compensation that the NCB are forced to meet for surface damage caused by their operations at the Beswick Pit amounted to 5s 6d per ton of coal, compared to a national average of just 6d per ton, this did not take into account the fact that the quality of the coal mined there was the highest premium grade to be found anywhere in Europe.

Not too long ago, the NUM argued, there had been plans to extend the workings further underground beneath neighbouring Collyhurst, Ancoats, Clayton and Cheetham, creating the possibility of a 'super mine', employing tens of thousands of men. These plans have now been abandoned, despite the fact that, at a conservative estimate, there are sufficient reserves of coal still waiting to be extracted that could last for centuries, a point vigorously made in a recent Commons debate when

Barbara Castle, Secretary of State for the newly created Ministry of Employment and Productivity, had to face a heated exchange of questions from MPs of all sides of the House, including some from her predecessor Ray Gunter, the former Head of the now defunct Ministry of Labour. Whither now, we ask Messrs Wilson, Shore, Cousins and Benn, the white heat of technology?

It was three and a half centuries ago that mining first began here, during the reign of King James I, and it was just forty years ago that the pit played host to another royal visit, by King Amanullah of Afghanistan.

Now the yard at Bradford Colliery is empty and silent, a place of memories and ghosts.

*

Three days after reading the article Sol decided he had to act. "It's time," he said to Nadia, later that night while they were in bed. Two months had passed since his release.

"I know," she said, lying in the crook of his arm.

"I've put this off for far too long."

"I'm proud of you," she whispered, kissing his fingers intertwined with her own. "Now go to sleep. You've got an early start tomorrow."

But Sol did not sleep. He watched the gentle rise and fall of Nadia's body next to his own, looking out towards the window. It was a clear night, and the orange glow of the street lamps mingled with the pale stars up above. It reminded him keenly of all those nights he had spent in

Walton Gaol, staring through the bars of the broken, smeared window in his cell there, when he had first begun to formulate this plan. But until he had read that article, the idea had remained incomplete, sketchy and uncertain. It was his mother who had thrust the newspaper in front of him three evenings ago, as he sat down for his tea after coming in from work. At first he did not make the connection. Coal mines were closing all the time these days.

"Bradford," she said. "See? Where your father and I met. When he went to see King Amanullah. When they took away from him what he'd been given. Look. They're pulling it down. Soon it will be all gone. Nothing left. You have to bring it back."

And he had understood. This was what had been missing from his own plan. What had been for him some kind of vague homage to the journey his father had made all those years ago – forty, he suddenly realised – so painstakingly reconstructed in his meticulous hand in the architectural drawing, traced with that faint blue line, had suddenly become transformed into a mission, a quest, a chance for salvation and redemption. He looked up at his mother and nodded.

"Yes," he said. "I will."

Now, as the dawn seeped slowly across the night sky, he got out of bed as quietly and carefully as he could, so as not to disturb Nadia, who was still sleeping peacefully, put on his clothes and crept in socks down the stairs towards the front door, where his boots, polished the night before, his coat and his rucksack, complete with sandwiches, an apple and a thermos, together with his father's drawing wrapped tightly in polythene, were all waiting for him.

Just as he was about to unlock the front door, he heard the soft pad of small footsteps behind him. Jenna. She was looking at him again, unblinking and stern, with her large brown eyes.

"You're going away," she said.

He put his finger to his lips and nodded.

"Again."

"Yes. But I'll be coming back."

"When?"

He paused. "I'm not sure. Tomorrow. The day after. Soon."

"Promise?"

"Promise."

"You'd better take this," she said, and she handed him an umbrella. "It might rain." Her expression was solemn and serious.

"Good idea," he replied, taking it from her. "Thanks."

"Will you write?"

He shook his head. "But I'll tell you all about it when I get back."

"You'd better get going then." And she padded back upstairs.

Sol watched her go in wordless admiration. Then he turned the handle on the front door, stepped out into the early morning light, and set off down the road, walking at a fast, determined pace. Everywhere was silent, except for the sound of his boots striding out towards the Canal.

He halts as he reaches the water's edge. There is less traffic these days flowing in and out of the Port of Manchester, and the surface of the Canal is slimier than he remembers it. A thick scum of oil-green sludge, clogged with weeds, shifts uneasily just a few feet below him. This is where things began forty years ago, when Sol's grandfather stood on the aqueduct as it swung open in honour of the visit by King Amanullah. Sol treads carefully now along the overgrown tow-path towards it, the start of his father's journey, tracing his route, first along the Bridgewater. Unlike his father, Sol shan't be travelling by narrow boat. No coal barges ply these waters now, and so Sol must walk the route instead.

A walk that is easier said than done. The path is neglected and has not been kept up for some years. At times the weeds are so thick that he almost slips in the mud and into the Canal. As he passes under bridges and railway arches, the ground lies strewn with broken bottles, empty cigarette packets. The walls are blackened from decades of smoke and soot, dripping with damp and covered in graffiti. This is going to be even more of a task than he had envisaged. What by road would be just over nine miles of fairly easy walking is, according to his father's drawing, almost fourteen by canal, and after an hour he has barely covered two, with the most difficult stretches still to come, when he has to follow the route of the Rochdale Canal from Castlefield to Ducie Street, where it passes through low tunnels beneath the city streets. Sol does not know whether this section will even be passable, but he has promised himself he will try. He turns up the collar of his coat against a sudden squall of rain, glad of the umbrella Jenna thrust into his hands just before he left, and, head bent, he leans into the wind.

He passes the Royce Trading Estate, the Dye Manufactory, various warehouses either side of Ashburton Road. He's on the edge of Trafford Park, skirting factories he's only previously seen from the road. He crosses the line of the Thirlmere Aqueduct, ducks under Mosley Road Bridge, encounters a dead dog, dumped in the nettles near Moss Road, rotting and wriggling, feasted on by crows that flap menacingly towards him as he nears them. Half an hour later, though only a quarter of a mile further in distance, as Sol has to clamber over a burnt out car and pick his way through ankle deep mud and rubbish, he reaches Taylor's Bridge, from where an embankment takes him onto welcome higher, drier ground. He disturbs a young woman sunbathing in a bikini, surrounded by litter at Waters Meeting, where an arm of the Bridgewater heads south. Sol continues east. The rain has eased. A pale, milky sun leaches through the clouds. He has been walking for several hours already. At this junction of the two branches of the Canal, he pauses. He sits on a mill-stone capstan, where narrow boats may once have moored to unload or pick up goods and materials when the waterway was busier, and takes out a sandwich from his rucksack. He looks out across a patch of gorse back towards Westinghouse Road and can just make out the back of Metro-Vicks. He thinks about his father, passing this same spot all those years ago. But on that occasion it had been night, and Sol imagines how differently the atmosphere must have seemed then, the Canal an even inkier black, a starless sky, when owls go hunting. Below his feet, by the water's edge, he sees a rat skirting the tow-path. It scratches in the dirt, ever watchful, its body quivering as a light breeze riffles its skin. Another cloud crosses the sun and Sol realises he will not reach his journey's end before nightfall, not with his current rate of progress. The prospect of attempting to follow the course of the Rochdale and Ashton Canals in the dark is not something he relishes, is not something he can take on. He nods slowly, reconciling himself to the thought that he will have to sleep rough tonight. He stands stiffly and stamps some warmth back into his feet. His movements send the rat scurrying back to the undergrowth.

From Taylor's Bridge, with the Foundry on his left, the wide basin of the Freight Terminal opens up on his right. There is only one ship docked there today, rearing up high above him, almost blotting out the sky. Chained like some ancient beast, its engines shut down and silent, it creaks and groans in the wind, rusted and immobile, destined for scrap. Sol sees two boys chasing one another round its empty decks, a ghost ship. Passing by Old Trafford and the football ground, beneath the Throstle's Nest Bridge, he reaches the Palmolive Soap Works, looks up and sees the Trafford Park Road Swing Bridge, Barton Dock's sister, from where he set off all those hours ago, and the junction with the Ship Canal once more, and there before him, stretched out like a giant oyster farm, the wharves and basins of Pomona Docks.

It is more than twenty years since Sol was last here, when, together with his mother and grandfather, he came to float rose petals along the surface of the waters, to say goodbye to his father, this family tradition begun by Yasser when their daughter died when just a child, named for this place, Pomona, the Roman goddess of fruit and orchards, and then returned to each time there is a family funeral. Did his mother come here after Yasser died, while he was recovering in a Djibouti hospital from his injuries sustained in Aden? In the recriminating silence that has hung between them for almost fifteen years he has never asked her, and she has never told him.

Pomona Docks.

He has only travelled here by bus before, crossing the wide Trafford Road Bridge, thundering above the Erie, Huron and St Louis Basins of Salford Quays, pointed out to him by Yasser, full of tales of pirates and adventure, then standing by a railing, leaning over and looking down upon the murky Canal, from which no reflection ever came back, before they scattered their petals. Now, approaching the Quays from where the waters of the Bridgewater join them, they tower above him, dwarfing him with their hulk and clanging. On this busy Saturday afternoon, although nothing like the hive and hustle of its heyday, he is nevertheless overwhelmed by the noise and clamour, the flying sparks from welders, the ceaseless press of cargo being unloaded onto drays and trucks, the crane-drivers grabbing, clutching then dropping the crates from huge rope nets, while overhead the massive metal containers glide along gantries. A hunting horn is blown to announce the opening of the lock gates to allow another ship to enter the dock. Men swarm up and down the ladders and gang planks from ship to ship, relentless columns of ants, and Sol moves unseen among all of this, as once more the rain and darkness begin to fall. He opens up his umbrella so that from above he resembles just one more piece of merchant cargo arriving to be processed.

He reaches the junction with the Hulme Locks Branch, only a furlong in length, which links the Irwell Navigation with the Ship Canal at Pomona Dock Number 3, now shut and overgrown, choked and airless, before eventually arriving at the Castlefield Basin, at the bottom of Deansgate, by Water Street, behind the Granada TV Studios, on the edge of Manchester, close by the remains of the first Roman fort and settlement there, where the Bridgwater finishes, where the Rochdale Canal begins, and where Sol will try to find somewhere dry and safe to hunker down for the night.

Running alongside the tow-path are a series of railway arches beneath an iron bridge carrying trains towards Piccadilly and Victoria. He could have caught one from Eccles, which would have passed directly over where he is now standing, had his father travelled that way himself back in 1928. But Jaz had journeyed on a Sunday, when no trains were running back then, or buses either, at least not until later in the day, and so the Canal had been his only option, and the bargemen making their way towards Bradford Colliery to pick up an order of coal all knew Yasser and owed him. It still feels important for Sol to be following the same route that his father did, despite the prospect of a night beneath these arches.

He walks beside them, hoping perhaps one of them may be open, not locked or shuttered, but accessible. He passes garages where men are still working in pits beneath broken cars being patched and mended, reaches a lock-up just as an acned youth is pulling down a metal shutter, who looks at Sol suspiciously, is drawn to where he sees the light of what might be a fire burning inside and stumbles into a forge, a bare-chested smithy hammering horse-shoes at an anvil with one hand, while pumping a large pair of bellows with another. He hears the distant whinny of a horse rising from behind an adjoining bricked-up builder's yard, until eventually he reaches an arch with a cobbled recess stretching back and in, several yards away from the street, before tapering down to the ground.

This will do, he thinks, as he curls up in the farthest corner of it, his back against the stone, and places his rucksack behind his head to use as a kind of pillow. He takes a firm grip of the umbrella and looks about him, his eyes adjusting to the shadows. Others have used this spot before him, he can see, from the evidence of discarded cigarette stubs and a few beer cans. He does not expect to get much sleep this night, but at least it will be dry and away from the wind and rain, and it will not be too many hours before light streaks the sky once more.

But he is wrong. The exertions of the day have taken their toll. More than ten hours of walking, some of it more like clambering and slithering, have exhausted him, and now that he has allowed himself to stop, he finds his eyes drooping almost at once, and before he can start to contemplate the rest of the journey that awaits him tomorrow, he is almost asleep. Some long buried instinct impels him to pick up a small sharp stone and carve his initials, SW, in the farthest corner of the recess, before he curls up into a foetal position for the rest of the night.

*

The light was fading in the western sky. He could just make out the curve of low hills, shaped like suckling breasts, which gave the settlement its name. Mamucium. Skirting the wooded rise, he saw the ring of fires smouldering in the valley of the three rivers. He had been marching hard all day, ever since he left the Oak River Fort at first light. There'd been times when he doubted he'd ever reach Redstones. But there it was, and as he drew nearer, he began to make out the shapes of men and horses. Dru was planning to rest a few days there, before continuing to stake out the road further north, beyond the Ribble, towards the Wall.

It felt like he'd been on the move for the last three years, ever since his capture by the Imperial Army when they cut their way through the villages of Galicia. A soldier had pinned him to the ground, a spear at his throat, and offered him a simple choice. Either march with us, or end up like your father, whose severed head was hoisted on a burning palisade. Since then he'd crossed the Weeping Mountains, wrestling with lynx and bear. He'd plodded through the wet marshlands of Southern Gaul. He'd endured a stormy crossing through the channel that separated Breizh from The Fleet. They'd marched in testudo as local tribes rained down sharpened sticks and stones from their hill forts. For the last year they'd sliced their way north, slashing and burning in broad, straight lines through field and forest, carving out the wide marches for the larger forces to follow on behind them. And now he was in desperate need of rest.

He sent on ahead a dozen men to scout the last mile and to warn the Camp Commander of their approach. A hunter's moon rose in the night sky. He waited till the last man had safely arrived before finding a place to sleep – a small hollow in the base of a dead tree close to one of the fires. Within moments of settling himself, he was asleep.

He awoke early to the smell of wood smoke. A raven croaked in the chill air. His bones ached. He heard the snort and stamp of tethered horses nearby, their hooves delicately balanced, their breath forming statues. He could hear the sound of water. Just beyond the circle of camp fires, which had all but gone out, the ground dropped away. He let his eyes accustom to the grey light. A pale sun was lightening the sky. He wandered down the slope, following the sound of the water. A young woman was lowering a bucket at the river's edge. She heard a twig crack as he approached and froze. She was kneeling, her back towards him. Dru carried on walking until he was right behind her. It was her reflection he saw first, slowly rippling in the water. Briefly their eyes met. He expected her to look frightened, or to bolt, like a hare startled from the thickets, but she held his gaze, before dipping the bucket into the water to fill it, obscuring both their faces as she did so.

He caught her by the wrist. He had a little of the native language, enough to ask her name and where she lived. "Bron," she said, and pointed. Her arm stretched away towards where the three rivers met. In their confluence was a small huddle of low huts with makeshift *roofs of earth.*

*Three days passed. The men were getting restless. They'd
drunk themselves into a stupor the first night, gambling
with the soldiers who were garrisoned there. On the
second night they'd sampled most of the local women. But
not Bron. Dru made it clear that she was off limits. By the
third night fights had started breaking out. Many of the
men were itching to be on the move again, while some of
those stationed there were keen to join them. It was a
small camp, barely meriting the name. The quarters were
basic. There were no baths, no temple, no villa. The
whole place felt impermanent, a way station only,
towards the bigger settlements of Ebor and Vinovia, and
it was clear the soldiers posted there felt forgotten by
Rome.*

*But Dru looked around and saw nuts growing on the
trees. He saw fruit being picked from orchards in the
valley. He saw pigs rooting for acorns in the copses. He
saw deer stripping bark from the saplings. He saw eels
coiled and wallowing in the ditches. He saw fish
gathering in shoals where the rivers met. He saw food.
He saw water. And he saw Bron. When he held her close
under the blood-red moon at night, and when he watched
the sparks from the fires dancing with the stars in the sky,
he looked in her eyes and saw more than just himself
reflected back, more than the sureness of her gaze. He
saw a future. They reared and bucked beside the
stamping horses, and the next morning, while the camp
still snored, Dru took his knife and cut the rope that*

326

tethered one of them. He climbed astride it and lifted Bron before him. She whispered something in the horse's ear, and, lacing her fingers through its mane, together she and Dru rode away towards the confluence of the three rivers, where a small family of rats foraged among the still-glowing embers.

*

He is woken with a start just before daybreak. Crazed, bloodshot eyes are staring at him right up close, caught in the flare of a recently struck match. Sol can just make out a mass of matted hair and a pair of hands reaching towards him. He can smell the man's sour breath as the blackened fingers of one of these hands reach slowly down towards Sol's rucksack, which has fallen to the ground and lies beside him. Propelled into life, Sol makes a grab for it with a sudden shout of alarm. The man springs backwards, snatches the umbrella lying at Sol's feet and dashes out of the archway and into the street. Sol hears his feet echoing along the cobbles, and, by the time he has picked himself up and followed him out, he is gone. The weak beginnings of a pale dawn are just becoming visible in a slightly lighter streak of grey in a corner of the sky. There will be no chance of further sleep and Sol dusts himself down as best he can, cursing the loss of the umbrella Jenna had made him take, especially now, as a thin, hard, stinging rain starts to fall. Hauling his rucksack back onto his shoulder, thrusting the other hand into his pocket, stiff and hunched, he begins once more to walk.

327

He makes his way back to the edge of the Canal, follows the narrow tow-path towards Duke's Lock, back beneath the railway arches and the iron bridge and on to Tunnel Lock, relieved to discover that his path takes him straight on, past the old Tunnel on his left, where the bricks are crumbling and the roof appears to have collapsed, only to realise that there is another tunnel he has to negotiate, fortunately quite short, right beneath Deansgate. The path is slippery and it is still dark enough for him not to be able to see exactly where he is putting his feet, so he turns sideways, using the damp walls as a guide, edging slowly, step by step, like a cumbersome crab. Emerging from the tunnel, he wipes his hands dry on his coat and heads on towards another lock, where the path momentarily fizzles out and he has to scramble around the lock gates, before finding the path once more as he trudges up the slabbed rise along the edge of Albion Mill, its looms lying still and silent this early Sunday morning. The rusting iron girders of Gaythorne Bridge shower flakes of grey and green metal upon him as he steadies himself from skittering down the still-slippery cobbles, the path widening slightly as he picks up more pace approaching Tib Lock. An opening into another now blocked canal on his right, the old Manchester and Salford Junction, forces him to retrace his steps to Gaythorne Bridge and cross to the other side, to a path which leads him back to a point where the lock can be climbed. He clambers over three sets of gates, looking right down the fag end of Tib Street itself, where he remembers going with his parents when he was still very small, probably about seven years old, on a rare trip to

Manchester, to see Santa Claus in Henry's Department Store, and how, afterwards, his mother had led them down Tib Street, and she had shown him all the market stalls with their caged birds, and how he'd longed for them to take one home, a cockatiel, a budgerigar, or canary, but how his mother had said it was cruel, and that she was showing him because she wanted him to understand that, but at the time he had only cried.

Light is growing in the sky now, but Tib Street is silent, as all the streets still seem to be, while the rain continues to slant in towards him. Looking ahead he can see once more how the tow-path peters out and so again he is forced to sidle across the lock gate back to the other side where the path continues towards another low arched bridge and the next set of locks, at Oxford Street, where what remains of the old Manchester & Salford Junction Canal delves underground. Tall buildings rise up on either side of him as he nears the bridge, almost blotting out the light, as if he is in some kind of canyon. He ducks his head as he reaches it and has to remain stooping low until he comes up for air once more at the back of Princess Street and another set of locks. A series of narrow iron footbridges require him to keep criss-crossing the Canal as he passes Sackville Street, Chorlton Street, then Canal Street and on towards Minshull Street, at times the tow-path merging with the streets, at others involving several drops down, which Sol must navigate carefully by way of steep stone blocks placed there for the purpose, to enable the bargemen of old, he imagines, to leap on and off their narrow boats as they approached each lock. On one of these Sol slips and nearly ends up in the Canal, saving himself at the last moment by grabbing at the remains of an old hand-rail.

He edges along a high brick wall, inching his way towards the first of the tunnels that his father had marked so clearly on his drawing. The Piccadilly Tunnels. Immediately he enters them the light drains away, apart from the twinkling reflections from the few electric lamps that were not there when his father would have passed through here, but thankfully for Sol are working this cheerless Sunday morning. Back in 1928, the narrow boat would have had a torch held aloft by the skipper as he steered through these dark and mysterious tunnels weaving their way between stone pillars beneath the heart of Piccadilly. But now Sol has to rely on the light bouncing off the murky water as he crawls his way through this cavernous underworld. The walls are slimy to his touch, he hears occasional scuttles ahead of him along the path, and soft splashes in the water alongside. After what seems an eternity he sees a pale light ahead of him and lengthens his stride to emerge into Dale Street, gulping for air.

He is now approaching what his father had labelled 'the Rochdale Nine', a series of locks in close succession enabling the coal barges coming down from the Ashton to make their way to the easier passageways of the Bridgewater and Ship Canals. Just before embarking upon this stretch of waterway, which his father had also labelled 'to be avoided, due to absence of tow-paths in places', the entrance to the Ashton appears on his right at the Dale Street Junction, by Ducie Street, on the edge of Ancoats. The rain begins to ease slightly, as the sky continues to lighten. Sol can make out the chimneys of huge redbrick mills stretching out ahead of him – Decker, Dolton, Paragon and Pin, India, Beehive, Victoria and Phoenix – just beyond the Kitty Footbridge, as he turns away, following the curve of the Ashton Canal.

He now has less than two miles remaining. There are no more tunnels to face, for which he is thankful, but six more locks, and in recent years this stretch has fallen largely into disuse. Sol passes where old wrecked cars have been set on fire and tipped into the narrow channel, increasingly devoid of water, looking more like a ditch than a canal. Flies are buzzing all around him, there is the unmistakable stench of dead carcasses rotting and decomposing. Rats the size of tomcats run along the tops of walls that line what remains of the tow-paths, youths lob stones at him from the Store Street Aqueduct, an old man pushing a handcart piled high with items scavenged from the Thomas Telford Basin forces past him, almost knocking him down, a couple are having hard, loud sex standing against a smoke-black wall in a damp brick arch before the junction with the Islington Canal, until finally he reaches Beswick Locks 4 to 6, where he can still make out what once must have been a landing station, and a flight of stone steps, which he climbs, slowly and with relief, to reach the entrance to Bradford Colliery.

Unlike when his father climbed these steps forty years ago, there are no cheering crowds, no brass bands playing *God Save the King*, no line of dignitaries with chains of office waiting in line to greet him, no soldiers in dress uniform. Instead the rain has begun to fall again, clattering on the tin roofs of the deserted sheds and outbuildings, rooks caw on the telephone wires, water from the Canal slaps against the steps, the abandoned winding gear creaks and groans in the wind. A high fence bars his entry, with a sign saying "*Danger. Keep Out*", but he has not walked all this way to fail at the last. He straps his rucksack tighter onto his back and climbs the gate, landing heavily on the other side. He picks himself up, brushes himself down and walks towards the pithead. The mine is full of ghosts.

The shafts are sealed up and their entrances blocked, but coal wagons still wait on the rusting rail tracks. The wash-house, where the men could take showers after each shift, lies silent. Sol pushes against one of the doors and it opens beneath him. He wanders through it, reminded of a similar set-up back in Walton Gaol, and hears again the jokes and songs, the thwack of wet towels against bare backsides, imagines the slip of a soap bar falling from his fingers, feels the rush of water against his skin. Now all that remains is the drip, drip, drip from a broken tap.

Back outside he stops to look around and tries to get some sense of where things must have been. He sees the metal chutes circling the site like a big dipper towards the store houses, where tons of coal would have been deposited each day to be graded and sorted and then carted off for delivery by trucks to the train station, or transported by wagons down rails to the canal steps where the barges would have pulled up by the dozen, morning, noon and night. He locates where the administrative centre once was, a low brick building with a flag pole on the top, though no flag flies today, and heads towards it. The doors are locked, but all the windows are smashed, the lowest of which he climbs carefully through. Inside is a snowstorm of paper – memos, notices, invoices, reports – lifting in the breeze blowing through the offices. He walks on broken glass through this gently cascading drift.

What he is looking for is nowhere to be found, and in truth he hasn't expected it to be. Anything of value or importance must surely have been packed away before everyone left and the building was locked, but given how closely the whole scene resembles that of the *Marie Celeste*, with unwatered plants still in their pots, a scarf hanging on a hook by the door, it might have been possible to find it after all. He picks up a framed photograph from the floor, its glass mount cracked and in pieces, and studies the faces from a bygone age. Men in frock coats and top hats, an elegant lady cutting a ribbon, but nothing resembling a royal visit, and certainly no mounted lump of coal with accompanying brass plaque.

He wanders back outside. The rain is falling stronger now. In the distance he sees children running up and down the slag heaps, shrieking as they slide down the tumbling scree. On the far side of the yard he sees a pair of older men emerging from behind one of the sheds, pushing a pram into which they are piling everything they can lay their hands on, and beneath the coal chutes he notices women, whom he must have missed when he first climbed over the gate, crawling like crabs across the ground, bent low to the earth, trawling for pieces of coal, which they are putting into baskets strapped to their backs.

Suddenly a loud whistle pierces the air. Everyone freezes, and then simply vanishes into holes in the ground, all, that is, except for Sol, who turns about him, bewildered. Running towards him he spies a young Policeman, still whistling and shouting.

"Oi, you! Stay where you are! Don't move!" His helmet falls from his head in his haste, and Sol wonders whether he should make a dash for it. But where would he go? And if he were caught, having been warned, that would only make matters worse. The thought of having to return to prison floods through his veins like ice, so he remains where he is, rooted to the spot, until the young Constable reaches him, fixing his helmet back on as he speaks.

"Can't you read?" he says. "Property of the National Coal Board. No trespassing. Danger. Keep Out."

"Sorry," says Sol. "I'd read about the closure of the pit and I was just curious."

"Arms out," says the Policeman, and he proceeds to tap beneath Sol's arms, down the front and side of his coat, then down the outside of both his legs. "OK. What's in the rucksack?"

"Nothing. Just a flask and…"

"What's this?" He holds up Sol's father's drawings between the finger and thumb of one hand suspiciously, as if it might blow up.

"Please," urges Sol, "don't tear it. My father drew it. Before he died. He came here once, forty years ago, to please his own father…"

"What happened?"

"It's a long story."

"And why are *you* here?"

"To try and make amends, I suppose."

The officer nods, as if he understands, then hands the drawing back to Sol, who folds it carefully and puts it back inside his rucksack. "Thanks."

"My dad used to work here too. Till he got the black lung."

"I'm sorry."

"It's all wrong. Closing this place. There's at least a hundred years' worth of coal still waiting to be dug up right underneath where we're standing. Vast reserves. Premium quality too."

"I don't understand."

"Subsidence. Houses nearby. Walls started to crack. Whole streets threatened with collapse or demolition. It's just too expensive to keep mining it, so they say. Uneconomic. So people lose their jobs, a whole community ends up on the scrap heap, and I end up having to chase off trespassers. Like you."

Sol nods.

"So hop it."

Sol heads back towards the direction of the canal.

"Not that way. Over there." And the Policeman points towards a different gate, open, where his blue-and-white panda car is parked, engine still running.

Sol turns around, thanks the officer once again, and walks away from the pit. As he reaches the gate, he sees a large lump of coal, lying among the dust of smaller pieces, and bends to pick it up. He looks back towards the Policeman and raises his hand. "Souvenir," he says, then moves on.

Sol catches three buses back to Patricroft. On each one of them, the conductor is unwilling to let him board, and Sol can understand why. He is filthy. His trousers and shoes are caked with mud, his coat is creased and soaking, while his face and hands, he knows, must be plastered in muck.

When he arrives back at his front door it is late afternoon. He has been away for the best part of two days. He steps inside and at once takes off his boots. Nadia sees him and cannot help the look of concern that spreads across her face. He hangs his coat over the banister at the foot of the stairs and squeezes past her in the hall. "I'm fine," he says, "don't worry. Is Mum through here?"

Nadia nods and Sol walks through to the kitchen where Ishtar is sitting at the table with Jenna cutting pictures out of a catalogue.

"You're all wet," says Jenna. "What happened to your umbrella?"

"Somebody took it, I'm afraid, while I was asleep."

"Where have you been?"

"Just for a walk."

"It must have been a very long one. Will you tell me about it?"

"I'll draw you a picture."

But already Jenna's attention is elsewhere. She gets down from the table and skips over to Nadia, who is standing in the kitchen doorway, watching, as Sol walks towards his mother, takes the lump of coal from his rucksack and kneels beside her. Ishtar picks it up and holds it to the light, marvelling over every shining detail of it.

"Thank you," she whispers and pulls Sol close to her, oblivious of the mud and dirt and wet, and Sol buries his face in her arms.

*

The following week he starts his Art classes again with George at Salford Institute. "I have an idea," he says at the end of the session, and he tells George what it is. "Do you think I could do it?"

"Definitely," replies George, lighting up his pipe. "But it's going to take time before you're ready."

"How much time?"

"I'd say about ten years."

Sol is not phased by this response. Instead he nods and says, "We'd best get cracking then."

8

George in his forecast proved uncannily accurate. Ten years after his long walk to reclaim his father's lost heritage, Sol was ready to unveil his response.

He could only attend Art classes one night a week and so progress was perforce slow and measured. When George first heard Sol explain his idea to him, he was both excited and not a little daunted, for he understood just how important it would be for Sol, not only to carry out his plan to completion, but to execute it to the highest possible standard, given what were inevitably going to be compromises in terms of space and resources.

To begin with, therefore, George took Sol through a detailed crash course in public art, from its earliest origins in the Ancient World, right through to some of the more experimental, contemporary guerrilla activities coming out of the sixties. Together they pored over Greek and Roman mosaics, Renaissance frescoes, the paintings of Michelangelo in the Sistine Chapel, to the great civic commissions of the Victorian age, statues, carvings, tapestries, wall paintings. They went to the Town Hall to look at the Ford Madox Brown murals that Farida had chanced upon after Salim's inquest. George took Sol to meet Walter Kershaw, currently at work on the Trafford Park murals, including Denis Law, painted on a factory wall. Given Sol's not inconsiderable, innate talent for painting, allied to his growing skills as a draughtsman because of his work, George had a hunch that it might be the murals of Diego Rivera that would really fire his imagination, and so it proved.

Sol loved their energy, the sense of movement that surged through them, peopled by hundreds of characters, each individually identifiable, yet equally part of a unified group. He loved their humour, their passion, their vibrant sense of colour, but most of all he loved their sheer scale and size. George of course was driven to emphasise their politics, the way Rivera unequivocally depicted the heroism of the peasants, the factory workers, viewing the work as a revolutionary call to arms, while Sol, seeing all that, also loved how Rivera would insert images of himself and his wife, Frida Kahlo, right into the heart of them.

That, more than anything else, was what Sol was striving for, to create a mural that told the full story, not only of the building of the Manchester Ship Canal, the opening up of all the small towns along its banks to the rest of the world, the carrying of huge tons of coal and cotton and other goods out into the open sea, but also his own story, Yasser's, his father's, Ishtar's, Nadia's and Farida's, and now Jenna's, and all the untold thousands of others who lived and worked along it, right up to the present day, when it was falling slowly but inexorably into decline and disuse.

He wanted to show King Amanullah arriving at Barton Swing Bridge and then later hewing the coal at Bradford Pit. He wanted to show the labours of all those who'd been drafted in to excavate the first channels, from Ireland, China and the Yemen. He wanted to show the mountains of earth and the ingenious devices of the engineers to remove them. He wanted to show the factories at Trafford Park, and he wanted to show the ships, from all over the world, sailing its length, to the Royal Pomona Docks, where he finally wanted to show petals scattered on the surface of its waters in remembrance of love and loss.

For three years George passed on to Sol everything he felt he needed to make him ready to begin this vast undertaking. For the next three he helped him plan and prepare it, beginning with small-scale drawings, gradually increasing to larger and larger designs, until the whole shape and structure of it could be mapped out, like an architect's plan, section by section, frame by frame, scene by scene, figure by figure. Over the next six months George used all his contacts, pulled in every favour, to source materials, to organise storage and finally to secure the necessary permissions as to where the finished work could be placed. He found an unused basement cellar in the old Mechanics' Institute in Pendleton, where Sol had first attended classes. The space was interrupted by pillars and pipes, and the ceiling was quite low, but it was warm, it was dry, and it was theirs to use for as long as they needed it.

Sol was still in contact with Ray, who was now involved with house-clearances, as the demolition of the slums and the old back-to-back streets right across Salford was currently in full swing, and through Ray he managed to acquire literally hundreds of differently-sized lengths of wood, planks, old bits of skirting, floorboards, window-frames. Then, employing all of his

340

draughtsman's skills, he allocated each a number, recording them in endless lists, as he selected which pieces of wood to use for which particular tableaux. These were all mapped out separately over a period of two years and lay there neatly stacked in piles on the floor of the basement cellar, dry and warm beneath the gurgling pipes, as George waited for the final permission to come through.

One memorable Tuesday evening, while Sol was laying out several pieces to see how they might be joined together, George burst in, waving a piece of paper. "We've got it," he said. "Here. It's official. Signed by the Director of the Port of Manchester himself, no less. Permission to hang."

They cracked open a few bottles of beer George just happened to have with him, and the following week they began to plan in earnest how they would transport it all and assemble it once they had got it there. It took several weeks. Ray would let them use one of his vans whenever one was free, which sometimes Farida would drive, and Sol would bring Eric along to hump all the numbered pieces of wood and take them to where they were needed.

It was to be hung in one of the former Pomona Docks, which were gradually being closed as traffic along the Ship Canal was declining. Number 2 Dock, less than four hundred yards from where, as a family, they had traditionally gathered to scatter flowers on the surface of the water when someone had died, was due to be filled in, for safety reasons, within the next eighteen months, but George had been reliably informed that if they went there now, before the year was out, they would be undisturbed.

The piece of paper George had so gleefully waved in front of Sol secured them permission to come and go as they needed onto the site until the infilling began.

"You do understand," said George, "don't you, Sol, there are no guarantees your mural will survive once the diggers move in? They'll probably just clear everything away, breaking all this up as they go."

Sol nodded. "It's fine," he said. "It's all recycled anyway, and it's all in here," he added, tapping the side of his head. "There's something sort of right about the possibility of it all just being swept away."

"In Japan," said George, "they make the most exquisite ice sculptures, knowing that as soon as spring comes, they'll melt. And in Spain they build huge wooden statues of saints and devils, which take the whole community the best part of a year to create, only for them to be burnt during a single night."

"I have the drawings," said Sol. "When I look at those, I'll be able to imagine the rest."

"And I'll be sure to take lots of photos," said George. "It shan't be lost completely. Afterwards we can do a collage if you like. You know, like those joiner photographs of David Hockney I was talking about in class last week."

"Maybe," said Sol. "But right now we've got to get all of this down to the Dock, assemble it, and then finish painting."

"Agreed."

Between them, Sol and George had devised a method where Sol had drawn on every single piece of wood the outlines of each section, and had then laid down a first wash of what Sol had called an undercoat.

"I like that," George had said. "So would Rivera. Like being a painter and decorator. This is a job of work that has to be done."

"And it will have to be done quickly if the rain's not going to wash it all away before it's finished."

"Excellent," quipped George. "Nothing like a bit of urgency to create a sense of spontaneity. And best to use an all-weather paint, I think, don't you?"

"Already bought."

The year turned. 1977 gave way to 1978.

The following weekend, the first of the new year, they took everything down in Ray's van, including hammers and nails, screws and drills, as well as paint and tarpaulins. It took Sol the whole two days to assemble the entire mural, piece by piece, following his carefully worked out scheme of joining each individual piece of wood, number by number, letter by letter, eventually forming a single continuous sequence, which he attached to an old brick wall that still remained, from when the dock was originally built, back in 1894, when the Port of Manchester had first opened, the year Sol's father was born, just five years after Yasser had been burned in the chemical explosion here at Pomona.

By Sunday evening as the light began to fade, Sol had completed the entire construction. It was the first time he had seen the whole structure of it in a single sweep, apart from in his early drawings on paper. It spanned two chains in length, forty-four yards, two cricket pitches, one

343

yard for each year of his father's life when Sol was born, and fifteen feet in height, one foot for each year of Jenna's life, for whom, Sol had come to realise, he was creating this mural, as much as he was for himself, for his parents, for Nadia, for Yasser, and for Rose, whom he never knew. When he had finally arrived home, filthy and bedraggled, from his epic walk along the four canals to Bradford Pit to retrieve the fabled lump of coal, it was Jenna who had asked him to tell her the story, to which he'd replied that maybe he would draw it for her one day. And here it was, sketched out before him now, lit by the moon on this clear winter's night. He carefully covered the entire edifice with the sheets of tarpaulin he had brought with him for the purpose, made sure they were securely fastened, gathered together all his tools, before closing and padlocking the gate that secured the now shut down Dock Number Two.

Over the next eleven weekends he worked solidly, painting from first light until last, every Saturday and every Sunday, until eventually it was finished, all except for one tiny detail, which would have to wait, and the thought of it, of when he would add it, made him smile.

He stood back and surveyed it all. It was monumental. Everything he had hoped to include was there within it. All of the wound-up tension he'd been carrying inside him, since he'd first had to leave school when he was just fifteen, since the call-up papers for his National Service had arrived through the door, since Nadia sent him his first sketch pad when he was in Aden, since his first trip out to the desert when he saw the mountains his father had been named after, since the grenade blew away two of his fingers, since he waited outside Turner's for Nadia to finish work on his first day out of the Army, since she told him she was pregnant, since the Police came charging up the stairs to their flat above the fish and chip shop, since he opened the envelope and saw the drawing left to him by his father, with its map of the Manchester waterways, and its thin blue line tracing his route, passing this very spot, since all of those nights in his cell at Walton Gaol, staring up at the orange night sky as the years crawled by and his idea began to form, all of it left him as he stood before his now-completed mural, and he sank to his knees.

George put a hand on his shoulder and nodded with approval. "Aye, lad" he said. "It's finished."

*

On Tuesday 28th March 1978, exactly fifty years to the day since Jaz made his night-time journey by narrow boat from Barton Dock to Bradford Pit to meet King Amanullah of Afghanistan, Sol unveiled his mural to a small gathering of his family and friends. Nadia was there, having taken a day off from work; Jenna, at the start of her Easter holidays from school, fifteen years old and morose; Ishtar, now eighty, dressed in white from head to toe as usual; Farida, Salwa and Jamal. George was there too, standing to one side, smoking his pipe, his camera slung over his shoulder, with his friend Francis, having roared in at the last minute on his classic 1958 Dot Villiers 200cc motor bike – "made right here in Manchester, on Ellesmere Street," as he never tired of telling people – as well as Mr Tunstall and his wife; Eric and Ray; Susan and Brenda.

Once everyone had arrived, George stood on a beer crate and called for attention, then handed over to Sol.

"I'm not going to make a speech," said Sol.

"Good," called out Ray, only to be shushed at once by Brenda and Susan.

"I just thought I'd better show you what it is I've been up to all this time, and to thank you all for putting up with me while I squirreled myself away in the evenings and weekends these past few months."

"Years, more like," laughed George.

"For ever," added Jenna, rolling her eyes.

"But most of all, I want to thank *you*, Nadia, for believing in me, for encouraging me, for giving me a good talking to when I've needed it, and for loving me. Thank you," at which point Jenna stuck two fingers down her throat.

"I also want to dedicate this mural to my mother, for more than anyone's, this is *her* story."

He pulled on a piece of rope and the tarpaulins fell away to reveal the entire mural. Everyone applauded, gasping with delight and amazement. The day was cold and crisp. The sky was cloudless and a brilliant, clear blue. The sun shone down directly, illuminating the colours in a fierce brightness, and everyone surged forward, keen to examine every detail, exclaiming over each new discovery.

"Oh look," they said, and "See," they pointed. "Do you recognise this?" they wondered. "And that?" they asked. "And isn't this…?"

Ishtar clung to Nadia with such pride and joy. "He's done it," she said, her eyes shining. "He's captured it all. Every last detail."

Nadia linked her arm through hers and led her gently towards the centre of the mural. "Isn't that you, standing at the top of the colliery steps, about to go and speak to Hejaz for the very first time?"

Ishtar brought her eyes right up to the painting. "Was I really so certain he would turn round when I called?"

Nadia laughed warmly. "I'm so glad that he did."

Only Jenna hung back. Sol went up to her and led her towards the bottom right-hand corner, where a small child was offering something to a figure representing Sol, carrying a rucksack on his back, stepping out of a front door, onto a quiet street, with a distant view of the Barton Aqueduct.

"Do you recognise this?" he asked her.

She nodded. "There's something missing."

"I know," he said. "I lost it, remember?"

Despite herself, Jenna smiled.

"But I think I've found it now."

"What do you mean?"

"Here." And he handed her a small paint brush. "Fill it in for me."

Jenna's face broke into the broadest of grins. "Really?"

"Really."

Jenna frowned in concentration, and, with the brush her father had handed to her, painted in the missing black umbrella.

9

1981

It was a time of rejoicing, a time of lamenting. A time for celebration, a time for sorrow. It was a time for special birthdays and a time for dying.

As the years pass Salwa and Jamal settle into a comfortable routine. Having fully retired a year ago from the Steel Works in Irlam, Jamal spends his mornings in the Arab Workers' Union, whose headquarters had moved to Eccles, stops by at Abdul's for tea and conversation, before returning home for a late lunch, which Salwa prepares the night before, so that she can spend more time with the other ladies, who take it in turns to host coffee mornings, where they can exchange gossip and catch up on local news. This late lunch is their main meal of the day, and afterwards, especially when the evenings stay lighter for longer, she may drop in on Farida, or arrange to meet Nadia with Jenna in the park, or help with any of the other children Farida is looking after.

On this particular afternoon, a breeze blows off the Canal, making it feel rather cold for June, and so Salwa turns on their newly-acquired gas-fire in the front room, where Jamal goes to sit with his newspaper, while she prepares a final coffee. She finds that she is singing as she does so, an old Egyptian pop song that was a favourite of theirs when they first met, on The Esplanade Road back in Aden, when, even though their families had arranged their marriage, they would meet anyway, daringly unchaperoned, having each pretended to their respective parents they were somewhere else, until they were spotted one afternoon, so that they were then forbidden from seeing each other until the actual wedding, when this particular song by Leila Mourad, *Ana Albee Daleelee*, was all the rage.

"My heart is my guide
It told me that I'd fall in love
It always speaks to me
And I believe my heart..."

She carries the coffee through and shakes her head, smiling, Jamal asleep in the armchair. She puts the cup down beside him and gently pats his shoulder to wake him.

It takes her no time at all to realise that something is wrong. His face and brow are cold despite the gas-fire and she sees no reassuring rise and fall in his chest. He is no longer breathing. Quietly, calmly, almost as if she is still trying not to wake him, she creeps out of the room, walks to where their ivory-coloured telephone sits on a small purpose-bought table in the hallway, and calls Mr al-Haideri, speaking to him in a low voice, so quietly that he has to ask her to repeat what she is saying several times. He arrives just a few minutes later, goes straight to where Jamal is still sitting in the armchair, places two fingers gently against his neck, and, on finding no pulse, turns back towards Salwa, and bows his head.

"He is with God now. Your husband is sleeping with the angels."

*

Jenna turns eighteen.

Her bedroom wall is covered with posters of The Buzzcocks, whose music she plays loud and often. When the band splits during that year, she declares she will from now onwards only be wearing black, and she is as good as her word. Black lipstick, black eye-shadow, black fingernails, as well as her customary ripped black jeans, black T-shirt, and short, spiky black hair. The lyrics to their song *I Believe*, from which she frequently quotes, she has written out in black felt-tip pen and stuck to the outside of her bedroom door.

STOP. GO. WAIT HERE. GO THERE. COME IN. STAY OUT. BE A MAN. BE A WOMAN. BE WHITE. BE BLACK. LIVE. DIE. YES. NO. DO IT NOW. DO IT LATER. BE YOUR REAL SELF. BE SOMEBODY ELSE. FIGHT. SUBMIT. RIGHT. WRONG. MAKE A SPLENDID IMPRESSION. MAKE AN AWFUL IMPRESSION. SIT DOWN. STAND UP. TAKE YOUR HAT OFF. PUT YOUR HAT ON. CREATE. DESTROY. REACT. IGNORE. LIVE NOW. LIVE IN THE PAST. LIVE IN THE FUTURE. BE AMBITIOUS. BE MODEST. ACCEPT. REJECT. DO MORE. DO LESS. PLAN AHEAD. BE SPONTANEOUS. DECIDE FOR YOURSELF. LISTEN TO OTHERS. TALK. BE SILENT. SAVE MONEY. SPEND MONEY. SPEED UP. SLOW DOWN. THIS WAY. THAT WAY. RIGHT. LEFT. PRESENT. ABSENT. OPEN. CLOSED. UP. DOWN. ENTER. EXIT. IN. OUT.

She carries around with her a much-read, well-thumbed and underlined copy of *The Naked Lunch* by William S. Burroughs wherever she goes. When Nadia picks it up one time from the floor where Jenna drops it, she quickly snaps it shut, blushing, although Ishtar has read it all, and she and Jenna have on occasions energetically discussed some of its vignettes, or 'routines', as Burroughs calls them, to be read in any order, a notion Jenna really responds to, excited by the chance possibilities thrown up by such random collisions. Sol generally steers a wide berth around her, while Nadia finds herself frequently stopping to wonder at this cuckoo in the nest – when she and Jenna are not yelling at each other, that is.

Jenna is to be found at Farida's as often as she is at home, around whom she behaves with meek obedience. She loves helping out at *Busy Bees*, with the toddlers in the playgroup, who in return adore her unreservedly. She's developed this thing that, whenever she's there, everyone has to run around the space, buzzing loudly like bees, even the paid staff and students. One time, when Farida is about to re-decorate the main play-room, Jenna persuades her to ask all the parents to make sure that the children come the next day in their oldest clothes, ones that don't matter, and she spends a wild morning urging them all to hurl paint at the floors, ceilings and walls. The children cannot believe their luck and have the best time ever, their parents arriving to collect them at lunch time being greeted by a tribe of screaming, charging, whooping and hollering war-painted warriors.

When she stays out all night at parties, it's to Farida's,

as like as not, she'll roll up around lunch time the next day, who will make her shower off the smells of drugs and alcohol, before cooking her an enormous breakfast, then packing her off back home. "Don't worry about her," she tells her sister. "It's just a phase."

And when she gets 'A's in all her exams in the summer, and her place at Manchester is confirmed, Nadia can see that Farida has been right all along. Jenna will be the first person in all of their families to go to university. Sol, especially, is deeply proud.

*

Salford Advertiser

29th December 1981

LOCAL LEGEND DIES AS SHE LIVED

It is with great sadness that we report, in this, our first edition since the incorporation of the former much-loved *Salford City Reporter*, the passing of another much-loved local legend.

Last week, in a freak accident on Liverpool Road, Mrs Esther Ward, universally known as "Ishtar", was knocked off her bicycle by an oncoming florist's delivery van, while she was swerving to avoid a small child who had unexpectedly run in front of her.

Mrs Ward, who had celebrated her 85th birthday just six months before, was a well-loved and familiar sight, frequently to be seen

352

cycling the highways and byways of Eccles, Patricroft, Barton, Peel Green, Monton and Winton, in all weathers, clad in her distinctive all-white garb, including a long veil upon her head, as she rode to help those in need, whatever their background or circumstances.

Reverend A.E. Walker of Christ Church, Patricroft, described her as an "Angel of Mercy", while Mr al-Haideri, founder of Salford's first mosque and a long-time family friend, recalled her courage and compassion. She was warmly welcomed into the Yemeni community here in Eccles, which she so fully embraced after her marriage to one of its most well-respected members, Mr Hejaz Wahid, more than fifty years ago.

Mrs Ward, born Esther Blundell, the second of six children, grew up in Gorton in East Manchester, where she was an active member of the Suffragist Movement. After her brothers left, either to war or to get married, Esther stayed at home to look after her ailing father, whom she nursed uncomplainingly for several years, before finding work as a Canteen Supervisor at Bradford Colliery. It was there, shortly after the famous visit by King Amanullah of Afghanistan, that she met the man who was to become her husband and moved to Patricroft to be near his family.

During World War II Ishtar, as she then became known, volunteered as an ARP Warden, where she was widely praised for her quiet heroism, frequently risking her own life, cycling through unlit streets at the height of an air-raid, to come to the aid of someone who had lost their home or their loved ones. She continued her charitable work after the War was over and became a pillar of both the Christian and Muslim communities, helping anyone in need, while raising countless hundreds of pounds for a variety of worthy causes.

She was just returning from a local Bring & Buy Sale she had been supporting at the Holy Cross Community Centre in order to help raise much-needed funds for the *Busy Bees* playgroup that meets there every morning, when the accident occurred. Mrs Linda Billings, 23, of Peel Green, mother of the toddler who ran out into the road, told the *Advertiser* she "was devastated" by what had happened. "One minute he had hold of my hand, the next he was off. If Mrs Ward hadn't swerved as she did, my little boy would have been knocked flying."

Mr Alan Rees, 32, from nearby Urmston, the driver of the florist's van, was distraught. "She just appeared in front of me, suddenly, out of nowhere. I slammed on the brakes, but I couldn't stop in time."

Afterwards, traffic came to a standstill as ambulancemen tried to revive her, but were unable to do so. Lying surrounded by a sea of tulip flowers that had spilled from the delivery van, Mrs Ward died of the injuries she had sustained.

She leaves behind a son, Sol, 41, a draughtsman on Trafford Park, and a granddaughter, Jenna, 19, a student at Manchester University.

354

Burial will take place next week at Peel Green Cemetery, where she will be laid to rest next to her husband and father-in-law.

"Certainly those determining acts of her life were not ideally beautiful. They were the mixed result of a young and noble impulse struggling amidst the conditions of an imperfect social state, in which great feelings will often take the aspect of error, and great faith the aspect of illusion. For there is no creature whose inward being is so strong that it is not greatly determined by what lies outside it... Her full nature spent itself in channels which had no great name on earth. But the effect of her being on those around her was incalculably diffusive: for the growing good of the world is partly dependent on unhistoric acts; and that things are not so ill as they might have been, is half owing to the number who lived faithfully a hidden life, and rest in unvisited tombs."

George Eliot: Middlemarch

*

In early December, just three weeks before Ishtar's accident, Nadia turns forty.

After the usual jokes – life begins and all that, a delightedly pleased-with-herself Jenna handing her an elaborately wrapped bottle of *Philosan* – Nadia contemplates her life and where she is now with quiet disbelief, but also with immense satisfaction. At work she is Head of her team, overseeing Adult Literacy programmes across the whole of Manchester now, frequently having to travel to centres across the region, to set up new courses, recruit new staff, write reports for the Council. Sol has been as good as his word since he came out of Walton, quietly keeping his head down at Turner's, where he'd transferred after his training at British Westinghouse was complete, slowly working his way up to more challenging briefs, rarely complaining, regularly attending his Art classes at The Institute, now incorporated into Salford University's extra-mural department, George a family friend as much as a tutor. His relationship with his mother is repaired, and the four of them jog along quite comfortably in the old house on Stanley Road.

Ishtar is not as sprightly as she was, although she still goes out on her bicycle to the Community Hall most days, even now, when, earlier this year, having turned eighty five, they hung a huge banner the length of the hall to announce the fact, and a large party was held in her honour, with more than a hundred people present, including Nadia's parents, both smiling, her father singing as the evening wore on, almost the last time she saw him before he died.

They are having a quiet family party only to celebrate Nadia's 40th. Her mother will join them after Sol has come home from work. Jenna is back for the Christmas vacation, after the first term of her second year at university, where she is studying Politics and International Relations, no surprises there, and living in a bed-sit in Moss Side, even though she could just as easily live at home. Ishtar is polishing the lump of coal that Sol brought back from Bradford Colliery, returning it to the mantelpiece above the fireplace in the front room, where it still holds pride of place, beneath the drawing of the Hejaz Mountains he had sent from Aden for his grandfather. After they have eaten a meal cooked especially by her mother, after Jenna and Farida have turned out the lights and carried in a cake they baked together, slowly and ceremonially, giggling as they try to make sure none of the forty lit candles is extinguished before Nadia, whose eyes have been closed to make a wish, takes a deep breath and blows them all out, and after everyone has gone, Jenna and Ishtar upstairs to their respective bedrooms, Salwa back to her quiet, empty house, driven there by Farida, so that now only she and Sol are left downstairs, Sol goes quietly towards the record player in the corner, requests Nadia not to look, while he takes a record from the rack he has inserted while Nadia wasn't looking, removes its sleeve, places it on the turntable, then turns back towards her as it begins to play.

"Remember this?" he says.

And out of the silence Nadia hears again, for the first time in over twenty years, the crackling sound of Johnny Ray:

"Look homeward, Angel
Tell me what you see
Do the folks I used to know
Remember me…?"

Sol holds her close to him and they begin to dance. "What did you wish for?" he whispers into her ear.

Nadia smiles. "This," she says, and kisses him.

10

2016-18

Molly is wiping glasses behind the bar of *The King's Arms*, a pub where she works several nights each week, on Bloom Street in Salford. It's handy and flexible. It fitted in well when she was a student, and now that she's just finished, it suits her while she works out what to do next. She is about to finish her shift and has told Paul, her boss, that she is meeting someone there afterwards.

"And you're telling me this why?" he asks.

"Just in case he turns out to be a weirdo."

"First date then?"

"I'm not calling it a date."

"Fair enough. I'll be here till we close."

"Thanks."

She scans the room seeing if she can spot anyone who looks as though he might be waiting for someone, when a rather tall young man in a jacket and tie walks in and nervously approaches the bar.

"I am looking for Molly. I understand she works here."

Paul points in Molly's direction, who waves the fingers of her left hand towards the tall young man, gesturing with her right the table she is leaning against.

"You must be Michael?"

"Yes. Michael Chidi Promise Adebayo." He hands her a card.

"Wow."

"And you must be…?"

"Molly. Just Molly. Would you like a drink?"

"Thank you. Yes. Water please. But let me."

"It's OK. I can get discount. One of the perks of working here. Paul? An iced water please, and a Villa Maria for me." She sits at the table opposite Michael, who is removing clips from his trousers. "You came by bike then?"

"Yes. Straight from my last lecture."

"Risking life and limb with the rush hour traffic."

"It wasn't too bad."

They pause while Paul brings their drinks across. He gives Molly a thumbs-up behind Michael's back. She looks away and back towards Michael. "Cheers."

"Thank you."

"So?"

"So."

"Michael Chidi Promise?"

"Yes."

"Which one do you prefer?"

He frowns, as if not understanding the question.

"Of your three names?"

"Oh. Well, Michael is the name I am known by, Chidi is my Yoruba name, and Promise is… something my mother wanted."

"And have you?"

"What?"

"Lived up to it?"

"I hope to. Soon."

"Good answer."

"If I work hard."

"And do you?"

"Oh yes. Always."

"You're certainly persistent." He shakes his head. Molly elaborates further. "All those texts."

"Ah. Yes. When I say I'll do a thing, I do it."

"How did you get my number?"

"You gave it to me."

Now it is Molly's turn to frown and shake her head.

"What I mean is that I picked it up. From your show, your final year exhibition."

"You saw it?"

"Yes. I love art. Back home my mother designs fabrics and prints them."

"But you don't study it?"

"Oh no. I have no talent. Just an appreciative eye. I teach."

"What?"

"History."

"Really?"

"You're surprised?"

"I suppose I am. I thought Science. Perhaps Engineering. I'm sorry."

"Please don't be. They are what most students from my country come over here to learn. My own father would have been much happier if I had done so too."

"So why History?"

Michael pauses, then leans forward, smiling broadly. "Because… because History is at the back of things. It tells us what happened, and why. Like a story. Except that it's true. It really happened. First this, then that, and then, because of that, this. And then it repeats itself. I love that about it, how we can learn from the past. It explains why things are the way they are, who we are, and how we got here."

"And where we might go next?"

"Exactly."

They are quiet for a moment. Molly sips her drink. Michael waits until she puts her glass down.

"That is why I texted you, why I wanted to see you. I went to the exhibition like I said, and when I saw your work, it... well, it stopped me in my tracks."

Molly's eyes widen.

"You seemed to be painting what I am trying to understand in my doctorate."

"How? Was it a particular piece?"

"Not one. All of them. All of those birds. Flying across empty skies. Sometimes alone, sometimes in thousands. Where were they going? Where had they come from? Who were they?"

Molly nods eagerly. "I've always drawn them. From when I was little. My mother's called Jenna, which means 'a bird in flight'. My grandfather used to say that even as a baby I was fascinated by them, even the scraggy little sparrows in the park he used to take me to, squabbling in the holly bushes. Sometimes, when I was a bit older, just as it was getting dark, we'd catch a bus to the city centre to watch the starlings roosting on the buildings. I loved the way they wheeled about the sky, thousands and thousands of them, all in a great flock, and the sudden way they'd all change direction at once, in a heart beat, as if one of them had given a signal, but you could never tell which one, and all that noise... It was thrilling, and then, before you knew it, they all dived down onto the rooftops and ledges, and clock towers and chimney pots, and it was suddenly silent, as if none of it had happened at all." She picks up her glass again and finishes it. "Sorry. I get carried away sometimes."

"Please don't apologise. I love hearing you talk about it. Would you like another drink?"

"Yes please."

"Same again?"

Molly nods as Michael gets up and goes back towards the bar, where Paul catches Molly's eye and winks. She tuts and shakes her head, and looks away until Michael returns.

"Thanks."

"You mentioned your grandfather before."

"Yes."

"He sounds a very special person."

"He was."

"Was?"

"He died. Earlier this year."

"Oh. I am very sorry for your loss."

"Thank you. Actually, I think that's what set me off." Michael inclines his head, unsure of what she means. "Well, let me think. Where shall I start…?

Michael leans back in his chair and spreads his hands. "Wherever you like. Take your time. We're not in a hurry, are we? Unless, perhaps, you have somewhere else you need to be?"

Molly smiles. "No. I don't."

"Okay then. Whenever you're ready"

Molly takes another sip and looks down, as if

calculating just how much she is prepared to say at this stage to someone she has only just met, but who, somehow, seems to invite confidence.

"My grandfather was an artist," she begins. "An amateur one, but exceptionally good. And that's not just me being biased. Lots of people think so. But he had a difficult time growing up. He was one of the last batch to be called up for National Service and he was posted to Aden, which is kind of ironic really, because we're from Yemen. Originally, I mean. While he was out there, he started making sketches, and he sent these back home. I've got some of them, they're incredible, the way he looked at things, not obvious, you know, but somehow he got right to the heart of things – faces, wild life, mountains, people. He was especially good at capturing those moments when you're just waiting, you know, caught in between things. A bit like *he* was, I suppose…" She looks down before continuing. "He'd always wanted to pursue his Art, but he had to leave school early to help out at home, where money was tight, so when he came back to England, out of the army, he got a series of dead-end jobs that he hated, and ended up getting into some kind of trouble. Anyway, to cut a long story short he went to prison – what he did doesn't matter, but although it wasn't a terrible thing, it *was* against the law. His wife, my grandma, stood by him. She was amazing – still is actually – and while he was inside she encouraged him to keep drawing and take it up properly again when he came out. Which he did." She takes another sip from her Villa Maria. "By day he was a draughtsman, a good one, though not as good as his own father was, he'd say, and smile." Molly, too, smiles, remembering, and then turns back towards Michael. "Before I was born, when my mum was about five, I think, he made this special journey, a long walk, like a kind of pilgrimage, to the place where his parents, my great grandparents, had first met, but there was more to it than that, something about a King of Afghanistan and a piece of coal. I didn't pay it much attention when I was growing up. My dad wasn't around much, and my mum had to go out to work all the time, which meant that I was brought up by my grandparents as much as I was by her. More than, really. My grandma still worked too at first, and so it was my granddad who was around most of the time. He'd been made redundant when the place he worked at went into administration, and, because he was reasonably close to retirement age, they'd offered him a package, so he took it. I'm sorry – this is too much information."

"No. Not at all. Please carry on."

Molly shrugs, as though to say, "if you're sure", and, encouraged by Michael's smile, continues. "We had great times together. He'd take me with him everywhere, and then later pick me up from school. And always, always, he'd draw for me." She smiles at the memory. "Then, a few years back, he got ill. He started coughing a lot. My grandma blamed it on the asbestos where he'd been working. She was really bitter about it because nothing could be proved, but she was sure of it. She'd worked there once too, as a girl, when the two of them had first met, and *he* had warned *her* about the asbestos back then, but she'd just laughed about it. When he got really ill, she blamed herself terribly, because it was she who'd got him the job in the first place, you see, while he was still inside, but he used to tell her not to be so daft, and ask her to fetch him some more paper and pencils, and she'd sit by his side, while he drew sketch after sketch of her…"

She pauses and Michael waits expectantly. She says nothing for a long while, as if what she is about to say next is what she's been building up to all this time, but that now she has reached it, she is suddenly unsure whether she can carry on.

Michael tentatively breaks the silence. "Yes?"

Molly rouses herself. "Just before he died, he asked me to take down the piece of coal that occupied pride of place in the downstairs front room and bring it up to him. He gripped my wrist tightly and told me that it wasn't really the piece of coal hewn by King Amanullah. I said I'd never thought it was, that that was just a story, but he pulled me closer to him, it was really important, he said, that I understood him. 'I want you to take it back,' he said. 'I stole it. I thought it was my birthright somehow, my story, but it was so many other people's too. I tried to tell them with my mural, I did my best, I really did, but it's all gone now, broken up and smashed to bits, like a jigsaw you can't put back together, because you haven't got the picture any more to guide you. Draw a new picture, Molly…' he said, and then…"

Her voice has become quite shaky, and she pauses once more, while she tries to regain her composure. "Nadia came in – that's my grandmother – and told him he needed to rest now, and that he wasn't to bother me with all that kind of talk – I think she must have heard some of what he'd been saying – that it was up to me what I did, and I wasn't to trouble myself with what couldn't be helped, with what was past…"

She looks hard at Michael, who holds her gaze.

"But it isn't all past, is it?" she says. "It's everywhere. Like those starlings he took me to see, all those millions of voices, all shrieking at once, all clamouring to be heard, then before you can pick out a single one, they've dropped out of sight, silent in the darkness."

She is trembling, on the edge of tears. Michael passes her a handkerchief.

"Here. Take this."

She considers it a moment, smiles thinly, then blows her nose and dries her eyes. "Thank you."

"And that's why you draw birds?" asks Michael.

Molly shrugs. "I wish he'd seen them. But he died before my finals. Nadia came, though. She didn't say much. She just looked at them a long time, then tapped me lightly on the shoulder. 'Yes,' she said, that's all. 'Yes.' But it was enough."

She blows her nose once more and regards him with an amused smile. Michael shakes his head. "What?"

"You are a most surprising man. I can't remember the last time I ever *saw* a handkerchief, let alone used one. I'll wash it, then give it you back next time."

"I like the sound of that," says Michael.

"What? That I'm going to wash your handkerchief?"

"The thought of a next time."

They pause a long time, each trying to read the other's expression. Molly is the first to speak. "Wait here."

She stands up and walks behind the bar, from where she comes back with a splintered piece of wood, on which

366

some pale flakes of old paint can just be made out.

"After my grandfather died, after my show, I started looking up all the different things he'd said. I went to museums and libraries. I went to Salford Quays and out on to Pomona Island, which still hasn't been developed. It's quite a sanctuary. You wouldn't believe you were just a few minutes walk away from the centre of town. Butterflies, bees, flowers. Everywhere overgrown and tangled. And I found this."

She holds up the piece of wood.

"I can't be certain, but I'm pretty sure this is from the mural he was talking about." She hands it across to Michael, who holds it with great reverence. "If you look really close," she continues, "you can just make out the outline of a child handing an umbrella to a man. I showed it my mum, and she went very quiet – which if you met my mum, you'd realise was something she never did – and she said, '*I* painted that. Your granddad left that bit for me to complete.' And now I have it. It's possibly the only bit of the mural left. And I'm not sure what I'm meant to do with it…" She exhales deeply.

Michael nods, handing the piece of wood back across the table to Molly. "I'm in the final year of my PhD," he says, "and I teach some first year courses to help fund it. Before I begin each class, I ask the students: 'What's your story?' I look out at this sea of eager faces, from all parts of the globe, and I ask them: 'How did you get here? *Here*?' I say. 'This room.' Someone usually jokes and says 'by bus', or 'bike', and we all laugh, but then I say, 'No. Not just this morning. This century. What are all the different forces that have brought each and every one of

367

us to be sharing this exact same moment? Me from Nigeria, and you from… where?' 'Japan,' someone shouts. 'Spain'. 'Poland'. 'Lithuania'. 'Libya'. 'Somalia'. 'Sheffield', 'Leicester', Leeds', 'York'. 'Mumbai'. 'Hong Kong'. 'Sydney'. 'Saigon'."

Molly grins and puts up her hand. "Eccles."

"Eccles?"

"By way of the Yemen and St Kitts."

"St Kitts?"

"My dad."

"And Nevis?"

"Most definitely."

"A citizen of the world."

"I suppose. I don't know him. My father. Never have. Don't know where he is."

"I'm sorry."

"Don't be. There's no need. I've been raised by two incredibly strong women."

"And your grandfather?"

"Yes. My mother never really let him in when she was growing up, kept him at arm's length. I think he saw me as an unexpected second chance – to redeem himself, I suppose."

"And did he?"

"Oh yes." She looks away for a moment, down towards the piece of wood that leans against the side of her chair. "I'm sorry," she says. "I interrupted you. Please carry on."

Michael waits a moment, allowing her to regain her composure, then says, "If you're sure? It's something of a hobby-horse of mine. You must stop me when you've heard enough."

"Don't worry. I will."

They laugh.

"Well," he says finally, "after we've established where we're all of us from, I say…"

"What? What do you answer them, your students?"

"History," he says, almost triumphantly. "History brings us together. History breaks us apart. It explains us."

"That sounds like none of us have any control over what happens to us. I'm not sure I like that idea."

"But we do. We all of us have our individual stories, and together these stories make history."

Molly says nothing for a while, thinking. After a while, she speaks. "Doesn't that depend on who's doing the telling? Our stories get appropriated, they become part of someone else's agenda, until they all get mixed up, and we can't tell what's authentic any more, it all becomes like fashion. You try on different clothes for a while, see if they fit."

Michael shakes his head. "That's the job of the historian, to pan the water for gold, looking for the real nuggets, throwing out the pyrites."

"Pyrites?"

"Fool's gold."

"That sounds like one of your lecture notes."

"It is. Sorry."

"But who decides? Who decides what we should keep and what we should throw away?"

"Time. It all becomes clearer over time."

"I don't think I can wait that long."

Another pause.

"So what are you going to do?"

"I don't know yet. I only know that I've been given *this...*" She holds up the piece of wood. "... And that my granddad asked me to return a lump of coal to a place that no longer exists. It just feels like it's my turn now, to make the next mark. But I haven't a clue what it should be."

"It'll come to you. Like those starlings. Suddenly. You'll know."

"I hope so."

"In the meantime, I have a proposition to put to you."

"Oh yes? Should I be worried?"

"It's why I wanted to meet you."

"Really? I'm intrigued."

"Now you're teasing me."

"Only a little."

Michael waits a beat, then asks, "Do you have an agent?"

Molly almost chokes in surprise. "What?"

"I know I'm not an artist, but I do know about fund-raising. How do you think I manage to stay on here year after year? What I'm suggesting is that I could be your agent, your producer. While you research your idea, get ready for it artistically, I will seek out galleries, curators, funders, promoters. I'll talk to the Arts Council, festival organisers, get your name known, introduce you to people who might want to support you, sponsor you, buy your paintings..."

"Whoa! Slow down. I've only just graduated."

"I knew as soon as I saw your drawings. They haunted

me." He searches for the right phrase to say next. "They took flight, and my feet haven't touched the ground since."

Molly looks down and picks at her fingers.

"Well…?"

"I'm thinking…"

"What?"

"That I'm glad I answered your text." She smiles.

"Do I take that as a 'yes' then?"

Molly nods. "Maybe."

Michael smiles. "Can I see you again?"

"Maybe."

"Tomorrow?"

"Tomorrow?!"

"Yes."

"Maybe."

"How will I know?"

"I'll text you."

"Will you?"

"Maybe."

He stands, puts his cycle clips back on. She remains sitting, watching and smiling.

"I'll be off then," he says.

"Right."

"Right."

He turns to go.

"Michael?"

"Yes?"

"I like your tie."

He beams. He walks out of the pub into the night, which has now grown dark. As he cycles back across town towards Rusholme, towards the house he shares with five others, he cannot stop smiling. As the wheels keep turning and the miles unfold before him, he has the distinct feeling that a ball of cotton is steadily being unwound, which marks the route he must travel, tighter and tighter, unstoppably reeling him in.

*

The Registrar smiled at them both warmly and said, "Repeat after me."

They looked at each other shyly.

"I do solemnly declare…"

"I do solemnly declare…"

"… that I know not of any lawful impediment…"

"… that I know not of any lawful impediment…"

"… why I, Molly…"

"… why I, Molly…"

"… may not be joined in matrimony…"

"… may not be joined in matrimony…"

"… to Michael Chidi Promise Adebayo."

"… to Michael Chidi Promise Adebayo."

*

 Michael Adebayo added <u>8 new photos</u>.

26 September 2017·

Molly and I would like to introduce you to our newest addition, Blessing Dawn Wahid Adebayo, born yesterday at 06:18 weighing 8lbs 3oz at home as planned. We are over the moon

372

and Blessing is already living up to her name. Molly never fails to amaze me! 💕💕💜💜

*

Michael was as good as his word. Over endless cups of tea they mapped out a vision. He encouraged Molly to try to put all of her dreams into words and ideas, and from these he pulled together a Business Plan, which he then showed to various gallery owners, art centres, cafés and bars that were interested in attracting a younger crowd, people who liked independent music, foreign films, artisan food, and convinced some of them that Molly's work was exactly what they needed to reflect their image on their walls. She was gradually becoming known, sought after even. *@madebymolly* was receiving daily hits on Facebook, Twitter and Instagram.

He met key people at the Arts Council, who encouraged Molly to apply for funding, so long as she could demonstrate that her ideas had a strong element of public engagement. "Apply," he urged, but Molly favoured caution. "Let's wait," she said, "till the right idea presents itself." She walked across to the book shelves they'd put together with bricks and planks of wood, where the lump of coal given to her by Sol sat wedged between Howard Zinn and Rebecca Solnit.

*

Radio Announcer:

This is MCR Live, coming to you from the heart of Manchester, on digital, on line or via your mobile. To find out what's going on in our city and discover the best in music, culture and radio, listen to 'Manchester Conversations', presented by Sophie Sveinsson and produced for MCR Live by Jim Salveson.

SOPHIE:

Good evening, everybody, and welcome to *Manchester Conversations*. 'Untold stories from the city's unheard voices.' You've just been listening to *Time's Been Reckless* by Marika Hackman on *The Afternoon Show* with Charley Perry this Friday between two and four. Thanks, Charley, for a great show. This evening we've a fascinating piece from our Roving Reporter, Chloe Chang, on an exciting new Reminiscence Project being hosted by Manchester City Football Club at The Etihad. What can you tell us, Chloe?

CHLOE:

Well, Sophie, I'm standing on the footbridge leading to the Manchester City Stadium here at Eastlands, but how many of the thousands of fans who cross this bridge every match-day ever stop to wonder about what used to be here, on this very spot, before these state-of-the-art facilities were built? Until fifty years ago this was the site of the world-famous Bradford Colliery, which produced some of the best grade quality coal anywhere in the world, but at too great a cost. Not only was it more expensive to mine it here than at most other working pits, there were also problems with subsidence, with several houses in the area threatening to collapse, and so, back in September 1968, the National Coal Board, as it was then, decided to close it. Today, descendants of people who once worked there are campaigning to have a permanent memorial erected, so that all those thousands of football supporters who cross this bridge will be reminded of the land's history and heritage. A leading figure in that campaign is recent Manchester Metropolitan University Design graduate, Lauren Murphy, and she's standing here with me now.

At this point, Molly, preparing dinner in her kitchen, who had only been half-listening to this on her radio, pricked up her ears. Lauren Murphy. Molly had known her when she was a student herself at MMU.

LAUREN:

My dad and granddad were both miners at Bradford Pit, and I just wanted to do something that would honour them and the thousands of others like them.

CHLOE:

What sort of thing do you have in mind?

LAUREN:

We're talking to schools, members of the local community, the football club and supporters, to get as wide a range of ideas that we can And we're also contacting artists, as well as students from Manchester Metropolitan University, like I was, to come up with some innovative and creative ideas. Every time we pass this spot, we're walking over the ghosts of Manchester miners, and I think there should be something here to remind us of the sacrifice they made, men like my dad and granddad, in order to keep us all warm in our homes at night.

CHLOE:

I believe that you started this project some years ago, Lauren?

LAUREN:

Yes, Chloe, that's right. For my final degree show I designed some jewellery that featured various small artefacts donated by former mine workers and their families, which could be worn round the neck, with red ribbon signifying courage, or blue ribbon signifying loyalty. We then held an exhibition here at The Etihad, and we're still inviting people to come to us with their stories, their photographs, or any actual objects they may have that are associated with the Pit, which we can keep adding to the archive, until we find a permanent place to house them all.

CHLOE:

And how can people get in touch, Lauren?

LAUREN:

Just visit our website – bradfordpit.com – and go to the Contact page.

CHLOE:

Thank you, Lauren, and now it's back to you, Sophie, in the studio.

SOPHIE:

Thanks, Chloe. Really fascinating stuff. And you can hear the full interview with Lauren by downloading our podcast after this programme has finished. OK, we'll be back again shortly, but right now it's *Changing* by Sigma, featuring Paloma Faith...

Molly switched off the radio and turned the gas down low under the vegetable chilli she was cooking. She sat at the kitchen table and thought.

Blessing was asleep in their bedroom upstairs and Molly could hear the soft snuffles of her breathing on the baby monitor.

She closed her eyes and thought some more.

She thought and she thought.

The light outside began to fade until eventually Molly was sitting in the dark, but she remained exactly where she was, just sitting and thinking, while the chilli cooked itself dry.

A smile began to pass across her lips.

Yes.

She had it.

The whole idea was forming right before her in her imagination.

She could see exactly how it would work, and she couldn't wait to tell Michael when he came home.

Blessing started to wake and at once began to cry, quietly at first, little more than a grizzle, but Molly knew that if she didn't go to her quickly, that grizzle would become a howl, one that would not be silenced, and she ran up the stairs with barely contained excitement.

*

The funding comes through.

Over the next few weeks Molly and Michael mastermind a meticulous social media marketing campaign, sending out a series of cryptic, enigmatic tweets with links to enticing five- or ten-second-only teaser trailers. Molly has, over the past two years, developed a large and growing number of followers. The championing of her by various clubs and bars in Manchester's Northern Quarter has given her a certain cachet, and a buzz has begun to swell, like the spread of the city's adopted icon, the bee, now everywhere on street corners and lamp posts.

Save the date, the tweets urge. *Sunday 1st*, they cry. *This is No April Fool.*

High Noon at Eastlands.

She finds it difficult to say *Etihad*. Home of

Manchester City, the team she has always favoured. The civil war rages on in the country of her ancestors, the Yemen, where she herself has never been. She is not *Houthi*, and she is certainly not *Wahhabi*. This proxy war between Saudi and Iran, with no victors, but tens of millions of losers, starving and desperate in the desert, the lee of the Hejaz Mountains, a famine caused in part, it could be argued, by Sheik Mohammed bin Zayed Al Nahyan's billions, Crown Prince of the Royal House of Abu Dhabi, Saudi's allies in the war, and brother of Sheik Mansoor, owner of the football club, which is to be the Mecca for her installation. Eastlands. *The Etihad*.

She has quarrelled fiercely with her mother, Jenna, over this, who thinks she's selling out by even stepping foot on the bridge towards the stadium, but Molly holds firm. Her mother has always tended to over-simplify, to polarise, to look for conflict, where she, Molly, seeks resolution. Tribal loyalties. The followers of Manchester City stretch back much further than its current owners, to its first beginnings, as a club built on coal and cotton, carried by canals no longer clogged, but confluent and clean. If her art makes people think, if it reminds them of all who've passed this way before them, the countless thousands who marched this way to mine, or mill, or factory, who walk this way still, seeking their fortunes on streets paved not with gold, but blood, if it helps them honour the bones of those still buried underground, and helps others to remember and to heal, then she'll raise her head above the parapet and take what comes.

And so she sends out more tweets, more trailers.

#thinblueline
#whatsmineisours
#underourfeetoverourheads
#whosestory
#cottontales
#coalangel

*

There was one last thing she had to do before the day, and so, the week before, she got Blessing dressed and ready early to walk towards the bus stop by *The Blue Bell* pub, just around the corner from their tiny flat in Harpurhey that Michael had found for them just before they got married. "They're calling this 'Little Lagos' now," he'd grinned, and it was true, for a whole string of Nigerian shops were springing up along Moston Lane, where Molly now waited opposite the pub for the Number 100 bus to Piccadilly Gardens.

It came in a few minutes, already overcrowded, and, after manoeuvring Blessing's push chair into the last remaining space available, she stood, seeing little of the route through the steamed-up windows, so that she almost missed her stop at Shudehill, where she had to wait another ten minutes for the 81 bus for Warrington. This was less busy, and she even managed to find a seat. She wiped a section of the window with her sleeve and looked out.

The route, the same as that taken by Farida more than forty years before, after the Coroner's Inquest had declared Salim's death to have been accidental, when the idea for the *Busy Bees* nursery had first begun to form, was circuitous, taking in Pendlebury, Swinton and Walkden before dropping down past Worsley, skirting Monton and finally into Patricroft itself. It took Molly past mill after mill, or what remained of them, the occasional solitary tall brick chimneys, standing like sentries on duty, with nothing now left to guard. Those that were still standing had been turned into warehouses, or retail outlets, or gyms, or, in some cases, converted into highly desirable apartments, or, where they had been demolished, as so many of them had been, even Engels Mill on Weaste Lane, smashed through by the march of the M602 motorway, their names had been preserved in street names. Like this one, which Molly was passing now, Monton Mill, where modern houses had been built, around a green, each with a small garden of their own, light years away from what the women and girls who'd toiled there when it was still a working mill could ever have dreamed of living in themselves.

Molly could hear her mother's firebrand voice ringing in her ears. Jenna. She'd made the decline of the cotton mills in Manchester and Salford the subject of her thesis at university, not so much as a document of social history, like Lauren was doing around the former Bradford Colliery, but as an unapologetic political rant. As a result she'd been marked down, for "lacking the necessary perspective", a point with which Michael would have no doubt concurred. He and her mother had already crossed swords on more than one occasion, though in ways which both of them seemed to enjoy. But she was still awarded a First nevertheless, and, on graduating, she'd been immediately offered a research job with the local Labour party, had contested and lost two campaigns to be selected as a candidate for Openshaw, and subsequently worked in the Manchester office of the Institute for Public Policy Research, the IPPR, heading up its report *Taking Back Control in the North*, as part of the think tank's *Manifesto for Change*, which she had co-authored, before taking up her current role with the Refugee Council.

Molly wondered now, as she wheeled Blessing's push chair off the bus at Milton Street and began the short walk to her grandmother's house, a house which was so much more familiar to her than any of the various flats Jenna had lived in over the years, just what her mother would make of her installation event coming up in less than a week's time, whether she'd regard the political slant her tweets were taking as being an unmistakable chip off the old block, or whether she'd still think she was taking the softer option. The difference between them, she hoped, was that Molly didn't want to tell her audiences what to think. The thin blue line, she thought again, and smiled. Let people follow it or cross it, make of it what they will.

She reached her grandmother's house on Stanley Road, knocked on the door and began unstrapping Blessing, who was already wriggling in protest and threatening to let the whole street know. Nadia opened the door and beamed.

"Here she is," she said, opening her arms and then taking Blessing from Molly, still juggling the pushchair and her bag, and immediately Blessing's face was wreathed in smiles, as Nadia led them both down the hall and into the sitting room. "Come on in," she said. "I thought we'd go in here, and then Blessing can lie on the carpet."

"You'll be lucky," laughed Molly. "She won't let go of you, you know what she's like, a proper Granny's girl."

"*Great* Granny," corrected Nadia, who then turned her attention back to Blessing, who was gripping her Great-grandmother's finger with no intention of letting go. "I think *you'd* better make the tea," she called back to Molly. "Leave your stuff in the hall. You know where everything is."

After they'd finally settled, and Blessing had drifted peacefully off to sleep against Nadia's shoulder, Molly tentatively asked what had been preoccupying her. "You're sure you don't mind, Nani?"

"Now why on earth would I?"

"It's just that… well, that piece of coal is like a family heirloom."

"Given to you by Sol."

"Yes, but…"

"He wanted you to have it, Molly. He knew you'd find a proper use for it. He always felt it was too important to be just sitting here on a shelf, but he'd made a pledge to his mother to bring it back."

Molly was silent for a while, thinking, wondering how she would say what was in her thoughts. "You do know," she began nervously, "that it's not…" but she found she could not continue.

"What? The actual piece dug up by King Amanullah? Of course I do. We *all* knew. Even Ishtar. And who's to say that the piece Sol's father picked up and handed back

383

to the King all those years ago had actually been hewn by him in the first place? It's all speculation. And it doesn't matter. It's what the coal stood for that counts. For your grandfather it was a promise he'd made as a small boy that he felt he'd failed to keep. It brought him back to himself, and to me. For his mother it was simply a reminder of how she'd found love, when she wasn't looking for it."

"Wow," whispered Molly.

Nadia waved away her free hand. "Take no notice of me," she said. "I talk too much."

"No. You're right, I'm sure."

Blessing began to stir and burrowed into Nadia, nuzzling her.

"Here," she said. "You'd better take her. She's hungry." She lifted Blessing away from her body. "You won't find what you're looking for with me," she laughed, and handed her across to Molly, who sat her on her lap, while she lifted up her T-shirt and settled Blessing on to her breast.

Nadia stood up and patted Molly on the shoulder. "I'll be back in a minute. I'm just going to fetch something."

Molly looked around the room. The drawing Sol had made for Yasser of the Hejaz Mountains still hung above the fireplace and on the opposite wall was the joiner-photograph George had taken of the mural. Molly transferred Blessing on to the other breast. She continued studying the mural for several minutes, until Nadia returned with something wrapped in tissue paper.

"I wish I'd seen it," said Molly. "For real, I mean."

"Yes," said Nadia, pausing to stand in front of the

384

photograph. "It was unforgettable, truly a life's work."

"I've hung that small piece of it that I found, do you remember..?" Nadia nodded. "...on the wall above Blessing's cot."

"Oh." Nadia's face lit up. "What a lovely idea."

Blessing had finished feeding and was gurgling contentedly.

"Here," said Nadia, handing across the tissue paper. "I thought you might like this. Let me take Blessing again so that you can have a proper look at it."

Molly spread it across her knees and carefully opened it up. Inside the tissue paper was a folded piece of white cotton. Molly held it up against the light. It was so thin, so threadbare, she could almost see through it, yet its weft was still tough and strong. Delicately woven through it was a repeating pattern of a moth alighting upon laurel leaves, white on white.

"Is this…?"

"Ishtar's, yes. She had a number of them. One she was buried with. Some I gave to Charity Shops – that's what she would have wanted – and this one, I kept. It was Rose's originally. Given to her by Yasser when they got married. But it's a lot older than that, I think. I washed and ironed it, then put it away. It seems a pity for it not to have a use. Why don't you wear it for your event next weekend?"

Molly's eyes widened. "That would be perfect," she said. "Are you sure?"

"I wouldn't be offering it if I wasn't."

"Thank you." She sprang to her feet and arranged it round her. "Is this how she wore it?" she asked, turning back towards Nadia.

"I can't remember," she said, "and anyway, you should find your own way. It's yours now."

They spent the next hour happily playing with Blessing, until Molly looked at the time and said she had best be getting back.

"How long does it take?" asked Nadia.

"An hour and a half if I don't miss the second bus."

"Listen," she said. "I've been thinking, and I'd completely understand if you said no, but why don't the three of you come and live here?"

Molly's jaw dropped, but before she could say anything, her grandmother was speaking again.

"There's plenty of room. I'm rattling around in it all by myself, and I'm guessing you haven't got anything like enough room in that flat in Harpurhey, which I imagine is costing you the earth in rent, so that you can't save anything, and you probably don't have anywhere to do your own work, whereas here you could, and I'm sure it would be easy for Michael to get to the University, with the Metro Link, and there's a park across the road, and my sister could help with the baby, just till you find your feet and you've enough for a deposit for a place of your own, or... What do you think? You don't have to say anything now. I've rather dropped this on you, haven't I? I didn't know I was going to say any of this myself till just now, and you'll need to talk it all through with Michael, of course, but..."

"Nani, stop." They looked at each other, breathless.

"Well...?

Molly wrapped her *qurqash* around her head, began to

strap a cranky Blessing back into her push chair in the hall, picked up her things, including the white cotton shawl that had belonged to Ishtar, which she placed, wrapped back up again in its tissue, neatly into the pocket at the back of the chair, and turned once more towards Nadia, whose narrow, bird-like shoulders felt strong in Molly's close embrace.

"Thank you," she whispered, as she kissed her papery cheek. "I can't think of anything better."

All the tension left Nadia's body as she watched Molly and Blessing walk away down the street, knowing that they'd soon be coming back, and the last piece of wood from Sol's mural would hang above Blessing's cot here in the house where it had been started. Molly was stooping to point something out to Blessing, whose starfish fingers reached out towards an untrimmed privet hedge by one of the houses on the street. She was mesmerised, endlessly fascinated by every single leaf, scrutinising each one minutely, sniffing, stroking, licking, testing their uniqueness. Molly bent beside her, trying to share in the wonder of seeing something so commonplace as if for the first time once again, savouring the specialness of it. A wind was picking up from the Canal, and Nadia pulled her cardigan tighter round her chest as she continued to watch them, seemingly unperturbed by the sharp bite in the air, completely absorbed, their breath coalescing into statues, until they'd nothing more to show her.

*

Sunday 24 September 2017

To the accompaniment of the opening bars of 'By The Sleepy Lagoon' by Eric Coates, mixed with the sounds of herring gulls and waves from the sea breaking on the shore, Kirsty Young prepares to introduce her latest castaway on 'Desert Island Discs'.

KIRSTY:

My castaway today has been described as "intelligent but challenging" by her school headmistress, "wayward but brilliant" by her university professor, "a menace to society" by a Manchester magistrate, "a powerful voice for change" by the leaders of more than one political party, and "a source of pride and concern" by her mother! She has been a lecturer, a journalist, a member of the influential left-wing think tank, the Institute for Public Policy & Research, advisor to several Cabinet secretaries, Chair of a number of charities and NGOs, and has recently set up the Manchester branch of the NRC, the National Refugee Council, for whom she has written various influential policy briefings. This year she visited the Yemen to report on the growing humanitarian crisis there, with many of her audio diaries featuring on programmes such as *Today*, *PM* and *The World At One*, and for which she received a prestigious 'Woman of the Year' Award. She is – Jenna Ward. Welcome.

JENNA:

Thank you. It's lovely to be here. (*She can be heard chuckling*).

KIRSTY:

Why are you laughing?

JENNA:

I'm thinking about those words my mother used to describe me.

KIRSTY:

"A source of pride and concern"?

JENNA: (*laughing*):

Yes. There was quite a lot of concern, I seem to remember.

KIRSTY:

Indeed. I've read, Jenna Ward, that when you were younger you were quite a naughty girl?

JENNA:

Oh yes. I still am, I hope.

KIRSTY:

Let's have your first piece of music.

JENNA:

I Believe by The Buzzcocks. This was my creed when I was a teenager. I pinned the lyrics onto the outside of my bedroom door at home, and once, at school, I sneaked into the Reprographics Room and made hundreds of photocopies of them. I then climbed up onto the school roof and proceeded to shower them over all of the teachers when they arrived the next morning.

KIRSTY:

So a punk and a rebel?

JENNA:

They're one and the same, aren't they?

An extract of the song is played.

KIRSTY:

That was *I Believe* by The Buzzcocks, and while it was playing my castaway, Jenna Ward, was jumping all around the studio. You don't believe in doing things by halves then?

JENNA:

Never have. Never will. What's the point? If you believe in something, why pretend you don't? I believe in passion, and I love it when I see it expressed. By anyone.

KIRSTY:

Even if you don't agree with them?

JENNA:

Sure. So long as I can be just as passionate back.

KIRSTY:

This propensity for being passionate about what you feel, what you believe in, has at times, though, got you into trouble, has it not?

JENNA:

Many times. At school, university…

KIRSTY:

… and the police?

JENNA:

Oh yes.

KIRSTY:

Haven't there been times when you've wished you'd bitten your tongue?

JENNA:

Sometimes. I said some pretty harsh things to my parents which I wish I hadn't.

KIRSTY:

Let's talk about them, shall we? You're an only child. Did you mind that?

JENNA:

No I didn't. I was quite a handful. I don't think there'd

have been much room for anyone else.

KIRSTY:

You were born in 1963, near Eccles, on the edge of Salford, close to the Manchester Ship Canal, and your parents, Nadia and Sol, were from Yemen, I understand?

JENNA:

Not exactly. Both my mum's parents were, while my dad was a quarter Yemeni. But they were born in Eccles and saw themselves as British. Proud Mancunians, both! My mum's parents were quite strict, very much part of the wider close-knit Yemeni community that came to work in Trafford Park between the Wars, but they only ever wanted what was best for their children, both daughters, and so when my mum got her first job, as a typist, they were delighted.

KIRSTY:

You sound very proud of her?

JENNA:

Yeah. She's amazing. Until she retired she set up Adult Literacy programmes right across the North-West. She's been a big influence on me, the choices I've made. I've been very lucky to have grown up with such remarkable strong women as role models.

KIRSTY:

Let's have disc number two.

JENNA:

My mum's sister, Farida, adores Egyptian pop songs. She'd play them on her record player in the front room of her house on those afternoons she'd pick me up from school while my mum was at work, and she'd paint henna on my hands and give me bits of material to drape around me, and I'd dance to songs like this, which my Aunt would sing along to while she cooked my tea.

This second selection is now heard.

KIRSTY:

That was *Alba al Dalili* from the album *Aini Batref* sung by Leila Mourad, with visions of my castaway, Jenna Ward, dancing like an Arabian princess. A far cry from the punk rebel we met earlier?

JENNA:

Oh, I don't know – Leila Mourad was a bit of a pioneer too, championing women's rights in a very male-dominated world.

KIRSTY:

You've spoken briefly already, Jenna, about your mother and your aunt, but I believe your grandmother was another strong influence in your life?

JENNA:

Ishtar, yes.

KIRSTY:

Tell us a little about her if you can.

JENNA:

She was incredibly clear about who she was and why she did what she did, which was far from conventional. She grew up during the early part of the 20th century, the only girl among six children. She was just thirteen when her mother died, and so she had to look after five brothers, all miners, and her father, throughout her teenage years and into her twenties, until two of them were killed in the 1st War and the rest all left to get married or, in her father's case, died. After the War there was a surfeit of young single women, and I think she had settled for a life as a spinster, until events took a different and surprising turn. What really impressed me is the way she always grasped the nettle, seized the moment, never allowed herself to just drift. She took life by the scruff of the neck.

KIRSTY:

Is that something you've inherited from her?

JENNA:

I'd like to think so.

KIRSTY:

She undertook a great deal of community work, I understand?

JENNA;

She did. She was tireless. Nothing was too much trouble. But what drove her most was the desire to see people who might have experienced setbacks get back up on their own two feet again. She was quite tough in that way. She recognised that generally people like to manage for themselves if they can, but sometimes they might need a bit of support to help them get started. She never judged. Be true, she would say to me, be clear, be honest.

KIRSTY:

Time for disc number three.

JENNA:

Ah yes. The eighties. Hedonism and *The Hacienda*. And this is New Order.

The third piece of music is played.

KIRSTY:

That was *Here to Stay* by New Order, which takes our castaway back to the 1980s and the whole 'Madchester' music scene. So, Jenna Ward, what can you tell us about those times?

JENNA:

Not a lot! I was wasted for much of them, and what things I do remember are not fit to be broadcast before the watershed.

KIRSTY:

I see. Safe to say, then, that you packed a lot in?

JENNA:

You could say that.

KIRSTY:

Though perhaps you're being just a tad disingenuous? You graduated from Manchester with a Double-First in Politics and International Relations, and you won the prestigious Sir Bernard Crick Prize?

JENNA:

I think I scared people mostly.

KIRSTY:

In what way?

JENNA:

I was always angry, complaining about this, or arguing about that. I think they hoped by giving me a prize it might shut me up.

KIRSTY:

But it didn't?

JENNA:

> Not in the slightest. If anything it just gave me the
> licence to say what I felt, whenever and wherever I got
> the chance. So, when I received my award, instead of
> being gracious and just saying thank you, I went off
> on a rant about Mrs Thatcher.

KIRSTY:

> Let's have your next choice of music.

The fourth disc is duly played.

KIRSTY:

> That was The Smiths and *There is a Light that Never
> Goes Out*. And you were telling me, Jenna Ward,
> while we were off air just now listening to that track,
> that it's a song that means even more to you now than
> it did back when you first heard it as a student. Why is
> that?

JENNA:

> Because Manchester is a light that never goes out. One
> of the reasons that *The Hacienda* was so successful
> was that it was a place you could go to really let off
> steam, have a party, and forget about just how crap
> Manchester had become in those years. All the things
> that had made it what it was – the mills, the mines, the
> factories – they were all closing down, and nothing
> was replacing them. I used to walk to lectures from
> my student flat in Moss Side, and it was like a ghost
> town. Whole streets were boarded up, there were

squats everywhere, huge numbers of homeless sleeping rough, blocks of flats going up that nobody wanted to live in, that were riddled with damp, and no jobs. Unemployment topping three million, and this song just spoke to us, all of us, at the time. *"Take me out tonight where there's music and there's people and they're young and alive"*, and there was Mrs Thatcher seemingly oblivious. "The lady's not for turning", while Morrissey was singing, *"I never, never want to go home, because I haven't got one any more"*. Is it any wonder there were riots up and down the country.

KIRSTY:

And I believe that you were caught up in the ones in Moss Side?

JENNA:

Yeah, I was. *"In the darkened underpass I thought, oh God, my chance has come at last."* It was terrifying, but also kind of exhilarating. There were fires in the streets and barricades and chanting and marching, but there was also looting and burning and all kinds of violence – on both sides. I got hit over the head with a truncheon, but then another Policeman found me in the gutter and took care of me. It wasn't all us against them. I remember this Policeman telling me, while he helped me to an ambulance, that his father had been a miner, and that when the pit closed and they took away his job, they took away his sense of who he was too, so he could understand all this rage and anger, but there had to be a better way than simply smashing everything up. It got me thinking.

KIRSTY:

About what?

JENNA:

What that better way might be, and how to make it happen. Sometimes direct action *is* necessary, but sometimes you might have to play a longer game, and I've not always been the most patient of people.

KIRSTY:

Disc number five...

... is now played.

KIRSTY:

That was *Lust for Life* by Iggy Pop, played beneath the opening monologue from the film *Trainspotting*, written by John Hodge, based on the original novel by Irvine Welsh, directed by Danny Boyle...

JENNA:

...another Mancunian –

KIRSTY:

– performed by Ewan McGregor. And you chose that, why, Jenna Ward?

JENNA:

Because it highlights, I think, what that Policeman said to me after the Moss Side riots. Things are never black and white, nothing's ever that simple or straightforward, but in the end we must all of us try if we can to "choose life". And also, it's a great piece of music.

KIRSTY:

So – after you graduated, with that Double-First and a prestigious award, you could have had your pick, I imagine, of any number of jobs, but you chose instead to try and become what would have been the youngest ever female MP. You stood for selection, un-successfully, to be the Labour parliamentary candidate for Openshaw in Manchester?

JENNA: (*laughing*):

Twice. And failed both times. Talk about the hubris of the young!

KIRSTY:

But you don't, as far as I understand, advocate for positive discrimination or all female short lists?

JENNA:

No.

KIRSTY:

Why is that?

JENNA:

Because ultimately it undermines women. It makes us feel that that is the only way we can ever make progress, and I don't believe that to be case. It's divisive, and I'm all about people working together. I look at what my mother and aunt achieved, and my grandmother, and I know I'm right.

KIRSTY:

But is it really possible for women to, as they say, have it all?

JENNA:

I believe so.

KIRSTY:

In which case, I wonder what it is you say to those who have questioned your decision *not* to raise your own daughter?

JENNA:

That it's none of their business.

KIRSTY:

Quite. But if I may play Devil's Advocate for a moment, it's hardly surprising the question comes up when you are someone who has so consistently and vociferously challenged both business and government to be more flexible when it comes to supporting the rights of working mothers?

JENNA:

And I stand by everything I've said and written on the subject. I… I could, I suppose, have cited post-natal depression – and there would have been some truth in that – but…

There is a slight jolt in what Jenna says here, as if there has been a subsequent edit, so that some of what she said is not included in the final transmission but has been removed. She continues after a slight pause.

… the real reason is I simply wasn't very good at being a mother, not at first. My own mother and aunt and grandmother were so much better, so much more patient than I was. And then there was my job. It was better for Molly that way. In so-called developing countries a child is often raised by a whole village. That seems a much healthier approach to me.

KIRSTY:

So did your daughter live with you?

JENNA:

For some of the time, yes, though I moved quite a bit, and so sometimes she stayed at my grandmother's house.

KIRSTY:

The house you yourself grew up in?

JENNA:

Yes. I think the continuity which that provided gave my daughter the stability that I wasn't always able to offer.

KIRSTY:

And it worked?

JENNA:

Yes, I think so. Molly and I get on really well now, although at times the sparks can fly between us. She's an artist, and going to be a very good one, I think. She's just starting out.

Pause

KIRSTY:

Let's have some more music.

JENNA:

Yes. This track is from another brilliant Manchester band. I love the way they just stick two fingers up to the rest of the world, yet at the same time they can be so tender and insightful. Like here.

Jenna's sixth choice of music is now played.

KIRSTY:

And that was *Don't Look Back in Anger* by Oasis. And I get the impression, Jenna Ward, that that is a sentiment you abide by?

JENNA:

I do. I try, if I can, always to look forward.

KIRSTY:

And when you look forward today, what is it that you're hoping to see?

JENNA:

Change.

KIRSTY:

Can you be more specific?

JENNA:

Manchester.

KIRSTY:

Yes. The city seems to run through your life so far like a constant stream.

JENNA:

Perhaps 'canal' would be more appropriate.

KIRSTY:

Indeed, for the house you grew up in was very close to the Manchester Ship Canal, was it not?

JENNA:

That's right, and sometimes these canals get clogged up with all manner of stuff, which you just have to clear away, if the water is to flow smoothly and cleanly once more.

KIRSTY:

And so is that how you see your role? Unclogging canals? Is that what drew you to taking up your position ten years ago as Head of Policy for the Northern branch of the IPPR, the Institute for Public Policy & Research, back in Manchester, when you could, I am thinking, have gone anywhere?

JENNA:

I love Manchester. I always have. Whenever I travel anywhere else, for work or pleasure, I always find myself comparing it with Manchester, and Manchester always wins out. And so when the opportunity came up at the IPPR I seized it with both hands.

KIRSTY:

And it was you, I believe, who first coined the phrase 'the northern powerhouse' in a briefing paper you prepared for the previous coalition government?

JENNA: (*laughing*):

Oh, I don't think I can claim credit for that, Kirsty. There were lots of people bandying it about – David Cameron, Lord O'Neill, George Osborne, and more recently Chris Grayling – and to be fair, they were all talking about a whole swathe of what they call 'core cities' right across the north of England, but in that paper you referred to I was talking specifically about Manchester, which has always been a powerhouse, the engine that has driven the nation's wealth and prosperity. People were saying that as long ago as Peterloo. We were arguably the first truly world-city, but over time, as our traditional industries of coal and cotton have been swept away, we've been starved by successive governments of the resources we need to carve out a new 21st century identity for ourselves. When the Commonwealth Games were held here in 2002, we once again showed the rest of the world that while we have a past and a heritage that we can truly be proud of, we're also a contemporary, dynamic, forward-looking city of genuine world-class, a cultural leader, a *setter* of trends, not a follower. So when it comes down to it, I'm not really interested in whether a new High-Speed Rail-Link can knock twenty minutes off how long it takes for a train to reach London, or thirty, or forty minutes. That to me is missing the point. A much more telling statistic is that as a nation we are still currently spending an average of nearly fifteen hundred pounds per head on infrastructure improvements in London, compared to less than five hundred per head up here in Manchester. That's why I, and many other Mancunians like me, retain a healthy scepticism about all this current talk. We've always been Radicals up here, Non-Conformists, doing things our own way. So just give us our fair share, and then stand back and watch us amaze you.

KIRSTY:
Time now for your seventh choice.

JENNA: (*taking a deep breath*):

Yes. Sorry about that. I have a habit of getting on my soap box at times. I'm passionate about this city, as you can tell. And what I'd like to hear now sums up that unique spirit of Manchester that makes us who we are. Earlier this year, following the terrible terrorist attack on the Manchester Arena after the Ariana Grande concert, this city came together like it always does in times of crisis. We wept together, grieved together, and stood together, determined not to exercise revenge or recrimination, but to continue to look forward together to an even stronger future. A City United, defiant and proud, gathering in Albert Square, in the heart of the city, less than twenty-four hours after the bombing, to demonstrate that wherever we came from to begin with, we are all Mancunians now. Two hundred languages are spoken here. Mosques, temples and gurdwaras share streets with synagogues, chapels and churches. And so I'd like to hear *This is the Place*, an Ode to the City of Manchester, by the poet Alan Walsh.

"If you're looking for history, yeah we've a wealth
But the Manchester way is to make it yourself
And make us a record, a new number one
And make us a brew while you're up, love, go on..."

KIRSTY:

That was an extract from *This is the Place* by Alan Walsh, reminding us of the common humanity we all share, after the tragic events that took place in

407

Manchester earlier this year, recalled so passionately and eloquently for us by my castaway this morning, Jenna Ward. Which brings us neatly to your current role as an ambassador for the National Refugee Council. How did that all come about?

JENNA:

I was invited to serve on the Board of CARE International, which is a remarkable organisation, doing incredible work in, currently, seventy-four different countries around the world, but this number's growing all the time. Our primary aims are to find long-term solutions to poverty, support women and young girls to overcome inequality and fulfil their potential – something which is very close to my heart – and essentially to save lives. I remember my grandmother telling me a story of how, when she was a young woman, she went to listen to Queen Surayya of Afghanistan speak at the Town Hall. This was ninety years ago. The Queen was in Manchester as part of a state visit to Britain by her husband, King Amanullah, who'd recently been deposed. She felt this was partly her fault – there'd been a great deal of opposition to the reforms she'd encouraged the King to introduce to improve the lot of women and girls back in their home country. But she was passionate in her belief that it was the right, the only, thing to do. I've never forgotten the impression her words made on my grandmother. In the past few years, as everybody knows, we've witnessed the most appalling human tragedies right around the world, with wars and all of their collateral damage, displacing millions and millions of people, forcing them to flee their homes. Some figures put it as high as nearly forty percent of the world's population being on the move at any one time. This mass migration of people, like the birds my daughter draws endlessly, is the single most pressing issue of our time. It threatens to overwhelm us and it can seem very frightening – uncertainty always is – but nothing like as frightening as it is for all those currently on the move, risking their lives in overcrowded, unsafe boats, trying to make a better life for themselves and their children. And isn't that in the end what we all want? And so I'm doing what little I can to see if there are ways that can be found to offer more of these refugees a fresh start here.

KIRSTY:

And you yourself recently visited the Yemen, the country of your grandparents, to see the situation there at first hand?

JENNA:

I did, yes, and it's inconceivably terrible. Human suffering on a truly biblical scale. This spring *Médecins sans Frontières* estimated that more than seven million people there are threatened with famine, with three and a half million children and lactating women already suffering acute malnutrition. Meanwhile the civil war there continues, threatening the shipments of desperately needed aid from reaching those who need it most. Already thousands of migrants are clogging the ports, trying to find ways of escaping these unimaginable horrors. Inevitably some of those will make it here. As both the Bible and the *Qur'an* say, '*Be not forgetful to entertain strangers: for thereby some have entertained angels unawares.*'

KIRSTY: (*after a respectful pause*):
Time for your last piece of music.

JENNA:
I have a childhood memory, of creeping downstairs late at night, when I was meant to be asleep, drawn by a piece of music. I peeped through the rails of the banister and saw my parents dancing, slow and close. Although I was trying hard not to make a sound, so that they wouldn't know I was there, a part of me wanted them to hear me, to see me looking at them from the stairs, and then carry me over to dance with them.

KIRSTY:
And did they?

JENNA:
No. But I wish they had. This is the song that was playing.

'Look Homeward Angel' by Johnnie Ray.

KIRSTY:
And so, as well as the eight discs, you can take one

book with you. We give you The Bible and The Complete Works of Shakespeare.

JENNA:

Might I have the *Qur'an* instead of the Bible?

KIRSTY:

Certainly. And what else?

JENNA:

I'm going to choose *The Manchester Man* by Isabella Banks.

KIRSTY:

It's yours.

JENNA:

Might I read a short extract?

KIRSTY:

By all means.

JENNA:

This quote is on the headstone by the grave of Tony Wilson, the founder of *Factory Records* and *The Hacienda*, and so it felt appropriate: "*Mutability is the epitaph of worlds. Change alone is changeless. People drop out of the history of a life as of a land, though their work or their influence remains.*"

KIRSTY:

And you're permitted one luxury.

JENNA:

I'd like to take a black umbrella. If I'm allowed.

KIRSTY: (*pretending to scold*):

I'm not sure the rules permit that. It sounds rather practical.

JENNA:

In which case, one of the drawings of my mother that my father did.

KIRSTY:

Your father? You haven't mentioned him before.

JENNA:

Oh? Haven't I?

KIRSTY:

And unfortunately there isn't time now. But of course you can have the drawing as a luxury. And if the waves came in and threatened to take away all of your discs, which one would you try to save?

JENNA:

That's tricky. Oasis, or perhaps New Order. Yes – New Order, I think.

KIRSTY:

Here to Stay.

JENNA:

That's me.

KIRSTY:

Jenna Ward, thank you for letting us share your Desert Island Discs.

JENNA:

It's been a pleasure. Thank *you*.

The music for 'By The Sleepy Lagoon' returns.

RADIO ANNOUNCER:

Desert Island Discs was created by Roy Plomley and was produced for the BBC by Leanne Buckle. Kirsty's castaway next week will be...

Kirsty watches Jenna leave the studio and thinks what an unsatisfactory edition this has been, apart from that one instance when, for a brief moment, she caught a fleeting glimpse of a more vulnerable, more complex and, as a result, more interesting person than the one she presented for the rest of the programme, which she'd turned into a kind of platform for her various hobby-horses, and Jenna had insisted that that section had to be cut. Oh well, you win some, you lose some...

Pity, she thinks. She likes Jenna, especially her feisty 'take-no-prisoners' combativeness, and feels people would warm to her far more if she'd let them get a little closer, but this armour-plating she's encased herself in makes her seem cold-hearted and not a little manipulative. That chink she'd almost revealed, if only she'd... And what was that last minute reference to her father all about? Hmm...

But she has to break off from considering these alternative scenarios further for her producer is beckoning her into the control room. It seems the recording has over-run its allotted forty-three minutes, so some cuts will have to be made. Some of that rant about the Northern Powerhouse perhaps...?

Meanwhile Jenna hurries out of the studio without once looking back. As soon as she steps outside, onto the concourse of Salford's Media City, she pauses, lights up a cigarette and inhales deeply. She is almost shaking.

That was close, she thinks. She's not ready to tell the world her full story. Not yet. That will have to wait, she tells herself, till another time, till later, before she heads off towards the Metro Link station to catch the tram back to her newly-converted waterfront apartment at the Grade II-listed former Daily Express Building on Great Ancoats Street.

*

Michael ran the lead-up to the installation with meticulous attention to detail, leaving Molly free to take care of the concept and the execution. The Arts Council funding enabled them to employ more than a dozen assistants, most of them even more recent graduates than *she* was, to help her set it up, and at precisely half an hour before midnight on Saturday 31st March, they all assembled at their various starting points across the city.

Fifty years since Sol had walked the tow-paths from Barton Bridge to Bradford Colliery, and ninety since Jaz had made the same journey overnight by narrow boat, Molly proposed to recreate it once again, only instead of walking it she would take the tram, which now linked Eccles and Media City, (where Jenna had just finished recording her edition of *Desert Island Discs* and from where Molly had first begun to conceive her idea, coming out of the Imperial War Museum, sitting across the Canal from Old Trafford), with *The Etihad Stadium*, built on the site of the former pit. She would be travelling across the city from one footballing powerhouse to another, and instead of embarking from a single jumping off point, she and her assistants would be starting from seven, from each of the final stops on all the separate branches of the Metro Link network – from Bury, Rochdale, Ashton and Altrincham, from East Didsbury, Manchester Airport, plus herself from Eccles.

At exactly 11.30pm they gathered in pairs at the entrance to each of the branch terminuses, connected via their mobiles to the *thin blue line* app Molly had set up specifically for the project. When each had checked in, Michael clicked on *Go*, and they separately entered their various stations to board their allocated tram, to arrive at their next rendezvous point, which was to be St Peter's Square, where each of the different branches all converged, just after 1am.

Each pair was armed with a large ball of blue cotton tape, the twine approximately five centimetres wide, measuring the miles, and a strong pair of scissors. Their task was a simple one, but extremely precise. At every station along their particular route they had to leap out of the tram as it stopped, attach the blue tape to a pre-arranged fixing at one end of the platform, then run the length of it, letting out the cotton twine behind them, until they reached a second fixing point, where they tied it tightly, before jumping back on to the tram as it departed. On each platform were a further two volunteers, whose job it was, after the tram had pulled out, to make sure that the trail of twine was securely attached at a height that was visible, but just beyond the reach of even the tallest person. They then continued the trail with blue cotton tape of their own along the stairs, escalators and walkways to that station's entrance, or, where the stations were at street level, to the nearest tying-off point. This was repeated at every one of the network's ninety-nine stations, a draughtsman's blue pencil marking the route.

By 1.15am all of the pairs had arrived at St Peter's Square, opposite the Central Reference Library, in the heart of the city. There they joined their individual, separate lengths of remaining twine into a single seven-way braid, weaving them together into one much stronger thread. This took almost an hour, while they sat, huddled close together for warmth in the adjoining Peace Garden. When they had finished they carefully looped it through the hands holding the dove on Barbara Pearson's bronze statue of *The Messenger of Peace*, from where they took it up high to the top of a nearby street-lamp, and from there back to the platform in the Square.

All but one pair then boarded the next tram to come along, and a further pair left at each of the next four stations – Piccadilly Gardens, Piccadilly, New Islington, Holt Town – so that when the tram pulled into Eastlands, the remaining two pairs, including Molly, alighted together. One stayed at the station, while Molly and the final pairing made the short walk towards the stadium and the footbridge, unravelling and attaching the cotton twine as they did so. This final pair then stood at either end of the bridge, keeping vigil and guard over this thin blue line, as did everyone else at their allotted station, with instructions to replace the tape if anyone tried to take it down, and to photograph on their mobiles people's reactions to it as they began to arrive the following morning, posting their images onto a range of social media platforms, encouraging members of the public to do the same.

Molly, now alone in the centre of the bridge, tied the thin blue line to herself. With another series of large balls of white cotton thread she set out to fashion a pair of giant wings. She had, she calculated, about four hours to complete them before the bridge would begin to fill with people arriving for the lunch-time kick-off. She was nervous but excited. She had practised the process a hundred times in her rented studio on Moston Lane and knew exactly what to do.

She had brought with her a bundle of thin bamboo canes, sturdy but flexible, which would form the wings' basic structure, which she then began to cover with the white cotton thread, being filmed by one of the assistants as she did so, to form a strong but delicate latticed pattern, a gridded network of lace, closely bonded while still allowing the light to show through, light which, as she finished, was just beginning to slant across the grey expanse of former industrial waste-ground either side of the bridge, on land that was still not developed, where the Bradford Colliery had once stood, where the precious coal, tons and tons of it, another hundred years' worth at least, lay beneath her. She could just make out where the Ashton Canal flowed past, the light now hitting the stone steps by the landing station, which fifty years before her grandfather had climbed, before scaling the wire fence and stealing a piece of coal from the abandoned workings. She fetched that piece of coal now out of her bag and placed it at her feet. Then she draped the white cloth that had been Ishtar's, and before that Rose's, across her head and shoulders, the caught moths fluttering against the stitched laurel leaves.

She stood up, the wings rising from her back, quivering, feathers rippling in the early sun, so that she resembled one of the many birds she drew taking off in slow, graceful flight, or an angel perhaps, looking down on where, once, so many countless pairs of feet had walked their way to the pithead, the winding gear, those twin towers a cathedral to commerce and labour, where thousands more would walk in a few hours' time, converging from every corner of the city, following the thin blue line, towards a different kind of temple.

At 8am precisely, the final contingent of Molly's team started to arrive, in ones and twos to begin with, then in larger numbers. Mobilised by Lauren Murphy, whose help and guidance Molly had sought when first planning her installation, descendants of the last miners in the colliery walked across the bridge towards her, the unworked seams still under their feet, the thin blue line of cotton still over their heads. They each carried their own piece of coal, which they ceremonially placed around Molly's, until they had built a significant cairn, reaching up to Molly's waist, out of which she appeared to rise, phoenix-like, wings outstretched.

High Noon at Eastlands...

Crowds for the match began to pour across the bridge. One of Molly's assistants pressed play on her smart phone, which was connected by blue tooth to speakers at either end. Shaun Ryder's irreverent *Reverend Black Grape* filled the air.

*"O Come, all ye faithful
Joyful and triumphant..."*

There was joy and celebration, there was bewilderment and anger. People paused to look at the installation. Some applauded, some scratched their heads in puzzlement. A log-jam began to form, with some people pushing and jostling to get through and see for themselves what was causing the commotion, while others simply wanted to get on their way to the stadium and the match. There was shoving and shouting, cries for help and appeals for calm.

"Don't talk to me about heroes..."

Molly stood stock still and silent throughout it all. She thought of her grandfather fifty years before, and his father forty years before that, each of them occupying this same spot, and felt this same thin blue line linking them together, a flight of birds across the sky, a stone skimming across the water, a moth opening then closing its wings, the trace of footprints in a disappearing path, a faint pencil mark placed across a map, a web stretching across the whole city, a magnet to the world...

Eventually stewards called in the Police, who, though steadfastly friendly, were nevertheless firm in carrying Molly bodily from the scene, to a mixture of boos and applause. Within seconds images of the scene had gone viral.

#whosestories
#whatsmineisours
#coalangel

After the match, after the crowds had all made their way back home, radiating out from *The Etihad* along the separate branches of the Metro Link to all corners of the city, the bridge was silent. The pieces of coal that had formed the cairn lay kicked and scattered, the sky-coloured cotton threads of the thin blue line trailing and tangled in the dirt, Shaun Ryder still singing on endless replay.

"It's a big day for the north..."

*

Early the next morning, as the sun poked through a pale bandage of cloud, illuminating a scattering of rats scuttling along the underpass beneath the bridge, a wake of crows was picking its way through the litter and detritus left from the previous day. A pair of them, attracted by the light reflecting from its shiny surface, flew down upon the neatly rebuilt cairn.

Ragged feathers plumped into the wind, they croaked defiantly to the sky. It was as if an army of unseen ghosts had risen from below, broken the seals of their tombs deep within the earth, and returned to the surface, each of them carrying a single piece of coal they had individually hewn, which they set upon the ground in a simple pile, before melting in the morning air.

Cairn: a mound of rough stones, built as a memorial, or a landmark, placed against a skyline, to signpost a way, across unfamiliar terrain. (OED)

*

A month later Molly is retracing her steps. She steps out of the tram at Pomona Station and rides the escalator towards the upper air. Beside her stands Michael, pushing a supermarket shopping trolley, which contains all their worldly possessions in a jumble of assorted bags, cases, rucksacks, hold-alls and bin-liners. Like a pair of new arrivals. Molly carries Blessing in a crow-black baby-wrap sling, facing forwards. She is flicking her tiny tongue in and out between her lips, tasting the wind, experimenting with wordless sounds. "Lera, lera, lera,

lera…"

They glide together towards the light. Molly and Michael smile at each other, the start of a new chapter in an old book.

Waiting for them outside, as they reach the top, are Jenna, hastily stubbing out a cigarette, Nadia, stretching out her arms in greeting, Farida, standing by the new MPV people-carrier that she now drives, and Salwa, sitting in a wheelchair, just a few weeks shy of her ninety-ninth birthday. The four of them are waving as Michael, Molly and Blessing step off the escalator.

Overhead a small straggle of starlings skits across the sky.

Looking down, they will see a young man taking out his camera, arranging the others into a group. "Smile," they will hear him call out, as six women, spanning five generations, linked by a piece of white cloth, threaded through and between them, this length of cotton, woven with moths and laurel leaves, which preceded and would outlast them, lift their eyes to watch the birds flying up and up, higher and higher, until they are just dots.

*

Two hours ago on Instagram:

Photograph of Salwa, Farida, Nadia, Jenna, Molly and Blessing holding a white cotton shawl standing beside the Metro sign saying 'Pomona'

#ornamentsofgrace

Ornaments of Grace continues in:
Book 2: Tulip, Volume 1: Enclave

Dramatis Personae

(in order of appearance)

CAPITALS = Major Character; **Bold** = Significant Character;
Plain = appears once or twice

MOLLY WARD , later Adebeyo; daughter of Jenna;
granddaughter of Sol & Nadia
King Amanullah, deposed ruler of Afghanistan
Queen Surayya, wife and consort of King Amanullah
YASSER WAHID, father of Hejaz, grandfather of Sol
HEJAZ, known as 'Jaz', son of Yasser
Rose, Yasser's wife, mother of 'Jaz'
ESTHER BLUNDELL, later Ward, husband of 'Jaz', mother of Sol
aka **ISHTAR**
Mr Lomas, Under-Manager Bradford Colliery
SOL, aka Sulh, Solomon, Solly
Eric, friend of Sol from work
Ray, friend of Sol from work
Susan, Eric's girl friend
Brenda, Ray's girl friend
NADIA RAQEEB, daughter of Salwa and Jamal, sister of Farida,
later Sol's wife
FARIDA, Nadia's sister, wife of Salim
Mr Meakin, teacher at Sol's school
Salim-ul-Haq, Farida's husband
Salwa, Nadia's mother
Jamal, Nadia's father
Cliff Mitchelmore & Jean Metcalfe, presenters of Two Way
Family Favourites
Mr Hassan-al-Haideri, Muslim Spiritual Leader in Eccles
Captain Jackson, Aden Protectorate Levies
Captain Michael James Bradley, C/O/ 4th Brigade Yorks & Lancs
Regiment
Hakkim, Arab National Police

Corporal Roy Carter, Sol's army friend
Taii, Yemeni boy
JENNA, Sol and Nadia's daughter
Mr Tunstall, Nadia's boss at Turner's
Terry, Caretaker at Turner's
GEORGE WRIGHT, Sol's Art tutor
Cadge, Sol's co-worker at Cussons
Pat, gang member
Judge, Manchester Crown Court
Attending Officer, Crown Court
Anita, Nadia's co-worker at Kendal Milne's Department Store
Miss Gresty, Shop Window Designer at Kendal Milne's
Sir James Peter Coatman, Prison Governor, Walton Gaol
Sheila, Corporal Roy Carter's widow
Lenny, Sol's cell mate
Prison Officer at Front Desk
Farida's Doctor
Mr Godfrey Callan, Manager of Martin's Bank
Mrs Margaret Pullen, Farida's next door neighbour
Mr Alan Carmichael, Coroner
PC Brian Kempson
Clerk of Coroner's Court
Dru, a Roman Soldier
Bron, a woman of the Brigantes tribe
Policeman patrolling Bradford Colliery
Mrs Linda Billings, mother of toddler
Mr Alan Rees, delivery van driver
Paul, manager of The King's Arms, Salford
MICHAEL CHIDI PROMISE ADEBEYO, later Molly's husband
Marriage Registrar
Blessing Hope Wahid Adebeyo, Molly & Michael's daughter
Sophie Sveinsson, MCR Live Presenter
Chloe Chen, MCR Live Reporter
Lauren Murphy, bradfordpit.com
Kirsty Young, presenter of Desert Island Discs
BBC Radio Announcer

The following are mentioned by name:

[Sir Edward Manville, Deputy Chairman, BSA, Birmingham]
[Lieutenant-General Sir Francis Humphries, Honourable Artillery Company]
[Sir J.E. Kynaston Studd, Lord Mayor of London, 1928]
[Outriders of Grenadier Guards]
[HRH Edward, Prince of Wales, later Edward VIII]
[Escort of Royal Horse Guards]
[Escort of Irish Guards]
[King George V]
[Queen Mary of Tek]
[Duke of York, later King George VI]
[Lord Birkenhead, Frederick Edwin Smith, Lord Chancellor]
[Marquis of Salisbury]
[Field Marshall Sir George Milne]
[Sir Frank Dyson, Astronomer Royal, Greenwich]
[Grakle, Koko, Billy Barton, Tipperary Tim, runners in the Aintree Grand National]
[16th Service Battalion Band of The Manchester Regiment]
[Ernest Terah Hooley, Owner of Trafford Park Estates]
[Marshall Stevens, General Manager Manchester Ship Canal Company]
[Lieutenant-Colonel George Westcott OBE, Lord Mayor of Manchester]
[Abraham Williamson, Civic Mayor of Salford]
[Sir Edward Leader Williams, Chief Engineer Manchester Ship Canal Company]
[Charles Heathcote, Chief Architect British Westinghouse Electric Company]
[Sir Philip Nash, Chair Metropolitan-Vickers]
[Aide to King Amanullah]
[Bargemen]
[Alice Blundell, Esther's mother]
[Walter Blundell, Esther's father]
[Freddie, Esther's youngest brother]
[Miss Frangleton, Colliery Canteen Assistant]
[Lady Mayoress of Manchester]
[Esther's brothers' wives]
[Mr T.H. Fisher, Owner of Bradford Colliery]

426

[Bradford Colliery Brass Band]
[Children of Christ Church Primary School, Clayton]
[Constables controlling crowds at Bradford Colliery]
[Mr Puncknowle, pronounced 'Punnel', Managing Director Metro-Vicks]
[Neville Chamberlain, Prime Minister]
[Doctor and Nurse attending Jaz]
[Major K.G. Birkett DSM]
[Ron, lock keeper at Barton Swing Bridge]
[Sailor on board SS Pioneer]
[Yasser's parents]
[Thomas Walker, proponent of Manchester Ship Canal]
[Hilal, Nadia's brother who died in infancy]
[Stephen, Ray's older brother]
[Sol's Sgt Major]
[Aunts, Uncles, Cousins of Nadia]
[Mrs Ahmed, neighbour of Yasser and Esther]
[Mourners, Gravediggers at Yasser's funeral]
[Major-General Douglas Harrington, Commander-in-Chief Yorkshire & Lancashire Regiment, Aden]
[Taii's Mother]
[Office Girls in Typist Pool]
[Mrs Tunstall, Mr Tunstall's wife]
[Salim's male friends at Abdul's Café]
[Courting couples kissing in the cinema]
[Salwa's sister, Farida's Auntie]
[Wedding Guests at Salim & Farida's wedding]
[Ladies at Salwa's talk to the Women's Institute]
[Secretary of local W.I.]
[Whit Walkers]
[Sailor on board Hejira]
[Helen Shapiro]
[DJ at The Majestic]
[The Hollies]
[Francis, George's friend]
[Bookmakers and punters at The Albion Greyhound Track]
[Prince Monolulu, tipster at Castle Irwell Racecourse]
[Police officers who arrest Sol]
[Roy, Anita's husband]
[Lance, Anita's son]
[Peter Anthony Allen, convicted murderer]

[Gwynne Owen Evans, convicted murderer]
[John 'Jack' West, murder victim]
[Detective Sgt Bagnall, Cumberland & Westmorland Police]
[Neighbour of West]
[Tenant of Builders Yard in Ormskirk]
[Mary Allen, wife of murderer]
[Mrs Allen, Mary's mother]
[Manchester Constables searching West]
[Detective Inspector Byrnes, in charge of investigation]
[Judge Justice Ashworth, Manchester Assizes]
[Lord Chief Justice Lord Parker of Waddington, Justices Winn and Widgery, Appeal Court]
[Right Honourable Mr Henry Brooke MP, Home Secretary]
[Robert Leslie 'Jock' Stewart, Executioner, Walton Gaol]
[Harry Allen, Executioner, Strangeways]
[Albert Pierrepoint, Chief Executioner to the Crown]
[Mrs Pierrepoint, publican and Albert's wife]
[County Sheriff of Lancashire]
[Walton Gaol Doctor]
[Walton Gaol Governor]
[Walton Gaol Chaplain]
[Other prisoners in Walton Gaol]
[Winston Churchill]
[Yuri Gagarin]
[Yuri Gagarin's Interpreter]
[Woman Hand Bell Ringer
[Alexei Leonov]
[Sergei Korolev]
[TV Commentator for First Walk in Space]
[Kenneth Wolstenholme]
[Geoff Hurst]
[Nobby Stiles]
[Evelyn Waugh]
Margery Allingham]
[Foinavon, winner of 1967 Grand National]
[John Bickingham, Foinavon's jockey]
[Vienna Boys Choir]
[Marshall MacLuhan]
[The Beatles]
[John Masefield]
[Vivien Leigh]

[Alexander Dubcek]
[Antonin Novotny]
[Nguyen van Lem]
[Martin Luther King]
[Enoch Powell]
[Student Protesters in Paris]
[Manchester United's 1968 European Cup Winners]
[Robert Kennedy]
[Sirhan Sirhan]
[Board of Trustees of Martin's Bank & Wives]
[Bus Conductor, Monton]
[Ambulencemen at scene of Salim's accident]]
[Dr Julius Sandler, Physician at Hope Hospital]
[Mrs Mabel Monks, Florist]
[Sgt Bernard Banks, Kempson's Supervising Officer]
[Town Hall Official]
[Anonymous Miner's Wife, Bradford Colliery]
[National Coal Board Representative]
[NUM Spokesperson]
[Barbara Castle MP Secretary of State for Employment]
[Ray Gunther, Minister of Labour]
[Harold Wislon, Prime Minister]
[Peter Shore MP Secretary of State for Economic Affairs]
[Anthony Wedgwood Benn MP Minister of Technology]
[Frank Cousins, TUC General Secretary]
[King James I]
[Dead dog]
[Woman sunbathing in bikini by canal]
[Dock workers, Port of Manchester]
[Acned youth in car repair workshop]
[Bare-chested smithy beneath railway arch]
[Dru's father]
[Roman soldiers]
[Tramp with bloodshot eyes]
[Youths lobbing stones]
[Old man pushing a handcart]
[Couple having sex in railway arch]
[Children running up slag heaps]
[Old men with prams]
[Women scavenging for coal]
[Walter Kershaw, mural artist]

[The Buzzcocks]
[Children and Parents at Busy Bees Nursery]
[Reverend A.E. Walker, Christ Church, Patricroft]
[Ambulancemen at traffic accident]
[George Eliot]
[University Students in Michael's lecture]
[Molly's Caribbean Father]
[Gallery Owners, Arts Centre Directors, Café Managers in Manchester]
[Crown Prince Mohamed bin Zayad Al Nahyan of Abu Dhabi]
[Sheik Mansoor]
[Leila Mourad]
[New Order]
[The Smiths]
[Iggy Pop]
[John Hodge]
[Irvine Welsh]
[Danny Boyle]
[Ewam MacGregor]
[Oasis]
[Margaret Thatcher]
[David Cameron]
[Lord O'Neill]
[George Osborne]
[Chris Grayling]
[Ariana Grande]
[Alan Walsh]
[Johnnie Ray]
[Isabella Banks]
[Tony Wilson]
[Desert Island Discs Producer]
[Art students assisting Molly]
[Barbara Pearson]
[Descendants of Miners at Bradford Colliery]
[Football Crowds]
[Shaun Ryder]
[Stewards at Football Ground]
[Police Officers at Football Ground]

Acknowledgements

(for *Ornaments of Grace* as a whole)

Writing is usually considered to be a solitary practice, but I have always found the act of creativity to be a collaborative one, and that has again been true for me in putting together the sequence of novels which comprise *Ornaments of Grace*. I have been fortunate to have been supported by so many people along the way, and I would like to take this opportunity of thanking them all, with apologies for any I may have unwittingly omitted.

First of all I would like to thank Ian Hopkinson, Larysa Bolton, Tony Lees and other staff members of Manchester's Central Reference Library, who could not have been more helpful and encouraging. That is where the original spark for the novels was lit and it has been such a treasure trove of fascinating information ever since. I would especially like to thank Jenny Marsden and Jane Parry, the Archives and Neighbourhood Engagement & Delivery Officers respectively for the Local History Dept of Manchester Library Services – Jenny for introducing me to the inspiring *Stories of a Manchester Street* project coordinated by Phil Barton and Elaine Bishop of the Park Range Residents Association, and Jane for her support in enabling me to use individual reproductions of the remarkable Manchester Murals by Ford Madox Brown, which can be viewed in the Great Hall of Manchester Town Hall. They are exceptional images and I recommend you going to see them if you are ever in the vicinity. I would also like to thank the staff of other libraries and museums in Manchester, namely the John Rylands Library, Manchester University Library, the Manchester Museum, the People's History Museum and also Salford's Working Class Movement Library, where Lynette Cawthra was especially helpful, as was Aude Nguyen Duc at The Manchester Literary & Philosophical Society, the much-loved Lit & Phil, the first and oldest such society anywhere in the world, 238 years young and still going strong.

In addition to these wonderful institutions, I have many individuals to thank also. Barbara Derbyshire from the Moravian Settlement in Fairfield has been particularly patient and generous with her time in telling me so much of the community's inspiring history. No less inspiring has been Lauren Murphy, founder of the Bradford Pit Project, which is a most moving collection of anecdotes, memories, reminiscences, artefacts and original art works dedicated to the lives of people connected with Bradford Colliery. You can find out more about their work at: www.bradfordpit.com. Martin Gittins freely shared some of his encyclopaedic knowledge of the part the River Irwell has played in Manchester's story, for which I have been especially grateful.

I should also like to thank John and Anne Horne for insights into historical medical practice; their daughter, Ella, for inducting me into the mysteries of chemical titration, which, if I have subsequently got it wrong, is my fault not hers; Tony Smith for his deep first hand understanding of spinning and weaving; Sarah Lawrie for her in-depth and enthusiastic knowledge of the Manchester music scene of the 1980s, which happened just after I left the city so I missed it; Sylvia Tiffin for her previous research into Manchester's lost theatres; the sonic artists Kathy Hinde and Matthew 'I-am-the-Mighty-Jungulator' Olden for their skills, expertise and generosity in helping me to envision aspects of Molly's final installation, and Brian Hesketh for his specialist knowledge in a range of such diverse topics as hot air balloons, how to make a crystal radio set, old maps, the intricacies of a police constable's notebook and preparing reports for a coroner's inquest.

Throughout this intensive period of writing and research, I have been greatly buoyed up by the keen support and interest of many friends, most notably Theresa Beattie, Laïla Diallo, Chris Dumigan, Viv Gordon, Phil King, Rowena Price, Gavin Stride, Chris Waters, and Irene Willis. Thank you to you all. In addition, Sue & Rob Yockney have been extraordinarily helpful in more ways than I can mention. Their advice on so many matters, both artistic and practical, has been beyond measure.

A number of individuals have very kindly – and bravely – offered to read early drafts of the novels: Rachel Burn, Lucy Cash, Chris & Julie Phillips. Their responses have been positive, constructive, illuminating and encouraging, particularly when highlighting those passages which needed closer attention from me, which I have tried my best to address. Thank you.

There are many references to particular songs, occurring throughout the twelve books. These are all available to listen to on various platforms, as are the jazz and classical pieces also mentioned. Two songs, however, have been written specifically for *Ornaments of Grace*. The first, *The Song of Weights & Measures*, with music by Chris Dumigan, appears in both Books 4 and 12, while the second, *Marks on the Land*, with music by Phil King, features in Book 12. This latter is available to listen to by going to: vimeo.com/165425043. I am extremely grateful for both Chris's and Phil's contributions.

I would also like to pay a special tribute to my friend Andrew Pastor, who has endured months and months of fortnightly coffee sessions during which he has listened so keenly and with such forbearance to the various difficulties I may have been experiencing at the time. He invariably came up with the perfect comment or idea, which then enabled me to see more clearly a way out of whatever tangle I happened to have found myself in. He also suggested several avenues of further research I might undertake to navigate towards the next bend in one of the three rivers, all of which have been just what were needed. These books could not have finally seen the light of day without his irreplaceable input.

Finally I would like to thank my wife, Amanda, for her endless patience, encouragement and love. These books are dedicated to her and to our son, Tim.

Biography

Chris grew up in Manchester and currently lives in West Dorset, after brief periods in Nottinghamshire, Devon and Brighton. Over the years he has managed to reinvent himself several times – from florist's delivery van driver to Punch & Judy man, drama teacher, theatre director, community arts co-ordinator, creative producer, to his recent role as writer and dramaturg for choreographers and dance companies.

Between 2003 and 2009 Chris was Director of Dance and Theatre for *Take Art*, the arts development agency for Somerset, and between 2009 and 2013 he enjoyed two stints as Creative Producer with South East Dance leading on their Associate Artists programme, followed by a year similarly supporting South Asian dance artists for *Akademi* in London. From 2011 to 2017 he was Creative Producer for the Bonnie Bird Choreography Fund.

Chris has worked for many years as a writer and theatre director, most notably with New Perspectives in Nottinghamshire and Farnham Maltings in Surrey under the artistic direction of Gavin Stride, with whom Chris has been a frequent collaborator.

Directing credits include: three Community Plays for the Colway Theatre Trust – *The Western Women* (co-director with Ann Jellicoe), *Crackling Angels* (co-director with Jon Oram), and *The King's Shilling*; for New Perspectives – *It's A Wonderful Life* (co-director with Gavin Stride), *The Railway Children* (both adapted by Mary Elliott Nelson); for Farnham Maltings – *The Titfield Thunderbolt, Miracle on 34th Street* and *How To Build A Rocket* (all co-directed with Gavin Stride); for Oxfordshire Touring Theatre Company – *Bowled A Googly* by Kevin Dyer; for Flax 303 – *The Rain Has Voices* by Shiona Morton, and for Strike A Light – *I Am Joan* and *Prescribed*, both written by Viv Gordon and co-directed with Tom Roden, and *The Book of Jo* as dramaturg.

Theatre writing credits include: *Firestarter, Trying To Get Back Home, Heroes* – a trilogy of plays for young people in partnership with Nottinghamshire & Northamptonshire Fire Services; *You Are Harry Kipper & I Claim My Five Pounds, It's Not Just The Jewels, Bogus* and *One of Us* (the last co-written with Gavin Stride) all for New Perspectives; *The Birdman* for Blunderbus; for Farnham Maltings *How To Build A Rocket* (as assistant to Gavin Stride), and *Time to Remember* (an outdoor commemoration of the centenary of the first ever Two Minutes Silence); *When King Gogo Met The Chameleon* and *Africarmen* for Tavaziva Dance, and most recently *All the Ghosts Walk with Us* (conceived and performed with Laïla Diallo and Phil King) for ICIA, Bath University and Bristol Old Vic Ferment Festival, (2016-17); *Posting to Iraq* (performed by Sarah Lawrie with music by Tom Johnson for the inaugural Women & War Festival in London 2016), and *Tree House* (with music by Sarah Moody, which toured southern England in autumn 2016). In 2018 Chris was commissioned to write the text for *In Our Time*, a film to celebrate the 40th Anniversary of the opening of The Brewhouse Theatre in Taunton, Somerset.

Between 2016 and 2019 Chris collaborated with fellow poet Chris Waters and jazz saxophonist Rob Yockney to develop two touring programmes of poetry, music, photography and film: *Home Movies* and *Que Pasa?* In 2020 Chris was invited by Wassail Theatre Company to be part of a collaborative project with 6 other writers to create the play *The Time of Our Lives* in response to Covid 19 as part of the *Alternative Endings* project.

Chris regularly works with choreographers and dance

artists, offering dramaturgical support, creative and business advice. These have included among others: Alex Whitley, All Play, Ankur Bahl, Antonia Grove, Anusha Subramanyam, Archana Ballal, Ballet Boyz, Ben Duke, Ben Wright, Charlie Morrissey, Crystal Zillwood, Darkin Ensemble, Divya Kasturi, Dog Kennel Hill, f.a.b. the detonators, Fionn Barr Factory, Heather Walrond, Hetain Patel, Influx, Jane Mason, Joan Clevillé, Kali Chandrasegaram, Kamala Devam, Karla Shacklock, Khavita Kaur, Krishna Zivraj-Nair, Laïla Diallo, Lîla Dance, Lisa May Thomas, Liz Lea, Lost Dog, Lucy Cash, Luke Brown, Marisa Zanotti, Mark Bruce, Mean Feet Dance, Nicola Conibère, Niki McCretton, Nilima Devi, Pretty Good Girl, Probe, Rachael Mossom, Richard Chappell, Rosemary Lee, Sadhana Dance, Seeta Patel, Shane Shambhu, Shobana Jeyasingh, Showmi Das, State of Emergency, Stop Gap, Subathra Subramaniam, Tavaziva Dance, Tom Sapsford, Theo Clinkard, Urja Desai Thakore, Vidya Thirunarayan, Viv Gordon, Yael Flexer, Yorke Dance Project (including the Cohan Collective) and Zoielogic.

Chris is married to Amanda Fogg, a former dance practitioner working principally with people with Parkinson's.

Printed in Great Britain
by Amazon